THRAX ANNIVERSARY EDITION

BOOK FOUR OF THE ANGELBOUND ORIGINS SERIES

CHRISTINA BAUER

COPYRIGHT

Brighton, MA 02135
www.monsterhousebooks.com
ISBN 9781946677174
First Edition

CONTENTS

SHARKIE AND SNICKERDOODLES

ALSO BY CHRISTINA BAUER

APPENDIX

DEDICATION

For All Those Who Kick Ass, Take Names
and Read Books

COLLECTED WORKS

Angelbound Origins

About a quasi (part demon and part human) girl who loves kicking butt in Purgatory's Arena

1. Angelbound
2. Scala
3. Acca
4. Thrax
5. The Dark Lands
6. The Brutal Time
7. Armageddon
8. Quasi Redux
9. Clockwork Igni
10. Lady Reaper
11. Reaper Wars
12. Angry Gods

Angelbound Lincoln

The Angelbound experience as told by Prince Lincoln

1. Duty Bound

10. Rapunzels and Powers

Dimension Drift

Dystopian adventures with science, snark, and hot aliens

1. Scythe
2. Umbra
3. Alien Minds
4. ECHO Academy

* This is a finished series.

Pixieland Diaries

About sassy pixie Calla and her love-crush-nemesis, the elf prince Dare

1. Pixieland Diaries
2. Calla
3. Dare

* This is a finished series.

Beholder

Where a medieval farm girl discovers necromancy and true love

1. Cursed
2. Concealed
3. Cherished
4. Crowned
5. Cradled

*This is a finished series.

THRAX

*F*or the record, there's no better way to spend your honeymoon than lounging naked in bed while playing a little game I like to call, "No, I hated *you* more."

Here's how it works. My now-husband Lincoln and I positively loathed each other when we first met. Back then, Lincoln thought I was a reckless quasi-demon. Meanwhile, I thought *he* was a super-uptight part-angel demon-hunting douchebag. That's ancient history now, so today we're sharing the "best of the worst" moments from our rocky past. Plus, the game is extra-fun because Lincoln is ripped in that lean way swordfighters are, and the comforter is pooled around his hips. *Yum.* My guy is tall and broad-shouldered with wavy brown hair and lips that scream, *kiss me* without saying a word. Go, honeymoon!

For Lincoln's last turn, he just reminded me how I wore sweats to a formal thrax event as a lame means of protest. I agreed that my attire was not in the best taste. Still, in the end I had to remove said sweats and then wear the ugliest white dress ever. Total mitigating factor. Long story short, Lincoln gave a decent entry, but we still don't have a winner.

"You're up," says Lincoln with a sneaky smile. He totally thinks I don't have a good story for my turn. And he's way wrong. I am about to crush him like a cute itsy-bitsy-yet-mega-ripped man-bug.

"I have such a good one, you're going to cringe when you hear it." I really drag out the word *cringe.*

"You don't say." Lincoln rolls over to face me. Now, we're nose-to-nose under the covers of our incredibly fluffy bed. For the last three weeks, we've spent our honeymoon camped out in this fancy-shmancy bedroom inside one of Lincoln's hidden palaces. My guy is the high prince of the demon-fighting thrax, and his people have a tradition and glitzy hangout for everything. This particular mansion is just for royal honeymoons. The place is decked out with hefty wooden furniture, tapestries, and porcelain knickknacks. It's pretty, but I'd happily spend the time in an abandoned truck stop, so long as Lincoln and I were alone.

"Oh yeah," I say. "Prepare to lose."

"Please continue. The anticipation is almost beyond endurance."

"Anticipation almost beyond endurance? Who talks like that?"

"I do. And if you keep stalling, you'll forfeit the game."

In case you were wondering, Lincoln always uses huge vocabulary words. As a prince, my guy got educated by an entire league of smarty-pants tutors. Meanwhile, I'm a quasi demon—mostly human with a bit of demonic DNA—so my "education" was more of an attempted brainwashing by the ghouls who once ruled my homeland of Purgatory. That said, although being quasi means that my school years were crap, it *also* means that I have a tail. Every quasi-demon does, only mine is extra great with a side order of awesome. It's even covered in dragonscales and has an arrowhead-shaped end.

The tail of tails, my friends.

As if it knows I'm thinking about it, my tail pops out from under the covers and waves to its imaginary audience in the bedroom.

What a ham.

Lincoln chuckles. "Is that a sign that you forfeit?"

"Never," I say. "Here's my turn. I hated you more when you were in the library at the Ryder mansion, and I had to listen to Lady Adair coo all over you."

"She cooed?"

I roll my eyes. "Please. She was all *Oh, Prince Lincoln, I want to touch your muscle-y muscles*. It was infuriating." My tail pats Lincoln's biceps as a demonstration of the action in question.

"We recently killed Adair," says Lincoln.

Which is true. Not sure where he's going with this, though.

"Yeah," I retort. "And she was possessed by the King of Hell at the time. Why bring that up?"

"Her death takes some of the bite out of your story, that's all."

Okay, Lincoln does have a point. Armageddon, the King of Hell, essentially forced us to take down Adair. I still wish we could have saved her. The whole situation sucked. Hard. Best to skip that entry. However, I still have a long list of "I hate you more" moments.

"I get one do-over per turn," I say.

"That is true."

I tap my chin until a better memory appears. "Okay, I've got one."

"Enlighten me." Amusement dances in Lincoln's eyes. Like

all thrax, Lincoln has one brown eye and one blue. It's a sign of his dual nature as angelic and human. Like his battle scars, I've come to love Lincoln's mismatched eyes. I stare into them deeply as I drop my verbal bomb.

"For my turn, I hereby submit the first time we met."

"No." Lincoln closes his eyes and groans. "I was such an anti-demon douchebag."

By the way, I'm totally proud of Lincoln for using the word "douchebag." I consider it a serious sign of my positive influence on moving him into the current century.

When I next speak, I take care to add a mock-nostalgic tone to my voice. "I remember the night so well. It was a formal ball at the Ryder mansion. You approached me."

Lincoln groans again. "I was wearing a tux. Does that change things?"

"Nope. Even though you looked cute, you were still all, *You should be so grateful that I, the amazing thrax dude, am asking you to dance, you lowly scummy demon you.*"

"In my defense, my people are demon killers."

"I'm aware."

"And I live miles under the Earth's surface in a very traditional society."

"Know that, too."

Lincoln's people, the thrax, do in fact live deep underground on Earth in Antrum, where they refuse to get television and generally stay stuck in their own version of the Middle Ages. In fact, I'm in one of his underground palaces right now. Plus, it's true that thrax are part angel and have a mandate from the Almighty to kill demons on Earth. So, yeah, not a lot of quasi-demon awareness there with Lincoln at first. These days, my guy has totally moved beyond the whole quasi-demon-loathing thing. Unfortunately, the thrax as a people are still a major work in progress.

"Is that your defense—you were just being thraxy?" I ask. You get one defense per story.

"Not much of a defense, is it?"

"Nope." I make sure to smack my lips hard on the P sound.

Lincoln shakes his head. "I can still try to top that with my turn."

"Ha!" I grin from ear to ear. "I'm so winning this bet."

Lincoln and I are always turning things into bets. In this case, the winner gets our traditional prize: naming the time and place of our next kiss. Normally, this is a big thing since the winner can call their kiss anytime, anywhere, and the loser has to comply. When we're in a formal diplomatic thingy, it can get pretty awkward. But since we're on our honeymoon, Lincoln could call his kiss anytime, and that's fine with me. It's just the principle of the thing.

I like to win.

"I concede nothing." Lincoln leans forward and rubs his nose along mine, which sends nice shivers of yummy moving through my insides. "I have the perfect example of when I hated YOU more." Lincoln rolls onto his back and laces his fingers behind his neck. This shows off his bare chest with all the battle scars that I love. Still, I keep my focus on his face. I won't be lured into ogling him and falsely losing. Both parties have to agree who the winner is, and Lincoln's abs are designed to distract me.

And yes, I have serious distraction issues.

As a quasi-demon, I get two demonic powers: lust and wrath. Lust is the side of me that wants to stare at Lincoln's abs. Wrath is the part that likes to win. Guess which one is driving the bus right now? That would be wrath, which is why

I'm keeping my gaze locked on Lincoln's face as I speak once more. "Let's hear it, big guy."

Lincoln's sly look returns with a vengeance. "I happen to remember a moment when I was at battle practice, minding my own business and educating some of the nobility on the finer points of swordplay."

"Oh, I love this story."

"All of a sudden, a woman dressed in a dragonscale fighting suit bursts onto our practice ground—"

"I had a very important diplomatic message."

Lincoln keeps right on going. "And flattens every one of my nobles in quick succession."

"I was being viciously attacked." Not really, but that's my story and I'm sticking to it.

"One of them did suffer a concussion."

I purse my lips, considering. "A concussion is a serious thing, but the guy in question is a warrior, and he came at me first. I don't see anything here that beats you being an anti-demon dope."

Lincoln scrubs his hands over his face. I know that particular move. I'm totally winning.

With supernatural speed, I move to straddle Lincoln, pull his hands from behind his neck, and pin them above his head. "Give up, loser."

Lincoln's gaze moves down my naked torso. My stomach tightens. *That's one hot look, right there.*

When he speaks, his voice is deep and husky. "I concede. You win."

"Good." My voice is a little husky, too. It's been a few hours since we last had sex, and we quasi demons have a quick recovery time. As it turns out, partly angelic dudes like Lincoln recover quickly, too. Total marital bonus.

"So, when are you calling your kiss?" The way Lincoln stares at me, I can tell he's ready now.

For the record, impulse control has never been a strength of mine. But three weeks ago (aka the first time I ever had sex with Lincoln), I became pregnant. Since then, my impulse control issues have no gone from "not so great" to "major disaster."

In other words, I am absolutely calling my kiss right now. My tail bobs happily behind me. It's totally on board with this plan.

I don't even bother replying. I just lean down and give Lincoln a deep and soul-satisfying smooch. For one full bliss-filled minute, we're all about tongues sliding. I'm really looking forward to what comes next when it happens.

Ethereal singing echoes through my mind.

That would be my igni.

And damn, those little magical critters have the worst timing.

Here's what's up. I'm a supernatural being called the Great Scala. That means my body can house, process, and direct igni, which are tiny lightning bolts of power that move souls to Heaven or Hell. The actual "moving souls around" part is a real energy-suck, but that's just one challenge of being the Great Scala. In my opinion, the far trickier bit is what I call "igni management." Those little lightning bolts are a super-needy bunch.

Take now, for instance.

Lincoln and I are about to get busy, and the igni decide to start singing inside my head. At least, these are the light igni whose power draws souls to Heaven. That means they're going "la-la-la" in childlike voices, which isn't too painful, but it *is* distracting. There's also some indistinct murmuring in the mix. Bottom line? It's an art form to translate that babble into actual useful communication.

"Myla?" asks Lincoln. "Have the igni started talk to you again?"

"Why do you ask?"

"You stopped kissing me, for one thing."

I roll onto my back and slam my head against the pillow. "Yeah. They're yodeling away in my brain. They must have a message for me."

Lincoln kisses my cheek and slides away. "Duty calls. I can wait."

"Bleugh."

At that moment, the lovely music of the light igni is ruined by the cacophony of the dark igni who—you guessed it—send spirits to Hell. Think about a thousand toddlers playing broken recorders, and that's the general idea behind "dark igni-speak."

This is so not good.

My light igni are sweethearts. They're always jumping into my consciousness to tell me about some new and awesome soul they want sent to Heaven. They also alert me when good things happen, like when Dad proposed to Mom.

But my dark igni? They only pop in with bad news. Unfortunately, much of it is misleading. For instance, they freaked me out once by saying Mom was dead, but they only meant dead wrong about installing a bidet in all the bathrooms in my parents luxury mansion. (I agreed with that call, by the way.) Still, dark tidings and a honeymoon do not mix. And considering how these igni made sure I got knocked up three weeks ago? This could be about some risk to the baby.

I really don't want their bad news. At all.

2

*T*he voices of both the light and dark igni grow louder. Soon, they're babble-singing inside my brain at an earsplitting volume. *Yow.* Wincing, I pull the covers over my head. Listening to igni is like asking a million four-year-olds to name their favorite ice cream: they all talk at once, and it does zero good to tell them to quiet down and choose a spokesperson. My father says it's because igni have to take a multifaceted form while in the after-realms. I'm not sure what that means, but I believe him.

A quick note on my father: Dad's an archangel named Xavier who's been alive since the beginning of time. In all those eons, he never fell in love with a woman until he met Mom. Say it with me: *awwwww!* Trouble was, in order to keep Mom alive, Dad made a pact with Armageddon, the King of Hell, and agreed to be imprisoned in Hell. Not fun. Most of my life, I never knew who my father was. All that changed when I turned seventeen, became the Great Scala, and freed my dad. Go me.

The voices hit a level I like to call double-screech. Yes, I've made up my own naming system for their noises, and yes, double-screech is way painful. It's also nearly impossible to make out anything they're trying to say. I grit my teeth and hope it all goes buh-bye. It doesn't. Whatever my igni are worried about, it's a big problem. I just wish they'd calm down to single-screech level so I could understand them.

Within seconds, the noise grows so overwhelming my brain feels ready to burst. Somewhere through the haze of sound, I hear Lincoln's voice.

"What happening?" he asks. "Are you all right?"

I force out words through my clenched teeth. "Igni...still giving...message."

"What are they saying?"

"Can't tell...yet."

Now, I can't order the igni around, but I can quiet them if I send good images and energy their way. Sweat beads along my forehead as I focus on mental pictures of chubby bunnies. For some reason, the igni love fat rabbits. But picturing this while I'm in major pain? It's not easy. Eventually, I can make out a single word in their babble: "man." As terms go, that's not too helpful, but it *is* progress. I double down and try adding a few baby seals into my mental bunny images. It helps a little.

I must be picturing stuff for quite some time, because the next thing I know, I'm wrapped in a plush robe and sitting on Lincoln's lap. My guy has pulled on a pair of jeans, and based on the way his bare chest is soggy, I've been crying against his pecs for a while now. Sadly, this isn't the first time this has happened on our honeymoon. Pregnancy hormones are the worst. Three days ago, I saw a picture from some old movie where an orangutan wears a diaper. I lost it for like five minutes solid. Yesterday, the smell of broccoli with dinner made me puke. I only cried for a few minutes after that, but still. I'm a warrior. Being weepy makes me nuts.

Lincoln rubs my back in soothing circles. "What level is it?" He knows all about my igni rating system.

"Double-screech."

Lincoln lets out a low whistle. "And it's been going on for hours."

"Never this bad...before." Normally, double-screeching rarely lasts for more than a few minutes.

Lincoln's voice is steady and clam. "You can do this, Myla. Once you interpret their message, the igni will go away."

I sniffle against his skin and try to concentrate. Hours have passed, and the "bunny and baby seal" combo isn't working. It's time to try something new. I decide to tap into my warrior energy, which is part of my demonic wrath powers. Mostly I use warrior mojo to hyper-focus during battle. However, this experience is turning into one of my worst fights yet, so I'm pulling out everything I've got.

Closing my eyes tightly, I leverage every ounce of my supernatural concentration and go into "warrior mode," which is when everything else disappears except my opponent. In this case, "warrior mode" doesn't make the pain go away, but I can move it to the back of my mind. Little by little, my thoughts clear. Soon I can sift through all the noise, looking for something useful. Finally, four clear words appear within the garbled sounds.

"Mirror Man."

"LK Route."

After that, the igni go blessedly silent. I curl into Lincoln's body and exhale.

"You did it," says my guy. "I knew you would. What did they say?"

"It was something about a person and a place. The first is someone called the Mirror Man. Does that name mean anything to you?" *I've certainly never heard about him before.*

"No." Lincoln kisses the top of my head. "And the place?"

"The LK Route. Is that a street or something?"

Lincoln's eyes widen a fraction. For him, that's as good as a gasp. "It's a secret spot in Antrum. Not even my mother knows about it."

"Seriously?" Lincoln's mother, Octavia, has an amazing spy network. I seriously thought she knew everything.

"She doesn't know about the LK Route," confirms Lincoln. "Walker found this place when I was a kid. It's a royal escape path that was built in the thirteenth century. With it, royalty can make a quick getaway in times of trouble. Walker asked me not to tell anyone, and I never have."

"Nice." Even though he's a ghoul, Walker's a super-cool guy, brilliant engineer, and incredibly good liar. If anyone could find a hidden escape route and keep the secret, it's Walker. "So does the LK part stand for?"

"Lime Kiln."

"Wow. I have no idea what that is." Insert comment here about ghouls and crap education.

"Lime is a stone that's used in medieval construction. Kilns are little ovens to heat it up. Thrax call those ovens LKs. We have a line of them behind Arx Hall, so we can quickly make repairs to the palace. The last in line is also rigged for an emergency escape. You touch the top, say "in thrax sic hunt," and it turns from a fiery oven into a mini-Pulpitum transfer station that takes you anywhere you want to go."

My brows lift. "How many does it fit?"

"Only one. Lime kilns aren't that large."

"Huh." When it comes to secret passages and escape routes,

I'm like a crow with a bright shiny object. I could talk about this stuff all day. "And what if someone tries to follow you?"

"I asked Walker the same thing. He thinks it's booby trapped."

"Since Mirror Man isn't ringing any bells, maybe we should check out this lime kiln."

Lincoln opens his mouth to answer when a knock sounds on our door. "Hello? It's me. I came as quickly as I could."

My eyes widen. My mother's here. With that realization, all thoughts of the lime kiln evaporate. My father may be an archangel, but my mother is the president of Purgatory. She shouldn't be zipping over to Antrum to check on me.

But lately, that's exactly what she has been doing. A lot.

As I peep at Lincoln, I can't help but cringe. "You called her again?" Over the last three weeks, I've been having mood swings galore, and sometimes a girl just needs her mother. Lincoln's been really cool about it, but it's still a little embarrassing.

Okay, a *lot* embarrassing.

Lincoln pulls me closer to him. "You're carrying a child of incredible supernatural power, right?"

I nod into his chest. I'm carrying the Scala Heir, and yeah, that's a big deal. At any one point in time, there can only be two people in the after-realms with the blood of a human, demon, and angel: the Scala and the Scala Heir. Sadly, there are no real records on Scala Heir pregnancy. My mother is my solo source of information. Unfortunately, finding out that I'm in any way uncomfortable transforms her from the awesome President of Purgatory (which is her new day job) into freaked-out mom (which was how I knew her growing up.)

"It's just embarrassing, that's all," I say.

"But you'll talk to her?"

"Sure. Thanks for calling her in." Now that I know Mom is here, I really do want a chat. Does Lincoln know me or what?

"No problem," says Lincoln. "Would you like some privacy? There are messages I can review in the study." He pinches the bridge of his nose. I know what that move means.

"Don't tell me. You got more letters from the so-called Supreme Leader?" I stifle the urge to roll my eyes. Supreme Leader…that's the title Lincoln's childhood friend Ethan has given himself, along with a lifelong mandate to write annoying letters to my husband. Long story.

I take that back. Actually, it's a short story. Some bad shiz went down when Lincoln and Ethan were kids, and now his Supreme Annoyingness lives on the Earth's surface where he sends a never-ending tirade of letters begging for extra guards to protect him.

"It *is* Ethan, isn't it?" I ask.

Lincoln sighs. "I have to accept his messages. I'm still his king. Besides, our annual diplomatic summit with Ethan's almost here." And by almost here, Lincoln means tomorrow.

My heart sinks. Not only does my honeymoon end today, but I also have to hang out with Ethan the Irritating tomorrow. Only one thing can make this summit palatable. "Can I kill him?"

The ghost of a smile rounds Lincoln's mouth. "No, and you're leaving your mother waiting."

Mom pipes up through the door. "Yes, you're leaving me waiting." Our chambers in Arx Hall are magically sound-proofed. Guess that's not the case here in the honeymoon palace.

Lincoln chuckles and kisses my cheek, which is my cue to slide off the comfort of his lap. And away I go, but I do take my time about it. Lap-snuggling with Lincoln is a definite marriage perk. We're sitting side by side on the mattress when Mom speaks through the door again.

"I need to see you, Myla-la."

Uh-oh. Things are getting serious if Mom's cracking out childhood pet names. I give Lincoln a gentle nudge with my elbow. "You better take off."

Lincoln rises and stretches. For the record, I love watching the play of muscles across his bare chest. "Fine. I'll be in the study." Although the bedroom has been our favorite hangout, this palace is huge. The study's in the adjoining chamber.

"I'll give you two your privacy," he adds.

"That's right," says Mom through the door. "Myla and I need girl time."

Lincoln guides me to my feet and straightens the lapels of my fancy black robe. "I'll be close."

One nice thing about thrax palaces is they all have hidden doors to adjoining rooms. Arx Hall even has a ton a secret passageways. In this palace, Lincoln only has to touch a panel of wall to open an archway to the study. The panel closes behind him with a soft click. I can't decide if I'm relieved to have time with Mom or sad to see Lincoln go.

I tap my chin. *Sad, definitely.*

"Is he still in the room?" asks Mom through the door.

"He's gone. I'm coming over."

After pulling my robe more tightly around me, I cross the fancypants chamber and open the door. Mom rushes in, looking panic stricken. She resembles an older version of me, so she has long auburn hair, a curvy figure, and a long black tail that's covered in dragonscales. She's wearing one of her classic purple skirt-suits, which means she just came from being presidential somewhere. A lead weight of guilt settles onto my shoulders.

She should be running Purgatory. Not coddling me.

After kicking the door shut behind her, Mom wraps me in one of her too-tight hugs. It feels great. "What happened?" she asks. "Did you see more orangutans in diapers?"

"No, this time it was my igni. They wanted to give me a message."

Mom leans back and inspects my face carefully. "They've done that before."

"Never this loudly, though. They pounded in my head until I figured out what they were saying."

Mom sighs and slips onto a nearby chair. "Some days, I wish I'd been the Great Scala instead of just pregnant with one."

"The igni choose who gets to be the Great Scala and Scala Heir. Consider yourself lucky. It's not that choice of a gig."

"That's just the problem. I could be far more helpful to you in cases like this if I had personal experiences with igni."

"You're sweet." I slump into a seat beside hers. "Talking to the igni was tough, but there's more bugging me. Everything feels so intense now. Is that normal?" For the record, I've asked this question a hundred times, but it helps to hear her answer.

"Being emotional is very common in pregnancy, even when you're carrying a so-called typical child."

I nod slowly, taking in this news again. It's good to hear how all pregnant ladies have mood swings. "Anything turn up from Dad's research?" My father's been using his "from the dawn of time" connections to find out more about Scala pregnancies.

"Yes, Xav uncovered a few items." Mom says this while making an *eek* face, so I know this isn't good.

"Lay it on me."

"Every Scala pregnancy is different. Some last years; others are over in a matter of a few months. It seems that the stronger the supernatural power, the shorter the pregnancy."

"Is there a baby power rating scale or anything? I'd really like some idea of the timeline here."

"I'm afraid not." She leans over and pats my hand. "Don't worry, Myla-la. I was pregnant with you for three months. I bet your pregnancy will last that long as well. Plus once the baby is born, things will get easier. I'm setting up a nursery right next to our bedroom."

"*Our* bedroom?"

"The one your father and I use. You still plan on living with us after the honeymoon, don't you?"

That would be no, not that I'm sharing this info right now. Lincoln and I plan to split our time evenly between Purgatory and Antrum. And even when we're in Purgatory, there's no way we're permanently living with my parents. Don't get me wrong; I love my parents. It's just that being around them all the time would quickly get super-awkward. As soon as we can, Lincoln and I plan to buy our own home.

"You are moving in, correct?" Mom is so not letting this drop.

Instead of answering, I dig into my years of mom management and make a noncommittal "umm" noise, which my mother takes for agreement to her "live at home forever" plan.

"I'm thrilled that you'll stay with us," she gushes. "Are you sure Octavia won't mind? I know she's wanted you in Antrum full time."

Every thrax alive knows Lincoln's mother wants us in Antrum full time.

"Lincoln and I will deal with Octavia."

"You two know best." Mom bobs a little in her seat, she's so happy. Cue additional guilt loading onto my shoulders. Mom grips my hand. "The remodeling has already begun, by the way. All our rooms will be in a row."

"A row?" I slowly slip out my hand from hers.

"First, there'll be our room, then the baby's room, and finally a room for you and Lincoln. We're even building a guesthouse in the yard for his parents."

"Ummm." For some reason, that's all I can get out again.

Sure, I knew Mom and Dad would want me and Lincoln to live nearby, but they're actually doing renovations at this very second?

"When will you move in?" asks Mom. "Tomorrow night, maybe?"

Thank Hells I have a good answer to this question. "Oh, Lincoln and I have a summit that starts tomorrow, remember? It lasts for a week."

"Ah, yes. You're talking with that thrax who wants guards so he can live on the Earth's surface. Bethan." For the record, Mom hates Ethan almost as much as I do. She makes a point of forgetting his name. I never correct her. "What house is he from again?"

"Viator." Thrax life is divided up into houses. There are four major houses—Acca, Horus, Kamal, and Striga—and a bunch of minor ones. Viator is one of those minor houses, as in *very minor*. In fact, their big claim to fame is that they were the first thrax to use Pulpitum platforms in order to transfer to the Earth's surface. Not sure what else they've done, other than create a mega-loser like Ethan.

Mom folds her arms over her chest. "Tomorrow you start a week of negotiations, but what about after that? When will you move in exactly?"

My jaw falls open. Mom is pushing this super hard. Time to change the subject. "Honestly, Mom? I can't focus on the future right now. I'm still stuck on something the igni just said."

Mom's eyes light up with concern. "What's that, honey?"

"They gave me a name. Mirror Man. Is he some Purgatory guy?" I cross my fingers, hoping for good news here. My tail pops up and does its own modified version of a finger-cross, which involves curling its arrowhead-shaped end. I appreciate the support.

"Mirror Man." Mom shakes her head. "That's a name that I've never heard before."

"Oh."

My disappointment must be obvious because Mom gives me an extra-bright smile. "But I will ask your father."

"Thanks." I squirm in my chair, thinking how Mom is constantly running around for me. "You know, I really appreciate you coming over on short notice. I do realize that you have all of Purgatory to lead."

"It's fine. I always keep a transport Pulpitum on standby for Antrum." She does that mom-thing where she beams at me like I hung the moon and stars. It's pretty awesome.

"You're the best."

"Of course, I am." Mom winks. "I gave birth to you." She stands up, takes a step toward the door, and pauses. "Oh, I almost forgot. Your rooms will be ready tomorrow, so you and Lincoln can move in once that silly diplomatic meeting with Kethan is over." She fans herself with her hands. "I can't believe it. My baby will be home again—and with her own baby, too."

My heart sinks. Sure, it's no surprise that the rooms will be ready so quickly. My father is general of the angels, and he has all sorts of magical folks with feathers who build things quickly. In addition, it's no shocker that my honeymoon is ending.

It's just a total bummer.

I try to slap on a smile. "Thanks, Mom." My tail rises behind me to give her a modified wave. It's much better at pretending happiness than I am.

"Excellent. See you in a week!" She practically skip-walks out of the room.

Once Mom is gone, I stare at the closed door. Lincoln and I haven't really chatted about our plans after the honeymoon is over. Of course, we'll split time between our realms. That said, we haven't discussed which one we'd hit first. Getting married was a drama—Armageddon crashed our wedding ceremony after all—and our honeymoon has been spent doing important things like playing kissing games. Now, reality looms large.

And it will be here tomorrow.

The idea makes me want to cry, and for once, I don't think it's all pregnancy hormones. The actuality of being a ruler, wife, and mother becomes overwhelming. Take the queen stuff, for instance. I have no idea what's needed from me, other than a laundry list of projects. For instance, we have problems with the magical flow of oxygen to Antrum. To help out, I promised to review plans for a new system. If I screw that up, no big deal, everyone just dies a painful death without air. So that's what I know about queenly stuff.

When it comes to being a wife, all I know is that there's

some nutjob who's decided to plague my husband with daily messages. How do I stop Ethan? Even more importantly, how I prevent Lincoln from feeling responsible for every little thing in Antrum? No easy answers there, either.

And last but not least, there's the baby. I haven't even thought about anything maternal. For example, I don't know what crib I'll get for the baby's room. Mostly because I haven't made a final decision on what room or rooms to put said baby into.

Hells Bells.

Standing up, I go off in search of Lincoln. Sometimes, a girl just needs a hug from her husband.

3

J find Lincoln in the study, which is an oak room lined with leather-bound books. Every so often, the many tall shelves are separated by a single floor-length mirror. Comfy club chairs and round tables dot the floor. It's a classic thrax space, really. If it has a ton of secret passageways and silencer spells, it could be just like Arx Hall, our main palace.

Lincoln stands in the chamber's center, his arms braced onto a round wooden table that's piled high with white envelopes. A few medieval parchments lay rolled off to the side. My throat tightens with anger. I know exactly who sent all those white envelopes. Ethan.

What a creep.

Lincoln still wears his jeans and nothing else, which is great to see. Most thrax stay "medieval traditional" even when they're hanging at home. However, Lincoln's logged so many hours doing demon patrols on Earth, he likes to dress mortal-style. It's one of the many things I like about him: my guy isn't afraid to do his own thing.

I step closer, and sure enough, the many large envelopes sport the insignia of Ethan's company, Hunter Enterprises. All the messages have been opened, except for one. It rests on the table between Lincoln's braced arms.

My tail whips behind me in a predatory rhythm. "Are you going to open that new letter from Ethan?"

"Opening things from Ethan?" Lincoln shakes his head. "I have far bigger things to worry about." Lincoln scoops up a parchment, unrolls it, and pretends to be fascinated by its contents. *Riiiiiight.* I know my guy. That unopened letter is bugging him. It always takes him a while to work up to reading these nasty missives.

I stand behind Lincoln and wrap my arms around his waist. "Hey, I get that you and Ethan were buddies, but he needs to leave you alone now."

Lincoln and Ethan hung out when they were kids. Then everything changed. Ethan's parents became possessed while on demon patrol. After returning to Antrum, they killed Ethan's only sister and then offed each other. It's a truly horrific story.

Still, something about the whole thing has always struck me as strange.

I mean, the entire reason thrax live underground is to screen people for stuff like demonic possession. Case in point: Lady Adair was possessed, and she set off alarm bells all the time. In her case, she had a good cover story. Everyone thought she was the Scala Heir, and that role is *supposed* to be partly demonic. But Ethan's parents just waltz into Antrum with demons inside them, and not a single alarm goes off? I don't get how that happened.

Lincoln is still pretending to be fascinated by his scroll. He gives the parchment a little shake. "What an interesting analysis of food distribution between the houses."

I go on tiptoe and peep over his shoulder. "Really? Because you're holding it upside down."

Lincoln resets the parchment on the table and sighs. "Ethan is my subject. He has every right to send me messages. It's *my* problem that I allow his requests to bother me."

"You can't blame yourself for what happened."

"Yes, I can. I was on Pulpitum-training duty when Ethan's parents came through. I should have detected their possession."

"How? You were ten years old."

"Someone could have looked into their eyes. With that level of possession, their irises had to be glowing."

I rest my cheek against his back. "You can't take responsibility for everything. There's a whole magical system for detecting demons when thrax transfer in and out of Antrum. It should have set off alarm bells without anyone checking eyeballs."

"Well, the alarms didn't sound, and I was there. As the ranking noble, that makes it my responsibility."

Now, I want to ask whether the thrax engineers found anything wrong with that particular Pulpitum afterwards, but Lincoln always gets super-grouchy whenever I raise this issue. So, I silently vow to keep my mouth shut.

Aaaaaaaand my vow lasts all of two seconds.

"Did they ever find anything wrong with the transfer station?" I ask.

"No."

"So, it's been successfully detecting demons ever since then?"

"Myla, you know it has."

"The whole thing doesn't make sense, that's all I'm saying."
I mean, the odd demonic item can come in and out without
setting off alarms. But people? Never.

"We're a traditional society and our rulers *always* take
responsibility."

*Don't point out Lincoln's father. Don't point out Lincoln's father.
Don't point out Lincoln's father.*

Screw it. I'm pointing out Lincoln's father.

"When your dad was king, he didn't take responsibility.
Like ever."

Lincoln pinches the bridge of his nose. "Myla." He's getting
exasperated, and yeah, I feel for him. But if I don't tell him the
truth, who will?

I step to the side and take Lincoln's hands in mine. That
way, he has to face me when I say my next bit. "Please, all I ask
is for you to consider the possibility that you've been raised to
take on way too much. There's something fishy about Ethan."

"He's a great leader," counters Lincoln. "No thrax settle-
ment has ever lasted this long on the Earth's surface."

And this is true. Sort of. After his family died, Ethan
decided that Antrum wasn't secure, and he built his own
colony on Earth. In some ways, Earth life is easy for the thrax.
Humans are totally oblivious to angelic and demonic stuff.
Like when I join demon patrol, I don't need to hide my tail or
anything.

But the hard part for thrax? That would be staying not-
dead on Earth for any length of time.

Thrax are part angel, and that angelic energy draws
demons like a magnet. Plus, nothing makes a demon happier
than killing a thrax demon hunter. Rogue thrax rarely last
more than a week or two on Earth before a demon offs them.
And yes, Ethan's colony has lasted for years.

That said, I'm still not buying the "Ethan is a great leader" line. I go into my classic retort. "If Ethan is so awesome, why don't we hear more from his so-called followers? Who's actually living in that colony, anyway?"

"I've raised that same query to Ethan," answers Lincoln. "He promised to bring some of his subjects to the summit tomorrow, as well as a sampling of the technology he's developed. He claims it's revolutionary."

"Huh. Like what kind of tech is he bringing, do you know?"

Lincoln shakes his head. "I'm aware of some new Earth weapons, but too much happens for me to stay abreast of everything. How about you?"

"If it was state-of-the-art twenty years ago, then the ghouls picked it out of a Dumpster and brought it to Purgatory. Other than that, we haven't gotten much new tech, even after we kicked the ghouls out."

Lincoln's mouth thins. That's his worried face. "I wish I knew more about Earth devices."

I snap my fingers. "I know who's an expert. Cissy." She's been my best friend since forever and now serves as diplomatic senator in Purgatory.

"Really?"

"Oh sure. Since she's part envy demon, it's in her DNA to shop. You can't have the best of everything if you don't know what's best, right?"

"I never thought of it that way."

"And Zeke is running the senatorial guard these days." *That's Cissy's boyfriend.* "She stays up-to-date on weapons so she can help him be safe. She's even become a wiz with computers. To her, it's all just another category of shopping."

Lincoln picks up a blank parchment and scribbles out a

note. "Done. I'll have her invited to the summit." He strides over to the main door, calls a guard from the outer hallway, and hands off the message.

Once the parchment's on its way, Lincoln closes the door and returns his focus to me. "How about we get back to our honeymoon?" His mouth is smiling, but his eyes stay filled with worry.

"Ethan's letter is still bugging you." I press a gentle kiss to his cheek. "I love the fact that you want to take the world on your shoulders. But now that I'm here, I'm going to make sure you don't *actually* do that." I shoot him a sly grin. "It's really bad for your back."

Lincoln gives me a look of a pure adoration. "I love you, Myla. Never get serious and stuffy on me. Promise?"

"I love you, too. And I'm not sure serious is possible for me anyway."

For a long moment, we do nothing but share smiles and feel awesome that we're together. Unfortunately, after a few seconds, that look of concern returns to Lincoln's eyes.

I give his fingers a squeeze. "Why don't you open the envelope?"

A muscle feathers along Lincoln's jawline. "I absolutely loathe the idea of my people up there, unprotected." He eyes the sealed envelope from Ethan. "I'll open it in the morning."

I stare at the message as well. "It says *Code Orange* on it. Doesn't that mean you could have thrax at risk?" All of Ethan's other messages have been marked *Code Yellow*.

"It does."

"So, it'll bug the crap out of you until you open it."

Lincoln nods. "True."

"Then open it up, see that it's nothing, and write him

another message to hold his horses until tomorrow. That way, you can enjoy the rest of our honeymoon."

Lincoln leans in until our foreheads touch. "When did you get so smart?"

"It's just my natural state of being."

"Quite." Lincoln turns and swipes the envelope from the tabletop. "Here goes." He tears open the message.

A sheet of paper falls out. I scoop it up and scan the contents. "It's more blah-blah *send me troops* blah-blah."

Lincoln tips the envelope over. A small arrowhead slides out onto his palm.

Wait, what? Who sends an arrowhead to their king? I know I'm supposed to be Queen of these people, but sometimes I really don't understand them at all. Meanwhile, the black metal gleams against Lincoln's pale skin. The ghost of a smile rounds my guy's mouth.

"Ethan made this," says Lincoln.

"How do you know?" I ask.

"There are tiny runes carved into the black metal. It's his mark."

"Wow. I don't think of Ethan as making anything but you crazy."

Lincoln chuckles. "When we were kids, Ethan washed out of thrax warrior training, so he started into the trades. He was always making little gadgets and models of weapons. It was a hobby we both shared."

"You made little models?" I can't picture Lincoln and handicrafts.

"I didn't say I was good at it." Lincoln fiddles with the small black arrowhead. "Everything Ethan crafts has a little trick to it. When we were boys, he used to make things for me all the time." Suddenly, the end of the arrowhead telescopes out, transforming it into a full arrow. "How clever. I wonder what kind of metal he used."

For a moment, a carefree and joyful look shines in Lincoln's mismatched eyes. I can picture the child he once was, and how that little kid loved sharing models with his buddy. It was a nice move for Ethan to send this arrow. For a moment, I decide that I almost like Ethan.

Emphasis on the word *almost*.

Lincoln sets the arrow down. "I suppose I should get started on that reply. It's a thoughtful gift, but we're still not sending any troops."

At those words, our world falls apart.

The arrow explodes into a column of black flame. A wall of heat and dark fire engulfs both me and Lincoln. Neither of us burns, however. Every cell in my body goes on alert. Black fire? No burning? That can only mean one thing.

This is a spell, no question about it.

And even worse, it's black magic.

Black magic is illegal in Antrum and for a good reason. To cast it, you need to drain someone's soul, preferably someone strong and angelic. It's really complex, not to mention disgusting. How would a lowly thrax like Ethan learn how to do something as tricky as drain souls? The flames lick around the room, but I can't focus on them. Instead, a single question keeps rolling around in my mind.

Why would Ethan send Lincoln a booby-trapped message?

The answer comes quickly. The entire room shudders as one of the floor-length mirrors bursts outward. Shards of glass fly in our direction. I crouch into a defensive stance; Lincoln curls his body around mine.

The room seems to flip. Instead of gravity pulling us toward the floor, everything's now being drawn into the broken mirror. Books, tables, tapestries, and knickknacks…it all gets pulled into the blackened hole where the frame once held the mirror.

Adrenaline surges through my veins. Acting on instinct, my tail jams into the floorboards, becoming an anchor to keep me in place. A vortex of wind whips about the room, extinguishing the magical fire and causing my robe to billow about my legs. Lincoln tumbles toward the open hole. His face and chest are scratched all over by broken glass. Reaching forward, I grab his hands in mine.

I won't let him go.

The din of wind grows louder. I scream over the noise, "What's happening?"

Lincoln's face twists with the effort of grasping my hands. "Summoning spell."

"Where?" I don't know a lot about legal magic, let alone the black stuff.

Lincoln keeps his voice carefully controlled, but I can see terror sparkling in his mismatched eyes. "Don't know."

I'm now standing and grasping Lincoln as more stuff gets sucked into the blackened window-hole. Mirrors tumble off the walls, shattering as they fall into the darkened space. Books tear apart as they spiral away. All the while, my entire body strains with the effort to hold Lincoln's hands. The arrowhead end of my tail stays spiked into the floor. Still, I'm not sure how much longer it can hold out.

With every passing second, the pull into the broken mirror-hole grows stronger.

All of a sudden, my tail loses its anchor-grip into the floorboards. Lincoln and I tumble forward a few yards before my tail punches through the floor again, holding us both in place once more. The movement makes me lose my two-handed grip with Lincoln.

Damn. I only hold Lincoln by a single wrist now. My fingers ache from clutching him so tightly. The wind howls in my ears and whips through my hair. Bits of wood splinter as my tail cuts through the flooring.

Lincoln's gaze locks with mine. "You can't hold me much longer." His mismatched eyes now glint with determination. "Too much weight."

I know what he's thinking. He wants to let go and get pulled off to Hell-knows-where. I won't allow it.

"No!" I cry. "Hold on!"

All of a sudden, my igni appear out of nowhere. Both light and dark voices echo in my mind and materialize around my body. Instantly, they multiply into thousands of tiny lightning bolts of power, whipping around me like a school of fish. I'd know that shape anywhere. It's a soul column. The igni create these to move a spirit to Heaven or Hell.

And they are circling around me.

I remember the name they spoke before. Mirror Man.

The igni aren't anywhere near Lincoln, only me. Is this their way of saying that I have to let him go?

Well, screw my igni. Even if they are supernatural, I am not releasing Lincoln for anyone. He's twenty. I'm nineteen. We're expecting. This can't be the end.

"Hold on!" I call again.

"We both know the igni don't want that!" yells Lincoln.

"You can see them?" They rarely show themselves to anyone but me.

More bits of glass and debris fly past us. I'm protected by my igni, but Lincoln's beautiful face becomes crisscrossed with fresh cuts. "You and the baby must be safe."

"No!" I try to keep my grip solid, but the pull from the mirror-hole is too strong. My grasp on Lincoln slips from his wrist to his fingers. All the while, my tail is losing its battle with the floorboards. The pull from the mirror-hole has us steadily slicing through more and more wood. Some small part of me knows this is an impossible situation. A dozen thoughts fly through my mind at once. There are so many things I want to tell Lincoln. How much I care about him. The many ways he's changed my life for the better. Why our child needs him. I only get out a single cry. "Please!"

"I love you, Myla."

With that, Lincoln lets go of my hand.

I can only watch in horror as the love of my life tumbles through the broken mirror-hole and into the darkness beyond. All the while, he keeps his gaze locked with mine. The igni grow brighter as I scream my head off.

Then the igni's white light turns incredibly strong, blocking out my vision. My mind quickly fades into nothingness as well. The last thing I'm aware of as I lose consciousness is a single fact.

I do not stop screaming.

hen I become aware again, I'm still yelling my lungs out. It takes me a moment to realize I've returned to my honeymoon bedroom. Lincoln's beside me. I'm lying on my back. While resting his weight on his left elbow, Lincoln gently shakes my shoulder with his right hand.

"Myla, wake up," he says softly.

I pant in a few rough breaths, but I do stop screaming. "What happened?" I ask.

"You're having another bad dream."

I sit upright and check my clothes. Yup, I'm still in my robe from last night. I scan Lincoln carefully. All the bloody scratches are gone, and he's wearing blue silk pajamas. I cup his face in my hands. "Are you all right?"

"Of course, I'm fine. The bigger question is…are you feeling okay? You've been nothing but trouble these past few weeks." He winks. "Not that I'm complaining. You are carrying my kid and all."

I freeze. This is so screwed up it isn't even funny. Lincoln never acts like my pregnancy is a burden. And he certainly doesn't ever refer to me as a Myla-shaped vessel that exists solely to carry his child. I drop my hands from Lincoln's face. "What happened last night?"

"Don't you remember?" He chuckles. "More pregnancy hormones."

"Answer the question, please."

"Your mom stopped by to help with your latest baby freak-out. I went to the study. When I came back, you were snoozing." He eyes me hungrily. "Come here and give me a good morning kiss."

That's not happening. At least, not until I get some answers.

Instead of moving in closer, I scooch farther away. "Why are you wearing pajamas?" Lincoln's mother Octavia constantly buys him nighttime wear, but that's only for show. Lincoln always sleeps nude. Yet another reason why this is so screwy.

"This is what people wear when they sleep, Myla."

"You don't."

Lincoln shakes his head. "What? You're an expert on me after a three-week honeymoon?"

"You do realize that everything you're saying is an insult, right?" I tick off the comments on my fingers. "I'm crazy with pregnancy. I'm nothing but a baby carrier for you. I'm overestimating how well I know you. This isn't the normal Lincoln here."

He sighs. "I'm sorry if I'm acting a little crazy, Myla. It's just that hearing you scream threw me off this morning. Whatever I'm saying, it's only because I'm worried about you and our child. I'm truly sorry if it came off as rude or whatever."

"You've never acted this way before."

"I've never almost been a father before." He slides closer to me on the mattress. "Why, did something else happen last night? I mean, you've been having wild nightmares ever since you got knocked up. Did you see stuff in your dreams? Anything bad?"

Normally, I'd never lie to Lincoln. But this whole situation is beyond strange. My inner warrior sense says, *Danger*, and I always listen to that part of my soul. After all, it's what's kept me alive since I first stepped out onto the Arena floor at the tender age of twelve. I force my face into a carefully neutral look. "No, it's just as you said. My mother stopped by and I went to sleep. I don't remember anything specific that happened in my nightmares."

"Good. If that changes, let me know." He gives me a sweet smile. "You and the baby. That's my world, Myla. You know that, don't you?"

His mismatched eyes are so sincere. And that voice? It's the deep tone I've come to love. "I do, Lincoln."

"Why don't you get cleaned up, and I'll order us some food. Does that sound like a plan?"

"It does, thanks." How very like Lincoln to know how much I value my meals. Maybe things will look different once I've showered and eaten. I slide out of bed. "I'll start getting ready."

"Awesome. I can't wait to see my beautiful wife in her Scala robes."

He seems so kind and honest that I can't find the words to reply. Instead, I leave the room, pad down the outer hallway, and feel a heavy sense of guilt tumble in my stomach. What is happening to me? Did I really just lie to Lincoln? This supernatural pregnancy has me all kinds of whacked out. What if I'm remembering my made-up nightmares as real? What kind of person lies to her husband about something like that? I ponder that for all of twenty seconds before coming to a firm decision.

No way am I questioning myself on this one. I'll stay true to my warrior instincts. Something is definitely wrong here. I just need to figure out what.

Fortunately, I do some of my best thinking in the shower, and this honeymoon palace has an amazing one. It's all white tile, burnished steel fixtures, and—best of all—it holds an enchanted mini-waterfall. Most of the time when I wash up in Antrum, the servants fill a tub for me. But in this palace, the experience is just like back home in Purgatory, only better because a waterfall in a shower stall is just that cool. The moment I turn the handle, the perfect temperature of liquid cascades from the top of the stall.

Now, I like to putter around a little before getting into the water. So I check the drawers and pull out my toothpaste. Meanwhile, the bathroom quickly fills with heated vapor. Stepping over to the sink, I find the mirror covered in condensation. I wipe away the mist with my sleeve. My face looks as it always does: full lips, blue eyes, amber skin, and auburn hair.

All of a sudden, my reflection disappears. In its place, I see Lincoln. He's bare-chested and pounding against the opposite side of the mirror with bloodied fists. Worst of all, he's screaming with rage.

I slap my hands over my mouth. It takes all my strength not to scream as well.

The image is gone as quickly as it appeared. But the vision of Lincoln—*my* Lincoln—trapped and enraged still fills my mind.

For a long moment, I can only stare at my own reflection. The igni had warned me about the Mirror Man. That must have been their way of saying that this would happen to Lincoln. He somehow got trapped in another dimension or something. I shoot a wary look at the closed bathroom door.

I don't know who's out there, but one thing is for certain.

That's not my husband.

5

I march out the bathroom door and enter the main hallway. Steam billows in behind me from the shower. I shudder, remembering the image of the real Lincoln screaming in the mirror. He looked hurt. In agony. Bands of worry tighten around my head.

Where is my husband?

An image appears in my mind: the smarmy creepster I woke up next to this morning. I decide to give him a new name, *Evil Lincoln,* mostly because Douchebag Lincoln is too much of a mouthful. All my anxiety instantly transforms into white-hot rage. How dare someone kidnap my guy? I head off in search of my fake husband and some real answers. The last time I saw Evil Lincoln, he was in our—excuse me, my— bedroom. I kick open the door. "Howdy, honey."

No one is there.

"Lincoln? Sweetums?"

Still no answer.

That's a bit of a bummer, but it's a big palace, after all.

With that, I hunt through the rest of the honeymoon

castle. Room after room, closet after closet. I leave no area unexamined. There's no one around. Not unless you count the guards, in any case.

Fine. Evil Lincoln took off. I'll still track him down.

I don't memorize the guard rotations like *my* Lincoln, but I do know the captain will be hanging out by the front gate.

That's my next stop.

I march up to the main entrance. It's basically a huge stone room sporting a massive oak door with one of those iron grates over it. A small red door sits to the right of the main gate. I try the handle.

Locked.

I pound on the door. "Hey there, it's your Royal Me-ness out here. Open up. I need to speak with the Captain of the guard."

There's a bunch of rustling and whispering, but finally the door swings open. An older guy stands on the threshold. I can tell by the extra jewels sewn on his Rixa tunic that he's not only the Captain, but he's also one of Lincoln's private guards. I scan him carefully. This Captain's a lean guy with brown hair that holds flecks of gray at his temples. He's named...uh, something.

Note to self: get better with names.

"Your Majesty," says the mystery Captain. "Is anything amiss?"

"Why yes, there is, as a matter of fact. Where is the guy who was here this morning?"

His eyes widen, which make the crinkles around them smooth out a little. "You mean the High, uh, King?" Lincoln used to be the high prince. Now he's King and I'm Queen. The staff still gets the titles mixed up sometimes. Hey, at least I'm not alone in forgetting stuff.

"Whatever," I say. "Where did that guy go?"

"I'm not at liberty to tell you."

"No?" My tail arches menacingly behind me.

"I'm afraid not."

The guy's name appears to me in a flash. "Williamson."

"Yes?"

"Do you value your job?"

"Yes."

My tail makes jabby motions at his head. "How about your life?"

"Obviously, as do my wife and three children."

Okay, that tidbit of information takes some of the rage-wind out of my anger-sails. "Can you please tell me where the, uh, King has gone?"

"He just stepped out for a few minutes. There are some matters of state that he didn't want to burden you with. I'm instructed to get you anything you need. He'll rejoin you in the main receiving room as soon as he can." He lowers his voice to a whisper. "Please, Your Majesty. We have orders to restrain you if you try to leave."

"You do?"

I go on tiptoe. Outside the palace, about a dozen guards are flanking the main entrance. I can take down that many, easy-peasy, but I really should lay low with the pregnancy and all. The reason? My fighting style is pretty physical. Normally, I give and receive body blows all the time. But that's not something I want to risk while pregnant. Besides, most these warriors are from Lincoln's private guard. It doesn't feel right to hurt them for doing their job.

At length, I let out a long breath. "Fine. I'll wait in the receiving room. You're sure that he'll join me right away?"

"That's what the King said."

"Got it. I'll get dressed and meet him there." *Not that I have much choice.*

I take off at a quick walk and try not to worry too much.

Just a few minutes.

I can handle that.

A few minutes, my ass.

After talking to Williamson, I changed into my Scala robes and hit the receiving room. Since then, three freaking hours have slowly ticked by while I've waited. I'm now overly familiar with every tapestry, floor plank, and porcelain knick-knack in this stupid chamber.

It's making me crazy.

At times like these, I wish we had telephones in Antrum. Why must absolutely everything stay stuck in the Middle Ages? I mean, this room doesn't even have an old-time wall phone where you talk into a black cup. Outside of screaming from a window, I have no way of contacting anyone.

And yeah, I've thought about screaming.

Trouble is, the honeymoon palace is surrounded by acres of what's called the Crystal Woods. Here the trees made from white stone, which make for a nice postcard (if the thrax used postcards). Still the place is mega-huge. I'd have to yell for a helluva long time before anyone would hear me. And although I could still attack the guards and make a run for it, I honestly don't know where I am. Lincoln and I rode a carriage to get here. At the time, I was too busy kissing my new husband to plan an escape route.

That doesn't mean I don't have any options, though. I cross my fingers, close my eyes, and mentally call my igni.

They haven't responded all morning, but there's always a chance this time will be different.

Come to me, my little ones.

A few seconds tick by as I wait for my supernatural buddies to reply.

They don't.

Again.

I grit my teeth with frustration. Why aren't my igni answering? I've been calling them for hours without any response. And the worst part of this situation? There are two mirrors in this receiving room and—although I check them constantly—I have yet to see my Lincoln.

What's happened to him?

For the umpteenth time, I yank open the door to the main hallway. Two warriors step onto the threshold, blocking my exit. The guards have taken to hanging right outside the receiving room door. Why? My many visits to the main gate were freaking them out. They didn't want a woman "in my condition" to be traipsing around the palace any more.

Sheesh. Like pregnancy means I can't walk five minutes to bug my own guards. Not for the first time, I wish I were back in Arx Hall. That place is lousy with secret passages. There's no way I could be held in one room for long. This stupid reception chamber doesn't even have more than one door in or out. That has to be a fire code violation of some kind.

Note to self: get this palace inspected as soon as possible. Install more doors.

All of which brings me back to the present moment. I'm now staring at the two young warriors who block my exit. Both carry the look of the House of Rixa: tall and lean with sharp cheekbones. They remind me a little of Lincoln.

Okay, they remind me a lot of him. My eyes sting with held-in tears.

My Lincoln. The love of my life is locked up somewhere, and I can't help him. I don't even know where he's being imprisoned. I open my mouth, but no words come out.

"Yes, Your Majesty?" asks the first guard. I'm pretty sure his name is Manfred, but who knows? Memorizing guard rotation schedules was always firmly on the Lincoln-side of our relationship.

"I want to—" I begin.

"Are you certain you're all right?" asks Maybe Manfred. The gentle way he asks the question, you wouldn't think I'd been opening the door every two minutes for the last three hours, asking where my fake husband was.

But I have. And my naturally thin patience is almost completely worn out.

"Can we get you anything to eat, Great Scala?" asks the second guard. Unlike Maybe Manfred, I have no clue what this guy's name is, nor do I have the internal bandwidth to retain that information right now. As a result, I've been thinking of him as Could Be Bob.

"No," I say slowly. "What I want is to leave."

"You know we can't allow that," says Maybe Manfred. "Your husband sent orders."

"Would you like some demon bars?" asks Could Be Bob. "Our King said you could have as many as you want."

Demon bars. The very mention of my one-time favorite snack makes my inner wrath monster growl with frustration.

"Come on. My Lincoln would *never* want me to have demon bars. You're on his personal guard. He trained you. You know the man lives on carrots and raw nuts. Do you really think he'd send his pregnant wife demon bars?"

The guards stare guiltily at their feet. My warrior sense kicks in. I can tell when I'm gaining an advantage, and that foot-staring routine? It means these guards suspect something is wrong, too. I lower my voice to a conspiratorial tone. "Have you seen anything *strange* in mirrors lately?"

Both of their heads snap up. The guards stare at me like I'm insane. Okay, maybe the mirror-thing was a stretch to lead with. I decide to veer back onto firmer Lincoln ground. "Forget the mirrors. Look at me." I gesture across myself. "I've been sitting around for three hours, and the King sends orders to you, but not a single word to me? You know that's not Lincoln. So let me leave and go talk to him. Or at least, get the so-called King here, so I can confront him."

The guards go back to staring at their feet once more. I decide that I hate Maybe Manfred and Could Be Bob. I need to try someone else.

"Get me Captain Williamson."

"He's busy," says Maybe Manfred.

I lower my voice to a deep rumble and decide to call in the big guns. That would be my Scala powers. "Find him or you both will rot in Hell. I'm talking burning. With Armageddon. Forever." With that, I slam the door.

Okay, the Hell thing was harsh, but I really need to get out of here.

A few minutes later, Williamson steps into the room. My heart lightens. Guess the Hell thing might have been rough, yet it was still pretty darned effective. Williamson gingerly closes the door behind him.

"You asked for me, Your Majesty?"

Now, I've been doing a lot of "Old Myla" stuff, which has involved attitude and threats. Hey, my husband got sucked into a mirror, and an impostor took his place, so sure, I lost it for a while. But outside of getting Williamson in here, the Old Myla hasn't been too effective. It's time to give my Queenly side a try.

A small voice in the back of my head says there's a lot more to being Queen than acting regal, but I push those thoughts aside. I need to find my husband. Tilting my head, I offer Williamson what I hope is a truly regal smile. "Why don't you have a seat?"

"If you insist."

"I do." With that, I plunk my butt onto the same chair my mom used.

Williamson sits across from me. "How can I be of service, Your Majesty?"

I lower my voice to a whisper. "You must know something's wrong with the King. I need your help."

Williamson rubs his neck. "It's not my place to do anything."

I take care to keep my voice low. There's no way I want the guards outside to hear us. This is the honeymoon palace, not Arx Hall, and my chambers aren't soundproof. "If you won't help me, who will? The summit with Ethan starts shortly. The supposed Supreme Leader will ask for more thrax warriors to protect him on Earth."

Every line in Williamson's body stiffens. "But none of the guards who go there ever return. Our King would never authorize more troops for Ethan."

"The guy who's calling himself the King is not my Lincoln. I must confront this impostor. It's the only way to find the true King. But I can't do that while I'm sitting in here alone. Again, I need your help. Please."

Williamson runs his hand through his loose brown hair. "We've sent a number of runners asking for an update from the King in terms of when he'll come back. His replies have been...odd."

"Like what?"

"Ordering demon bars for you to eat. Keeping you locked up. Insisting we restrain you if you try to leave."

"Exactly."

Williamson bounces his knees in a nervous rhythm. "At first, I suspected the King had encountered something on his last demon patrol—perhaps he ran across an enchantment of some kind. But we have royal mages who check for such things. They've reported back."

"And?"

"They say he's clean. No enchantments."

"But you're still not convinced that everything is fine."

Williamson doesn't reply. In my book, that's as good as a yes.

"Where is Octavia in all this?" I ask.

Lincoln's mother is notorious for knowing everything that happens in Antrum, sometimes before it even takes place.

"All morning long, the King has been communicating with the major houses in Antrum. Most of the minor ones, too. All his messages say the same thing: you're in a crazed mental state due to your pregnancy."

It takes an effort to keep my voice calm as I ask my next question. "And what does everyone think about that?"

"With so many requests for your mother to help you, I'm afraid that the King's explanation has been accepted by every-one, including the Queen Emeritus. To be honest, I might have believed it too, only I can see the truth with my own eyes. You're perfectly fine."

The door swings open. It's Maybe Manfred. "The King is en route."

Williamson exhales. "It seems you'll be able confront him without my help."

"It seems." I force another smile and try to think of something Queenly to close off with. "You may return to your duties."

Williamson bows before retaking his place in the outer hallway alongside the other guards. For a while, I pace around the receiving room. After that, I step out into the hall myself. At last, Evil Lincoln is coming.

This, I have to see.

A drumroll of footsteps sounds on the polished wooden floor as Evil Lincoln saunters toward me, all smiles. Along the arched ceiling, pennants with the Rixa crest sway slightly as Evil Lincoln strides beneath them. The sight makes my hands clench. Whoever this stranger is, he has no right to walk under the mark of Rixa. Plus, Evil Lincoln is now wearing the full kingly get-up. I'm talking tunic, crown, tall boots—the works. He has no right to that, either.

Evil Lincoln strolls past me and into the receiving chamber. There's not even a fake hello; I'm just expected to follow. I shoot Williamson a glare that says, *See? This is not my husband.* A flicker of sympathy shines in Williamson's eyes before he's back to standing at attention against the wall. The other guards keep staring guiltily at their feet.

At least I have a possible ally in Williamson. That may be useful in the future.

However right now, I have a fake husband to deal with. Anger corkscrews up my spine. How dare Evil Lincoln march past me without a word? I take in a series of deep breaths, trying to soothe the rage monster inside me.

Calm down, Myla. This is about saving my Lincoln, not

squashing an impostor. Well, actually it's about both. But saving my Lincoln is the first priority.

I nod once to myself, my plan set. I'm still Queen Myla, and I'll manipulate the truth from this impostor with my superior brainpower. With that resolution firmly in place, I saunter into the receiving room. Behind me, my tail gently closes the door.

Evil Lincoln turns to me, throwing his arms open. "Hello, gorgeous." He gives me a smarmy grin, hikes up his tunic, and starts to loosen the waistline of his leather pants.

I point at his hands. "What's that all about?"

"I've been gone for a while." He gives me what's supposed to be a sexy wink.

"Thought you might want some alone-time with me."

Of all the things I expected from Evil Lincoln, him waltzing through the door and looking for sex wasn't on the list. At all. "Slow down there, bub. I do not want any alone-time with you. What I want is *out* of this freaking palace."

He blinks innocently. "You do?"

And with that, the "New Queen Me" starts to fade under a barrage of Old Myla fury. "You just locked me up. Do you seriously think I want to fool around with you right now?"

Evil Lincoln shakes his head. "Your mouth is saying no." He eyes me slowly from head to toe. My Scala robes are made of skin-tight white fabric. "But your body's saying yes."

That does it.

Whatever Queenly sanity I had? It vanishes into thin air. Using my mind, I command my Scala robes to change into heavy white body armor and kickass boots. This is a major perk of being the Great Scala, by the way. Instant battle readiness.

Once the change is complete, I lunge straight for Evil

Lincoln. Sweeping his leg, I knock him onto the ground. Once Evil Lincoln is flat on his back, I take a seat right on his sternum. My tail arcs over my shoulder so its arrowhead-pointed end is aimed right for Evil Lincoln's jugular.

He gasps. "What's the problem, babe?"

"If you so much as flinch the wrong way, my tail will take you down. It hates you." To emphasize the point, my tail does its scary snake-slither move, where it shimmies in a zigzag.

By the way, my tail normally has a thing for Lincoln. In fact, it'll sometimes do stuff for my husband that it'd never do for me. So the fact that my backside has gone straight for the jugular? It's even more proof that I'm dealing with an impostor.

"Call off your tail. I'm your husband. You don't want to kill me."

"You are *not* my husband and we both know it. Death is the least you deserve."

Honestly, I wouldn't really murder Evil Lincoln at this point. Even so, I don't want *him* to know that. A frightened enemy is a blabby enemy. This impostor simply must tell me where my real husband is hidden. To emphasize the amount of danger, I force my irises to glow demon red. "Tell me where my real husband is being held, and I won't kill you."

Evil Lincoln's eyes go even wider. "I don't know, I swear."

I press my tail more firmly against Evil Lincoln's throat. It's not enough to break the skin, but it does show that I mean business. "Talk."

"No, no... Don't hurt me."

The tip of my tail slides farther down my fake husband's jugular. The muscles in his neck twitch. I decide to use Evil Lincoln's line right back at him. "Your mouth says no, but your body says yes."

At that moment, the door swings open, and Lincoln's parents step into the room. Both are in their thrax medieval best, so Connor is tall and barrel-chested in his velvet tunic. His white hair hangs gracefully to his chin. Octavia wears a long black gown with her silver hair curled into a neat bun. The two stare at Lincoln and me.

"What's going on here?" asks Connor.

"Foreplay," I say. At the same time, Evil Lincoln shouts: "She's crazy!"

Connor and Octavia share a long look. The pair of them do this a lot. It's like they have entire conversations without saying a word. After nodding to each other, they stare pointedly at my stomach.

"How are you feeling today?" asks Octavia.

I refuse to move from the throat-threatening situation I have going with the impostor. "This is not Lincoln."

Connor takes a cautious step backward. Wise move on his part. I'm already not a fan of his.

Octavia gives me a calm and regal smile. "Of course it's Lincoln. You've been rather unbalanced lately. Don't you remember? The doctors say that you must live here in Antrum, even after the baby is born."

My brows lift. "They did?" I look down at Evil Lincoln, who starts over-blinking. I'm guessing this is his default *I'm so innocent* face.

Not buying it.

"Don't you remember, Myla?" asks Evil Lincoln. He twists his neck to get farther away from my tail, but the arrowhead end just follows his every move. "We asked the physicians over last night after your mother left. They told us how your pregnancy's at risk due to your moods. They want you to stay here with Octavia and Connor. Forever."

Now, it's true that my mother wants us to live in Purgatory, but she's got nothing on Octavia. Lincoln's mom is on a mission to have us in Antrum. And yes, forever is the timescale she's pushing for.

I hate to admit it, but telling Octavia that we'll always stay in Antrum? That's a brilliant move from Evil Lincoln. Octavia has a gift for ignoring unpleasant realities when it concerns someone she loves. Just look at her marriage to Connor.

Octavia steps closer. If she's shocked that I'm still restraining her son, the Queen Emeritus doesn't show it. And since Evil Lincoln still isn't talking anyway, I decide to stand up and release him. As Evil Lincoln sits there, dumbfounded, my tail gives the impostor a little smack across the kisser. *Good tail.*

Turning to Octavia, I greet her with a little wave. "Hello."

"So good to see you, my dear." Octavia air-kisses my cheeks.

Lincoln huffs as he slowly stands up. "She threatened me, Mother."

At this point, I feel like Evil Lincoln and I are a brother and sister who're fighting over "who punched who" in the back seat. Again, something the real Lincoln would never do.

"She's a warrior," counters Octavia. "Of course, she'll become physical. While I was pregnant with you, I once broke three of your father's ribs." Octavia used to be a fighter herself, and a good one.

Connor guffaws. "Don't surprise your pregnant warrior wife with tickles, my son. I learned that one the hard way."

Octavia refocuses on me. "We're so pleased about the news that you're staying. I've already got the royal carpenters fixing up a baby's room right next to our suite."

Wow. This sounds way too similar to the conversation I

had with my own mother. Don't get me wrong—I'm happy everyone wants to spend time with the baby. It's just they can do that and then *leave*.

"I know this must be overwhelming for you," adds Connor. "Months ago, you were a senior at Purgatory High School. Now, you're the Great Scala, Queen of the Thrax, a wife, and a mother. It's a lot for anyone, even without your demonic heritage. And now, all these baby hormones? It's amazing you're acting sane at all." He gestures around the room. "And Antrum is so safe! I love this idea of you staying here twenty-four-seven." He turns to Evil Lincoln. "Great thinking, son."

"Thank you, Father."

There are so many things I want to say to Connor at this point, starting with a critique of the whole *"demonic heritage"* crap and ending with his *"amazing you're acting sane at all"* line. But I have bigger fish to fry. Instead, I round on Evil Lincoln. "Clearly, you've had a busy morning, my little lamb chop. It seems you talked to your parents and got everything lined up, eh?"

"That's right." He looks so smug when he says that, I want to punch him in the throat.

"So what am I supposed to do next, according to your plans, oh my dearest?"

This ought to be good.

"Well, the summit with Ethan starts in a few minutes. However, I figured that man-stuff might go right over your head. Plus, you haven't been in—*how do I put this?*—the most sane condition. We need to show Ethan our very best selves. He's a critical ally."

"Huh." The way Evil Lincoln speaks the word *"ally,"* he might as well say *"co-conspirator." Makes sense, really.* Evil Lincoln showed up right after Ethan's black magic took my guy away. All of a sudden, I want in on this summit and how. Ethan and I need to talk.

"I am attending the summit, end of story."

"But you must understand—" starts Evil Lincoln.

Octavia jumps right in. "The King and Queen rule jointly in Antrum. If Myla wishes to attend the summit, then she should go."

I can't help but smirk. Okay, maybe I could help it, but Octavia is giving Evil Lincoln a smackdown. That's just too awesome.

Evil Lincoln frowns. "It's going to be terribly boring, though."

"I can always play rock, paper, scissors with my tail." My tail arches over my shoulder while rounding its arrowhead end into a fist-shape, just to make things clear.

Octavia's mismatched eyes narrow. "What's really bothering you, my son?"

For the first time since they walked in the room, I'm very glad that Lincoln's parents are here. Or at least, that Octavia showed up. The fact that she's seeing through Evil Lincoln in this moment is beyond sweet.

"It's just..." Evil Lincoln sighs. "What if Myla attacks me again?"

"You're a trained fighter." Octavia sniffs. "That's a ridiculous concern."

I want to pump my fist in the air, but I'm trying to be more Queenly. Instead, I lift my chin in what I consider to be a most regal pose. "I'm Queen of the Thrax. I don't shirk my duties. Let's go speak with Ethan."

Octavia grins. "Well said, my dear."

Evil Lincoln steps closer. "If you're sure." His voice has a soft yet menacing tone.

Meaning: if you join me at this summit, you will regret it.

"Oh, I'm positive," I reply.

Translation: bring it on.

I return my attention to Octavia. "Where are the negotiations taking place?"

"The Chamber of Reflection," she replies.

That's in Arx Hall, our main palace. I know where the room's located, even though I've never been inside it before. And now that I have Octavia to back me up, I can get a carriage there, easy-peasy.

"Got it." I whip open the door and call to the guards. "Send a runner to the stables. I want a fresh carriage outside in two minutes."

Williamson steps forward. "Absolutely, Your Majesty."

I return to the receiving room, make my goodbyes, and then march off for the main gate. Evil Lincoln run-walks to stay close. "Wait up, Myla. It's unseemly for us to be apart."

I don't bother answering him. The most seemly thing in the world will be when I'm as far away from this creep as possible. I want my real husband back, and to do that, I need information.

In other words, it's time to confront Ethan.

*a*n hour later, I'm marching down the southwest passageway in Arx Hall. The place is an ornate corridor made of gilded walls and marble floors.

Next stop: Ethan and the Chamber of Reflection.

"Not so fast, my sweetling." That would be Evil Lincoln, who is currently huffing and puffing his way behind me. Whoever this loser really is, the dude is not in shape. My Lincoln would be disgusted.

I consider replying to His Evilness, but then pick up the pace instead. There's no point interacting with my fake husband. I've interrogated my share of criminals. When my tail was against Evil Lincoln's neck, the creep looked frightened enough to wet himself. In that moment, if Evil Lincoln had known anything about my *real* husband's whereabouts, it would have come a-tumbling from his lips.

But Evil Lincoln said nothing. Zero. Zip. Nada.

And that means my best option for information is to visit the Chamber of Reflection, which is at the end of this very passageway. In there, I'll find the annual summit and Ethan the Supreme Creepster.

AKA the dude who sent the magical arrow that kidnapped my husband.

AKA the dead man.

As an extra bonus, Cissy should be joining us. Sure, Lincoln and I invited her to this summit because my bestie knows a lot about Earth technology. But now, her presence will be extra awesome. Cis is Purgatory's Senator for Diplomacy. As such, she has contacts all over the after-realms. In other words, no matter where they're holding my Lincoln, Cissy can probably help me rescue him.

My fake husband pipes up again from behind me. "Dear heart, please slow down."

"Humph." For the record, there's only one reason why Evil Lincoln gets any kind of reply from me: his last statement marked the first time he used his "big-boy manners" and actually asked "please" before demanding that I slow down. You have to reinforce good habits with the selfishly minded.

After a few more strides, I reach a set of gilded doors. The words "Chamber of Reflection" are inlaid with glittering stones. Evil Lincoln rushes to stand beside me. Am I happy that's he's red faced, panting, and covered in sweat?

Why yes, yes I am.

"Now, my love." Evil Lincoln pants a few more times. "It's best if you stay quiet while I run the summit."

Say what? I didn't think I could hate this guy more, but it seems that Evil Lincoln is always full of surprises. *Did he really ask me to shut up while he runs the summit?* I purse my lips and glare at him. "Come again?"

"You're here to learn statecraft. You know, take notes from

the master." He gestures across his torso, in case I didn't understand how he was the "master" in this scenario.

There's a moment that lasts a million years where I contemplate having a round two of pinning Evil Lincoln to the floor and threatening his jugular. However, I'm working on being more patient and mature, so I don't attack.

For now.

After forcing myself to take in a few breaths, I once again address my fake husband. "Let's be honest with each other, okay? I'll make it really simple for you."

"Yes, my dearest heart. I'd adore that."

In the spirit of making things clear, I decide to talk Tarzan style. "Me Myla." I tap my chest. "Great Scala. Queen. Know what doing." My tail arches to point straight at Evil Lincoln's nose. "You impostor. Loser. Nobody. You shut up. Me run show. Got it?"

All the blood seems to drain from Evil Lincoln's face. "Is that all?"

I bob my head from side to side, thinking. "Only that I'm probably going to kill you before this is all over."

He staggers a step backward, which is good to see. "But I was sure you thought… Don't you find me attractive?"

My eyes almost pop out of my head. "And *this* is where your mind goes? Do I find you attractive?" I flash him my palms. "Please, it's best if you don't talk to me for awhile. I have business with Ethan."

Evil Lincoln's eyes widen, and that's when I notice it: some of the skin under his right eye is droopy. I point at the orb in question. "Hey, what's up with your face?"

Moving more quickly than I thought possible, Evil Lincoln presses his palm over his right eye. "It's nothing." The way he says those two words, it's definitely something. "You're acting crazy again."

"There you go with the crazy talk." Although, as much as I hate to admit this, the "let's focus on nutty Myla" program has worked pretty well for Evil Lincoln. At least, so far. My fake husband has infiltrated the guards and even the royal family. For the record, Williamson's the only one who thinks anything is off with the new Lincoln. But having Lincoln's face melt off his face? That may be unavoidable evidence.

I tap my chin. "Eye drooping isn't a human condition. Well, not one that I've ever heard of. Could it be something magical?"

"Just give me a second."

I can't help but notice that Evil Lincoln didn't answer my question. My mind whirs through everything I know about magic. "You're not under an enchantment. I had that confirmed." I rub my neck, thinking. Even if Ethan is the one I want to interrogate, it wouldn't hurt to know more about Evil Lincoln. My thoughts flip through every magical ailment I know about. "Besides, enchantments don't cause skin to melt like that."

"Do you mind? I've been checked out by the royal mages. I'm not under any spells." Evil Lincoln lowers his hand, and his eye looks normal once more. "All better now, see?"

I tilt my head, my mind still stuck on the mystery of Evil Lincoln. "If you're not enchanted, what are you, exactly?" I'd started to discuss this with Williamson back in the sitting room, but we got interrupted.

"I'm late, unless we get inside this chamber. We need to speak with Ethan as soon as possible."

Wow, I may actually agree with him on that point.

Whatever may be the mystery of Evil Lincoln, he's not the

big magilla here. My main job is getting info out of Ethan. I turn to face the golden door. "Time to do this."

Evil Lincoln starts to creep up behind me. "Allow me to—"

"Back off, buddy." I throw open the golden doors and step into the Chamber of Reflection. Inside, I find about a dozen Earls sitting around a long mahogany table. Cissy's not here yet, which is a bummer. That said, it's not surprising. She's a busy lady and we only invited her last night. But if I know my bestie, she'll show up soon enough.

Back to the summit.

At the head of the table sits a youngish guy with a round face, upturned nose, and small button eyes. A smattering of freckles covers his cheeks. His straight sandy-blond hair looks like someone slapped a yellow chimney sweep brush on top of his head. When I step into the room, he flashes me a grin, showing square teeth with wide spaces between them. It's like someone ripped out his regular choppers and replaced them with Chiclets or something.

"Greetings, Myla." The guy rises, which reveals he's wearing one of those blue jumpsuits normally used by gas station attendants, only his has an embroidered—and overly loopy—H-E on his chest. That's the logo for Hunter Enterprises. "I'm Ethan von Essen, Supreme Leader of the Thrax. You can also call me Ethan the Great or the Supreme Legal Ruler on Earth. Just don't call me one of the Supremes." He gives me an exaggerated wink. "My singing voice is terrible."

All the Earls start laughing their asses off. I count the major houses seated at the table, including Striga, Acca, Kamal, and Horus. Plus, a bunch of minor houses showed up, too. My Lincoln didn't say any of these folks would be joining the summit. It was just supposed to be me, Cissy, Lincoln, and Ethan. What's going on here?

Ethan snaps his fingers at me. "Myla? Did you hear what I said? I gave you a wide variety of greetings to choose from." The Earls look between Ethan, Evil Lincoln, and me, their attention rapt. Ethan is clearly testing me, and Lincoln is not backing me up. It's like the best show they've seen in forever, especially since we don't have television in Antrum.

Whatever. Color me not worried.

Ethan just let his soft spot show, which you should never do off the bat in a battle. It's clear that the guy is obsessed with having his ass kissed. Which means that Queenly-Myla isn't the right fit for this situation. Nope. I need to push Ethan's buttons, and that's a job for the old me.

"You gave me a variety of greetings?" I arch my right brow into my best bitch face. "All those fake titles, you mean?"

Ethan's nostrils flare. "They are not fake."

"Look, Eth." I pull out the chair beside his and slide on in. "Let's get things straight. For the record, I call you whatever I want, and you call me Queen Myla or Your Majesty." Normally I'm not one for titles, but this guy brings out the worst in me.

Ethan's thin mouth quivers with rage. It really is too easy to push his buttons. This is just like being back at Purgatory High. Ah, how I used to love working over my ghoul teachers until they cracked. *Such good memories.*

"Here's what I have to say about that." Ethan slams his palms against the tabletop. "Guards!"

Once more, the doors swing open. A half-dozen humans march into the room. At least, I think they're human. It's hard to tell because they have black bandages wound across their faces. Besides that, they're all wearing long dark coats, tall jackboots, and shiny brimmed hats. It's like they fell out of a black and white movie about Nazis.

I point at each of the men in succession. "Those are your guards?"

"They are my Razor Guards, to be exact. Each one's a human warrior that I've trained personally."

"Isn't that interesting?" I scan the thrax leaders around the table. "What do you think, my Earls?"

No one replies. Instead, they all keep looking to Evil Lincoln for guidance on how to act. For his part, my fake husband stands casually beside my chair. It's like Razor Guards march into our meetings every day. He's way too calm.

Clearly, I need to double-down on my disrespect.

"Let me put this another way," I continue. "Does anyone else think it's really weird that Ethan's guards are all dressed like Nazis with bandaged-up faces? I mean, I go on demon patrol all the time, and this is *not* a look that is sweeping the human world."

The Earls all decide that now is a great time to stare at the ceiling and pretend that I didn't use the word "Nazis" in a sentence. My back teeth lock in frustration.

Sometimes, my subjects suck.

Evil Lincoln moves to crouch by my chair. "Ethan's only bringing in a little extra help in case you lose your temper again." He shoots the Earls a knowing look. "What did I tell you, boys? Pregnant women."

All the Earls share secrets smiles and knowing nods.

Correction. Sometimes, my subjects suck *hard.*

Still, I have to try to save them. Even if it is from themselves.

I glare at Evil Lincoln. "Seems you were quite the busy boy while you had me locked up. Visiting the Earls? Telling 'crazy hormonal wifey' stories?"

"I did visit the Earls, and yes, I absolutely informed them of your condition," answers Evil Lincoln. "But I did so only for your safety, my dearest." He gives me a simpering grin. "My sole concern is for you and the baby."

"Really." I lean back in my chair and kick my feet onto the tabletop. "The baby and I want to talk to Eth. Alone."

Ethan narrows his eyes. "You still haven't addressed me properly, you know."

And again, this situation reminds me so much of Purgatory High, I almost want to change into gray sweats and ask for an Arena battle. Been there, tortured that. All I need to do is push the "disrespect" button on Ethan until he lets something slip. And if verbal shoves don't work, I'm not above the real thing.

I set my feet back onto the floor with a thud. Leaning in closer to Ethan, I lower my voice so only he can hear. "I'll call you anything I want."

Ethan replies in a tone that can't be heard by others, either. "Not for long." After that, he sits up straight, forces a smile, and gestures across the table. When he next speaks, his voice is super-loud. "Now, I'd like to share my dazzling achievements."

I can't believe this. "Back to you, are we?"

Ethan lifts his rounded chin. "That's why everyone came to this summit, Myla. It is all about me." Now that he's showing off, Ethan seems calmer.

Boo. Ethan's getting happy again? That means I need to up my game.

With so much going on, I hadn't paid attention to the tabletop. For the first time, I notice how it's covered in model trains, tanks, and helicopters. If I need to needle Ethan, then this makes it just too easy. "Toys? You brought a bunch of toys to Antrum?"

"These are not toys." Ethan's voice quivers with rage. I feel confident I'm making real progress again. Ethan will crack soon for sure.

I pick up a helicopter. "This really looks like a toy." It also seems to be made of the same dark metal as the arrowhead that stole my real husband away. I hold the item closer. Tiny runes have been carved onto its surface. "This thing is lousy with black magic."

Ethan laughs. "What did I tell you, guys?" All the Earls guffaw right along with him. Ethan wipes under his eyes with his knuckles, brushing fake tears away. "I knew she'd be frightened of my models."

I mouth one word: *Toys.*

Ethan's laugher dies right down. "For your information, these items came from Earth, where all sorts of things can get contaminated with demonic aura. Honestly, we'd never go on demon patrol if we worried about every little thing getting a touch of darkness. No, the only thing we really need to focus on is when thrax get possessed. Trust me, I know all about this."

This is totally true, by the way. Having an item with a little demonic something-or-other won't set up the Pulpitum alarms. Plus, Ethan just got to veer the conversation onto his tragic—if somewhat sketchy in my opinion—past with his family. I need to get things back on track. "Whatever you choose to call these things, I don't know why they are here."

"These are small replicas of actual prototypes that I've created on the Earth's surface," snaps Ethan. "Behold my glory." He gestures across the table once again, just in case we missed it last time. "I have merged human technology with thrax magic."

My eyes narrow. "Thrax magic? You mean from the House of Striga?" I stare at Lucas, the Earl of that house. "You were in on this?"

Lucas is an older dude with pale skin and long gray dreads. "No, Ethan has found a new strain of thrax magic." He nods excessively, which makes the beads in his dreads jingle. "It's most exciting."

I eye Lucas carefully. The Earl has been a great supporter in the past. Most recently, he helped Lincoln and me sneak off to Earth. Based on the childlike glimmer in his eyes, I don't think he's being a traitor here so much as really, really gullible.

Smacking my lips, I refocus on Ethan. "We've got machinery in Purgatory. Trust me, technology doesn't make things easier. It just pushes the problems around."

"That doesn't happen when you use my tech." Ethan next raises a toy tank above his head. "Machines from Hunter Enterprises are infallible. We send them out on demon patrol, and they do all the dirty work while my people stay safe in a master skyscraper."

At the mention of the words "master skyscraper," all the Earls' eyes go wide. It's rare for an Earl to go on demon patrol. Their lives are simply too important. As a result, most of these dudes have never set foot on the Earth's surface. Based on the hungry looks on their faces, these Earls clearly believe that Ethan's inventions will be their "get out of jail free" card from Antrum.

Plus, demon patrols are pretty self-sufficient. Thrax make their own calls on the Earth's surface. The most these Earls can do is play post-game quarterback on the big show of thrax life: killing demons. How much would these egomaniacs love to have more hands-on control? A whole lot.

"Look, there's no way to avoid this." Ethan sighs dramatically. "This is the way of the future. We will fight demons with tech. Right, Linc?" My fake husband nods enthusiastically. "And I need the Earls at my side. We aren't the only ones who can dream up new technology. What if the demons find someone to build them new machines?"

"None of the demons can plan their way out of a paper bag." I shrug. "Except Armageddon, that is."

"We're not talking about Armageddon," says Ethan. And I can't help but notice the fear that gleams in his mismatched eyes. You only get that look if you've met the King of Hell face to face. "My point is that these machines exist. Either we use them or the enemy will." Ethan gestures across the table. "Am I right, men?"

And in a not-so-shocking move, all the Earls agree that Ethan is right.

Yipes.

The Earls are fanboying again, so Ethan is retaking control. I need to shut down this Ethan love-fest and fast. "Look, I don't care what you say, Eth. No machine can replace a trained thrax on demon patrol."

Ethan's shoulders vibrate with rage, and with that, things are back where they should be: with Ethan losing his mind. I haven't broken dozens of ghoul teachers not to know the warning signs. Any second now, Ethan will crack and blab something incriminating in front of the Earls.

"We don't replace thrax," snarls Ethan. "We put them into a high-tech control room where they can monitor everything from a safe distance. Besides, things cloud-side have changed. Demons are becoming visible."

I wave my hand. "No way. It's a basic fact of life that anything demonic and angelic can not be seen by the human eye."

"They're visible, I tell you!" Ethan slams his fist on the tabletop. All the toys bounce. "They're infiltrating everything. Even my own tech isn't safe. I have a huge event coming up, Touch The Tech, where all my best machinery will be on display. What if demons infiltrated some of my weaponry? We'd need a counter-strike with even more tech, all of it manned by my Razor Guards and these Earls. They must be ready to go on a moment's notice."

"That's a rather specific scenario."

"Only because it's very possible," offers Evil Lincoln.

The plan here comes into better focus. "Let me get this straight. You could have some kind of event that 'visible demons' infiltrate." I make little quotation mark with my fingers when I say the words *visible demons.* "And what would you do then?" As the answer appears, I snap my fingers. "I've got it. You'll shut down the thrax demon patrols and send in your Razor Guards on this souped-up magical tech."

"Now, you're talking sensibly," says Evil Lincoln. "Ethan is proposing a new way to manage demon patrol. The Earls work directly with the Razor Guards and this new machinery in order to protect everyone."

Ethan's plan is coming into focus, except for one blurry item. "But that still doesn't explain why you keep asking for thrax troops."

Ethan huffs out a breath. "You can't expect my Razor Guards to do all the work. Some thrax would be needed to bolster my troops. From the minor houses, mostly." Ethan then goes on to list out the houses involved. I can't help but notice none of them have Earls represented at this table.

I've heard enough.

"This isn't improved demon patrol," I state in a loud voice. "It's an attempted coup."

"Please, dearest." Evil Lincoln flashes his palms in the universal movement of *calm down*. "There is no coup. I'm in full support of this plan. Can't you see it's a major improvement." He blinks a lot. That's quickly becoming my least favorite look on him. "You approved this as well, don't you remember?"

"No."

"You'd remember if you were thinking clearly," says Ethan. "This is about improving things in Antrum. We need to join the current century. Simply put, we must use our best teams and technology." He fiddles with one of the helicopters, and it starts to fly.

Watching the tiny toy hover over the table, all the Earls go "ooooh" in unison. I can almost see Ethan's ego plump back up to its regular globe-shattering proportions.

Damn.

This situation is beyond belief. The room is filled with Nazi wannabes, small plastic toys, and a nutjob with a death wish. Meanwhile, all the Earls see is the fact that they can play demon patrol leader while someone else dies for them.

Bottom line: the Earls still need an attitude adjustment.

"What happened to the soldiers we gave you?" I ask. "We never hear from them."

Ethan shrugs. "They all love Earth life so much, they simply retired with the humans. Can I help it if they don't want to write?"

My mouth falls open. "That is a total crock."

"Try to calm down, my little lamb." Evil Lincoln sets his palm on my shoulder.

I pluck his hand away. "No touchie."

After that, Ethan picks up a toy motorcycle and starts to blah-blah-blah about how every Earl will get their own bike. A few of them actually start to drool.

Sitting upright, I drum my fingers on the tabletop. I have to hand it to Ethan. Unlike the ghouls, he has figured out a way to defuse my smart mouth. Each time I push Ethan toward Rageville—which should quickly lead to Spill The Beans Land—he just cracks out another toy. Enough is enough. I've found out all I can from Ethan by playing Little Miss Disrespectful.

It's time for my pushing to go from verbal to physical.

I stand up right so quickly, the chair falls down behind me. The room falls silent. A model blimp topples over with a sad little plunk. I turn to Ethan, my tail arched over my shoulder, ready for attack. At my mental command, the threads of my clothing realign from Scala robes into battle gear.

Everyone freezes in surprise. In my opinion, the face-wrapped Nazi guards should have brought out this level of shock, but maybe that's just me. For their part, the Razor Guards reach into the coats, no doubt getting ready whatever weapons they brought with them.

I shift my weight onto the balls of my feet, ready to lunge straight at Ethan. The moment is perfect. My enemy looks like a frightened little man-bunny. No way did he think I would do anything this aggressive.

That's when I notice the mirrors.

The walls here are covered with them...dozens of mirrors in different frames and sizes, fitting together in a complex mosaic. All these mirrors...that's why this room is called the Chamber of Reflection. I was so cranked up about Ethan, I just didn't remember it before.

My throat tightens with anxiety. Will I glimpse my Lincoln again? Last time, I checked the mirrors in the honeymoon palace, but maybe there was something wrong with them.

Evil Lincoln moves to stand beside me. "Are you all right?"

"I'm fine, just give me a minute."

My fake husband says something again about women and pregnancy, but I'm too distracted to really hear the words. I have bigger things to worry about.

Like seeing my true husband once more.

With careful steps, I make a slow circuit around the room, checking out each mirror as I go along.

Ethan takes my silence as the go-ahead to keep right on talking. I don't care. From every corner of my soul, I crave even the smallest glimpse of my Angelbound love. The first set of mirrors show nothing, but there are far too many to give up hope.

I move on to the second wall.

Meanwhile, the Earls go back to playing with their toys and ignoring yours truly. Long story short, no one bothers me. At this point, that's just fine.

As I scan each mirror in turn, I'm vaguely aware of Ethan talking to the Earls. He's handing them some line of garbage about his new magic combining with human technology to create an unstoppable force.

And they're lapping it up with a spoon.

"Look at this." Ethan carefully lifts a cell phone from the tabletop, cradling it in his hands like it's a precious relic. "This device can act as a communications console, portrait recorder, and entertainment center. It can even allow you to play games."

The Earl of Kamal's eyes grow wide. "Like chess?"

Ethan nods sagely. "Especially chess."

I move on to a new wall and scan more mirrors. *Portrait recorder? Chess?* Ethan hasn't even gotten to the good stuff, and the Earls are already putty in his hands. This is precisely why my Lincoln didn't allow flashy contraband tech into Antrum. It gives good thrax bad ideas. Like, you know, the concept that living a glamorous life on Earth is worth a swift and painful death. Demons always find thrax sooner rather than later. I shiver. It always results in a grisly end.

Ethan next picks up a model plane. "Here's one of our new luxury jets." He smiles another Chiclet grin. "It's enchanted to be invisible. No need for Pulpitums to get around Earth. You can fly around in one of these!"

The Earls lean forward, their faces locked in rapt attention.

Ethan picks up the toy blimp. "And here is my magic dirigible. I use it to float high above the fray, as any Supreme Leader should."

This time, the Earls all go "ahhhh." At least, they are mixing up their noises of adoration.

"So, what do you say?" asks Ethan. "Do I have your support?"

"Of course, Supreme Leader," replies Evil Lincoln quickly. "Our troops and resources are at your disposal." The Earls glare at Evil Lincoln. "And by troops, I mean from other houses. None of the houses here would be affected, obviously."

And although I want to keep checking mirrors, I simply can't let that slide. I turn to face Ethan. "Forget it. You won't receive a single thrax solider from *any* house. That's what *my* Lincoln wanted." My voice cracks a little when I say that last bit, but just picturing my lost love is making me weepy. I'd say it's pregnancy hormones, but I'd be losing it even without that.

Plus, there's more to this whole scene than missing my guy. The Earls just saw their King kowtow to some loser who looks like he belongs on the cover of Freckle-Faced Mean Kid Grows Up magazine.

Not on my watch.

Ethan gives me what can only be called an indulgent smile. *Creep.* "I realize that learning new things can be overwhelming, especially for someone in your condition…" He goes on to say more incredibly insulting junk, but I don't care.

Every mirror now displays an image of Lincoln. My Lincoln. My attention is entirely focused on the walls. Once again, no one else seems to be able to see this vision of my true husband.

Last time, I saw Lincoln pounding on the mirror like he was trapped inside another dimension. Now, I realize that wasn't the case. The mirror is actually acting like a window to where Lincoln is being held. He must have been pounding on the walls before. This time, I see my husband is imprisoned inside a large white room. People in hazmat suits are strapping him to a table while he struggles and screams.

I lose my fucking mind.

"You bastard!" I leap forward, knock Ethan out of his chair, and pin him to the ground. My tail does the same move it did with Evil Lincoln and points right at Ethan's jugular.

"What is your problem?" cries Ethan. "Have you lost your mind?" His features tighten with genuine fear.

Even through my haze of rage, I know Ethan's reaction means two things. One, Ethan can't see my Lincoln in the mirrors; otherwise he'd know why my mind is toast. I've no doubt Ethan is behind my Lincoln's disappearance. However, my seeing in mirrors must be something he didn't expect. Second, Ethan is terrified of me.

As he should be.

"Where is my husband? Tell me now, or I use your neck as a kabob."

A calm kind of sneaky washes over Ethan's face. "Why, your Lincoln is right here beside you, Myla. Don't you see?"

Voices echo behind me. Some small corner of my brain recognizes that Cissy has finally entered the room. I'm still too stuck on getting information out of Ethan to care, though.

"Start talking, Eth."

Evil Lincoln kneels at my side. He has the good sense not to touch me this time around. "Myla, we've talked about these episodes of yours. They're getting worse and they risk the baby. Don't make things harder on yourself. Just go back to your chambers like a good girl, and everything will be fine."

I keep my gaze locked on Ethan and his very puncture-friendly neck. If Evil Lincoln thinks that threatening me with house arrest will stop me, he's way wrong. Those words only validate the fact that I have one shot at getting information from Ethan.

That would be now.

I'm taking it.

The arrowhead end of my tail makes a slow journey along Ethan's jugular. "You better get chatty soon, Eth."

The Razor Guards all reach into their jackets once again. Moving in unison, they pull out small guns. The Earls gasp and leap from their chairs.

Glad I have some kind of value here.

"Stand down," orders Ethan. The Razor Guards replace the firearms into their long jackets. His gaze locks with mine. "What do you want?"

"Information." My mind races through everything I saw through the mirrors. Those images—along with the toys Ethan has been so proudly displaying—combine to give me an idea. "You develop machinery on Earth." My gaze flickers from the toy tanks to Evil Lincoln's now not-so-droopy eye. An idea appears. "Tell me. Do you do create things that change people as well?"

"My Earthly business is clean." Ethan's pupils widen. "I don't run any illegal labs."

"Interesting. I didn't say you did."

For the record, there's nothing more damning than denying you engaged in a crime that no one's accusing you of. Ethan is definitely experimenting with people on Earth. Maybe that's how he created Evil Lincoln in the first place.

The pieces start to fit together. The illegal labs...new magic combining with technology...and my Lincoln being strapped to a table for who knows what. Every nerve ending in my body goes on alert.

I know exactly why Ethan has my husband. Hunter Enterprises is doing some illegal stuff to thrax in these labs. My Lincoln is the latest test subject.

I grip Ethan's chin. "You said before that you mixed magic with technology. What kind of magic are you using?"

Ethan's face becomes the image of adult menace speckled with childish freckles. "Something of my own creation."

I glare at him for all I'm worth. "Black magic isn't anything new. And we both know how it's powered." When I next speak, the words feel torn from the bottom of my soul. "You must drain angelic souls to get it to work. That's why you have those labs." My voice cracks. "It's why you took my Lincoln."

Ethan has the nerve to roll his eyes. "You're letting your

imagination run wild. How would someone like me master black magic enough to drain someone as powerful as your husband?"

Evil Lincoln raises his hand. "And I'm right here, sweetness. Don't you see me?"

"Talk," I snarl at Ethan. "How did you get this magic? Tell me!"

The Razor Guards had been hanging back before. Now, they start to close in. They even pull out their guns.

All my Earls go into action. Moving as a single unit, they pull out their weapons, surrounding me and Ethan in a circle. Within seconds, the Earls create a human shield between the Razor Guards and yours truly.

A bubble of warmth moves across my chest. *Awwww.*

It's nice to see the Earls have some sense of preservation for my well-being. I'm debating the best ways to make Ethan suffer when I realize there's a female presence beside me.

It's Cissy. She must have some in with the guards. I didn't notice her in all the excitement.

"Myla, you don't want to do this," she says gently. "Let's go for a walk."

From the corner of my eye, I scan Cissy's familiar outline —she's tall and willowy with blonde curls that hang to her shoulders. Today she's wearing the purple Senatorial robes of her office.

"Listen to your friend," stammers Ethan. "Leave."

"Please, Myla." Cissy tugs on my shoulder. "We have to go."

Now, I have no idea where Cissy wants to take me, but I do know one thing. I just got some decent intel. Chances are, my Lincoln is being held in a Hunter Enterprises lab somewhere on Earth. At this point, my chances of getting even *more* useful information out of Ethan are slim at best. Plus, the longer I straddle Ethan with my tail at his throat, the more I validate the lies about my being hormone-crazy.

I stand up, reform my garment into a robe, and address the room. "Thank you for protecting me, my Earls." I gesture regally to Ethan, who's still sitting on the floor and rubbing his neck. "I must admit, I did lose my temper on old Eth here."

Ethan looks up at me. His eyes positively blaze with hatred. "You should apologize and use my correct title."

Yeah, that is so not happening.

I ignore Ethan and keep my focus on the Earls. "Please know that my fury came in part due to my genuine concern for your safety. Mark my words: going to the Earth's surface is a dangerous idea. No matter what technology has been developed, there is no protection from demons that's superior to our defenses in Antrum. Lincoln and I have always been clear on this point."

Evil Lincoln gestures toward the door. "Why don't you take a break, babe? Let the real leaders handle this."

I turn to him. "I am a real leader and a powerful one, too. Consider yourself lucky that I'm not zapping you off to Hell this second."

The Earls gasp, and I realize that the longer I stay in this room, the more I put my plans in danger. If they think I'm crazy, they might just go along with Lincoln and his house arrest scheme. And while I can fight a lot of people, there's no way I can take on all of Antrum. And with my igni out of commission? I can't rely on their help, either. For whatever reason, I keep calling to my little supernatural buddies, and they keep not answering. No wonder they went into double-screech mode last night. It was probably the last time they could talk to me for a while.

Still, all those realizations don't help me in my present

situation. Only one thing will: and that's exiting the room. Working my most Queenly vibe, I turn to Cissy. "Perhaps we should take a breather."

"I know the perfect spot," says Cis. "There's a Pulpitum near here that can take us to Purgatory."

"Ah-ah-ah," counters Evil Lincoln. "Myla must return to her chambers. That way, the royal physician can check her out at a moment's notice."

"We have doctors in Purgatory," says Cissy.

The temperature in the room goes up about twenty degrees. I know what my Earls think about partially demon doctors treating the royal heir. None of them are fans.

Clearly, Evil Lincoln has the same thought. "Perhaps it might help if a few of the Razor Guards accompanied you to your chambers, my sweet. You need to be seen by Antrum doctors and safely."

"I'll pass, thanks." I loop my arm with Cissy's. "My best friend and I will go right back to my chambers. The guards can alert you when we arrive. Good enough?"

A muscle twitches by Evil Lincoln's eye, and I wonder if it will start drooping again. "Of course. Be safe, my dearest love."

"Sure thing." I address the room. "Goodbye, everyone."

As Cissy and I march out the door, I know one thing for certain.

There is no way I'm being held hostage. Cissy and I are finding a way to Earth and after that? I am rescuing my Lincoln.

7

*C*issy and I turn down another corridor in Arx Hall. While the honeymoon palace was all dark wood and earth tones, everything in here sparkles with gold. I'm not really focusing the scenery, though. I can't wait for me and Cissy to reach my chambers. Once we're alone, we can lay out a plan to leave Antrum and find my Lincoln.

As we speed along, Cissy shoots a nervous glance over her shoulder. "This place gives me the creeps," she whispers.

When I reply, I take care to keep my voice low as well. "That's because a pair of Razor Guards are following us."

"How do you know?"

"Let's just say I've learned a lot on demon patrol." Actually, my education on tracking comes from Lincoln, who's simply the best hunter in the after-realms. But I can't mention my guy's name without tearing up, so I don't add in that part.

"What should we do?" asks Cis.

"Ignore them. Once they confirm we've gone into my chambers, they should go back to the summit. There are other thrax guards around who can ensure we stay put." *And those are easier to avoid.*

Cissy purses her lips. "But we aren't staying in your chambers, are we?"

"What makes you say that?"

"I know my Myla."

In reply, I give her a wink. Cissy knows that means, *Hells no, we aren't staying put.*

Cissy and I pass a bunch of thrax guards, enter my royal chambers, and shut the doors tight. I call it my chambers, but this place is more of a mini-house than anything. Cissy and I make our way into what would be a living room back in Purgatory.

I plunk down onto a comfy leather couch. "We can talk freely here. Lincoln and I put in ton of silencer spells."

Cissy sits down beside me and launches into a rapid-fire series of questions. "Why were so many people at that summit? Who's that freckle-faced guy? And what's wrong with Lincoln?"

It takes a while, but I explain how Lincoln's been replaced by an evil body double with a droopy eye; that this whole summit thing is just a ploy to get thrax troops onto Earth; and how Ethan is the creepy mastermind behind it all. After that, I tell her how Ethan has lured all the Earls to his side by promising them easy demon patrols. It all starts with Touch The Tech, an event Ethan is holding on Earth.

"So what's this event about, exactly?" asks Cissy.

"It's Ethan's first demon patrol with his souped-up technology. The Earls are so excited to run the patrols, they're ignoring red flags right and left. Ethan is not planning to improve demon patrols for our people. He kept talking about new kinds of demons that humans could see—he said they were a threat to his company." I close my eyes tightly, trying to put the pieces of information into a larger picture. For now, I can't. "There's something else going on at that event, but I can't worry about that now. I need to find Lincoln."

Cissy rubs her forehead. "I don't get it. Why would Ethan put Lincoln in a laboratory? I mean, if he wanted to replace your Lincoln with a fake, why would he keep the real deal alive?"

I take in a deep breath and force the words from my mouth. "Ethan's building a bunch of machines—tanks, planes and other human stuff—that he's combined with thrax magic. Supposedly it's all for demon patrol and uses good magic." I make little quotation marks with my fingers when I saw good magic. "But it's really black magic."

Cissy narrows her eyes. "I don't know a lot about black magic. How would that affect your Lincoln?"

"Black magic works by using the essence of an angelic soul. Real angels are hard to capture, so the most common sources are thrax. It's best to drain them in their prime, just after adulthood." A knot of grief tightens my throat. "That's why Ethan took my Lincoln and is keeping him. Ethan wants to take my guy's soul energy. I must find my Lincoln before his energy is drained. Once that's gone, he'll die."

"Oh, Myla. That's terrible."

Normally, I'd enjoy a few minutes of sympathy from Cissy. But right now? Nervous energy zings through my body. It's like I could crawl out of my own skin. I scrub my hands over my face. "Look, sitting on the couch is making me crazy. You want in on helping me?"

"You know I do."

"Then, it's time for us to leave Antrum and find Lincoln. Let's hit the Arx Hall Pulpitum."

"Okay. How will we get past these guards, though?"

I stare at Cis for a few seconds before the little gears in my mind put things together. "That's right. You and I mostly hang out in Purgatory." I gesture around the room. "Arx Hall is lousy with secret passages."

Cissy gives me the side eye. "No way."

I stroll to the far wall and knock on one of the doors. "See this? It looks like a regular closet." Turning the handle to the right, I open the door.

Cissy leans forward on the couch and squints. "It *is* a regular closet."

"Only when you open the door by turning the handle to the right." I glance inside the opened space. The closet is lined with shelves of bottles that are filled with cleaning goop.

"So, what's the trick?" asks Cissy.

"In this case, it's all in the handle." I close the closet door and tap the handle in question with my pointer finger. "Now, most handles only turn clockwise. But with this one, when you turn it to the left, the shelves slide away and—voila—you have a passage."

"Excellent." Cissy stands, too. "I'm ready."

"Let's get out of here." I grip the handle. "One, two three." I turn the handle to the left and open the door.

But no secret passage appears.

Instead, a wall of black fire rolls out to meet me. On reflex, I crouch to the ground. Like last time in the study with Lincoln, dark flames engulf me, but they don't actually burn. My gaze locks on Cissy. She was too far away to be affected, so she just stares me, her mouth open.

For a moment, my mind returns to the last time I saw a display of black magic power: when Ethan took my Lincoln.

My mind blanks. Fear and hurt zing through my nervous system.

Once the smoke has cleared, I force myself to focus again. There should be a passage beyond the opened door. There isn't. What should be a hidden corridor is a solid wall. My jaw tightens with frustration.

Damn you, Ethan.

Cissy rushes to my side. "Myla, are you all right?"

"Yes, I'm fine." I start pushing on the black plastic wall with my palms. My tail tries jabbing it as well. "There shouldn't be a wall here."

Cissy touches the dark surface. "How did this happen?"

"Ethan did it somehow. It's just like when he sent that arrow to Lincoln. We saw a wave of black fire, and then the mirror turned into this vortex."

"But there wasn't an arrow this time. How did he do it?"

A realization appears. "Wait a second." Leaning over, I examine the door. Sure enough, the handle is not some old-fashioned L-shaped job that's the standard here in Arx Hall. Nope, this is now a sleek metallic number, all black, with little rune notches in it. I've seen that exact pattern before. Ethan carved it into the arrow that took my Lincoln away.

In other words, this handle is definitely one of Ethan's creations.

A sickly feeling crawls up my throat. Ethan probably sent Evil Lincoln in here with a bunch of hardware that could block up every secret passage. He's been planning to trap me for ages.

My inner rage demon roars to life inside me. "That butthead!"

Cissy gasps. "Did you say *butthead*?"

"I'm trying to be more Queenly," I growl. "And Queens don't swear." *Much. I think.*

"Okay," says Cissy slowly. "Which particular butthead are we talking about here?"

"Ethan." I rattle the door. "He made this handle and laced it with black magic."

"Got it." Cissy nibbles on her thumbnail for a few seconds. "Wait. Maybe he didn't get to all of the doors. You said your chambers had lots of secret passages."

I snap my fingers. "Good thinking."

With that, I rush from one secret passageway to the next. First, I check on the one in the pantry. Then the bedroom floor. After that, the hallway closet. None of them have any obvious machinery like the first handle. Unfortunately, all of them are still totally booby-trapped. The second I pry them open, I get a poof of black flame and an impassable wall.

Double-damn.

Once I'm out of secret passages to check, I plunk my butt back on the couch. Cissy slides in beside me. "I take it you've tried every secret passage?" she asks.

I scrub my hands down my face. "All the ones that I know of."

"So we're back to where we started." Cissy sighs. "How do we get out of here?"

"I'm working on it."

Cissy lifts her chin. "How about we fight it out?"

Considering how my friend is a crap warrior, I've never loved her more than I do in this moment. Cissy has my back. But for once, fighting isn't the answer.

"There are too many guards between here and the Pulpitum. And even if I could kill them all, that's bad PR. Plus, it's dangerous to get into hand-to-hand combat fighting while I'm pregnant. That should only be a last resort."

"I've got it. How about trying your igni?"

I grab a couch pillow and hug it to my stomach. "I've been calling my igni for hours. They haven't answered me once." I pick some stray threads from the tapestry-style fabric. "I think that's why my igni were so insistent on getting me a message last night. They must have known they wouldn't be able to reach me today."

"So no transport help from igni."

"Not this time."

My igni don't exist like other beings do. I still don't understand what makes them come and go, let alone talk to me. This isn't the first time they've gone silent on me for no reason. My father says it's because they must take a fractured form in the after-realms in order to move souls.

"Hold on a sec." My eyes widen with a realization. "My igni did give me another message last night. They were trying so hard for me to listen to them, I think they knew it would only be my only way to escape today."

"What's that?"

I worry my lower lip with my teeth. Sure, I want to tell Cissy all about the LK Route, but based on what Lincoln said, it only has room for one person. That means I'm going solo. Sure, Cissy has other ways to leave Antrum, but she might get interrogated for information about me. The less she knows about certain things, the better.

"Come on," urges Cissy. "What did your igni tell you? How are we going to escape?"

"This escape route is just for one person. And honestly? It's best if you don't know the particulars, just in case anyone asks you where I went. And when I say *ask*, I mean in the sot-so-nice way."

Cissy's mouth rounds into an O shape. "Got it."

"What's important to know is that I can reach any spot on Earth that I wish in, say, about an hour or so."

"Awesome." Cissy sits up straight. "How can I help?"

Did I mention that Cissy is amazing? *She is.*

I tap my chin as I think through our options. "You should definitely go to Earth first. Say you need to return to Purgatory for diplomacy stuff. After that, take a few wrong turns in case you're followed. Then we can meet..." I rack my mind, trying to think of a good place on Earth for me and Cissy to reconnoiter. Beyond a sketchy island in Nova Scotia, I'm not what you'd call an expert on Earth geography.

"How about we meet at the top of the Empire State Building?" offers Cissy. For the record, Cissy loves two old movies that feature the Empire State Building: *An Affair to Remember* and *Sleepless in Seattle*. I've seen both more times than I'd care to admit.

Still, I know the spot. Tapping my lower lip, I think through the suggestion. The Empire State Building is a touristy place, so strange people come and go. It won't look weird for one of us to hang out and wait for the other. "That's perfect, Cis."

Cissy frowns. "But will you be safe in Antrum without me?"

"Oh, I'll be fine. The Razor Guards left. All I need to do is ask my regular thrax guards to keep me safe while I go on a walk to parts unknown." I mime my fingers strolling away.

"Will they really let you walk around?" Cissy makes her 'eek" face. "Ethan and Evil Lincoln seemed pretty set on keeping you in your chambers."

"But that was before Octavia got involved. I'll throw her name around and say I need some exercise for the baby. They'll agree, I'll sneak off, and no one will get hurt. Everything will be fine."

"If you say so."

"I do." Mostly because I don't have another choice, not that I share this part with Cissy.

With our plan in place, I walk Cissy to the main doors. Outside, I find that Maybe Manfred and Could Be Bob are still on duty.

"Hey, uh, you," I say to Maybe Manfred. "Can you please make sure my friend gets safely to the Pulpitum?"

"As you command, Your Majesty," says Maybe Manfred.

I turn to Could Be Bob. "Where's Williamson?"

"He had to step away," replies Could Be Bob. "He should be back any minute."

I screw my mouth to one side of my face, thinking. What I need to do doesn't really require Williamson. "If I wanted to take a walk, can I do that?"

Could Be Bob frowns. "I'm not sure that's allowed."

I cup my hand by my mouth. "Maybe I should call for Octavia, then." Here in the main palace, the hallways are loaded with her spies. They'll get a message to her in no time flat.

"On second thought, that will be fine" says Could Be Bob. "I'll just need to accompany you. And maybe bring along some other guards as well."

"How many?"

Could Be Bob winces a little. "Six, all from the thrax royal guard."

I run though the process in my mind. Earlier, Lincoln said that I should find the last lime kiln in the row, touch the top, and say "in thrax sic hunt." With that, the fiery oven turns into a mini-Pulpitum transfer station with room for one and some kind of booby trap to stop anyone from following me.

In other words, it doesn't matter how many guards there are; none of them will expect me to enter a lime kiln. Plus, it will be too small for them to follow, and the booby trap will keep them off my trail.

I shoot the guard a thumbs-up. "Six is fine. Whatever. I'll be right back."

Could Be Bob bows slightly. "As you command."

Cissy and I give each other a quick hug good-bye. Once I'm back inside my rooms, I scrounge around for a carrier and some necessities. It doesn't hurt to be prepared.

I soon find a canvas satchel that the servants use to bring in stuff for the pantry. It makes the perfect backpack replacement. Into that sack, I add a hairbrush, toothbrush, a few more necessities, and I'm done. There really isn't time to do a thorough packing job. Besides, I'm heading to Earth, the land of buying stuff. I grab some lesser jewels to pawn in case of emergency.

This is going to work. It has to.

With my satchel slung over my shoulder, I saunter up to the front door and swing it open, expecting to see Could Be Bob waiting for me with six of his buddies.

They aren't there.

Instead, a dozen Razor Guards wait outside. My heart sinks. I give them a little wave. "Hey, guys. Where are all my thrax warriors?"

A Razor Guard steps forward. "They went with the Senator to the Pulpitum station."

Huh. "Do you have a name?"

The Razor Guard takes a half step backward. "What?"

"It's not a trick question. What's your name?"

"Ethan Unit 126-X."

"That's a name?"

"When we entered into service for the Supreme Leader, he gave us all new names."

"After himself, of course."

"It's my honor to be named after him."

"Whatever. I'm calling you X."

"X?"

"Trust me, it's a step up." I set my fist on my hip. "Now look, X, I'm going on a walk right now. If you and all the other Ethans want to join me, that's fine. But I am going."

I start to step away, but X moves into my path, blocking me. "The Supreme Leader has ordered for us to guard you here. Your beloved Lincoln agreed. Our mission is to keep you safe until the doctors come for your procedure."

There are so many things wrong with that series of statements, I don't even know where to begin. The Supreme Leader shouldn't be ordering anything. Evil Lincoln might be the fake king, but he should be running the show. And that's not even the worst part.

Huh. Maybe I heard that last part wrong.

"Did you say procedure?" I ask.

"I did."

"And what procedure would that be?"

X chuckles behind his black bandages. I'm not going to lie; it's a creepy sound that sends cold tendrils of fear up my spine.

"Why," says X, "it's my understanding that your husband explained this to you already. You're a danger to the baby. Everyone's agreed you must be sedated until after you give birth."

For a long moment, I can only stare at him. If Ethan didn't expect my attack, then I certainly didn't expect this counter-move from him. Doctors? Sedation?

The world takes on a dreamlike glow.

Ethan is sending doctors to sedate me.

My own thrax guards have vanished.

And my real husband is still trapped somewhere in a sketchy research lab on Earth where they're trying to drain his soul.

In such situations, there's only one thing you can say.

Fuuuuuuuuuuuuuuck.

8

There's a moment that lasts forever where I'm staring at the bandaged faces of not only X, but all the Razor Guards. My mind spins over everything I could do in the moment to escape them and reach the LK Route. With each passing second, fighting my way out is looking like the only viable option.

The rumble of voices and footsteps fill the hallway. I glance toward my left. Sure enough, Evil Lincoln and Ethan are marching toward me, accompanied by a bevy of very worried-looking royal physicians. Even from a distance, I can see the fear in the doctors' eyes, along with the light glinting off the syringes all of them grip in each hand.

My jaw falls open. *Come on.* Do they really need a dozen Razor Guards and ten physicians to get the job done here, not counting Evil Lincoln and Ethan? And adding onto that, must every last doctor carry a pair of massive syringes…and all just to subdue little old me?

My palms slick over with sweat.

Actually, that math seems about right. *Fuck-fuck-fuckity-fuck-fuck.* I am in deep trouble here.

At that moment, something flickers on the right side of my peripheral vision. I swipe my hand across my brow, all the better to hide my sneaky peep down the opposite side of the hallway.

Bingo.

There, in the shadows, lurks Williamson. Evidently, the dude is back from his break.

Thank Heavens.

My thoughts spin through possible next steps. Demon patrol training flashes to the forefront of my mind. To save time in battle, thrax warriors learn different code words for attack scenarios. For example, a classic one that I've used with Lincoln is Assault Plan Delta. It involves turning his baculum fire sword into a big net made of white flame.

I nod once to myself. *This could work.*

Williamson is a trained thrax fighter; the Razor Guards aren't. Also, I know for a fact that Ethan washed out of warrior training, so he won't know the assault plan codes. And as for Evil Lincoln, I'm guessing that he's some kind of lab experiment gone wild. Bottom line: I can call out the assault plan of my choice to Williamson. Hopefully, he'll back me up.

Question is, which plan do I call?

The docs step closer. All them wear the long tunics or gowns of their various houses. Ethan and Evil Lincoln flank the jittery group on either side. It's like they're afraid the doctors will bolt at any second.

Not an unreasonable fear, really. I'm a tough Arena warrior who's about to be cornered. They know an ass kicking is coming.

As the group moves closer, Ethan shoots me his "freckled bad kid" smile. Evil Lincoln arches his brows in a look that can only be called snide. The faces of the doctors all twitch with terror.

Closing my eyes, I do my best to ignore them all.

I need to pick the perfect fighting scenario and fast. At best, I'll get one shot at calling out a plan to Williamson. Assuming he helps me.

He's got to help me.

Besides, if my plan doesn't work, I'll become a pincushion for the doctor's syringes. Or worse. Williamson won't let that happen. Otherwise, why would he have been the only person to believe me? And he did sneak off on a sketchy break and is lurking behind a wall while scoping out my attackers.

He's definitely going to help me.

Attack plans flip through my mind like pages in a book. There's a whole category dedicated to being surrounded by enemies while one of your fellow thrax warriors is still free. Of these, there's another subset that focuses on indoor situations. At last, the perfect option appears in my brain.

Assault Plan Beta Epsilon.

This particular scenario involves the non-surrounded warrior creating a diversion of the explosive variety. Most thrax fighters carry an array of charms on them for all sorts of occasions. I can only hope they have a few options for blowing up intruders who try to raid the royal chambers.

I tap X's shoulder. "Beta Epsilon."

I can't see his face, but the double-take move is a universal one, even if you are covered in black bandages. "What did you say?"

"I said, Beta—"

An eardrum shattering kaboom rocks the hallway. Bits of

rubble tumble from the ceiling. Massive chunks of stone slam into the floor. Smoke and dust fill the air. Voices cry out, mostly the doctors. My brows lift.

Williamson did help me, and damn, he's a fast worker.

Someone grabs my hand in through the smoke. "Your Majesty, this way."

Even through I can't see squat, I recognize that voice. It's Williamson. I stumble along in whatever direction he's dragging me. We dodge around Razor Guards and freaking-out physicians. Moans echo all around. A pang of worry tightens my insides. Whatever I think of the Razor Guards, they didn't deserve to have the ceiling fall down on them.

I run a few more paces down the smoky hallway before deciding: actually, the Razor Guards totally deserved to have that happen to them. Who restrains a pregnant lady so she can be sedated against her will? Plus there are only a dozen physicians around them. I'm sure they'll all be fine.

It's impossible to see, so I sense Williamson pushing open a section of wall. I smile. Evil Lincoln only blocked the secret passages inside my chambers. Dumbass.

Williamson and I step into the hidden passageway. The door-sized section of wall slams shut behind us. In the dim light, Williamson unclips his baculum from his sword belt. It's a welcome sight. Baculum are two silver rods that can take any shape with angelfire. Only thrax from the House of Rixa can wield them.

Oh yeah, and me.

Lifting his baculum high, Williamson ignites the weapon into a torch blazing with white angelfire. Flickering light illuminates the passageway. It's like others I've seen before: a cramped space that's carved out of gray rock. Sometimes, the passages are also framed with wood, but that's less common.

Williamson scans me from head to toe. "Are you all right, Your Majesty?"

"Yes, thank you for saving me."

"What happened to the rest of your thrax guard?"

"The false King sent them away."

A light coat of dust has settled on Williamson's hair. He rakes his hand over his scalp. A cascade of gray motes dances through the torchlight. "I'm so sorry. I had no idea your guard would be sent away."

"Did you know about the doctors?"

Williamson straightens his stance. "We'd just heard about the sedation plan. But we wouldn't allow it to happen."

"We? Because all the other guards left their posts pretty easily."

"You're right. I wouldn't allow it to happen."

"So you said you needed to step away."

Williamson nods. "And I waited." His mouth thins to a determined line. "You can't blame the other guards, though. None of them have interacted with you the way I have. They think the King is correct in finding you insane."

"Hey, I'm just thankful you stayed on my side. That was a great risk. I know you have a family. If the false King figured out that you helped me—"

"My family knows the risks of my role here in the castle." Williamson straightens his stance. "What can I do to help you?"

"I need to go to the Lime Kilns."

Williamson shakes his head. "I don't understand."

"Honestly, it's better if it stays that way. Just find a way to sneak me to the Lime Kilns behind the castle. I'll take it from there."

"As you command, Your Majesty." Williamson turns and heads down the empty passage. "This way."

As I follow Williamson through the cramped space, raised voices echo in from the castle. Evidently, they are pulling in more Razor Guards and warriors. Yuck. To keep my focus, I remind myself of all the tight spots I've been in. On the Arena floor. With Lady Adair. While fighting Armageddon. I've been in tougher places and escaped. I simply have to do it again.

And even though my internal pep talk helps, I know that although I've always made it in the past, the risks have never been higher.

My husband. My child. Williamson. His family. Hell, if Ethan and Evil Lincoln take over Antrum, all the thrax could be at risk. And if the thrax aren't able to protect humanity, what will happen to the mortal world?

Memories appear in my mind. I picture Lincoln holding the arrowhead from Ethan back in the library. That was more than a weapon to steal away my husband. The memory slicing into my soul, opening up the question I've been avoiding.

What does it really mean to be Queen of the thrax?

Guess I need to find that answer and fast.

Shaking my head, I focus on the path before me. Before I solve the riddle of what it means to rule, I first need to find my Lincoln. To do that, I must reach the LK escape route. Once I'm out of Antrum, we'll see what's possible.

This simply has to work.

Williamson and I maneuver through the hidden passageways of Arx Hall. These routes are new to me, although I can't be sure. The many corridors start to merge into a single blurred experience.

Another cramped passageway.

Williamson's torch casting flickering light on the gray rock walls.

Stale air filling my lungs.

Dust motes and cobwebs tickling my face.

All the sameness is only broken by the fact that, every so often, we pass a doorway that leads to a different path. These passageways snake throughout the castle. Only one leads to the LK Route.

With every second, fresh waves of anxiety twist up my spine. The voices echoing into the passageways grow louder. Ethan, Evil Lincoln, and their Razor Guards seem to be every-where at once. The entire palace is on alert. How much time do I have to escape Antrum?

At last, we pause by a stone door that's set into the wall. "We're here," announces Williamson. The torchlight casts deep shadows on his lined face.

I pause. You'd think that arriving would ease the ropes of tension across my shoulders, but somehow, they've only gotten worse.

"And where's here?" I ask.

"This door opens onto the Dark Forest. It's the closest I can get you to the lime kilns."

This is just like the Chamber of Reflection, part two. I know all about the Dark Forest, although I've never been there before. The Dark Forest was an early attempt to add some Earth life to the underground. Ages ago, the House of Striga enchanted a real forest and moved it into Antrum. Things worked out well for the first hundred years or so. After that, the woods just got huge, dark, and creepy. No matter what they tried, the spell didn't have the mojo to keep up with the decay. That's why they built the next forest, the Crystal Woods, out of white stone. It stays bright and inviting. These days, the Dark Forest is where we shove things that don't really fit in other spots.

Like lime kilns.

"How far to the kilns?" I ask. On reflex, I run my fingers through my hair. A small cloud of dust and cobwebs tumble to the ground. These secret passageways aren't necessarily a hotspot for dusting.

"It's a short walk through the Dark Forest. A path leads you right to the kilns."

The "Dark Forest and oven" combo reminds me of a fairy tale. "This all seems very Hansel and Gretel to me."

"You're not the only one to think so. The stone path is called Breadcrumb Alley. It ends in a small clearing where the lime kilns are kept."

"Got it. Let's go."

Williamson heaves open the door. We step outside into a shadowy forest filled with huge trees and wide dark leaves. Behind us, there looms a stretch of tall stone. We must be somewhere along the south wall of the palace. I scan the ground, looking for any sign of Ethan, Evil Lincoln, or the Razor Guards.

No one is here.

Perfect.

Just as Williamson said, a path of brown stones winds off through the trees. Taking off at a run, I follow the trail, Williamson at my side. I haven't gone too far before a thought occurs to me.

I forgot to ask about Cissy and her escape.

"If you had orders about me, did you have any for my

friend?" I ask.

"Who?" Williamson scans the forest as we race along. His mind is clearly in his own kind of warrior mode, scanning for intruders.

"This is important. Did you and the rest of my guards get any orders about Cecelia Frederickson, Senator of Diplomacy for Purgatory?"

"We did. She's not allowed to leave Antrum. The orders were jointly signed by both Ethan and the King."

That stops me dead in my tracks. I open my mouth, ready to complain that I asked my guards to ensure she got safely away…and they promised to do so. And since when does Ethan countersign anything? But there's no point whining. I have to focus on what I can do to change things. "You need to find her. Help her leave Antrum as soon as possible."

Williamson shakes his head. "But I must ensure you get to the lime kilns."

"My destination won't mean anything if I can't get Cissy out of here. I wish I could explain more, but there really isn't time. Can you do this for me? Cissy simply must leave Antrum."

Williamson pauses for a moment before answering. "As you command."

"Thank you." My voice breaks as I reply. What would I have done without Williamson? "For everything."

"It's been an honor." Williamson turns about, running in the opposite direction. I take off again on the Breadcrumb Alley.

If this is another fairy tale, I hope I'm Hansel or Gretel. They escaped the witch and her evil oven. Too bad my final destination is that oven.

Things aren't looking good.

9

I keep running along my path through the Dark Forest. I can see why no one likes hanging out in these woods. If trees could be zombies, that's the dark Forest: both dead and alive at the same time. Even worse, the trees don't seem too happy about that fate. It's hard to pull air into my lungs, like the atmosphere is choking with barely-contained rage.

Or maybe the anger is just mine alone. How did I go from a happy honeymoon to running for my life to escape Antrum?

The path takes a sharp turn through the massive black tree trunks. The barest sound echoes through the Dark Forest.

Footsteps.

And worse, they're the tread of someone who's trying not to be heard.

There's a short list of who could be sneaking around the Dark Forest at this time. Ethan. Evil Lincoln. Razor Guards. My guards. Doctors. None of them have good intentions.

I pick up my pace. Beads of sweat roll down my back. Some of my steps become louder and more obvious, but it's a chance I have to take. I simply have to go at full speed and Williamson said this trail was short.

Let's just hope Williamson was right.

Still, no matter how hard I push myself, there's no break in the trees. No clearing. And certainly, no lime kilns.

"Myla, I know you can hear me." That would be Ethan, calling to me through the forest.

No way am I responding to this guy. I just try to run faster.

"I brought my toy planes," adds Ethan. "They do more than decorate a tabletop. These are miniature working prototypes where I've swapped out the ammunition for something else. Tranquilizer darts." He makes a tut-tut noise. "You scared away all my doctors, Myla. You left me no choice."

Fuuuuuuuuuuck. Tranquilizers, again?

I run so hard that a stitch starts to bite into my side. I do my best to ignore it and keep up the pace. This kind of thing never happened to me before, though. Being pregnant must be messing with my warrior mode.

"Please, my love." Now, it's Evil Lincoln's voice that sounds in the forest. "You must see reason. Stop running. Where will you go, anyway? Turn yourself in, and the sedation process can be far more pleasant."

Did Evil Lincoln just say the words *"pleasant sedation process"* as a lure for me to turn myself in? Wow. What this guy doesn't know about me is a lot.

"Ethan is merciful. He could have brought more arrowheads, you know. There are Razor Guards here with composite bows. Be thankful you'll only be put to sleep."

Like an animal. Thanks.

I follow another turn in the path, my sandals slapping against the brown stones. The thought occurs to me that this trail does look like giant-sized breadcrumbs. There are large flat stones separated like rocks in a river, only here the water is actually the dark earth of the forest. I'd think it was pretty if I weren't running for my life.

A mechanical buzz sounds behind me. I risk a quick glance over my shoulder. About twenty toy planes zoom toward me through the heavy branches. Even worse, I'm running at full tilt and they are gaining on me. A faint whirring noise fills the air as the miniature guns angle in my direction.

Unholy Hell.

My tail arcs behind me, ready to deflect any projectiles that come my way. Trouble is, with that many planes and so many miniature tranq missiles headed at me? That might be too much, even for my tail. I will my Scala robes to change into body armor. The threads change form and cover me from head to toe. It's bulkier for running, but I should be better protected.

Popping noises sound as the tiny tranq missiles are launched in my direction. Fresh waves of adrenaline pump through my system. My body gets jerked a little as my tail moves wildly to bat away the missiles. None break through, though.

I'm tempted to give my tail a high-five, but there will be time for that later.

The miniature planes veer off into the treetops. I'm pretty sure they've given up the fight, when they all swoop in for a frontal assault.

Oh damn. My tail can't be nearly so helpful from this direction.

A barrage of needle-like missiles fly at me, embedding in the front of the body armor. Prickles bite into my skin.

Some of the needles have broken through.

The planes veer off. My head starts to get woozy. I step through a cluster of trees and into a small clearing.

At least, I think it's a small clearing.

There are four igloo-shaped ovens all in a row. They are made of white brick with round mouths that spew red fire. My body feels weightless with triumph—I made it! Forcing myself to move even faster, I head toward the last kiln in line, just like Lincoln told me.

As I wobble closer, workers in cotton pants and matching tunics pause to stare, open mouthed. What I sight I must be: covered in cobwebs and dust, with a look of confusion on my face. I scan my body, looking for the needles. The tiny projectiles have all disappeared, which is no shocker. Magical weapons often do that once they've completed their job. Unfortunately, the fact that there's no obvious reason for me to be stumbling around only makes me look stranger.

The workers step back as I approach. A few let out whispered greetings of "Your Majesty." All of them keep staring at me like an alien landed in their back yard, which isn't too far from the truth.

I step past the first line kiln. The heart from the furnace sears into my skin. I keep going.

"Stop her," calls Evil Lincoln from the forest. "I command this as your King."

I pass the second and third kilns. No one comes near me. Man, I must really look a mess for no one to even approach me. I pause at the fourth kiln and rest my hand on the fiery stone.

"In thrax sic hunt," I whisper. The furnace turns cool under my touch.

Behind me, Ethan, Evil Lincoln, and a ton of Razor Guards step out of the forest. They mean business, too. A few of the

Razor Guards carry compound bows and quivers of arrows. If those arrows can do the same thing to me as they did to Lincoln? There's no way I could fight getting dragged off somewhere like Lincoln did through the mirror. Hells, I'm having enough trouble standing upright at this point.

"Stop her!" cries Lincoln.

I glare at my subjects, careful to make my irises glow red. "Touch me and die."

My subjects, to their credit, stand perfectly still.

Some small part of me wonders if there was a more diplomatic way of putting that, but I have bigger things to worry about now.

Like how to wiggle into this furnace.

Ethan and company take off toward me at a run. Leaning over, I wiggle my head and shoulders in through the mouth of the furnace. From there, it's easy to slip inside and crouch in the center. The furnace's mouth closes up tight. I have the weird sensation that this is what it must be like to get swallowed by a giant fish.

A gentle purple glow lights up the cramped space. Purple, that's Striga magic. The floor beneath me hardens into a metal circle. I exhale. A round disc means a Pulpitum platform. A young female voice sounds in the cramped space.

"Where can we take you?"

My head feels like it's stuffed with cotton candy or something. "Take me to...to..."

Pounding echoes outside the oven, which snaps some of my brain back into functioning again. "Earth." I curl up onto my side in the tiny Pulpitum. It takes all my focus to speak the next four words. "The Empire State Building."

"As you command," says the voice.

The Pulpitum platform lurches deep into the round. There

are the muffled sounds of an explosion followed by something about death and the Queen, but my brain is too fried to process that information. A hazy memory appears. Lincoln said something about the lime kiln being booby-trapped to prevent anyone from following me.

That information seems important now, but not as critical as staying on the platform. Pulpitum aren't exactly designed with safety in mind. If you get too close to the edge of the metal transfer disc, you can get caught in the transfer process. And considering how I'm now riding a small round platform past dirt, rock, lava and gemstones, the possibilities for injury seem endless.

The platform lurches again. Instead of heading downward, I start hurtling toward the surface. My mind starts to fog over from the drugs in my system. I can't fall asleep though.

I simply have to make it to the Empire State Building and Cissy.

10

*T*he next thing I know, I'm crouched on a metal grating. Humans stroll all around. For some reason, the air tastes like exhaust fumes and lemon. A bit of sun peeps out from the clouds overhead.

My hazy brain tries to process this fact. We never get direct sunshine in Purgatory. I must have reached Earth.

Someone crouches beside me. It's Cissy. Thank Heavens.

A few humans have started pointing in my direction.

Cissy leans in closer until we're almost nose to nose. "Myla, are you all right?"

"Mostly." The word comes out garbled, even to my ears.

Cissy glances nervously over her shoulder. "Those humans saw you appear out of nowhere. They're freaking out."

"Tell them I've been here for ages and be snippy about it. When it comes to the supernatural, humans never believe what they see."

"Okay, good plan." Looking over her shoulder, Cissy glares at the crowd. "What? You've never seen a woman pass out before?" The staring stops.

Cissy wraps her arm around my shoulder. "Can you stand up?"

I try to shift my weight, but my body feels like its made of noodles. I don't need to pretend to pass out—I'm actually going to pass out. "Get me to a hospital. Don't tell anyone in the after-realms where I am."

My last thoughts are of Lincoln and the baby as all my consciousness fades.

My dreams are vivid and gut wrenching. I transport in the lime kiln Pulpitum once more. Voices echo around me. "The Queen is dead." I pound on the kiln walls, trying to tell them that I'm alive. No matter how much I scream, I can't make a sound.

After that, I find my parents in their home, weeping in a room that's covered in drapes and paint cans. A half-assembled crib sits on the floor. Guilt and sorrow weigh down my bones. Once again, I try to tell them that I'm all right, but it's like I'm a ghost. They can't see or hear me. From the corner of my vision, I see a small glowing creature running through the house. I follow it.

"Who are you?" I call out the words, but no sound comes from my mouth. Stupid dreams. For what feels like years, I chase the little glowing man around my parent's home. Every time he seems close enough to catch, he slips away once more.

When I become aware again, I realize two things. First of all, I'm lying in a hospital bed. And second, Cissy's standing over me. It takes a few seconds for my memories to return. Then, I know.

The last time I saw Cissy, she and I were atop the Empire State Building. My head was woozy from Ethan's toy attack, so I'd asked her to get me medical help. I scan the cinderblock room. It looks like I definitely made it to a hospital, but who knows what happened once I arrived? Tranq meds and pregnancy don't mix.

I grip Cissy's wrist. "Is the baby okay?"

"The baby is fine and you're fine."

I close my eyes, trying to force Cissy's news through my brain. *The baby is fine and I'm fine.*

Nope.

Not believing it.

I open my eyes and squeeze Cissy's wrist harder. "But Mom said that the doctors don't know how far along the baby really is. It's all based on how powerful the child becomes in the supernatural sense. So maybe the baby looks fine to the humans, but they don't know because it's the wrong size or whatever."

Cissy's brown eyes hold a look of infinite patience. "I'm not sure I follow your logic, Myla."

She's not wrong, but that doesn't mean I'm dropping my point. "I just woke up, and I'm panicking. Give me something here."

Cissy nods. "Well, the human doctors checked you out thoroughly. They say you're three weeks along and everything looks perfectly fine for that stage of pregnancy." She wiggles her arm. "And I can't feel my fingers anymore."

"Right. Sorry." I release her wrist and do the pregnancy math. "Three weeks. That's right."

"Do you feel better knowing all that?"

"Much better. Thank you." I lean back onto my pillow and really soak in my surroundings for the first time. I'm in a private room, which is cool. The place has white cinderblock walls, a tiled floor, and a fancy color TV. The lights here even have actual dimmer switches.

Whoa.

This is Earth, all right. We don't have fancy light switches in Purgatory, and Antrum doesn't even use the cotton gin, let alone electricity.

Cissy drags a plastic chair beside my bed and sits down. Fortunately, the seat's one of those with an open backside, so it's perfect for her golden retriever tail. I notice how she's wearing a neat white sweater, black pants, and spiky boots. A huge Prada satchel sits on the floor beside her. No shocker there. Of course, my bestie found time to both organize my life and shop up a storm.

That's my girl.

Leaning over, Cissy fishes around inside her satchel. A second later, she pulls out a fancy laptop from her bag. It's so thin, you'd think the thing was made of paper. "I have a list of things for us to review. Do you feel well enough?"

In this moment, I love Cissy to pieces. This is why my bestie kicks ass as a Senator, even though she's the ripe old age of nineteen. The girl is an organizational force of nature.

I tuck the sheets under my arms. "I'm ready."

"You're been recovering for a day now."

"Only a day?" The way my dreams dragged on and on, I would have thought I was out for a week.

"Yes, a little under a day. It's now early Thursday morning, which means I've had plenty of time to review reports and organize my questions." Cissy gives me her puppy dog eyes, which are her specialty, considering her golden retriever tail and all. "To start off, I just have to say this. I'm so sorry about Ethan trying to sedate you through your pregnancy."

"Thanks for the sympathy, but don't worry too much." My tail arcs over my shoulder. "Ethan is a dead man."

"I'd expect nothing less." Cissy types a few keys and fixes me with her "I'm getting this shiz organized" stare. "Now, first question. You asked me before not to tell anyone where you are. Is that what you still want?"

My eyes widen. "Everyone in the after-realms doesn't know where I am?" I think back to my dreams. In them, my parents thought I was dead. Even so, I figured it was just that: a dream. And I remember some strange stuff before I took the Pulpitum out of Antrum, but I was heavily sedated at the time. A sinking feeling churns through my insides. "There's more to this question, isn't there?" I ask.

"Well, the way you left Antrum was..." Cissy taps her nail against the edge of the laptop in rapid-fire style. She only taps like crazy when she's super nervous.

"You can tell me anything, Cis."

"I've received some bizarre intelligence from my diplomatic team back in Purgatory." She clears her throat. "The reports say that you climbed into an oven?" She stares at me like that's the craziest thing she's ever heard.

"It was a lime kiln."

Cissy's jaw drops. "Lime kiln."

"I didn't say anything because Lincoln asked me to keep it a secret. Lime kilns are like medieval fix-it thingies. My igni told me to climb into one and escape. Lincoln said it was super-safe."

"My reports say it was lit to like, a million degrees inside."

"It got magically cooled when I said a secret pass-phrase."

Okay, that sounds totally insane even to me. "Whatever. I crawled in and everything was fine."

"Got it." Cissy screws her mouth up to one side, and she types onto the keyboard again. "Actually climbed into lit oven." She looks up from her typing. "Then what happened?"

"Umm, maybe I heard an explosion or something."

"Maybe?"

"Definitely?" I shrug. "At the time, I was shot full of tranqs and trying to escape. What do your report say?" I sit up a little higher, trying to peer onto her screen.

"My information says there was definitely an explosion. Everyone present saw the lime kiln blow up." Cissy shakes her head. "This is all very strange."

"Not really. It was an escape route."

"Escape route."

"You keep repeating what I say."

"This is a lot to take in."

"Here's the deal. The lime kiln was a secret way to leave Antrum. Walker found it ages ago and didn't tell anyone. The kiln also included a booby trap so no one would follow. That was the explosion. I get how this seems strange, but come on. Who would really believe that I crawled into a super-hot oven and got myself blown up? I was acting crazy, but not that nuts."

Cissy snaps the laptop shut and folds her hands neatly atop the closed device. "Myla, everyone absolutely believes that you crawled into a super-hot oven and got yourself blown up."

"Everyone? Really?"

"Everyone."

Now it's my turn to have a hard time accepting things.

"What about that thrax Captain, Williamson? He helped me find the kiln. He knows it was only an escape trick."

Cissy scans her sheet. "There's nothing in my reports about any Williamson."

I worry my lower lip with my teeth. *Dang, I hope that guy is all right.* If Ethan or Evil Lincoln found out that Williamson helped me escape, that loyal guard could have big trouble. And the man has a family, no less.

"That said, my reports are filled with notices of your, uh, passing."

I wave Cissy off. She's making a big deal about nothing. "Please. Nobody thinks I'm dead." The words come out as more of a question, though.

"Oh yes, yes they do."

My shoulders slump. "Really?"

"Really and for truly."

Whoa. All my family, friends, and subjects think that I've passed away. It's a strange sensation, like being freed and tied down at the same time. I settle more deeply onto my mattress. "You know, I heard some people yelling *'the Queen is dead'* as I was transported away. I thought it was all a dream, though."

"It wasn't. What else did you think was a dream?"

"I had visions of my parents mourning, and then I saw this…" I eye Cissy, debating whether or not to describe the little glowing guy. Based on how Cissy is still tapping her laptop and looking at me like I'm nuts, I decide to pass on the gleaming dude part of my dreams. My bestie is having enough trouble adjusting to the lime kiln thing.

"So if everyone thinks I'm dead, how is my family taking it?"

"Not well. In Antrum, there's a special ceremony that happens when a Great Scala dies unexpectedly."

"Thrax and their traditions. Color me not surprised. What's it about?"

"They shut down the gates of Heaven and Hell for a time. It's supposed to give the igni a chance to mourn."

My brows lift. "I had no idea that would happen."

Cissy glances at her sheet. "Your father was the one who insisted on reviving the ceremony. Didn't they do anything like that when the last Scala died?"

"When the last Scala went, it was totally expected. You remember him. Dude was older than dirt." The last great Scala was a thrax who'd done the job for a thousand years. He looked it, too.

"Right." Cissy raises her pen again. "All of which brings me back to my original question. Do you want me to inform your family that you're alive?"

I tap my cheek and contemplate my options. "If they know I'm alive, then they'll be here in a heartbeat. And you know what they'll do, too: drag me right back into the after-realms. I need to stay here and find Lincoln."

Cissy screws up her mouth. "They might not take you back."

"Cis. They think I just crawled into a freaking oven and got my pregnant self BLOWN the Hell UP."

Cissy leans back in her chair. I'm glad to see she's stopped tapping her pen. It's a sign that she's accepting things now. "You know, the whole oven scenario is kind of a Hansel and Gretel move, if you asked me."

"That's what I said, too." Cissy and I think so much alike sometimes, it's not even funny. "And you know my mom. There's no way she'd let me stay on Earth."

"True. She still gets a little off balanced when it comes to you."

"Well, Lincoln's parents are just as protective. Together, they'll drag me right back to Purgatory or Antrum. Lincoln's fam might even be totally okay with Ethan's 'let's sedate her for the rest of the pregnancy' plan. Am I right or am I right?"

Cissy sighs. "You're totally right."

"Then it's settled. Telling anyone that I'm alive is off the list. Next item?" I love how organized Cissy is. The little homework I did in high school was totally copied from her, by the way.

A knock sounds at the door. "Hello, is the patient awake?"

I sit straighter on the bed. "Yes, I'm up. Who is it?"

A doctor strides into my room. The guy's a stocky dude with ebony skin that stands out against his white lab coat. His large brown eyes and closely-cropped gray hair give him the perfect image of "trustworthy physician."

"I'm Doctor Obianu. How's the patient?"

I twiddle my fingers at him. "Feeling great."

The doc flips through his clipboard. "Your blood work came back normal. Congratulations on the pregnancy, by the way. Now, we can do some additional tests, if you like. Although your results are normal, there are some interesting qualities in your blood that might be useful to test merely for scientific purposes…"

After that, the doc goes on about some blah-blah-blah testing stuff, but all I can really do is focus on the Hunter Enterprises logo that's embroidered on his lab coat. I didn't notice it before because it's white-on white, but now that he's closer? I can't miss it. I point at the emblem in question. "Why is that logo on your jacket? Doctors don't advertise stuff."

Note to self: Mom said I'd never learn anything useful from the Human Channel. Check out all that doctor outfit knowledge. Ha!

"Oh, this?" The doc looks down at his chest. "It's not advertising, really." His big brown eyes take on a dreamy look. "Hunter Enterprises is changing this hospital like they're changing the world." He gives us a half smile. "But you two know all about that, of course."

"No," says Cissy. "We don't know."

"Yeah," I add. "What's up?"

"No one develops technology like Hunter Enterprises," explains the doc. "They're even going to upgrade all our systems at no charge so they work like magic. We won't even need electricity even more." He grips his clipboard so tightly, the papers rattle. "Plus, have you seen what H-E is doing at the airport?"

"Uh, no." I'm still a little stuck on the phrase *"work like magic,"* but I decide to let that slide for the moment. The airport thing sounds much more interesting. "Go on."

"It's all happening at LaGuardia airport," explains the doc. "They have closed down the runways and filled them with jet planes and helicopters. There's even a dirigible."

"You mean a blimp?" Cissy frowns. "I thought those exploded."

"Nothing from Hunter Enterprises ever malfunctions." The dreamy look returns to the strong lines of the doc's face. "And no one calls them blimps anymore. They're Hunter Dirigibles now. Every inch of them is jammed with amazing tech. H-E kept it all top secret for ages. In fact, the only prototype in the world is hovering over at LaGuardia right now." He glances at his watch. "Once I'm off duty, I plan to check it out. They're calling it the Touch The Tech Event."

"You seem pretty excited." My brows lift. Ethan mentioned this event back in Antrum.

"It's H-E," says the doc. "So everyone is excited. It's been all over the news. Only, you know the risks out there."

My tail does its up-periscope move over my shoulder. "I do?"

"There are rumors of other worldly beings—demons—who might try to infiltrate H-E and use their power for evil. Of course, I don't believe a word of it." As he makes that statement, the doc looks one hundred percent convinced that demons exist. "Fortunately, H-E has Razor Guard troops at the ready for any kind of counterstrike, whether it's mortal or not."

I narrow my eyes. "Riiiiiiiiiight." This is definitely the event that Ethan mentioned at the Summit. It's supposed to be some Touch The Tech stuff followed by a thrax demon patrol run by the Earls. And what would happen if humans actually saw demons as part of that exercise? Ethan and his Razor Guards could swoop in to save everyone. And in the process, Ethan could take over both the human and thrax realms.

At that moment, the door swings half open, and a nurse pops her head in. She's young with big eyes, copper skin, and straight black hair pulled into a neat bun. "Doctor? I need your signature on this form."

Dr. Obianu turns around to examine the paperwork, and that's when I see it. There's a Grotus demon on his neck.

Grotus demons, ugh.

These slimy parasites sap the strength of whoever they latch onto. They're lime green, slimy, and incredibly painful to their host.

Oh, yeah. For once, things are looking up. That Grotus is going down.

11

*A*s I stare at the Grotus demon, heat pools behind my eyes. My irises brighten with the red of demonic wrath.

"Don't you dare," says Cissy.

Oh, I dare.

Thrax rank demons by letter; Grotus are Class D. In other words, they're not too hard to kill. That said, they're painful little buggers who drive migraines into the humans they latch onto. Since the doc healed me, the least I can do is kill the demon on his neck and skull.

And if it helps me blow off a little steam after my crap time escaping from Ethan?

Hey, that's just a bonus.

Once the nurse is gone, the doc turns back to face me. "Where were we?" he asks.

Cissy gestures to the door. "You were saying the patient here is dismissed and you're leaving. Now."

I rub my palms together in the *mwhah-hah-hah* movement

of super-villains everywhere. "The doc can hang out for a second," I say slowly.

"You wouldn't," says Cissy. But the exasperated note in her voice says she's already accepted the inevitable.

I leap out of bed. All I'm wearing is my hospital gown; it opens in the back. That said, Cissy's seen my butt before. And in front of me? It's all Grotus demon, all the time.

The doc rubs his neck. His hand slides right through the Grotus demon because, of course, the doc can't see or feel it. I roll my eyes. Here the doc is all worried about Ethan's fake demons when there's a real one attached to his skull. Oh, well. That's just one of the many downsides to being mortal. You can't see the demonic or angelic realms. But in my eyes? That Grotus looks all green and sluggy.

"I was going to leave, wasn't I?" asks the doc.

I step closer. "Neck giving you trouble?"

"Why, yes. It's been that way for years. I have a strained muscle."

"No, you have a Grotus demon at the base of your skull. Do you spend a lot of time in the woods?" Grotus like to hang out on pine trees. If a human gets too close, they drop down and latch on.

"How did you know that?" asks the doc. "I haven't gone camping for years, but I used to all the time. And did you say demon?"

Cissy's voice takes on a warning tone. "Myla."

"Wait a moment." The doc frowns and checks his paperwork. "You gave her name as Miss. G. Scala."

"Excuse me." I step up closer. Now, I'm almost toe-to-toe with the doc. In other words, I'm well within striking distance. My tail doesn't need any invitation. It arches over my shoulder and moves to spear the Grotus demon. The clever little bugger squirms out of the way, avoiding the arrowhead end of my tail. It has a tiny mouth filled with needle-like teeth. With every dodge, the demon keeps making awful squealing noises and trying to gnaw on my tail. Tough luck. Nothing can break through dragonscales.

Still, for a Class D demon, this little creep is putting up quite a fight.

The doc arcs his head from side to side. "Neck feels strange today."

I point over his shoulder. "Oh no, look at that!"

"What?" The doc turns around and I have my chance. The Grotus demon is less than a foot away now. With lightning speed, I punch the Grotus in the side of its sluggy head, knocking it clear off the doc's back. My punch was a good shot; it hit the demon without affecting the host at all.

As the Grotus tumbles down, my tail spears the slimy critter straight through its middle, holding it in place. With a swish of my hips, my tail flings the critter against the wall. The Grotus lands with a sticky *thwack* before slowly sliding to down onto the floor. The doc can't see anything, of course. But sometimes humans are sensitive enough to know something is going on, even if they can't see or hear it.

I step back so my tail can wipe itself off on my blanket. "Do you mind leaving so I can barf?" I point to my stomach. "Pregnancy, you know."

The doc frowns. "Do you need further medical help?"

"Nope. Definitely not." I shoot the doc a hearty thumbs-up.

"This happens all the time," offers Cissy. "I just feed her a cracker and she'll be all better in like a minute." For the record, Cissy is a really good liar.

"Are you sure *you're* feeling all right, doc?" I ask.

"I'm fine." That said, the doc doesn't look fine. In fact, he looks really, really, really confused. I don't blame him. Poor humans. They make up all sorts of reasons for their problems when half the time, it's totally demonic.

"Neck feeling better now?" I ask.

Cissy narrows her eyes at me. "You know it's feeling better."

The doc's voice takes on a dreamy tone. "How would you know my neck is better?"

"Call it a wild guess." I gesture toward the door. "How about you leave now?" I put my finger over my mouth and puff out my cheeks in the universal symbol for 'barf a coming.' "Privacy?"

"Leaving." The poor guy looks totally freaked. "Yes, I suppose that's best." The doc shuffles out the door. He closes it behind him with a soft click.

The second the doc is gone, Cissy rounds on me. "Myla!"

"What?"

"You can't go around killing demons. Some humans are sensitive. They can't see anything, but it freaks them out. If we're going to find Lincoln, we need to keep a low profile."

I open my mouth, ready to argue, but then I shut it just as quickly. "You're right. I need to save my killing energy for the times when it can help Lincoln." Sadly, there are too many demons in a big city like New York, anyway. I could spend a lifetime skewering Grotus creatures and never make a dent.

Cissy stares at me for a long minute, and then shakes her head. "Wow. You might be growing up a little, Myla Lewis."

I set my pointer finger across my lips into a *shh* face. "Don't tell anyone. I'm not even twenty yet. I don't want to lose my immature rep." I sit back on the edge of the bed, careful to stay far away from my tail's smears of Grotus slime. "Sorry about interrupting your list. We only got through your first item."

Cissy sits back down and pulls up her clipboard again. "No worries. We had to speak to the doctor anyway." She scans the document before her. "The second item is that, actually, not everyone thinks you're dead."

"I thought we established the opposite was true."

"Nope, in fact, there is one person who is totally aware that you're alive and in need of aid."

A sinking sensation moves down my insides. I can guess where this is going. "Who came here with you?"

The door swings open once again. This time, Cissy's boyfriend Zeke swaggers into the room. "Hello, kittens. Miss me?"

Zeke looks like he always does: pale skin, chiseled bone structure, blond hair, brown eyes, and a monkey tail. Today, he's working a preppy killer vibe with his khaki pants and commando vest. I've known Zeke since grade school. We used to have this sick love-triangle thing going where Cissy loved Zeke, but Zeke wanted to get my attention. I can't say that he loved me so much as thought I was an interesting conquest. Anyway, he finally noticed Cissy and learned about love with a capital L. For some reason, I still have issues with the two of them thinking I'm carrying a torch for Zeke.

Cissy rolls her eyes. "Zeke, I said to wait outside until I was done briefing Myla. She's not dressed, you know."

Zeke gestures at the door, game show host style . "Oh, I was listening at the door, and I thought you'd gotten to the part where Myla would get excited that I came along to help. I run the Senatorial Guard now, after all." He looks over to me. "But you knew that, didn't you?"

"Yup."

"Zeke," warns Cissy. "Go back outside please. You and Myla have a history."

Oh, no. Here it comes. The couple I like to jointly call Cis-eke have been convinced that I've been in love with the Zeke side of the relationship for ages. It's really getting on my nerves.

I flash my ring finger. "I'm married, in case you two didn't notice. Can we please move past this whole 'Myla is carrying a torch for Zeke' thing now?"

"Oh, I finally figured that out," says Cissy. "I know you don't like Zeke."

"You do?" I ask.

"She does?" adds Zeke.

"Obviously." Cissy rolls her eyes. "Myla, I'm much more worried that you hate him."

Zeke's features turn slack. "Myla hates me?"

"It's not that she hates you, babe." Cissy bobs her head, which is her way of thinking how to position something. "It's more that she thinks you're a mindless lust monkey who will be of absolutely no value on this mission."

I let out a low whistle. "Way to lay it out there, Cis."

Zeke leans against the closed door. It's as if his legs have turned all wobbly. His big brown eyes lock with mine. "You don't really think I'm a mindless lust monkey, do you?"

I stare at Zeke for a long moment. There could actually be a strategic advantage to having Zeke along. It's true that he's part lust demon, just like me. I've rarely use my lust powers to influence others, even in a battle. But Zeke? I've seen him throw his lust mojo around, big time. For example, when he wants a bunch of quasi-demon girls to surround his lunch table, Zeke can make it happen in a heartbeat. He hasn't used that lust power since he met Cissy, but that doesn't mean the skill isn't useful, especially on humans. They're way susceptible to demonic influence.

"Let me put it to you this way…" I start.

"Don't say it." Zeke kicks at the floor. "You'll just make me feel bad."

"No," I counter. "What I was about to say was that I think you'll be a key part of this rescue mission."

Zeke perks right up and gives me a million-watt smile. "Exactly. Cissy told me all about how Lincoln was taken. We'll go in guns-a-blazing and set him free."

Cissy makes her *eek* face. "No guns, honey."

"Then what?" asks Zeke.

"First things first," I say. "Before we attack anyone, we need to find out exactly where Lincoln is. He's definitely in one of Ethan's labs on Earth, and if I know my Cissy, she's probably already found a nearby lab that we can check out."

Cissy reopens her laptop and points at the screen. "That's item number three. Hunter Enterprises has a super-suspicious-looking lab right in Times Square. And with the Touch The Tech Event coming up, all their regular personnel are at the airport, manning some kind of expo tent. The place is pretty much deserted."

"Right." I shoot Zeke with my finger gun. "And that's where you come in."

"I do?"

"Sure. I need to sneak in there and look around. And to do that, I need a distraction. Your powers of lust mind control are extraordinary." That's a bit of a lie—I've seen true lust mind control at work with Dyad demons, who are Class A level when it comes to mental influence through lust. Still, it can't hurt to prop up Zeke's confidence.

"Extraordinary?" echoes Zeke.

"Sure," I say. "When we go to the lab, you'll be able to control the humans, so I can check out the building."

Zeke kicks at the floor again. "Mind control is really hard. All I do influence a little, and that's tough enough."

"But we're talking about humans here, not quasis," says Cissy. "I bet it will super-easy."

"I don't know." Zeke fiddles with a pocket on his commando jacket. "I thought we'd get guns. We can't use munitions in Purgatory."

My mouth forms a little O. *So that's what this is about.* Guns don't work reliably in the after-realms. It's got something to do with the concentration of supernatural beings and magic. Zeke came here to play cowboy. In fact, I bet that pocket he's fiddling with is made for ammo or something.

I decide to go for broke. I've known Zeke since the third grade. Sure, he may want to play with deadly toys, but he's totally got a soft spot for folks in trouble. While gripping my hands under my chin, I bat my eyelashes shamelessly. "Please, Zeke. I need your help. And not with guns, with human minds."

Zeke straightens his stance. "Of course, Myla. Whatever you need."

Cissy winks in Zeke's direction. "Thanks, hun."

He puffs out his chest. "I'll be glad to assist."

I return my focus to Cissy. "What else is on your list?"

"That was everything." After closing her laptop, Cissy resets it into her bag. "Do you want to sleep some more? I know this has been a trying time."

"Nope, I want to get showered, changed, and out of here."

An image returns to my mind: Lincoln screaming and thrashing while being tied down. The look of terror in his eyes sets fresh adrenaline pumping through my veins.

And one of those laboratories is a short cab ride away.

I am going to find him.

hirty minutes later, Cissy, Zeke, and I are riding in a cab. It pulls up to a street corner in Times Square. A chill moves over my skin as I stare out the window.

Wow.

I've never seen anything like Times Square. The place is filled with tall buildings and even bigger TV screens. Nothing looks worn down or crappy, like it always does in Purgatory. And the images on these huge monitors are nothing less than amazing. One shows a guy swimming. On another, a model struts down a runway with a sour look on her face. What's she got to be sad about? She's a model on a runway.

The cabbie twists about to face us. "This is as close as you get," she says. Our driver reminds me of an old hound dog, what with her brown hair, long jowls, and big eyes. "You better get out fast," she adds. "I don't want a ticket."

Cissy pays the cab using this built-in credit card machine thing. I shake my head in awe. This cab is more tricked out than the house I grew up in.

I scooch my way out of the cab and onto the sidewalk.

People stream in every direction. The scent of hotdogs and drain water fills the air. Some of the residents have demons on them, just like the doc back at the hospital. I spot a business guy with a Greed Tic sucking on his cheek. The thing is as big as my palm and G-R-O-double-S. A small pink Vanity Monkey sits on the shoulder of an older woman. Those things look cute, but they have pointed tails that jab into vertebrae, giving their host no end of back pain.

Cissy pulls me against a building. "You're not going to kill all those demons, are you?"

"No way."

She scrunches up her mouth. "Why should I believe you?"

"Those are summoned demons."

"In English please?" Unlike me, Cissy never took a deep interest in the demonic. I'm always explaining things to her. Difference is, this time she actually wants me to go on about this stuff. Mostly, I just talk, and I'm pretty sure she only pretends to listen.

"The humans summon those demons to them by the way they act. Even if I killed the demon, another one would take its place."

Cissy tilts her head. "And you've totally killed these kind of demons before."

"That too." Cissy knows my system. I hoard new demon kills the way she hoards shoes.

Zeke pops his head over Cissy's shoulder. "Are we sharing secrets?"

"As a matter of fact, we are," I answer. "Cissy was just about to share which one of these building houses the lab."

Cissy points at a huge screen. "There."

"Inside the screens?" asks Zeke with a smirk. He's moved to stand behind Cissy with his arms wrapped around her waist. They look cute and happy, which makes my chest hurt a little.

Focus, Myla. You're here for Lincoln.

"Not inside the screens." Cissy chuckles. "Inside one of the office buildings behind them."

I stop being amazed by all the moving pictures enough to really focus on the content of what the screens are showing.

And it's everything Hunter Enterprises.

The guy swims in a pool. Through the churning water, I can make out the H-E Gymnasium logo on the wall behind him. The models are showing off the latest from the Hunter Enterprises fashion division. Another screen shows live images of their blimp hovering over LaGuardia.

"Hunter Enterprises is running everything," I say.

Cissy frowns. "Do you mean they're behind the demons on all the humans?"

"No. Trust me, those type of demons have been clinging on to humans for a long time without any help from Ethan. I meant something else. Look at these screens. Ethan's company has really infiltrated human life. That's not right. Thrax are supposed to keep a low profile."

"I never thought about it that way," says Cissy. "I mean, I've seen reports about Ethan's company, but I figured it was no big deal."

"And another thing." I point to each of the vid screens in turn. "That guy who's swimming underwater? He has ventilator disk in his mouth. It's black metal. And those models? They're all wearing jewelry made from black metal, too."

"What does that mean?" asks Zeke.

"Ethan makes things out of black metal," says Cissy.

Zeke shrugs. "There's nothing wrong with that."

"His inventions are more than metal," I say. "Ethan infuses them with black magic."

Zeke's eyes widen. "You mean, the stuff that runs on soul power?"

"Yes, that's the stuff." It's an effort to get those words out. "He's had hundreds of so-called followers who have disappeared. And the thrax warriors we send never return either. We think he's draining their souls of angelic power." My voice lowers. "At this moment, Ethan's trying to drain Lincoln's soul, too."

The images on the main vid screen change. The blimp disappears, and the words *"Hunter Enterprises Military"* flashes across the massive monitor. Glamour shots of Razor Guards flash across the screens while text scrolls along the bottom: *"At Hunter Enterprises Military, we're creating the next legion of warriors. Smart. Strong. Pure leaders."* After that, the screens show various tanks and planes, all made from the same black metal. *"Our soldiers will be armed with the best technology."*

Next the screen shows a smiling guy getting strapped down to a table by folks in hazmat suits. The dumb dude is grinning from ear to ear.

All the warmth drains from my body. I've seen that table before. It's just like the one Lincoln was being tied to in my last mirror vision.

More text scrolls by: *"But to create the perfect warriors and technology, we sometimes need volunteers."*

My breath catches. *"The perfect warriors and technology."* *Riiiiiiiight.* All this PR crap is just so Ethan can cover his ass is anyone sees what he's doing to the thrax he captures. A pang of worry moves across my chest. *Thrax like my Lincoln.*

Cissy pulls at my elbow. "We need to go, Myla."

I stay glued to the spot as I watch the giant vid screen.

"This is what I've seen in my visions. Lincoln's in one of those labs."

Now Zeke steps in at my opposite elbow. "And if we're going to help him, we have to go."

Finally, I snap out of my stupor. Along with Cissy and Zeke, I move through the crowd to a set of revolving doors. The words *"Hunter Enterprises, Research Division"* are written on the front of the building. My mouth winds into an evil grin.

I can't wait to get inside this research building. In my mind, I picture myself as a secret agent, searching through the lab with maximum stealth until I get what I need or move on. Hey, I might even get my hands on a new sword for the occasion. A katana would be cool—those things are massive. And if this lab doesn't hold the answers I seek, I could trot across the rooftops and break into another building or two. I close my eyes and savor that image.

This is going to work.

Whatever it takes, I'll find my guy and set him free.

a s I step into the lobby of the Hunter Enterprises Research Building, it feels like I'm boarding a spaceship. That, or I'm becoming trapped inside some massive egg pod from the future. Everything here is curvy and made from white plastic. A receptionist sits behind her oblong desk. Other than that, there are no chairs, tables, or even other people hanging around.

Zeke, Cissy, and I step across the lobby floor. Actually, we do more of a squeak-walk, considering the way the plastic flooring sticks to our shoes.

Weird.

The receptionist looks up as we approach. "Thank you for visiting the Research Division of Hunter Enterprises," she says smoothly. "I'm Albinia. How can I help you?"

My brows lift. Albinia is a good name for this chick. She's short and petite with white-blonde hair and blue eyes that are so pale they might pass for white as well. Her porcelain skin perfectly matches her eggshell-colored pantsuit. For some reason, a set of black binoculars hangs from a cord around her neck.

More weirdness.

"We're here for our tour," explains Cissy. We'd planned this scam on the cab ride over. Basically, the three of us would say we'd scheduled a tour of the facilities to fake our way in. And if that doesn't work? We have a plan B.

Albinia sets the binoculars to her face. Up close, I can see all the gears and knobs along the side. She twists a few dials and scans the dark ledger before her. I stand on tiptoe for a better look at the book in question. The ledger appears to be nothing but black sheets of paper. Interesting. Those binoculars are made of the same black metal with tiny runes that I've seen before. More black magic, only this time, the supernatural power makes it possible to see the writing on the ledger.

At length, Albinia lowers her binoculars and addresses us once more. "You don't have an appointment. You need to leave."

"Are you sure?" I ask sweetly. "I bet if you check again, you'll find us."

"I'm not checking again." Albinia closes the ledger with a slam. "We're short staffed today. I have no time for this."

Ouch.

For a young chick, she sure has that anger thing down pat.

While Albinia glares at the three of us, Cissy and I share a pointed look of our own. There's no need for us to discuss next steps. It's obvious what must happen.

Plan B.

Cissy turns to her boyfriend. "Didn't you set up the tour, Zeke?"

"What?" he asks.

I elbow him gently in the ribs. "I bet if you focus really,

really hard on Albinia here, you could help her remember that we have a tour today."

Translation: start working your lust mojo, buddy.

"I get it." Zeke turns to face Albinia. When he next speaks, Zeke's voice is all whiskey-rough and enticing. Well, to other people it would be. "Albinia, yes?"

Zeke doesn't wait for her to reply, he just gestures at the black ledger. "My friend here is right. If you look again, I'm sure you'll see our appointment for today."

But Albinia doesn't say a word. She doesn't move to look at the ledger, either. Instead, her gaze stays locked on Zeke in what can only be called a look of pure adoration. In fact, if this were a cartoon, there'd be little hearts popping up around Albinia's head at this point.

Hoo-Wee. That lust demon mojo sure works fast.

To his credit, Zeke is working his powers like a pro. He's all Mister Handsome McHunky as he leans over the reception desk. He's got a point and he's not dropping it. "Did you say there's no appointment? Again, I bet you could squeeze us in for a little tour, even if we aren't on the books."

A dreamy look takes over Albinia's face. "Maybe I could do...something."

I lean in closer to Zeke and whisper out of one side of my mouth. "Way to work it, supermodel."

Zeke shoots me a quick wink before returning his attention to Albinia. "What's it going to take?" He leans against the white console. Waves of lust demon energy fan out around the room.

Albinia blushes. "Ta-take?"

"For you to give us a tour of this place," offers Cissy.

"You know you want to help us," adds Zeke. Next Zeke does that thing where he clicks twice from one side of his mouth. Normally, it bugs me, but this time? Since Albinia seems enchanted by it, I decide that it's the most wonderful noise ever.

Albinia giggles. "You're sweet, uh…"

"Zeke. Call me Zeke."

"But I really couldn't leave my post."

Zeke's face flushes as he sends out fresh waves of lust demon mojo. "Come on. It's only for a minute."

With that, it's official. I take back all the nasty comments I ever made about Zeke being a lust monkey.

Or at least, I take back half of them.

"I would, but…" Albinia's blush deepens. "There's no one here to watch the desk."

I set my hand on Cissy's shoulder. "My friend here can do it."

Cissy raises her hand. "I'm your girl."

Albinia shakes her head. "You don't know what to do, though."

"Like it's hard." Cissy strolls around the desk, pushes Albinia out of her seat, and parks her own carcass in the same spot. "Good afternoon, I'm Cissy, and I'm really super busy right now. I'll get back to you in a few minutes." Cissy starts opening and closing drawers in the pod-desk. I have to admit, that's a nice touch. "Don't you have a computer or anything? I'd look more convincing if I could use a computer." *Plus, Cissy could probably sneak around their network and do some sleuthing.*

"No, we don't use computers out here. Only the ledgers." Albinia reaches for Cissy. "Maybe you should get out of my chair."

I step in front of Albinia, totally blocking her access to Cissy and seating. "Come on. What are you worried about? My friend is totally convincing."

Albinia frowns. "I still don't know. I could get in big trouble."

Zeke struts up to Abinia's side, wraps her thin arm around his, and pats the back of her hand. "It will only take a few minutes. That will give us some time to get to know each other." A muscle is twitching along his jaw.

I never thought I'd think this in my life, but: *poor Zeke*. The guy throws his lust demon mojo all over the place, but I doubt he's ever used it to control someone's mind before. That's hard work for even a full-blooded lust demon, and Zeke is mostly human with a little demonic DNA. My heart warms to him just a little more.

Albinia's eyes glaze over. "Fine. You're so handsome and strong and smart. I'll follow you anywhere."

Ugh. I might have thrown up in my mouth a little.

Albinia shifts the binoculars on their strap. "We'll just need these to get around," she says in a dreamy voice.

"Whatever you say," coos Zeke.

I push him gently in the center of his back. Okay, maybe it's not too gentle, but we have things to do, and this is taking a while.

"Why don't we get started?" I ask.

"Sure." Albinia sleepwalks toward the wall. As we get closer, she does that thing again where she puts the binoculars up to her face and adjusts some dials. After a second or two, an oval door appears in the smooth wall. I purse my lips. That's a pretty funky trick, right there.

Albinia then presses her palm against the center of the door. It swings wide open. After that, Albinia, Zeke, and I step into another white and somewhat circular hallway. This must be how a red blood cell feels tooling around an artery. I take a few steps down the pristine and curved passage. *Huh.*

For a guy who uses black magic, Ethan sure is obsessed with white.

Once we're in the hall, the oval door closes silently behind us. Albinia releases Zeke's arm and starts to gesture around. "Welcome to the inner workings of our Research Division." Her voice takes on the singsong tone of a memorized speech. "This is where we improve humanity."

"That sounds awesome." I slap on my most innocent face. "Where would those labs be, anyway?"

"I can't take you there," says Albinia. "That's a restricted area."

I snap my fingers. "I've got an idea. How about you just point me in the right direction, and I'll go there. That way, you aren't breaking any rules and you can hang out here with Zeke?"

Her thin blonde brows pull together. "I'm not sure that's a good idea."

Zeke tugs Albinia against his side. "Of course, it's the best idea." He stares deeply into her eyes. "It will give us a chance to be alone." More lust demo mojo wafts down the hallway.

Albinia nods so quickly I'm surprised her head stays attached.

Zeke shoots me a quick glance. Beads of sweat line his forehead. "Take your time, Miss Gee. I can keep Albinia here occupied all day."

Those are the words he says, but in truth, I know what he's really saying.

I won't last much longer.

"On it." I focus on Albinia. "Which way to the labs?"

"End of this hallway. Make a right. You can peep through the observation window without being seen. Just don't go inside the lab, all right?"

"Absolutely." I shoot her a double thumbs-up and take off down the hallway at a run. At this point, I know two things for certain.

First, if there's information to be found in this building, I need to uncover it and fast.

And second, if I can get inside that laboratory, I'm totally doing it.

14

I race to the end of the hallway and pause. Another thing I learned from demon patrol: never go into an unknown area without checking first.

Time to check.

With maximum stealth, I take a careful look around the corner. Crud. A pair of Razor Guards blocks the next passage-way. One of them is wearing a composite bow strapped across his back. Evil Lincoln mentioned that before. A composite bow means that guard can shoot one of Ethan's black arrows and send me to who knows where. Not good.

I step away so I'm back in the main hallway. Leaning against the wall, I press my palms against my eyes and think. There must be some way to get past the guards and keep going to the labs. My thoughts speed through various options.

Hey, guys, Albinia told me I could come check out the labs.

Bad idea. Even if Albinia was *supposed* to show me the labs, chances are, she wouldn't let me go there alone. Maybe I could try a more dramatic entrance.

Run for your lives! Fire!

I consider that choice and toss it aside just as quickly. Totally won't work. There are no actual alarms going off, and I don't know how to start them, either. I ponder going for my classic approach in cases like this.

Eat death!

Much as I love that classic line, I really shouldn't kill anyone who isn't attacking. For all I know, these guards could be good people stuck in bad jobs. Plus, there's another thing that I need to stay wary of here on Earth. Guns. These guards probably have them. Although my body armor could deflect them, I still have never done much battle training with human armaments.

Honestly? I've done no battle training with human armaments. That's another rule of thrax demon patrol. Avoid situations with the unexpected. It will always bite you in the ass.

My words, not theirs.

Most importantly, it's one thing for me to jump into a fight without knowing what to expect. It's another thing to do it while I'm pregnant. Nope, *eat death* is not an option either. I just have to think of something else.

At last, the perfect solution appears.

Closing my eyes, I command the threads of my Scala robes to change into a different form. This time, instead of battle gear, I ask them to become the shape of the white hazmat suits I saw in my last vision of Lincoln. These things have a small slit in the plastic helmet that acts as a visor. That should hide my identity pretty well, even if these guards were shown a picture of me as the Queen or Great Scala.

My heart thuds harder in my chest. This will work. It has to.

Once the change is complete, I stroll around the corner with a sense of purpose. As I've learned from showing up to school late, the worst thing you can do when you're sneaking around is look like you're, well, sneaking around. Over years, I've mastered the art of the determined walk.

Every step I move past the guards seems to happen in slow motion.

One.

Two.

Three.

The Razor Guards look me over, but don't stop me or say a word.

Yes!

At the other end of this corridor, I see another figure in a hazmat suit. Based on the frame, I'm guessing it's a man. Hazmat Guy has a set of those funky binoculars hanging from a black cord around his neck and turns toward the wall.

Double yes!

I saw this routine before when Albinia got us into the labs in the first place. Hazmat Guy is opening a door. With any luck, it's a door that leads to a laboratory.

It takes everything I have not to run full out, but somehow I'm able to control myself. I sidle up behind Hazmat Guy and keep working my casual vibe, like, *hey, I just went to get coffee and don't feel like using my binoculars if you're opening up the lab anyway* kind of thing. Fortunately, Hazmat Guy is so focused on his binoculars, he doesn't really notice me.

I keep trying to work my casual vibe, but the clear visor part of my helmet is starting to fog up from body heat. Lincoln might be inside this very laboratory. Talk about your stressful situations.

For a time, Hazmat Guy fiddles with the dials on his binoculars. I notice that he's facing a stretch of wall right beside a one-way mirror...just like Albinia described before.

It's hard to see past the tinted mirror at this angle, but I do see that the room beyond is white.

This is the lab, definitely.

My tail whips behind me in an anxious rhythm. *Come on, Hazmat Guy! Open the fricking door already.*

The guards at the other end of the hall take notice. "Having trouble, Felton?" They take a few steps closer.

Unholy Hell.

Hazmat Guy—I mean Felton—waves them off. "Dials are stuck," he calls. "Give me a second." At last, Felton turns a few more gears on his binoculars and—BINGO—a door appears. Like the one Albinia revealed, it's an oval doorway set flush into the smooth wall. Once it's visible, the guards stop moving and go back to their post. Whew.

Felton presses his hand against the door, and it slides away, revealing the laboratory beyond.

My heart beats so hard, I feel the pulse in my neck. Could this be where they're holding Lincoln? I know it's crazy to hope that I'd get that lucky, but I can't help it.

Felton steps forward; I follow. The door slides shut behind us with a soft hiss. Once inside, what I see makes me gasp. It's another all-white room with curved walls. That's not what stuns me, though.

In the center of the room is another table covered in a curved glass top. If getting into the lime kiln reminded me of Hansel and Gretel, then this scene is definitely a high-tech version of Snow White. That table could totally pass for a glass coffin. Only instead of seeing through the clear covering to see a sleeping princess inside, I can't make out squat on this thing. The insides are filled with dark smoke.

There are two canisters positioned behind the table, one black and one red. A tangle of plastic tubing snakes out from these metal columns in order to connect to the bottom of the glass covering. On reflex, I step closer. Is someone inside that glass? Every corner of my soul freezes.

Have I found my Angelbound love?

I want to rush over, but Felton steps into my path while yelling his head off. "Who are you? What are you doing here?"

I glare at him. Whoever this guy is, he's the only thing standing between me and what might be Lincoln. My instincts tell me to just skewer the dude through the chest with my tail, but with all that smoke inside the case on that table? Felton might be the only one who can get rid of it without hurting whoever is inside.

If anyone is inside, that is.

Time for me to lie my ass off. This isn't necessarily my strong suit, but for Lincoln, I'll do my best.

I just hope it's good enough.

elton folds his arms over his chest. "I'll ask you one last time, and then I'm calling security. What are you doing here?" Based on the way his voice is warbling, Felton is really freaking out about me.

I set my fist on my hip. "What's your name?" When sneaking around, it's always important to act angry when you get caught.

"Senior Researcher Felton Weiner Junior."

"Really?" *That's one bummer of a name, really.*

"It's a family name." Felton slides his hand down the front of his white hazmat jumper, smoothing out the crinkly plastic. Like Albinia, Felton has a set of black binoculars around his neck and grips a dark ledger. My eyes widen. I wants me both of those things.

Binoculars and ledger, come to Momma.

"You still didn't answer my question," says Felton.

For once, the lie comes to me easily. "I'm an inspector." Back in Purgatory, I had a ton of inspectors in my life. They were always checking out the Ghost Towers where we store souls.

"I wasn't told you people would be here today." I can't see his face, but there's no mistaking the frown in Felton's voice.

I've used this line on inspectors myself, so I already know the perfect comeback.

"Wouldn't be much of an inspection if you knew everything, now would it?" I gesture to the glass coffin. "Empty out the smoke. Let's see what we're dealing with."

"I can't for another minute or so," Felton says slowly.

I gesture to the ledger and binoculars. "Then, tell me how to use those things."

Even through the slit in his helmet, I can see Felton roll his beady eyes. "You should already know how these work."

Another line I've tried myself. This is becoming fun.

"Of course, I know how they work. I'm an inspector. I'm here to see if *you* do."

"Fine. There are nobs and dials on the sides of the binoculars. You twist them and can open doors."

"Albinia the receptionist knows that. How do you use them for research?"

"If I twist the dials the right way, I can see live results from this subject"—he points at the glass coffin— "as well as from other related tests going on around the world."

"So, there's definitely a subject in there." I can't help the hopeful note in my voice.

"Yes. All the data from this case and others gets stored in Chuck."

"Chuck?"

"Computer Harmony Under Cosmic Kinesthetics. CHUCK."

"And where is this master computer named CHUCK?"

Felton's beady eyes squint through the slit in his helmet. "It's on display down at the Touch The Tech event, same as all our top innovations."

Humans think that Ethan is a great dude and Hunter Enterprises is an awesome company. I bet if I could get some of that information out of CHUCK, the mortal world would understand what they're really dealing with. I set my fists on my hips. "And how does one access this CHUCK computer?"

"What?"

"Passwords, Felton. Cough them up."

"As an inspector, you know I can't divulge that under any circumstances."

I roll my eyes. "Duh."

Felton gasps.

Oops. Act grown-up, Myla.

"I mean, obviously you can't divulge such things. I was just testing to see if you'd follow protocol."

There, that sounded mega-mature.

Felton lets out an exasperated sigh. "I have to test the subject now."

"Go on."

"Aren't you going to help?"

I point to my face. "In-spec-tor." *And I have no idea how to help, not that I'm telling Felton that.*

"You must know that we're on a skeleton crew today what with everyone at the Touch The Tech Event. You should really lend a hand."

"No, I should really inspect." I'm using so many lines from my Purgatory inspection team, I'm definitely giving them all a bonus.

"Fine. I suppose you want to see me finish the soul transfer."

"No, I'm more interested in seeing how you let someone go and leave their souls alone."

"We pull out the power in rounds. I'm mid round" — Felton scans his ledger— "seven right now. I can't stop mid-round. The subject could prematurely terminate."

"Oh." Every muscle in my body tenses. "I guess you better finish this round then. But after that, we're leaving this subject alone for today. I need to, uh, inspect him. Alive."

Felton shrugs. "As you request. I'll finish this round. Then you can inspect the subject to your heart's content."

"Good." I'm happy with how calm my voice sounds when I say that because inside? I'm screaming.

Felton lifts the binoculars to his face. Unlike with Albinia, his device starts to move and expand. Tiny metal clamps reach out from the sides and top of the binoculars, securing them to his head. He flips open his leather journal. The pages look all black to me, but I'm guessing that it's a totally different view with the binoculars on.

With his free hand, Felton starts twisting dials on the side of his new headgear. I try to memorize what he touches and how. Once I get those binoculars—and I will get them—I'll need to know how to use them.

Across the room, the mist leaves the glass coffin. Inside lies a man. Every nerve ending in my body goes berserk. The guy is lying on his side toward the opposite wall, so I can't see his face. But the outline of his body is too familiar: broad shoulders, messy brown hair, and strong limbs. Plus, the guy is wearing the black body armor that's used by the House of Rixa.

Please, let this be Lincoln.

I start to rush over, but Felton grabs my elbow. "What are you doing?"

"Inspecting the subject." The words come out as more of a question, though.

"You want to kill him? I'm in the middle of the transfer round. Your soul energy could throw off all my calibrations."

"Right. That's what I was testing you for." I step backward, but each movement feels like moving through cold water. "Well done. Finish out the round."

"Thank you." I can almost hear the gears of Felton's mind working underneath his plastic helmet and binocular head-gear. I screwed up by starting to walk over. Felton turns to stare at me, which is super-weird with those binoculars on. "What division do you work for anyway?"

I fold my arms over my chest. "Asking questions only makes my inspection last longer."

Felton focuses on his ledger once again. I resist the urge to cheer. He twists a few more dials on the binoculars that are stuck to his face. "Round seven finalizing." He starts typing onto the black ledger's page with his free hand. "Looking for soul energy transfer in three...two...one."

The black tubes sprouting from the curved glass all stiffen as the dark canister machine makes odd whirring noises. A sinking feeling tumbles through my belly. I don't like this. At all.

A second later, arcs of electricity jet out of the black tubes and into the prone form. I can't see what's happening, but a sickly sweet smell fills the air. The man moans something.

"What are you doing?" I ask. A note of hysteria is creeping into my voice, and I can't stop it.

"Trying to take his soul energy. This is a soul transfer, after all. But the subject is fighting it. That's why everything's becoming painful for him." He taps his ledger again. "Second attempt to finish round seven transfer starts now."

More electricity arcs through the patient. His body convulses as he mumbles another word. The foul-sweet scent grows stronger. My hands ball into fists. It takes everything in me not to freak out, break the glass, and free whoever is inside. Every corner of my soul wants to free this subject now, but I know it would kill the poor person who's in there. I can't take that risk.

After all, it could be Lincoln.

"How much longer are you going to do that?" I ask.

"As long as it takes," explains Felton calmly. "It always slows things down when they fight. Last round lasted two days."

The electric jolt stops, and I round on Felton. "Do not run the test again."

"Why? The subject isn't dead yet."

Fear and rage churn through me. "Isn't dead yet? I thought I couldn't approach the subject, or he'd prematurely terminate."

"Right, I said prematurely terminate. That's the whole point of this. We need soul energy from this subject, and we take it until he's dead. This subject has lasted seven rounds, which is fairly typical. He won't make it another round, though. Still, this one will take a while because he's fighting too hard. Either way, the man is dead. But he'll definitely die early if you throw off my calibrations."

"But he'll die without pain."

Felton tilts his head, which makes his Hazmat suit crinkle. "I don't gather data on pain."

In other words, yes, if I release the subject now, he'll die without pain versus in agony. No question what happens next, then.

"I want him out of that case, now."

"What?" Felton's voice quivers with disbelief. "I have a power quota to hit. This is the only living subject left in the entire lab building."

"That's all this guy is to you? A power source?"

"Of course. How do you think the world is now running? Soul power is the secret that makes all our machines go. We only drain criminals, though."

"Criminals." *I can't believe this guy.*

"That's only a stop gap. Soon, we'll have a fresh set of power sources. We need that soul energy."

I can't believe this guy, part deux. "Need?"

"For that."

Felton gestures toward a large window that's set into the right-hand wall. Beyond the plane of glass, I see a room filled with seven-foot-tall glass canisters. Each clear tube is filled with black mist, which swirls around the outline of a man.

"Cloning tanks." I glare at Felton. "You're cloning people?"

"We're cloning Razor Guards." Felton sighs. "We use thrax to power the process. Young adults work best. We tried some children, but the optimum time for draining is somewhere between the ages of eighteen and twenty-two."

I nod, not trusting my voice. *Lincoln is twenty years old.*

Felton shrugs. "Honestly, children really aren't worth my time to drain."

My hands clench into fists. How can he talk so casually about pulling the souls out of kids? Enough is enough. I round on Felton. "Turn off whatever you are doing. I need to approach the subject."

"The subject is almost dead." Felton is whining now. "We might as well finish out this round. Like I said, I don't have any other subjects here in the facility today...and the Touch

The Tech event is sucking up an unbelievable amount of power."

"Open it!"

"Whatever you say." Felton adjusts some dials on his binoculars. The glass coffin splits in two lengthwise, with both curved sides sliding into the table. I race over to the dying man. "Lincoln?" I rush to stand on the opposite side of the table and for the first time, I get a good look at his face.

It takes everything in me not to sob out loud.

This isn't Lincoln.

It's *Williamson*. No wonder Cissy didn't get any report of him when I escaped Antrum. Ethan and Evil Lincoln must have arrested Williamson and sent him up here. My heart cracks. That's why he looked so much like Lincoln from the back. He's from the same house.

Williamson opens his eyes a crack. "Queen Myla." His voice is a hoarse whisper that makes my eyes sting.

"They took you after you helped me and Cissy, didn't they?"

"Ethan and the false King did, yes."

"I'm so sorry." I glance over to Felton, who's busy typing data into his ledger. "And your family?"

"They're safe. Queen Octavia insisted they be spared, as they knew nothing of my so-called treachery. She also said they'd be cared for as if I'd died in battle defending the palace. It was most gracious of her." He wheezes out a breath. Blood begins to pool in his mouth. "She thought I'd helped you kill yourself."

"No, you saved me." Everything in me wants to scream with rage and dismay. This is all so wrong. I brush the backs of my fingers gently against his cheek. "You're a hero, Williamson."

"Hero." He forces out a ragged breath. "They have the King."

"Do you know where?"

"No." Williamson raises his fist. "I stopped a guard back in the Black Forest. He had a bow and arrow." He moves the fist closer to me. "This may help our King." His eyes roll into his head as he exhales a rattling breath. For a moment, the world seems to still.

I've seen enough battles to know when someone's dead.

Still, I check his throat. No pulse. My eyes bead with tears. This warrior gave his life for me and mine. He deserved a warrior's death at the least, not cooped up in some glass coffin.

Williamson's body falls slack. His hand opens, revealing the fact that he was clasping a small black arrowhead. This is the same weapon that was used to drag my Lincoln away from me. Evil Lincoln had warned me that Ethan's Razor Guards had bows and arrows. Before he died, Williamson said he took an arrowhead from a Razor Guard.

Leaning in, I take a closer look at the arrowhead in question. The projectile is made from the same black metal as all of Ethan's creations, only this one looks like it got crushed a bit in Williamson's hand. I turn it over and ponder.

Why did Williamson think this would help Lincoln? I shake my head. The man was dying. Who knows what he was thinking? And in the end, it doesn't matter. Williamson was a faithful guard, and he didn't deserve to end like this. I set the arrowhead under my Scala robes and by my collarbone. Since I don't have pockets, it's the safest place to keep it for now. The arrowhead seemed so important to him. It feels wrong to toss it away.

I pat the arrowhead in its resting place beneath my robes.

My throat constricts with worry. How many more will die like Williamson, if I don't succeed? Yes, I've worried about Lincoln, but the risk goes much further.

The reality of being a ruler begins to weigh so heavily on my back, it's as if my bones could snap. It was one thing to fight evil souls in the arena, or to down an attacking demon while on patrol. But this is something else entirely. I essentially sent a man to his death. His poor wife and children.

My hand slides to my stomach as I think about the life inside me. Williamson may be gone, but I can ensure that my baby grows up with his father…and that the thrax have their leader back.

I rise, turn toward Felton, and force my voice into some semblance of calm. "He's dead."

Felton sniffs. "And I missed the last set of data *and* power. Don't think I won't put that in my report."

"Right." I keep glaring at Felton. Based on the heat behind my eyes, I know my irises are gleaming demon red at this point. Rage courses unchecked through my bloodstream. I march over to the senior researcher with one thought on my mind. Well, three actually.

First, take Felton down.

Second, get those binoculars and that ledger.

Third, find and free my Lincoln.

And not just for me and my baby, but for Williamson and all the thrax.

16

*I*n the last twenty seconds, the laboratory room seems to have gotten much hotter. It's probably just my temper at seeing how callous Felton was about Williamson's death. Part of me would love to just conk old Felton on the head and grab his stuff, but he isn't attacking me. Plus, I'm still trying to avoid physical confrontation, so I try to use my words this time.

"I have another question for you," I say. I hadn't noticed before, but there are loudspeakers in each corner of the room. They crackle to life with a low hum. For a moment, I wonder if someone's going to make an announcement, but when nothing happens, I turn back to the task at hand. I tap Felton on the shoulder. "Question. You. Now."

Felton doesn't look up from his black ledger. "Shoot."

"The black smoke... What does it do?"

Felton keeps typing away without so much as a glance in my direction. "Is this another quiz of my knowledge?"

"That's right."

"Our black smoke sedates the subject."

My tail flicks behind me in a predatory rhythm, not that the very human Felton can see that. "Anything else?"

"Nope."

"You're sure about that?"

"Positive."

"Good." Twisting about, I turn to face the long coil of tubing that snakes from the black canister into the examination table. With a single swipe of my tail, I slice through one of the tubes. Black smoke pours out from the severed end.

At last, Felton looks up. "What are you doing?" Felton can't see my tail, but he sure can see the newly-sliced tubing.

"This."

My tail jabs into Felton's white hazmat suit, creating an opening that's large enough for—*you guessed it*—the freshly cut tube-o-black smoke. I jam the open end into Felton's suit. A dark haze quickly appears behind the clear plastic visor of Felton's helmet. The dude coughs a few times before falling over onto the floor, unconscious.

Couldn't happen to a nicer senior researcher.

I scoop up Felton's ledger from the floor and remove the binoculars from around his neck. All the while, I make sure that the smoke tube is still safely jammed inside his hazmat suit because, well, that's the least this guy has coming to him.

At this point, I'm feeling pretty good about my bad self when the loudspeaker roars to life.

"Miss G. Scala to reception. Miss G. Scala to—" The loudspeaker goes silent. Still, I heard enough to know one thing.

That was Cissy's voice. And the way her tone was shaking? She's in big trouble.

Crap. In all my interactions with Felton and Williamson, I forgot all about Cissy, Zeke, and Albinia. I rush out the door and head toward the lobby at a run.

I've no sooner set foot in the outer hallway than the building goes berserk. Lights flash. Sirens sound. Razor Guards and researchers run in all directions. The soothing all-white passageways become the equivalent of a mosh pit at a Bullet For My Valentine show.

Here's one situation where having a tail comes in handy. It's a double bonus that no humans can see it. As a march along, my dragonscale tail juts out left and right, shoving anyone and everyone out of my path. Out of the corner of my eye, I see a flash of light. It's such a shock I almost trip over my own feet.

Was that? Could it be?

No way.

I didn't actually see the little glowing dude again. Not possible.

Shaking my head, I refocus on sprinting back to the lobby. It isn't a long journey; all Albinia did was walk me down to the end of a hall and say, *"Turn right."* Within seconds, I'm stepping back into the lobby.

The place is packed with Razor Guards. Cissy and Zeke stand against one wall. All the guards are arrayed around them in concentric circles, like some crazy version of planetary rings around a pair of moons. Only in this case, the rings have guns. And they're all pointed at Cissy and Zeke.

A knot of worry forms in my throat. These are my friends. They came here to help me, not be target practice for Ethan's goons.

Once again, Albinia stands behind her pod-like reception desk. She wags her pale finger at Zeke. "He took over my mind!"

I scan the scene, smooth out the front crinkles in my hazmat suit, and saunter up to the guards. Hey, the inspection thing worked before. It's just got to work again. "Who's in charge here?"

All the guards head over in unison to stare at me. It's a really creepy effect. One of the Razor Guards closest to me steps forward. "I'm Ethan Unit 437-Q. I'm the lead warrior in this building."

"You did a wonderful job, Mister Q." I set my fists on my hips and nod in what I hope is an authoritarian way. "This was an excellent test of your abilities in a crisis." I raise my hand. "Especially impressive considering how we're short-staffed today. Well done."

Mister Q doesn't say anything. I hope that's because he's appreciating the new name I gave him (Mister Q is a much better name than Ethan Unit 437-Q, after all). Doubtful, but a girl can hope.

I saunter over to my friends and shake their hands in turn. "Agent Frederickson, Agent Ryder. So well done. Any suggestions for our guard team?"

Cissy lifts her chin. "I'll put my suggestions in the report."

"As will I," adds Zeke.

I turn back toward Mister Q and cup my hand by my mouth. "What part of 'these are Hunter Enterprises employees' do you not understand? Order your men to lower their firearms." Under my breath, I mutter to Zeke. "That's what they call guns, right?"

Zeke nods. "You're doing great."

Mister Q slowly lowers his own gun. The rest of the Razor Guards follow. My body feels light as a feather. This is really working.

I address the guards with my best Queenly voice. "Really well done, men." I raise the ledger in my right hand. "I'll be sure to make a note of your performance for CHUCK. But now, we must take our leave."

Cissy, Zeke, and I start walking toward the revolving front door. Trouble is, none of the guards are getting out of our way. I refocus on Mister Q again. "Do you mind? We'd like to leave some time this century. The three of us have a very important meeting with the Supreme Leader."

Mister Q rubs his chin. Or rather, he scratches at the black bandages there. "What's your name?"

"Mine?"

"Yes."

"Senior Researcher Felton Weiner. I was recruited for this special assignment." I adjust the binoculars at my neck. "Can't wait to see these two off, so I can return to killing people."

"You," says Mister Q. "You're Felton Weiner?"

"Don't be judgy. It's a family name."

"I suppose that's fine," says Mister Q slowly. "Carry on."

At those words, it's as if someone loosened a vise on my body. I can breathe again, move again. And there's only one place I'm going: out the damned front door.

Cissy, Zeke, and I step through the knot of Razor Guards. They don't make a path for us, but at least they aren't actively moving to block us anymore. Hey, I'll take it.

We're in the middle of the pack of guards when the back door to the lobby is thrown open. The real Felton Weiner bursts into the room. He's got his helmet off, and yeah, the guy looks like a Felton Weiner: he's tall and thin like a hotdog with a neck-head combo that doesn't really have a distinct separation point. And he's mostly bald with a few stray clumps of hair combed over his head.

The second he enters the lobby, Felton starts screaming his head off. "Stop her! She tried to kill me."

There's a moment where Cissy, Zeke, and I share questioning looks. We're all thinking the same thing: do we keep playing the charade, or do we run for it?

I turn toward the revolving door. "Run!"

If I thought the hallways were a mob scene, then the lobby becomes even worse. We get a few yards closer to our exit before the guards close in. Now, I didn't want to get into hand-to-hand combat, but this moment leaves me no choice. My tail wraps around the neck of one Razor Guard and slams that dude's cranium into the ground. He slumps to the floor, unconscious.

One down, about fifty to go.

This is not going to end well.

From the corner of my eye, I see that glowing form again. And then things get even stranger. Childlike laughter echoes through the lobby. For a second, I see a small humanoid form. Fire drips from its hands.

"Bigga boom," it says.

After that, the lobby explodes in a ball of red flame. The fire touches everyone except Cissy, Zeke, and me. The three of us haul ass out the lobby door and into Times Square.

Another explosion sounds. All the windows in the Hunter Enterprises building shatter, sending shards of glass out onto the street. The huge monitor attached to the structure itself sparks with flame and electricity as it loses its tether to the building's façade and crashes onto a sidewalk. Humans scream as they leap out of harm's way.

A cab pulls up to the curb. The passenger side window rolls down halfway. A voice sounds through the window. "What's going on?"

I shake my head in disbelief. We've been here all morning,

and not a single New Yorker has said a word to us, outside of Felton and Albinia. Now there's a fire, and everyone is chatty.

"You're taking us to our hotel, that's what's going on." I quickly usher Cissy and Zeke into the waiting cab. "We're staying at the— Where are we staying, Cis?"

"The Industrial Arms. Soho."

I slide into the back seat beside Cissy and Zeke. "Oh, and there's an extra five hundred if you most fast." I have no idea if that's a lot of Earth money, but it sounds good.

The driver peels away from the curb at almost supersonic speed, so I'm guessing $500 is pretty good, after all. Sirens sound behind us as we drive away.

"Did you guys see anything strange in the lobby?"

Cissy rounds on me. "You mean other than the Razor Guards, researcher and random explosion."

"Yeah." It's on the tip of my tongue to ask if they saw a little glowing man, but I hold off. Chances are, I'm having stress-induced visions or something.

"Nope," says Cis. "I didn't see anything else."

"Same here," adds Zeke. "Did you?"

"I'm going to catch my breath now." It's not an answer, and Cissy gives me the side eye. But with the cab veering through traffic and sirens still going off, it seems like she's willing to drop the subject. Which is fine with me. I don't need to share my wild imagination with her.

I slump back into the seat, clutching the ledger and binoculars to my chest. These are what's real and important.

They're my keys to finding Lincoln.

Once we get back to the hotel, I know we'll do just that.

17

*E*ight hours later, we're all still hanging out in the Industrial Arms hotel, only we're no closer to finding Lincoln. I'm trying to be patient, emphasis on the word *trying*.

I shift my position on the mega-uncomfortable couch of my fancypants hotel suite. It's like someone painted a bunch of cinderblocks, jammed them together into a couch-shape, and then decided to charge people two grand a night to sit on its chilly magnificence.

Come to think of it, I wouldn't be too surprised if that's the real plan here. After all, I *am* staying in the penthouse of a swank boutique hotel. For all I know, cinderblock couches are the latest thing.

Zeke sits at a massive table on the other side of my equally massive suite. At least, I *think* the thing is a table. To me, it just looks like a big blob of Plexiglas stuffed with rusted screws. Cissy calls it post-industrial chic.

Whatever.

She can call it anything she wants, so long as we figure out how to use those magic binoculars and the ledger soon. The three of us escaped from Ethan's research building more than eight hours ago. Once we showered the smoke away, we changed into new jeans and T-shirt combos thanks to Cissy's superior shopping skills. Ever since then, the three of us have been holed up in this hotel room, trying to get the binoculars and ledger to work.

Needless to say, that's been a big bust. I had the first go, and that's three hours of my life that I'll never get back. For the last ninety minutes, it's been Zeke's turn while Cissy sits by him for moral support. Mostly, every time he loses his cool, she pats his hand and says, "Try again." It's really cute.

I fiddle with the TV remote for the umpteenth time. It's my job to watch for any reports about Hunter Enterprises and their big Touch The Tech Event at the airport. It's all over the news, so tracking the latest info should keep me busy.

And it is.

Sort of.

I try to focus on the screen, but I keep sneaking looks at my friends. Are they making any progress? I'm trying not to hover and glare, but it isn't easy.

Plus, there isn't a whole lot else to check out in this hotel suite. Everything is black leather and rusted machine parts encased in Plexiglas. It may be industrial chic, but I keep worrying that I'll need a tetanus shot if I get too close to anything. Even so, what *really* has me concerned is how the suite is covered in old mirrors. I check them constantly, but I haven't seen Lincoln at all yet. Craning to look over my shoulder, I peep at the big mirror behind the couch.

Nope. Still no sign of him.

Again.

My stomach churns with nausea. It's been hours since I

last saw Lincoln reflected in the mirrors in Arx Hall. All the waiting and worrying is making me seriously queasy.

Although that could be the pregnancy, too.

Or the fact that I just escaped a burning building.

Right after I watched one of my guards die.

And let's not forget—all that happened after recently witnessing my husband getting hoovered out through a magic mirror.

Leaning back on my brick couch, I let out an exasperated sigh. The last twenty-four hours have really been a shit show. Tossing the remote aside, I give up on watching more television and turn to Cissy.

"Anything new?" I ask.

"Not yet." Cissy leans back in her chair. The thing looks like a rusted bucket with legs, but what do I know?

Zeke stays hunched over the table, twiddling with some dials on his binocular headgear. "How about you?" he asks. "Any luck scanning the news?"

I gesture toward the flickering screen. "They're still talking about Ethan's blimp—excuse me, dirigible—at LaGuardia. The entire airport is shut down so they can fill the runways with different tech from Hunter Enterprises."

"Sounds like a war zone," says Cis.

"Nope," I counter. "It's actually a big family thing with a kids' costume competition, face painting, balloon animals, all sorts of crap like that."

On the TV screen, there appears some video with kids dressed up as superheroes, princesses, and animals. To my eye, it looks everyone of them is a trio of two smiling parents with their small, beaming child. Everyone's waiting in line for the costume contest. I rub my hand over my belly and think of child inside me. Will I ever have that with Lincoln and Maxon—costume contests and smiles?

"What's up, Myla?" asks Cissy.

"Nothing, just looking at this costume contest. It's part of Ethan's Touch The Tech Event."

Cissy isn't buying that answer for a second. Not that I blame her. I really didn't put any energy into making it a good lie. She leaves the table with Zeke and sits beside me on the cinderblock couch. "You seem so sad, girlfriend. Have you seen...anything else?"

That's what she says, but I know what my bestie is *really* asking: have I seen anything in all the mirrors on the walls?

"No, Cis," I reply. "No sign of Lincoln yet."

Cissy tilts her head and gives me one of her sympathy looks. It involves her already-big eyes getting bigger as her lower lip puffs out. That look always undoes me. All day long, I've been trying to be brave, but now? I can't stop sniffling.

Cissy pats my hand. "Don't worry, Myla. We'll find him."

"Every minute that passes, that becomes less and less likely." Frustration boils inside me. My tail stabs into the couch and takes off a chunk of concrete. Cissy is smart enough not to make a comment.

On the television, the music from a commercial break fades. Another reporter appears on screen: an older, serious-looking dude who's standing in Times Square. Smoke and emergency vehicles are clear in the background.

"Authorities are still unclear how the explosion was initiated," says the newscaster. "Some are speculating that this is another example of demons in our midst."

I stare at the screen, my mouth falling open. That newscaster said demons in our midst with a totally straight face. Hiding this side of reality is why the thrax exist in the first place. If humans know about angels and demons, then their free choice goes out the window. I turn up the volume.

"We do have word from Hunter Enterprises," continues the newscaster. "If demons do infiltrate their facilities, then H-E has enough Razor Guards to protect us all. We can sleep well tonight." The newscaster smiles.

Unbelievable. The faith these humans have in Ethan is terrifying.

I stifle a groan. If we get through this, the magical clean-up is going to be nasty. Thrax will have to magically wipe millions of human minds in order to erase these memories of demons. It's do-able, but a pain in the butt. And now that I rule the thrax? That pain would land soundly on my shoulders.

And Lincoln's too. Because I will get him back.

Cissy stares at the screen. She's not as hip to thrax culture as I am, so the whole "seeing demons" thing doesn't set off her internal alarms. "The fire we started in Times Square office building," says Cissy. "Is that still smoldering?"

I lift the remote and mute the screen. "Yes, but some fires burn for a long time. It doesn't mean that anything supernatural went down from anyone." *Like the little glowing dude.*

"What?" Cissy's staring at me like I sprouted a second head.

Oops.

Nice job, Myla. Like that didn't sound totally suspicious.

Cissy leans across the couch and grabs the remote, which is a total danger sign. "So." She taps the device against her palm. "You were acting mighty strange when we first got into the cab after leaving Times Square."

"I was?"

"Yuh-huh. How about you tell me how we escaped from

those Razor Guards in the Hunter Enterprises lab building?" She tilts her head and stares at me without blinking. I know that stare. It means there's no way I'm getting out of this.

Which is a major bummer. We escaped Times Square without Cissy asking too many questions. After the whole thing with the lime kiln, I'm just not ready for another major interrogation. Plus, I really have no idea who—or what—the little creature was anyway.

Plus, maybe the newscaster was right. It could have been some kind of bizarre malfunction, and I just imagined a little dude running around and saying, "Bigga boom."

Cissy smacks her lips. "Talk to me, Myla."

I shrug. "Nothing to say."

In the back of my mind, some part of me shouts that when I'm stressed, my default position is to hide information. After all, that's how I survived more than a decade being both an Arena fighter and my mother's daughter at the same time. Sometimes these habits get extended to other people as well.

"Bull," says Cissy.

"We went over this," I say. "I monkeyed with one of the machines to knock that guy Felton out. It must have caused a chain reaction."

"And I told you." Cissy gestures toward my feet. "Your tail keeps skulking behind your ankle when you say that, which means you're lying. I didn't push it before because it seemed like we'd find out something from the ledger at any second, but..." She looks over her shoulder at Zeke. "It appears that we have time for a chat." She points at my tail. "And it's still skulking."

For the record, my tail has a special relationship with Cissy. Nothing like the near-adoration it holds for Lincoln;

it's more of a sibling-style relationship. And yes, it does act all guilty when I'm lying to her.

Which I am right now.

"Out with it," says Cissy. "What happened, really?"

I kick my heels onto the plastic rust blob that is the coffee table and give Cissy my pinky. "Pinky swear you won't freak out?"

Leaning forward, Cissy loops her pinky with my own. "Pinky swear."

"Okay. You know how I had weird dreams after I transported to Earth?"

"You mean when you exploded?"

Zeke looks up from the ledger. "Did you say explosions? Are we going to get grenades?"

I roll my eyes. "No, Zeke, we aren't getting grenades."

"Keep going," says Cissy. "You were just saying that something else strange happened after it appeared that you crawled into a fiery oven and blew yourself up like a bad soufflé."

"Soufflé?"

"You know what I mean." A muscle twitches my Cissy's eye. This is yet another warning signal. My bestie is not handling this story well.

"Cissy," I say in a warning tone. "You pinky swore not to freak out."

"Fine. Look at me. Totally cool." She slaps on a smile, but I can't help but notice that her tail is wagging in a weird lurching motion.

"Are you forcing your tail to wag so it looks like you're not freaking out when actually, you're about to lose it?"

"Ummm." Cissy bites her lips together. She's totally doing a forced wag with her tail. That shiz hurts.

"Forget it." I fold my arms across my chest. "I can*not*

handle you losing your cool." For Cissy, this process involves demon eyes and the silent treatment. I have enough on my plate right now.

"Hey," counters Cissy. "I'm a badass Senator these days. That means I can be a little concerned and yet, still not lose my mind." She tilts her head and gives me those puppy eyes again. "Honestly. How are we going to save Lincoln if we don't share important information with each other?"

"Especially about that explosion stuff," adds Zeke.

"Quiet, Zeke!" Cissy and I call in unison.

A long moment passes where Cissy and I say nothing. Well, we do say a lot, but not with words. I slump into my uncomfortable couch, feeling guilty for not sharing with Cissy. For her part, my bestie keeps right on staring at me with huge puppy-dog eyes. That only makes me feel guiltier.

Finally, I crack.

"You made a great point. We need to share info."

Cissy raises her pinky. "And I pinky swore."

I take in a deep breath. If I can't trust Cissy, who can I trust?

A little voice in the back of my head says, *Lincoln*, but that little voice is also really upset about what we saw in the labs. I mean, who traps people in glass cases so he can zap out their souls?

Focus, Myla. Thinking about Lincoln is not going to help.

I blink hard, forcing myself back into the present moment. "Okay, Cis. Here's the deal. After I got into the line kiln—which was totally *not* hot at all inside—I found that it had transformed into a small crawlspace with a round floor."

"A Pulpitum Chamber," says Cissy.

"Exactly." I squirm on the couch, and it's not just because the concrete is putting my butt to sleep. "After that, the

Pulpitum platform does its thing and starts transporting me to Earth. I'm lurching all over as I hurtle upward." I stare at Cissy as if this is a crucial piece of information and not just me stalling.

"Got it. Hurtling. Keep going." For the record, Cissy can always see through my stalling techniques.

"Then, I found you and passed out. I had a dream where I saw someone."

"Who?" asks Cissy. Her face looks totally open and eager for whatever I have to share. For his part, Zeke stops fiddling with the ledger and looks over intently too. No doubt, he's hoping that Rambo showed up in my dreams with a ton of ammo.

I swing my arm over the back of the rock couch, all suave-like. "I saw a little guy."

"A guy." Cissy twirls one lock of blonde hair around her finger. "That's all?"

"He was little."

"I got that part. But I know you. You wouldn't have held back on me if there wasn't something *really* off about this so-called little guy."

She's totally on to me here. Best to fess up.

"Fine. He was glowing like a lightbulb and had fire dripping off his palms. Whatever. No big deal. It was probably just pregnancy hormones." I make grabby hands at her. "Can I have the remote back?"

Please don't make a big deal about this. Please don't make a big deal about this. Please don't make a big deal about this.

Cissy gasps.

Ugh. She's totally going to make a big deal about this.

"A glowing little man? Dripping fire? Are you sure you're okay? Nothing wrong with your brain?"

"It was probably just hormones, that's all."

"And what does this glowing little man have to do with the laboratory?"

"I might have seen him again at the Hunter Labs. Maybe he was running around and laughing or something."

"Or something." Cissy narrows her eyes.

"Fine. After the Razor Guards had us cornered, I saw him out of the corner of my eye. He ran by, laughed, and said, 'Bigga boom.' After that, everything exploded."

"Whoa." Cissy slumps back against the brick couch. "Your life is so weird."

"I know, right?" I raise my hands, palms forward. "For the record, I was really hoping this was pregnancy hormones. It really is too bizarre otherwise."

"*Bigga boom.*" Zeke pipes up from the table. "Told you there were munitions involved."

"Quiet, Zeke!" Cissy and I say again.

My bestie hops to her feet and starts pacing around the room. I don't like this. At all. "You said you wouldn't freak."

"I'm not. I'm processing unusual information." She takes in three deep breaths and reseats herself on the couch. "Okay, I'm fine now." She pauses. "No, I lied. What is a little glowing man doing following you around?"

"I don't know. If it wasn't hormones, then it was probably a dream."

And again, from the corner of my eye, I see a little glowing figure in the kitchenette. My mystery lightbulb buddy has returned. And considering how Cissy is having trouble processing his ability to blow stuff up, I'm not ready to introduce the pair of them yet. Especially since I just had the mother of all realizations.

That little dude could be my igni.

Dad always said igni had a fractured existence outside the after-realms. Maybe on Earth it's a different story. If that's the case, then this is a meeting I want to have solo. I need to understand what I'm up against before I bring in Cissy and Zeke.

Time to encourage my friends to take a break.

Shifting my weight from foot to foot, I make a great show of yawning. "Wow, am I ever beat. Maybe it's time for you two to leave for a while."

Cissy wags her finger at me. "What's really going on?"

A clicking noise sounds in the kitchen. "What was that?" asks Zeke.

It wasn't a little glowing guy playing with my fridge. Nope.

I exhale another totally innocent sigh. "I just need a little break, guys. Why don't you both go hang in *your* suite for a while?"

Zeke fiddles with the binocular knobs some more. "In a minute. I'm making progress here."

Sadly, he's been saying that for more than an hour. I'm not holding my breath.

I snap my fingers. "I've got an idea. Maybe you two could look for costumes for us? We're going to need to hit the LaGuardia Touch the Tech Event. Ethan might be there with some of his thrax followers. We can't show up with our tails hanging out."

"The costume contest is for kids, Myla." While she speaks, Cissy's tail keeps up the corkscrew motion. That means she knows I'm lying again.

This is going to be harder than I thought.

Tapping my chin, I consider my options. There's still one way to get around Cissy. I just need to bring on the kryptonite to Cissy's super-anti-Myla-powers.

And that would be Zeke.

Here's the deal. When it comes to females, Zeke is mister smarmy and charming…except if the female in question is bawling her eyes out. In those situations, Zeke takes off so fast, you can almost see cartoon-style dust clouds behind him.

It's time to turn on the waterworks.

I rest the back of my hand against my forehead. "Oh, I'm just so worried about Lincoln. It's terrible!" I follow this up with a long "waaah" noise that is totally believable. "Also, I'm pretty sure I might puke soon."

Zeke whips the binoculars off and looks directly as Cissy. "Babe, maybe we should give Myla some space."

I force a dry heave. "Oh, that was close. I really think you both should go." I follow this up with a *sorry, girlfriend* look to Cissy.

Her tail has not stopped moving. "I can see right through you, Myla."

Zeke sets the binoculars on the tabletop. "Myla needs a break, kitten."

I let out another wail; Zeke visibly cringes. This is working out great.

"We should leave now," says Zeke. He pulls Cissy toward the door. She doesn't move.

I throw up my arms. "I'm just so upset here. I'm going to cry so hard, snot strings will come out of my nose. How about a little privacy, eh?"

"Forget it," snaps Cissy. "Something weird is going on here. Don't think I don't notice it."

Another little clink sounds in the kitchen.

Damn.

Thankfully, Zeke slides up to Cissy's side and gingerly wraps his arm about her shoulders. He even starts rubbing the sensitive part at the base of her neck. "Now, babe. We've all had a long day. Why don't we take a break for only twenty minutes or so? You and I go for a walk. I bet when we get back, everyone will feel better." He starts to guide Cissy toward the door and—YES—she allows him to guide her away. Sure, she glares at me over her shoulder the entire time, but the departure is imminent.

"Thanks so much, Zeke." I give him a wobbly smile and I mean it.

"No prob, Myla. How much trouble can you cause in twenty minutes anyway?"

Cissy shakes her head. She knows exactly how much trouble I can get into in two minutes, let alone twenty. Still, she's almost at the door. The girl waited since grade school for Zeke to notice her. All he has to do is crack out his "shoulder rub" routine, and she's Jell-O.

At last, Cissy and Zeke exit the penthouse. Pressing my ear to the main door, I wait for the telltale sounds of their footsteps receding down the hall, followed by the ding of the elevator opening and closing.

That's it.

They're gone.

Finally.

I tiptoe into the kitchenette. "Hello? Is someone here?"

I check all the cabinets. I know I heard something.

Scratching my cheek, I head back to the living room, where I witness something I'd never imagined possible. Before me, there stands a small creature that looks like your classic bumper sticker of a bug-eyed alien.

Waist-high humanoid? *Check.*

Big head and massive eyes? *Check again.*

A body with a round belly, long arms, stubby legs, and spindly fingers. *Oh, yeah.*

It's the classic "visitor from outer space" package. Except, while most aliens are green or gray, my new little friend glows like a humanoid lightbulb on the low setting.

"Greetings, Great Scala," it says in a childlike voice.

My mind blanks. "Uh…hi."

With every passing second, my heart sinks deeper and deeper until I'm sure it's tumbled through all seventeen floors of this snazzy boutique hotel. "Are you my…" I have to force out the word. "Igni?"

"Yes, Great Scala."

"Wow." What I see before me shouldn't be possible, but nevertheless it's happened: my igni have somehow smooshed themselves into the form of a lightbulb-alien-man-child.

Coooooooool.

Something tells me that if I want to get Lincoln back, then this little friend will come in mighty handy. At last, things are looking up.

18

*F*or a long moment, the little alien-looking dude and I stare at each other. He's got an oval face, big bulbous eyes, no nose, and a tiny mouth. Right now, those big eyes are staring at me. I can't get over it.

This is my igni in humanoid form.

Whoa.

Words start tumbling from my mouth, seemingly on their own. "So, what do I call you, exactly?"

"We are Ignationarona-leebahnawannah-polywolly-wangalla."

I open my mouth, ready to try that name, and then snap my yap shut. We'll never get around to finding Lincoln if I try saying *that* name all day long. I force a smile. "How about I call you Iggy?"

"Yes." The little guy glows more brightly. "We like Iggy."

I gesture across the little dude. "So, guys." I know I have other things to ask my igni about, but they have a humanoid form here. And they're not talking gibberish. It's really hard to get past that. I mean, one of the whole basic facts about being the Great Scala is that my igni only appear to me as little lightning bolts of power. Plus, I'm also the only one who can see or hear them.

What the Hell?

I clear my throat and try to organize my thoughts. "Why are you here exactly?"

"Iggy come to Earth for time of mourning when Great Scala dies unexpectedly."

"But I'm not dead."

Iggy shrugs his little shoulders. "No one knows this. They still close the gates to the after-realms." He waves one super-long finger from side to side. "But never for long. They must open the gates soon. Iggy bad for Earth."

I wince. Not sure I want to know the answer to this, but I do feel like I have to ask. "And why is Iggy bad for the Earth?"

"Iggy make things move."

"Like souls?"

"Iggy no move souls on Earth. That is what after-realms are for. No, Iggy move other things here. Make bigga boom." When he says the word *"boom,"* Iggy lights up even brighter while his voice splinters into what sounds like a thousand people talking at once. I also can't help but notice how the carpet under his wide bare feet has started smoldering. "Iggy make bigga boom at building."

My mouth falls open. "You did set the Hunter research building on fire."

"Yes. Make bigga boom for Great Scala. Melt all the nasty guns too." Iggy raises his palms. Small lightning bolts of power—what I traditionally think of as my igni—tumble from his hands. Before, I thought that was fire dripping from his palms. But now that I'm up close? It's igni. Definitely igni.

"That's how you looked when I saw you in the lobby. I

thought it was fire, but you had little lightning bolts dropping from your palms."

"Yes, that was Iggy." He tilts his bulbous head. "You want Iggy to do again?"

I flash Iggy my palms. "No more bigga booms, Iggy."

"As Great Scala wishes. No more bigga booms here."

I can't help but notice that he limited his exploding capabilities to "here." "Where do you want to let loose more bigga booms, then?"

"Lagaga Wa-ardia where the great birds fly."

My eyes widen. "Do you mean LaGuardia airport?"

"Yes. Lagaga Wa-ardia. Iggy go there. Iggy make bigga boom."

"No bigga booms, Iggy. Not unless Great Scala says so, okay? Good Iggy." For some reason, I'm talking to a supernatural being like he's a puppy in training. "You got that?"

Iggy's little mouth droops into a frown. "Great Scala very mean. Must save handsome consort."

"Hey, I want save Lincoln." My voice catches. "Just without, you know, random bigga booms." Although, to be honest, I'm open to the concept as a last resort.

"Iggy try."

"Thank you, Iggy." I heave out a long breath. "And I agree we probably have to go to LaGuardia, but I need my friends along as well. And we also need a plan. I don't know where Lincoln is."

All of a sudden, the mirrors in the penthouse come to life. I see my Lincoln, trapped inside his glass coffin.

He's screaming.

Molten-bright light churns under his skin. Alarm rolls through my nervous system. I've seen that happen once before. It was back at Purgatory High. Armageddon, the King of Hell, has visited us in what turned out to be preparation for his invasion of Purgatory. He'd touched one of our teachers and pulled out her soul, which was his favorite method of attack.

As she died, her skin looked just as Lincoln's does now.

I race over to a nearby mirror and scan it carefully, desperate for any clue as to where Lincoln is being held. My heart thuds hard against my rib cage. Lincoln is still trapped in a dark room inside the glass coffin. Lightning arcs into him, just like I saw before with Williamson. This time, my view is much closer, though. It's clear how red light churns under his skin, reminding me of magma.

They're trying to pull out Lincoln's soul.

I scratch at the image in the mirror. "Lincoln, where are you?" Tears stream down my face. "Give me something. Show me something. I have to find you."

From the corner of my eye, I see Iggy standing across the room. His body glows more brightly. "Great Scala sad. Iggy fix."

Crash...crash...crash! One by one, every mirror in the room bursts outward in succession. On reflex, I crouch down in a protective move. Glass jingles as it hits the floor. Nothing falls on me, though. I risk a look at Iggy. He stares at me with his huge eyes. Every inch of his body glows.

"Great Scala got upset again. Iggy fixed it."

I stalk over to him. "Iggy didn't fix the mirrors. As terrible as it was, I needed to see Lincoln. I don't know where he is, and that vision could have given me a clue."

"No, Great Scala can't be sad."

I stagger a half step backward. "Lincoln was screaming something again." I close my eyes and try to picture the words. "It was my name. And that wasn't the first time this has happened. Whenever I see him in a mirror, I swear, he's calling for me." I rub my forehead, thinking through the implications. "What does that mean?"

"Iggy knows. That magic comes from your love for each other. Consort calls your name."

My skin chills over with shock. "You mean when Lincoln calls out to me—that's when I see him in the mirrors?"

"Yes, Great Scala and consort connected. When consort is in pain and calling for you, that's when you see him."

Lincoln's been in pain. He's calling for me and I'm not there. Hells, I don't even know where he is.

My mind slips into battle mode. All my emotion fades into the background as I focus on the challenge of finding Lincoln. My gaze locks on Iggy. He may be able to help in ways that don't involve destruction. "You make souls move in the after-realms. And here, you make things move, too?"

"Yes. Not as fun as bigga boom, though." More lightning bolts drop from his hand. "Iggy good with bigga boom. And Iggy melt things with igni power, too. Like guns and bad men."

"I don't need any melting right now, thank you very much." Rushing over to the table, I pick up the binoculars and ledger. "Here's what I do need. If you can make things move, can you make these work for me?"

"Iggy can try."

"Okay, this will be just like when we move souls." I hold the binoculars and ledger in front of me. "I'll tell you where to go, and you make it happen."

"Yes, Great Scala."

"Good." I set the binoculars against my face. Like they did with Felton, clamps extend to hold the device to my head. I sit down at the kitchen table and spread out the ledger before me. "Iggy, make these things show me information about Lincoln."

"As the Great Scala commands."

With the binoculars on, I can't see much. I do sense Iggy moving closer to me. Warmth spreads across my body as tiny lightning bolts drop from Iggy's palms. Soon, the binoculars heat up as Iggy's power moves through them. The gears begin to whir and—at last!—words appear on the ledger page before me. Each letter glows with a golden light.

I read the text out loud. "Test subject 962-A. Lincoln of Rixa. Subject shows extraordinary levels of angelic power mixed with human DNA. Best harvesting rounds we've had so far."

The binoculars turn so hot they could burn my skin. On reflex, my tail whips up to hold them a safe distance away. I now have to squint to read the writing, but it's possible. "Subject fights harvesting process. This is not acceptable. The last step in our plan is to obtain enough angelic soul power in order to—"

The words turn blurry as the binoculars start melting in my tail's grip. "Iggy, can you use less heat?"

"Iggy try."

A few more phrases appear on the bottom of the page. "LaGuardia…portals in unexpected places…lead to cloning tanks…harvesting tables…"

Those last two words echo in my mind: *Harvesting tables*. That has to be where Lincoln is. The news announced that Ethan would be at the Touch The Tech Event. If I know his Supreme Atrociousness, Ethan won't want to be far from the number one source of soul power for his evil plans.

Whatever those evil plans may be.

But before I can read another word, the binoculars turn

into a molten pile of goo on the tabletop. After that the ledger flashes with a burst of lightning as well. For a moment, the dark pages glow as brightly as Iggy's skin before transforming into a pile of ash. My legs turn wobbly as I plunk down into a nearby Plexiglas chair. My limbs shake. Inside, I'm torn between pure joy at learning more about where Lincoln might be…and a heavy sense of despair at not having him rescued already.

Iggy taps my shoulder. "Did Iggy help?"

"Yes, thanks. You did a great job making the binoculars work."

"The bad men want something from consort."

"Yes, they're trying to pull out his soul." My voice breaks as my warrior-mode fades. When I saw Lincoln in the mirrors, he was in so much pain. "We have to stop them, Iggy."

I look around the once-funky suite. All the mirrors are busted, and half the couch is now rubble thanks to my tail. Before me, a large section of the floor is convex and melted.

We definitely need to leave a big tip.

"You're right, Iggy. I need to go to LaGuardia now."

"Yes, where the planes fly."

"The ledger says there are portal doors there that will lead to cloning tanks and the harvesting tables. I think that's where we'll find Lincoln." I press my palms against my eyes and try to mentally regroup. "But before we can go, I need to find my friends."

"Iggy like this plan."

I nod, my throat tightening with emotion. Lincoln always said I was great at battle plans. And that's what this is, a battle. "You'd better disappear before my friends get back. I'll summon you again at LaGuardia."

Iggy closes his eyes and scrunches up his face. "Uh-oh."

I don't like the sound of that at all. "What do you mean, uh-oh?"

"Great Scala remember time of mourning?"

"Sure. The gates of Heaven and Hell are closed. That's how you ended up here."

"Time of mourning is now over. Gates to after-realms now open. If Iggy goes away, he goes back to Heaven, Hell, or Purgatory. No come back to Earth."

"You can't return and help me again?" The words come out with way more shock than I would have thought possible. After all, one of the few facts I thought I knew about my job as Great Scala was that igni couldn't visit the Earth. Igni only focus on souls, and that means staying in the after-realms. I hadn't expected that Iggy would ever show up. Now that he's here, I can't imagine him leaving.

"If Iggy go, Iggy can't help Great Scala. Like Iggy said, time of mourning is over."

"So they opened up the gates of Heaven and Hell again?" I know I'm repeating this statement over and over, but I'm having some serious issues with it. Somehow, I thought the gates would stay closed a lot longer than a day. After all, I'm a pretty good at being the Great Scala.

"Gates are open. If Iggy goes, Iggy no come back."

I pinch the bridge of my nose. I'm having a hard time adjusting to all this. Plus, I want to eat a gallon of ice cream like it's my job. "But it's a basic fact of our relationship that I can summon you when I need to."

"Iggy can stay. Iggy can help. Just no go."

I lace my fingers behind my neck and run through the options. There aren't many. I return my focus to Iggy. "Okay, fine. You stay and help, but you have to come along. With Cissy and me and Zeke. In the cab. To LaGuardia."

Wow, does this ever have *disaster* written all over it.

Iggy starts skipping around the room, leaving a set of scorch-mark footprints on the wood floor. "Helping! Helping!"

While Iggy has his own fire-dance party, I contemplate how I can get him to LaGuardia without alerting every Razor Guard around. All of us still need a disguise, for that matter. Ethan will definitely be at the event. Since he's thrax, he'll see our tails in a heartbeat if we aren't careful. Plus, he'll probably have more thrax around him as well, and they'll see our tails, too.

Nope. We definitely need disguises.

Iggy rushes for the door. "We go now."

"Hold it there, buddy. I need to think a little first." There must be some way to hide Iggy.

At that moment, the door whips open. Cissy and Zeke stride into the room. Well, they stride until they spy Iggy. At that point, they both stop in place. Cissy turns pale. Zeke falls over in a dead faint.

Crap. Just when I thought things were looking up.

*a*fter two hours—and a lot of explaining things to Cissy and Zeke—we're finally ready to go to LaGuardia. Cissy didn't want to bring Iggy, but Zeke was in full support. In my opinion, I think Zeke just wants to see Iggy blow things up, but whatever. As long as we leave for LaGuardia, I'm good.

Trouble is, we're not leaving. And the problem isn't Cissy and Zeke, either. Iggy is stalling.

"Iggy no like hat." His muffled voice sounds from underneath the black Darth Vader helmet Cissy found to cover his head. "No, no, no."

I kneel beside him. Like Cissy and Zeke, I'm wearing a floor-length trench coat to hide my tail, along with overlarge Terminator-style sunglasses to hide any kind of glow from my eyes.

I'll be honest here. It's not a great look.

"This is the thing, Iggy," I explain. "The Event at LaGuardia is called Touch the Tech. It's all about kids. There are going to be trucks and stuff everywhere, as well as face painting. But the biggest deal is the costume contest. We've been watching it on TV all day. Most of the kids there are in costumes. This is really the best disguise for you."

Remember when I said Cissy could shop? Understatement of the week. All I said was that we would need disguises for Ethan's Touch The Tech Event, and the girl came back with a ton of stuff in less than an hour, including this Darth Vader costume for Iggy, which he hates.

Full disclosure: Iggy was much more into the Jar Jar Binks costume, but some lines just can't be crossed.

My little glowing buddy stomps his foot. "Iggy no like."

"But you can't walk around naked in public," I explain. "And I can't ask you to disappear."

"If Iggy disappear. Iggy go to after-realms. Then Iggy no come back and Iggy wants to stay!" His little helmet rattles on his shoulders.

"Don't worry, Iggy. We know you want to be here. That's why you're dressing up. This hides you from humans." And as long as Iggy stays calm, he looks like a really pale kid. At least, I hope that's the look.

"Wear it all, but no hat." Iggy wraps his cape closer around him. It's pretty clear that he digs the costume except for the headgear.

"The hat is the most important thing, Iggy."

Zeke steps closer. Like me and Cissy, he's wearing a long trench coat, baseball cap, and mega-sunglasses. In other words, we look like a trio of flashers. To make matters worse, today is a warm fall day, so there's no actual reason for us to be wearing trench coats, except to hide our tails.

It's like a conspiracy. Why couldn't Touch The Tech be a

mini con or something cool along those lines? That way, everyone could dress up, adults and kids alike? But no... We've watched the TV a dozen more times. The only people dressing up are children. There aren't even adults dressed up in parent-child matching costumes, either. Which means that Iggy looks like an odd-yet-cute Darth Vader kid, while we three look like his terrifying relatives.

I stifle a sigh. There's not much we can do about how we look at this point. Besides, this is New York. People will probably be fine with seeing three adults in trench coats dragging along a kid in a Darth Vader costume.

Maybe.

I swipe my hand down my face. This is such a bad idea. Unfortunately, it's the best one we've got.

Zeke whips off his sunglasses in true fashion-model style. "Maybe we should leave Iggy here."

"Iggy go!" His little body vibrates, and his skin starts to glow. Now, it looks like we've wrapped a kid-shaped lightbulb inside a Darth Vader suit. The eyes of the helmet start to glow in particular.

I slap on my most soothing voice. "You're going, Iggy. I need you to calm down now."

Cissy picks out a cell phone from her pocket and checks the screen. "Our limo has arrived. We need to move."

I frown. "Limo? I thought we were trying to keep a low profile."

Cissy gestures across our little group "Low profile? Us? Do you really think any cab driver in their right mind would take us anywhere? We look like a serial killer convention."

There's only one thing to say to that. "True. Thanks for ordering the limo, by the way."

"Do you have your cell phone?"

I pat my pocket. "Yup." Cissy got all of us cell phones so we could communicate at the Touch The Tech Event. After years of lusting after one of these devices, I'm a little overwhelmed by the actual item. I wanted something with clear buttons that say "dial" and "end." What I got is a small computer with a screen and all these little colored app thingies that make no sense. Still, Cissy put a lot of work into this, so I shoot her a hearty thumbs-up. "Thanks for the cell phones, too."

"You know how to use yours?" she asks.

"Absolutely." That's a total lie, but I'm feeling tapped out as it is. I just want to get to LaGuardia, find Lincoln, and go home. At this point, learning how to join the current millennium is not a good use of my time.

Zeke slides his sunglasses back on. "Let's hit the road."

Cissy and Zeke head toward the door. Iggy hangs back. I kneel down before him again. "What's up, little dude?"

"Iggy scared. Iggy no walk and talk around humans. Only Great Scala."

I wave to Cissy and Zeke. "You guys go ahead. I need to have a quick chat with Iggy."

Zeke and Cissy march out the door, and within a few seconds, Iggy and I are alone again. "Look, bud." I take care to use my most soothing voice. "I need your help. With being pregnant and all, I can't do my usual battle moves."

"Great Scala jump around and fight."

"Normally, that's what I do. But with the baby, I don't want to do that. I can jump, but other people jump too. I can't risk body blows. So, you have this great power—"

"Bigga boom."

"That's it. Or that's part of it, anyway. Let's see if we can't work as a team and fight without blowing stuff up, okay?" I offer Iggy my hand. The little dude slides his palm onto mine. Instantly, a warm sense of peace moves through me. My eyes widen. This is the first time I've touched Iggy.

"Iggy like holding great Scala's hand."

"I like it, too." A fluttering sensation starts deep in my belly. On reflex, my hand pops over my stomach. "The baby is moving."

Iggy giggles. "Little Scala is happy."

"Hey, do you know how long I'll be pregnant?" Now's not the time to ask, but it doesn't look like later will be any better. I'm getting my info while I can.

"Yes," says Iggy.

"Really?" My heart lightens. "How long?"

"Faster than a drakus, but shorter than a fitzercutter."

Huh. I'm not even going to try and translate that. "Got it, thanks." I raise our joined hands. "Is this safe for the baby? Us holding hands?" Maybe I'm getting a head start on being a nervous mother, but no one really knows what the rules when a Great Scala and the humanoid version of her igni are running around.

Iggy nods. "Oh, yes. Fine, fine. Holding hands makes us all feel better. Like moving souls."

I nod slowly. When I move spirits, the supernatural power of igni does seem to calm my soul. But then, I'm always in Purgatory when that happens. In other words, I'm in the after-realms. Perhaps holding hands on Earth is the closest we can get to that experience, which is why it feels so nice.

Whatever it is, I'm about to meander around an airport in the hopes of saving my husband from a psychopath. I'll take any good vibes I can get my hands on. Literally.

"Are we good then, Iggy? Ready to go?"

"Just keep hold Iggy's hand."

"You got a deal on that one, bud."

With that, I head off to save my husband with two friends and a little supernatural dude dressed like Darth Vader. It's a plan that has "crap idea" written all over it.

It's the only chance I've got.

issy, Zeke, Iggy, and I all stand on the tarmac of LaGuardia Airport. The setting sun casts long shadows over the asphalt. Just like it showed on the news, the place has been completely shut down from its regular airport duties. Now, the runways are all packed with the latest in vehicular awesomeness from Hunter Enterprises.

There are Humvees.

Helicopters.

Tanks.

High-tech motorcycles.

A tent for CHUCK the computer.

There's even a functioning warship held up by some huge black archy-things.

And last but not least, a great dirigible floats through the clouds.

All of this stuff is very black and badass looking. No doubt, it's also totally permeated with black magic. I mean, how else do you get a freaking warship on the tarmac at LaGuardia?

My shoulders slump with worry. Sure, I knew that Ethan

was saying how awesome his combo black magic and human tech was, but all he had to show in Antrum was a bunch of little models. I stare out over the long line of battle helicopters on a nearby runway.

This is so not good. If Ethan has this much battle equipment, surely he's got something he wants to do with it. A dozen Razor Guards march by in two neat rows. I shiver, remembering how Ethan talked about a demon sighting followed by a joint rescue mission by the Razor Guards and Earls. It's a good plan for a day, but somehow Ethan's scheme feels larger than that. I nibble on my thumbnail, trying to piece it together.

The full picture doesn't appear.

More Razor Guards march by, districting me. My senses go on high alert. Whatever Ethan is planning, he certainly has the manpower to act on it. This place is lousy with equipment and guards.

Yipes. Getting out of here alive with Lincoln just got a lot more complicated.

Iggy tugs on my hand. "All the humans stare. Iggy no like."

I can't blame the little guy for feeling uncomfortable. The runways are not only packed with tech, they are also filled with humans. And even though this is New York, the four of us do look mighty shady.

I motion Cissy and Zeke closer. "Look, we need to break up and look for that portal to Lincoln. It will be someplace large enough to hide a secret lab…or small enough to be the magical entrance to one." On the limo ride over, I updated Cissy and Zeke about everything I discovered with Iggy.

"Check," says Zeke. "I'll take the helicopters and Humvees."

"And I'll scan the tanks and the computer tent," adds Cissy. "I'd love to see what I can find in CHUCK."

"Who?" asks Zeke. For the record, Zeke is not an envy demon, but if he were? His eyes would be lighting up right now.

"CHUCK is a computer," I explain. "It holds all the research data, and I'm sure a ton of other stuff that humans need to know about Hunter Enterprises. If Cissy could expose Ethan for who he really is, that might make it easier for us to escape."

Zeke leans in to kiss Cissy on the tip of her nose. "That's my brilliant girl."

I scan the tarmac and frown. Cissy and Zeke are pretty much covering most of the good tech. "What are Iggy and I doing then?"

Zeke gestures behind me. "You two can check out the minivan display."

"Minivans? There are minivans?" It doesn't seem possible. I'd peg Ethan as high-tech badass kind of guy. Minivans aren't really that kind of thing. They're more of a soccer mom kind of deal. Like what I'm pulling to be someday. Only, you know, supernatural and ruling everything.

Wow, my life is strange.

I slowly turn about—it's not easy to move quickly, what with the heavy crowd and Iggy's death-grip on my palm—and then, I see it. Line after line of minivans, all of them in sweet pastel colors. A large sign above them reads: *The softer side of Hunter Enterprises.*

To add insult to injury, the minivan section is also right by the port-a-potty area. I look longingly over to the helicopters. Normally, I'd rush right over there no matter what Cissy and Zeke said. But I'm planning for two now. The minivan section is indeed safer. "I'll go check them out, no problem."

Cissy's brows lift. "I thought you'd fight me harder on that one."

I force on a smile. "I'm trying to be mature."

"I'm very proud of you, Myla-la."

I give her a thumbs-up. "Let's start exploring."

Cissy raises her pointer finger. "But I need to make sure you can use your phone first." Cissy had started a tutorial in the limo, but it wasn't going anywhere, mostly because it's hard enough to learn technology when you can use both hands. Iggy hasn't let go of mine since the hotel suite.

"Look, everything will be fine. You call me. I push the button. We talk. You explained it really well on the ride over." I shoot a glance at the crowd. Six human police officers are making a beeline toward us. "The law's heading our way. We really need to vamoose."

Cissy adjusts her sunglasses with trembling hands. "Okay, good luck." She and Zeke head off to the cool parts of the Touch The Tech Event. Meanwhile, I drag Iggy off to the dreaded minivan display. We aren't a few yards into the rows of vans when I notice something. Three things, actually.

First of all, it's a lot less crowded in the minivan section of the tarmac.

Second, the cops have stopped following me and are now tailing Cissy and Zeke.

And third, Ethan is hanging out right in the minivan area, along with all the Earls from the Summit meeting in the Chamber of Reflection. The thrax nobility are all wearing blue jeans with actual ironed creases down the front, along with black Hunter Enterprises long-sleeve shirts and super-white sneakers. Some stare wide-eyed at the minivans. Others lovingly pat down the fabric of their dark shirts. I'd guess it's a thrill to wear cotton when you spend your life either in chainmail or body armor. Lincoln is one of the few thrax I know who dresses like a regular dude on his days off.

My throat tightens. My Lincoln.

I count the Earls of Kamal, Striga, Acca, and Horus, plus a few of the minor houses. That's the same group from the Summit, all right. They stroll down the last aisle of minivans, the one that's right across from the port-a-potties. It's the best sight I've seen since this whole disaster started.

I'm getting closer to Lincoln. I know it.

While the Earls make their way down the aisle, Iggy and I try our best to follow without looking obvious. It helps that the minivans are all nice and block-shaped, so they provide good cover for sneaking around. Iggy and I crouch behind one that's especially large and pastel pink.

"Iggy hide good?" he asks.

"Yes," I whisper. "You're doing great. Now, we need to see where Ethan and the Earls go."

At last, Ethan's little group gets to the end of the aisle, whereupon they start lurking in the space between a sky-blue minivan and the final port-a-potty. Ethan speaks to the Earls with grand hand gestures. I can't hear what he's saying, but I can imagine it well enough: *"Move to the Earth's surface, and it will be nothing but port-a-potties, minivans, and sneakers, twenty-four-seven."*

Jerk.

Whatever Ethan's speech is, the Earls watch him with wide-eyed attention. After a minute or so, Ethan steps into the last port-a-potty in the line.

My mouth falls open. *Say what? Ethan is taking a bio break. Really?*

Another long minute ticks by. I stifle the urge to groan. When this whole disaster began, I imagined myself as a secret agent, fighting crime and looking badass as I leapt across Earthbound rooftops and rescued my Lincoln. I'd even pictured myself having a new badass sword for the occasion.

That's not exactly how things have turned out.

Instead of rooftops and katanas, I'm crouched behind a pink minivan with an alien dressed like a little Darth Vader, waiting for Ethan to do his business.

Welcome to my life.

Finally, the port-a-potty door swings open. But instead of Ethan walking out, another Earl steps in. And another. And another.

Whoa.

Now, I've never actually been in a port-a-potty myself, but the dimensions are pretty obvious. With a space that small, it could never fit Ethan and all those Earls inside. It must go somewhere else. My heart rate skyrockets.

A portal.

That black ledger talked about hidden magical doors at LaGuardia. Where better place to stash one than in a port-a-potty?

It's so stupid it's brilliant.

Once everyone has disappeared into the port-a-potty, I force myself to wait a full minute. It isn't easy. After I've given us enough time not to look too obvious, I give Iggy's palm a squeeze. "Let's go."

"Iggy help."

"You know it."

Iggy and I make a beeline for the last port-a-potty, which is a major no-no in a crowd-type situation. People instantly get the vibe that something special is going on and—whammo —a line forms before *my* port-a-potty. If you really want to sneak in somewhere, you're best off nonchalantly sidling over.

Note to self: be more stealthy.

Iggy and I wait outside the port-a-potty for a few humans to do their thing. No doubt, they're using it as a regular port-a-potty, which means it must be activated based on my demonic or angelic blood. All of which is cool, but there's only so long I can stand around before I start to fidget.

Too much time has gone by. Will I even find Ethan and the other Earls now? I shift my weight from foot to foot while the last human finishes up.

Finally, the mortal leaves, and it's time for Iggy and me to take a turn. I whip open the port-a-potty, hurry Iggy and me inside, and then slam the door behind us. For his part, Iggy spends the entire episode giggling. He's having the time of his life.

Glad one of us is enjoying this.

We wait inside the port-a-potty for a few moments before a mixture of black smoke and flashing red lights surround us. That's a spell happening, or I'm not the Great Scala. Once the haze clears, I can't believe what's happened.

Iggy and I are now inside a massive and deserted laboratory. In some ways, it's like the one in Times Square: the place has curved walls made of smooth plastic. What's different here is that everything is black instead of white, and tall glass tanks line the floor in neat rows. Inside each pillar, a humanoid figure hangs suspended in a dark haze. I've seen these before.

Cloning tanks.

Gripping Iggy's hand more tightly, I steal down one of the aisles. There must be hundreds of cloning tanks here, and inside each one is a naked Ethan.

Eew. Just eew.

I hold up my palm so I don't have to see Ethan's junk, and scan the nearest tank. The small black placard reads Ethan 9375-R. My blood chills over. Weren't all the Razor Guards given names like that one?

Yes, yes they were.

Which means all the Razor Guards are clones of Ethan. I wish I could say I was shocked, but that seems like a totally Ethan thing to do. Now, all the bandaged-up faces make sense. I stand on tiptoe and check one of the Ethans floating in the tank. Both his eyes are already drooping, just like Evil Lincoln's did back in Antrum. They're also sagging enough that I can see the irises match. These clones are definitely human.

But why would Ethan create so many Razor Guards?

Some small part of me says that this has something to do with the threat of visible demons, too. An image appears in my mind. Lincoln in pain as something that looked like magma churns under his skin. Only the King of Hell has used that trick. The hair on my neck stands on end. Ethan wouldn't be in league with Armageddon on this, would he? I mean, the guy's a thrax. He's not that crazy.

Speaking of the crazy one in question, a voice echoes across the huge room. It's Ethan. "This is where we store our clones," he says. The Earls murmur something. I can't make out exactly what they're saying, but no doubt it's along the lines of "you're so awesome Ethan."

Man, do I ever hate that guy.

Ethan's voice sounds once more. "These will become Razor Guard soldiers that you can order into battle without risking your own people."

My jaw tightens with rage. The Earls may not be risking

their own people, but someone else is paying the soul price to power these Razor Guards. That would be thrax from the lesser houses. And my Lincoln.

The Earl of Striga speaks next. "I've heard rumors that you're cloning demons as well. Is this true?"

For the record, I love the Earl of Striga right now. Yay, Lucas!

"That's nothing but lies." Ethan's voice warbles. "I'm not cloning demons, and certainly I've never been in league with Armageddon."

Wow. There goes Ethan again, volunteering that he's innocent of something he wasn't accused of. Only, why would Ethan be in league with Armageddon anyway? It's all too strange.

"Come along now," continues Ethan. "The next chamber is far more interesting." Footsteps sound as the group walks away from Iggy and me. I can't see them past the many rows of tanks, but there's no mistaking the squeal of a door opening and closing. After that, the room is filled with perfect silence.

They're gone.

Iggy starts dragging me across the floor. "We follow the bad men. Go, go, go."

I lean over. "This will be easier if I carry you."

"Yes, Great Scala."

I swing Iggy onto my hip and take off at a run. He doesn't weigh too much, so we make great time. The place is also totally deserted, which is a nice bonus. I'd think it was a little fishy, what with the room being empty and all, but honestly? I've had nothing but crap luck for days. It's about time something went my way.

About halfway across the darkened floor, I hear it.

The roar of a man's voice in pain.

It's Lincoln.

He's here.

Changing direction, I take off after the sound of my angel-bound love. Iggy's long fingers grip on to my trench coat. "Why we no follow Ethan?"

I don't answer him. The only thing I can focus on is the sound of Lincoln's pained roar.

Finally, this nightmare will be over, one way or another.

21

I run all out for a short while. Although the passages are deserted, a muffled voice echoes from up ahead.

Could be a guard.

I slow my pace, let Iggy slide down from my hip, and take his little hand in mine. Together, we tiptoe down a round passageway made of smooth black plastic. It's not so much a hallway, really, as a person-size tube. A shiver rolls across my shoulders. This always happens when I'm walking around one of Ethan's buildings. I get this creepy feeling like Iggy and I are a pair of blood cells making our way down an empty artery.

Weird.

A fresh scream rips through the air. My back teeth lock. I know that voice, and it's no guard. *That's definitely Lincoln.* Even worse, there's a hoarse edge to his cries that I've never heard before, like he's been yelling for hours. *My love must be in so much pain.* Somehow, I'm able to stop myself from taking off at a run. We haven't run across any Razor Guards yet.

Lincoln can't be unguarded. There's no way I can rush into things.

Be careful, Myla. This is too important.

Our blood vessel hallway takes a sharp turn up ahead. Lincoln's voice grows louder. Making a *shh* face with my finger, I let Iggy slip down to stand on his own again. After that, I plaster my back against the curved black wall. Iggy does the same. As I inch closer to the turn, I keep a death grip on the little dude's hand. What can I say? It's a coping mechanism. As long as Iggy and I stay palm to palm, a pulse of serenity moves through both of us.

In my case, it's the only thing keeping me sane.

Angling my head, I peer around the turn in the passageway. Up ahead, the artery simply ends in a round wall. There's no visible door. Even so, three of Ethan's Razor Guards are lurking around, so the door must still be there, only it's hidden with a binocular lock.

I scan the guards quickly. They stand in a row, each one in full Nazi-style regalia: tall boots, long jackets, and brimmed caps. Black linen bandages cover their faces. *So creepy.* One of them has a composite bow strapped over his chest. Felton told me about those guards. They use the same arrows that went after my Lincoln in order to send prisoners away extra fast.

Note to self: get rid of the bow guard fast.

A low moan echoes out from behind the dead-end wall, interrupting my thoughts. My heart cracks.

Lincoln's still in pain. I have to get through that door. Now.

Leaning forward onto the balls of my feet, I get ready to take off at a run.

I take a half step toward the guards before I pause. *What am I thinking?* This isn't the old Myla who can just charge in now and ask questions later. I need to consider the baby before rushing into battle.

After taking in a few deep breaths, I decide to regroup with Iggy in the concealed area of the hallway. Kneeling down, I turn to the little dude and speak in a voice only he can hear. "Remember when we talked before about fighting?"

Iggy nods vigorously. "Bigga boom."

Unfortunate fact: Iggy is *not* a good whisperer. I make a quick *shh* face. "No bigga boom," I say quietly. "Maybe we try something else, though."

Closing my eyes, I try to focus on what that "something else" could possibly be. Suddenly, the answer is so obvious I can't believe I didn't see it before.

I can fight with igni power.

Here's the deal. On earth, my igni have taken a human form. But in the after-realms, my igni always appear as little lightning bolts of power that swim around in the air. Every Scala develops specialties with how they mold the little guys. The last Scala made ropes to bind people up. Now, I haven't had my powers for very long, but maybe I can make the lightning bolts do something useful, too. I've seen the power dripping from Iggy's palms. Maybe I can help him focus it.

"You know how you've had little igni come from your hands?" I hold my thumb and forefinger an inch apart.

"Iggy melt the bad men's guns."

"You also blew up the research building."

Iggy shrugs. "Hard not to make bigga boom."

"This is where I think we can work together. Just melt the bad men's guns and not make bigga boom. What do you think?"

Iggy leans his Darth Vader head to one side. "Maybe. Great Scala would have to hold Iggy's hand, though."

That answer makes me so happy, I could cheer.

"That's great, Iggy." I don't say this, but there's no way I'm letting go of Iggy's hand any time soon. "Here's the deal. There are Razor Guards in the passageway up ahead. They have guns."

"Bah." Iggy sniffs. "Little boomers."

"Well, those little boomers can cause me big problems. Let's melt those little boomers, and then send more lightning bolts to knock out the guards and tie them up. What do you say?"

"Iggy try."

My left palm rests on my stomach while my right grips Iggy's thin hand. "Let's do this."

Closing my eyes, I focus my request with my mind. Sure, I could whisper again, but we've been noisy enough already. Plus when I'm back in Purgatory, I always use my thoughts when summoning my powers. Probably best to go with proven methods here.

"Come to me, my little ones."

Iggy raises his free hand and stares at his palm. For the longest moment, nothing happens. Then, one of the best things I've ever seen comes to pass: a tiny lightning bolt of power detaches from Iggy's hand.

Then another.

And a third.

The little igni have arrived. Sure, they haven't shown up with ethereal voices like I usually hear in Purgatory, but I'll still take it. I issue another silent command.

"Go melt their guns."

The trio of little lightning bolts swim through the air. As soon as the bright wisps round the corner, the Razor Guards go berserk, unholster their guns, and start shooting at my igni like they were rabid bears. Each boom from their guns is ear-shatteringly loud.

Of course, igni are immune to gunfire, which makes the guards' plan both useless and stupid. Not that I'm complaining.

While the bullets embed in the arched walls, my little lighting bolts zoom right into the muzzles of the guns. I think another command.

"Melt the guns."

Sure enough, the guards yelp as their guns turn to molten steel in their hands. I grin from ear to ear. This is getting fun. And better yet, Iggy and I are still hidden around the corner. We may actually be able to do this.

Giving Iggy's hand a squeeze, I issue another silent command.

"Go tie them up and knock them out."

More little lightning bolts detach from Iggy's palm. At this point, I'm feeling pretty good about my bad self, so I do what should *never* happen in battle.

I get distracted.

The next thing I know, the three guards have rounded the corner and are running straight at me with their arms outstretched. The long black blades of daggers gleam in their fists.

The world seems to freeze. *How could I have been so stupid?* Battle moves happen in seconds. Now that the guards know something is up, there's no time to issue more silent-n-blabby commands. Instead, I shout my head off.

"Knock them out, Iggy!"

Iggy lifts his free hand. Hundreds of tiny lightning bolts instantly fly from his palm. The slivers of power shoot toward the Razor Guards, and fast as a whip, they all burrow under the warrior's flesh.

After that, nothing else happens.

Hells Bells.

The whole "igni burrowing" thing bought us a few seconds with the guards, but that's about it. Now, the trio charges at Iggy and me again. Once more, all their daggers are raised high. I haul my little buddy onto my hip and get ready to run my ass off.

That's when everything changes.

Light blasts from the guards' eye sockets and nostrils, burning holes through the bandages covering their faces. More tiny beams extend like little searchlights from the pores of their skin. For a moment, the guards' bodies flare with light.

After that, all three explode in a poof of dark ash. My eyes widen.

I have to admit, I did not see that coming.

I rush over to where the guards once stood. The fact that they're dead is terrible, but they were coming after me, my child, and my Iggy. We did what he had to do. And now, I have to find Lincoln.

Trouble is, to find my guy, I need binoculars from that guard. I kick around the piles of cinders with my boot. Everything is ash. No binoculars.

Damn.

I pinch the bridge of my nose. "This isn't going well."

"Great Scala is upset?"

Now honestly, I'm not upset with the result, really. I mean, those guards were coming to kill us. Any loss of life is horrible, but I'm a pregnant chick with a lightning-bulb buddy, I have to take what I can get.

"I'm fine. Please don't worry."

"Iggy do wrong?"

This is a trickier question to answer. When it comes to using our joint powers, Iggy and I still have some work to do before we're able to fight without melting people. Oh, and let's not forget the whole "taking too long to do things" problem. But Iggy and I need to focus on one challenge at a time.

"That was a good job," I explain. "Still, we need to do better. We can't keep exploding stuff. And we definitely need to spare the people."

Now, I can't see Iggy's face under the helmet, but I'm pretty sure he's sarcastically mouthing my words back at me. I shake my head. Every time I think my life can't get stranger, the oddness finds me again.

Lincoln's moans sound once more from the far wall, reminding me that there are far more important things to focus on, like finding my husband.

Taking off at a run, I rush over to the far wall and its hidden door. All the while, I keep my hand firmly gripped around Iggy's palm. With every step, one thought echoes through my mind.

I'm almost there, my love.

22

Since we can't open the door with binoculars, there are a limited number of ways Iggy and I can break through the wall and get Lincoln. First of all, there's my tail. But that's a noisy and time-consuming option.

Second, I can summon more igni power. However, last time that ended up with an explosion-type-situation that killed three guards. I glance down at Iggy. I have no confidence that we can blow open this door and still be quiet at the same time.

The tail it is.

Then, for once in my life, a genuine miracle happens. For the record, I'm not talking about the day when I found out my father was an archangel, although that was pretty cool.

No, I'm talking about this moment right now, when the door to the lab where my husband is being held captive opens up *on its own*. A lab tech walks out in a white hazmat suit.

Whoa. I never get lucky breaks of the fortunate variety, so I'm taking this one. Some small voice in my head warns that it's just too convenient. I tell that small voice to shut the hell up.

The moment the lab tech steps out the door, I grab the dude, spin him around, jam my forearm against his throat, and pin him to the wall like a bug. I scan the dude's face under his white hazmat helmet. What I see is a major shock.

It's Felton Weiner.

Again.

"Felton?" I ask. "Is that you?"

His eyes widen with terror. "How do you know my name?"

Up close, I can see how it looks like his skin is drooping from his cheekbones. "What's wrong with your skin?"

"I'm not a clone." The guy's voice takes on a note of hysteria. "And I'm definitely not magically built to do Ethan Hunter's bidding."

I purse my lips. "That's a rather specific set of things NOT to be, Felton." I nod toward the now-closed door. "Here's the deal. You're going to tell me what's inside that lab, and then? You're going to open the door. And if you're a really good Felton Weiner clone, I won't have my little Darth Vader friend here incinerate you, hot-dog style. Do we have a deal?"

Felton nods quickly. "It's just me in the lab. I'm only performing routine experiments, I swear. I just left the room to pee-pee."

Normally, I'd make a snide comment about the pee-pee thing, but I'm in a rush. "Your bio break will have to wait. Open the door, Felton Not-A-Clone. Pronto."

I flip Clone-Felton around so he's facing what now appears to be a solid wall of plastic. After lifting his binoculars, Clone-Felton sets them against his face. Like before, a trio of prongs juts out, holding the device against his skin.

With shaking hands, Clone-Felton twists the dials on the side. Within seconds, a regular door-shaped hole appears on the dead-end wall. I smile my face off.

"Thanks, Felton."

My tail arches over my shoulder. The arrowhead-shaped end points at me as if to say, *Can I please, please, pleeeeeease?*

"Go for it."

Fast as a heartbeat, my tail wraps about Clone-Felton's neck and slams the guy's head into the wall. A low moan fills the air. Clone-Felton is now knocked out cold.

"Good job, boy."

Keeping my firm grip on Iggy, I march through the doorway and into the lab. It's a perfect match to the one in the Times Square, only everything here is black. It's still plastic and sterile-looking, though. A med table sits in the center of the round room, and on that table is Lincoln. The glass covering isn't on him or anything. My breath catches.

He's here.

I've found him.

That little voice comes back into my head, warning that life never is this simple for me. I tell it to take a hike and approach my Angelbound love.

For once, my life will be this simple. I know it.

I step closer, soaking in every inch of my husband's appearance. Broad shoulders. Bare chest. Messy brown hair. Torn jeans. My Lincoln.

He's here again before me. *At last.*

Rushing over to the table, I grip his shoulder. "Lincoln, can you hear me?" He looks bruised and bloody, but not too cut up. I'm taking that as another minor miracle.

His eyes flutter open. "Myla, is that you?"

"Yes, it's me." My tail slices through Lincoln's ties like they were tissue paper. Wrapping my arm around his shoulder, I help him sit up. "Is it really you?"

His mismatched eyes twinkle. "Of course."

I shoot an anxious glance at the door. "Can you walk? We have to get out of here."

"I can try."

We stare at each other for a moment, and then fall into a deep embrace. Well, as deep as I can get while still holding onto Iggy. I nuzzle into Lincoln's neck and inhale his scent. Forest pine and leather. Yes.

"I've missed you so much."

"I love you, Myla." Lincoln leans back. "I knew you'd find me."

My little buddy pipes up. "Iggy helped."

Lincoln's gaze locks on Iggy. "Am I seeing things...or is that a kid in a Darth Vader costume?"

"No kid. Me Iggy." Iggy lifts up his Dark Vader helmet for a moment and exposes his long face, bug eyes, and semi-glowing skin.

"Put that helmet back on the right way, Iggy."

He complies, which is yet another miracle to add to the pile.

"I take it back," says Lincoln. "Is that a spaceman in a Darth Vader costume?"

"Not exactly," I say. "I'll explain later. We have to vamoose, Lincoln." I link the fingers of my free hand with Lincoln's. Together, the three of us march out of the lab.

A memory appears: the TV showing all those families lined up for the costume contest. To my eyes, it seemed like they were all a mother, a father, and a dressed-up kid. Now, I have that for real, even if it is a little temporary until my actual son arrives. I straighten my spine.

My baby will be born, whole and healthy.

Lincoln, Iggy, and I will escape.

We're closer to victory than ever before.

The three of us march back into the main hallway. A sense of warmth and peace radiates through my veins.

Finally. I have my Lincoln. We're going home.

The mental celebration doesn't last for long, though. We get hallway down the outer corridor when more Razor Guards appear. Once again, these creeps have guns, and they aren't afraid to use them.

I give Iggy's hand a squeeze. "Little boomer time."

"Little what?" asks Lincoln.

"Just focus on trying to walk. Iggy and I will handle the rest."

"Little boomer," agrees Iggy. "Need Great Scala to help."

"You got it." I close my eyes and call out to my igni.

"Melt their guns, little ones. Set them to sleep."

This time, Iggy's power rushes through my body. I use the same focusing techniques I did when my igni first began screaming in my head at double-screech volume. Working in harmony with Iggy, I'm able to stop him from getting out of control. Only a handful of lightning bolts speed from Iggy's free palm. This time, the bolts wind up the guard's noses. A flare of brightness fills the hallway as the three guards drop to the ground.

"That was unexpected," says Lincoln.

"Are they alive?" I ask Iggy.

"Only sleeping this time."

I give his hand a little squeeze. "That's great, Iggy. We're getting better at controlling it together."

Lincoln tilts his head. "Who is this little creature again?"

"I Iggy."

"Iggy is the physical manifestation of my igni on Earth. It's a once in a lifetime-type thing."

"Aren't you worried someone will capture him?" asks Lincoln. "They have cages on Earth that can contain creatures like Iggy. I've seen them on demon patrol."

"No, I'm more worried about Iggy losing control and blowing stuff up."

"But don't you—"

I hold up my pointer finger in a *shh* motion across my lips. It's not normal for Lincoln to be so blabby during a mission. But considering what my guy went through? I can understand him being off his game.

Once we're all quiet once more, I scan the artery hallway ahead. It branches off in no less than three directions. I point to the one on the left.

"That was the passage we came from," I whisper. "It leads to this huge room of clone tanks. There's a portal in there that can get us back to LaGuardia." I rub my neck in a nervous rhythm. "If there's a safer way out, I'd rather go that way. LaGuardia is crammed with tech and Ethan's goons."

Lincoln shakes his head. "The clone tank room is the only safe exit."

I pause. "How would you know that?"

He shoots me a snarky look. "I was trapped in a glass coffin, not deaf."

I'm still not processing this for some reason. "What do you mean, exactly?"

"The guards and lab techs talk, Myla." He takes some halting steps toward the far left passage, and I let him. "I can explain more later on, too." He winks.

Normally, I'd grill him on what he'd heard from the guards and lab techs, but we don't have a ton of time. Plus, if anyone could mastermind a plan to find the safest escape route from an underground lab—all while tied down and pumped up with black smoke—then it would be my Lincoln.

My Lincoln. The very thought makes me giddy. It's beyond amazing to touch him again, even if it is only while we try to escape from our latest catastrophe.

Soon, we're back in the main clone room again. Lincoln leads us straight toward what looks like a typical door set in the far wall. He nods at the spot. "That's the secret portal. The guards were talking about it."

"It's the same one we came through." My tail pushes the door open. A wall of black smoke greets us.

"That magic," says Iggy.

"Right you are, my little friend." I give his and Lincoln's hands a squeeze. "Let's get out of here."

"Agreed." Lincoln steps through first, then me, and last but not least, there's Iggy. We're still holding hands, so we resemble those little kids you sometimes see on walks during recess. I don't care how we look, though. At this point, there's no way I'll let go of either of them.

For a moment, heavy black smoke and pulsing red lights surround us. Then the magic disappears in a heartbeat. The three of us now stand crammed into a small space. The scent of port-a-potty slams into my nose. Everything outside sounds pretty normal.

Kids screaming.

Music blaring over the loud speakers.

The roar of an engine as someone touches some tech.

My shoulders relax a little. Lincoln was right. This is the best way to safely escape. We shuffle-walk our way deeper into the port-a-potty. It's a tight squeeze, but after everything I've been through today? This is by far not the worst situation.

The door back to the laboratory clicks shut behind us, and that's when my luck runs out.

The walls around us start to bow outward. Someone is pulling this structure apart. Snapping sounds crackle in my ears as the seams start to tear. With a great thud, the walls of the port-a-potty collapse outward.

Yes, we're back at LaGuardia by the end of the minivan and potty aisle.

No, were not alone.

Sadly, the three of us are now surrounded by what looks like a small army. Hundreds of Razor Guards stand around us, along with just as many representatives of New York's finest. Beyond them, the crowd gawks, holding up their cell phones to take pics. But that isn't even the worst part. The drone of engines fills the air as a half-dozen helicopters lift off a nearby tarmac. They swoop about and head straight for our location.

I fight a groan. As if it weren't bad enough to be surrounded by police and Razor Guards. Now, a bunch of enchanted tech is heading straight for us.

Iggy lets go of my hand. Standing aside, he raises his palm. "Iggy make bigga boom."

"No, Iggy." I reach for him. "You can't do this alone. You could hurt the humans."

At that moment, none other than Ethan steps forward from the crowd. He's got on one of those zip-up onesies that race car drivers wear, only his is covered with Hunter Enterprises logos. With that, it's official.

My day has gone to hell.

Ethan tilts his round head. "Hello, Myla Lewis."

"Hey there, dickhead."

"Brave words from someone who has been clearly outwitted." Ethan's gaze locks on Iggy. "Although, I must admit, this little addition was quite unexpected. It took some quick thinking on my part, but I've found the perfect way to lock your little friend up, too. It's an enchanted cage."

Now, Lincoln had talked about something like this back at the lab. For my part, I'd never heard of enchanted cages that can lock up igni. But whatever it was, they've brought it in to capture Iggy. A pair of Razor Guards steps forward, carrying what looked like a coffin made out of metal mesh.

I frown. What is it with Ethan and coffins, anyway? First glass, now metal. The dude was creepy enough without any extra help. And speaking of creepy, when did Ethan find out I had Iggy along? It must have been a while ago for him to crack out this trap.

There's no time to ponder Ethan and his scheming, though. The guards drop the metal coffin on the ground before Iggy. I lose my freaking mind. "What are you doing? If you imprison Iggy, what will happen to every soul in the after-realms?"

Ethan sniffs. "I've seen plenty of odd creatures. I don't care what this one does or doesn't do. All I'm focused on is harvesting angelic soul power from specific targets. Now, if holding this little monster will inspire you to give me what I want, then that's what I'll do. Clear enough for you?"

I kneel by Iggy's side. "You have to leave. Go back to the after-realms."

"Iggy no go. No, no, no, no, NO."

"You have to. It's too big a risk if you're captured." My voice is borderline hysterical, and I don't care. If Ethan gets his hands on Iggy, he could stop millions of souls from moving to their final destination. Hell, he could shut down the entire after-realms. When I next speak, it's like every word is torn from my soul. "Get out of here, Iggy. I don't want you around."

There's a flash of light inside the Darth Vader mask, and then Iggy's costume tumbles to the earth. It feels like part of my heart has been torn out with him.

Ethan's brows lift. He leans over the spot where Iggy once stood. "I didn't know he could do that."

"What a shock. You don't know something, and yet you try to control it." I kick the metal coffin. It lets out a satisfying clang.

Lincoln rests his hand on my shoulder. "Don't provoke him, Myla."

"What?" I pluck Lincoln's hand off my shoulder. The movement triggers a memory, but I can't quite put my finger on it. "Provoking is what I do."

Ethan shakes his head. "Silly little demon girl. You're about to become intimately familiar with my laboratory. That can be pleasant or painful. It's your choice."

On reflex, my free hand covers my belly. Whatever Ethan has planned, it can't be good for my unborn son. I scan the grounds, my mind rushing through battle plans and options. There aren't many.

All of a sudden, an ambulance speeds across the tarmac, lights flaring. Ethan gestures to it. "Ah, your chariot has arrived. Just get inside without causing any trouble, and I promise not to hurt the child."

My eyes widen. "You know I'm pregnant?"

"Of course." Ethan grins. "What do you think this was all about, anyway? In time, your son will call me father. And once he comes of age, why, I'll have the biggest harvest of angelic energy ever." Ethan gestures between Lincoln and me. "After the pair of you, of course."

At those words, a chill crawls up my neck. Things may have been bad before, but I have a sinking feeling that they are about to get a ton worse.

23

*T*his is terrible.

Lincoln and I are at Ethan's mercy. Now, he's got some souped-up ambulance tooling across LaGuardia, ready to take us away so he can drain our angelic energy. Only in my case, he'll do that after the baby is born so he can ruin our son's life too.

What a disaster.

The ambulance careens across the tarmac. Something about the way it zigzags seems way too familiar. Squinting, I try to make out the driver. It's a Razor Guard, but some blonde curls peep out from under the Nazi-style cap.

Could that be?

The ambulance clips the back fender of a Humvee. I've seen that move before. No question about it. That's definitely Cissy behind the wheel. She's always been a crappy driver.

The ambulance pulls up beside us. The back door pops open, and someone else who looks like a Razor Guard steps out. Only it's definitely *not* a Razor Guard. How do I know this? The top of a monkey tail is peeping out from inside his jacket.

That's definitely Zeke.

Sure, his face is covered with bandages, but I've known the guy since kindergarten. I blink hard and try to process this turn of events.

Somehow, Cissy and Zeke took over an ambulance and found themselves some disguises. Cool relief seeps through my chest.

I officially have the best friends in the universe.

That said, I also have an army of Razor Guards and Ethan to deal with, but at least I've got backup.

Ethan keeps glaring at me. I don't mind because that means he hasn't noticed Cissy or Zeke. Ethan gestures to the open door. "Get inside."

I take care to look especially miserable—it involves lots of sniffling—as I mope my ass in to the ambulance. Lincoln follows in right behind me. The interior of the vehicle is pretty standard stuff. There's a cot on one wall and a bunch of drawers and tech on the other. Lincoln and I park on the cot. Once were both settled, Zeke steps in as well, slams the door shut, and pounds on the wall with his fist. "Move it out."

The ambulance lurches forward. Once we're a safe distance away, I turn to Zeke. "Nice disguise."

He pulls down the bandages to expose his eyes. "I thought you couldn't tell."

"Meh. I'm just that great of an actress." I lean forward. "Tell me. How did you guys do it?"

Zeke crouches on the floor beside our cot. "When you disappeared, Cissy and I knew something had gone wrong. We snooped and found out they were setting up this ambulance for a special pair of prisoners. After that, the rest was easy."

Up close, I can see the bruises on Zeke's face. Blood drips from his fingertips. It wasn't all that easy. "Thanks, Zeke. That means a lot."

Zeke notices how my gaze locks on his bleeding. He quickly jams his hand under his arm. "I'll be fine, Myla."

Cissy calls over her shoulder. "There's a checkpoint up ahead." By the quavering tone in her voice, I can tell that my bestie isn't sure how to pass this one. "Need your lust demon mojo, hun."

"Be right there." Zeke pulls the bandages over his face again. "I've been working my lust demon magic all day. I swear, once we get back to Purgatory, I'll sleep for a year." He squeezes through the small opening between the back of the cab and takes a seat next to Cissy.

I turn my attention to Lincoln. "How are you feeling?"

He lets out a low cough. "I've been better. You?"

"Ask me when we're out of here."

My heart starts thudding a mile a minute as the ambulance rolls to a stop. Leaning forward, I get a good peep out the windshield. We're at the end of a runway lined with tech. Before us, there are a bunch of empty runways followed by a small guardhouse. It's a pretty classic setup as guardhouses go: a small black structure for the guard, along with a wooden arm that swings up when you can leave. Beyond that, I see the highway and freedom.

We're so close.

All we need to do is pass this guard and checkpoint. And avoid Ethan and his Razor Guards until we can reach a Pulpitum, but one thing at a time.

Cissy slows down beside the guardhouse. A regular human guard steps up to the ambulance window. "No one is supposed to leave by this exit." She goes up on tiptoe. "But you're the special case I heard about from HQ, eh?"

Hope sparks in my chest.

The guard is a woman. Considering Zeke's specialty, that should be good for us.

"We totally have clearance," says Cissy. "Just let us go."

"Really?" asks the guard. "What's the password?"

Zeke leans across the front seat. "Hey, kitten." Even from the back of the ambulance, I can feel Zeke sending out waves of lust demon power.

The female guard stares at him like he grew three heads. "Kitten?" Her eyes narrow. "Only *my wife* calls me that, buddy."

Hells bells. She's not into men.

This is so very, very bad for us.

The guard moves to stand right in front of the ambulance, aka blocking our exit past the swing-arm and onto the main street. "Wait right here." She pulls a cell phone from her pocket. "Guard CK-90, requesting backup."

"Change of plans!" Cissy puts the ambulance in reverse and peels away from the guard station.

I lean forward on the cot. "Cissy, be careful!" She really is a crappy driver, as evidenced by the fact that we start doing a donut on the tarmac.

"I don't know where I'm going!" calls Cissy.

Craning my neck, I scope out the airport through the front windshield. "It's all right, Cis. There's another guard station on the other side of the airport." I point to the spot in question. "As long as there's no one dumb enough to stand in front of it, we can break through the arm and get out of here."

"Right. Good. We're off." Cissy punches the accelerator, and I fall back onto my bum. Still, it could be worse.

As we tool across the tarmac, the squeal of tires and whoop of sirens sounds behind us. That human guard just called in the cavalry.

Okay, it's definitely worse.

Lincoln takes my hand and guides me to lean back onto the cot. "Myla, listen to me. We may not escape. We may have to go back to the laboratory."

For a moment, I can only stare at Lincoln in shocked silence. What's wrong with him? Did they torture all the fight from his soul? I give his hand a gentle pat. "Have a little faith." I hitch my thumb toward the windshield. "We're only a three runways away from the other gate...and getting ourselves out of here." I cross my fingers. My tail crosses itself, which I appreciate as well.

Come on, Cissy.

Lincoln shakes his head. "I wanted to say something before, but there wasn't time. It's just so great to be back together, and I love you so much."

My mouth falls open. Lincoln must have gotten his brains scrambled in that lab. Any warrior worth his salt knows the rules: you do *not* start with gooey love-you talk in the middle of an escape.

The whump-whump of helicopters sounds overhead. My pulse goes through the roof. Souped-up motorcycles appear, approaching us from both sides of the ambulance. Cissy swerves left and right to avoid them. A bunch of wires and stuff break loose from the wall of meds before us. It's a small price to pay.

Only two more runways to go.

Lincoln grips my hand. "You must understand. If we must

go back, it might not be the end of the world. We'd be together. Isn't that the most important thing of all?"

I scrunch up my nose into my *you're acting crazy* face. "What do you mean? Do you need to lay down or something?" An odd chill creeps up my spine.

Something is wrong here. Very wrong.

Cissy calls from the driver's seat. "One more runway!"

"You're doing great, babe," says Zeke.

Lincoln cups my face in his hands. "Look, I'm serious. Ethan's work is important. They need you and the baby to finish it."

My breath catches. Inch by inch, I examine every line of Lincoln's face. The skin under his left eye is drooping.

Oh, damn. He's a clone.

Or maybe he just got his brains temporarily zapped out in the laboratory. A girl can hope, right?

I grip Maybe Lincoln's wrists and pull them down from my face. "Where was our first kiss?"

"Myla." A muscle twitches along his jawline.

"Answer me."

"*Our* first kiss was almost in the honeymoon palace, but you were too damned suspicious."

My heart sinks. An almost-kiss in the honeymoon palace? This is even worse. I not only rescued a clone, I rescued the original Evil Lincoln.

Hells bells.

I shake my head. "I should have guessed. That whole rescue was too easy. There were no guards at first, and then? A Felton clone waltzes right out of the lab." I want to face-palm myself. *Hard.*

"We're almost there!" Cissy's voice quivers with excitement.

That's when the biggest, baddest helicopter in the universe plunks down from the sky to block our path. It hovers right before us as its guns angle straight at our windshield. Cissy slams on the brakes, and we screech to a halt.

A voice comes over the chopper's loudspeaker. "Hold your hands up, and we won't shoot."

Cissy calls over her shoulder. "Myla, should we—"

"You can't drive into an attack helicopter. And based on the noises, we're surrounded. Don't risk your lives any more than you have already."

Zeke takes Cissy's hand, and together they raise their arms. It's so sweet, and it makes me feel guilty as Hell for dragging them into this. I turn to Evil Lincoln. "I hate you."

He sniffs. "We wanted you to do this willingly. It will be tricky to keep you sedated through the whole pregnancy. Ethan thought that since I knew you the best, I might be able to convince you—"

"Fat chance."

"I'm starting to see that." Evil Lincoln rubs his jaw, and it makes the skin under his eyes droop more. "You should do this willingly. It's safer for you and the baby."

At that moment, the back of the ambulance swings open. Ethan stands before me again, looking like a deranged and baby-faced gas station attendant. "You ruined my special day, Myla Lewis."

"Good." My tail pops up to give Ethan a modified version of a nasty hand gesture.

"How sweet," snarls Ethan. "Now, let's take you to your *real* husband, shall we? With you along as motivation, I know he'll surrender the rest of his soul. How I hate to lose any more power simply because he refuses to cooperate. But with his wife and child at risk? I think we'll achieve a far better result."

Icy dread fills my body. "You wouldn't."

Ethan simply grins his Chiclet smile. He totally would.

There's no way in Hell I'm going to be used as bait to drain my husband's soul. Rising to my feet, I'm about to bolt and try to escape on foot when I feel the cold barrel of a gun at my neck. That would be Evil Lincoln. He's at it again. "Come along, wifey."

"Bite me, creep."

"And don't think about changing your little robes again. We know how to puncture anything. If not with a gun, with a needle."

There's nothing I can say to that. I already found out that Ethan can drug me even through my body armor. I simply have to follow along and hope for an opportunity to escape.

Ethan points at Zeke and Cissy. "You two. We have reports of someone visiting the CHUCK tent and hacking in to get access to equipment."

Cissy's eyes go super large. She appears mega innocent as she asks: "Who's CHUCK?"

Ethan huffs out a frustrated breath. "Please. Everyone knows CHUCK is the supercomputer that runs Hunter Enterprises."

Zeke raises his hand. "I didn't know that."

"Someone visited the display tent for CHUCK, hacked into the system, and rerouted some equipment. A few of our guards were injured. Know anything about that?"

Zeke slips his injured hand deeper under his armpit. "Nope."

"Someone locked down our systems with a new password. Know anything about that either?"

There's no mistaking the proud gleam in Cissy's eyes.

"Wow, whoever that was must be an excellent hacker. Like a natural genius or something." My girl knows she's caught and is just living the moment. That's my Cis.

Ethan's face reddens with rage. "Both of you are going right back to the CHUCK tent and fixing whatever you did. In return, I promise your death will not be painful."

My hand pops over my mouth. "I'm so sorry." Cissy and Zeke came here to help me, and now they're in worse trouble than ever.

Cissy gives me a sad smile before lifting her chin and turning to Ethan. "I'm still not sure what you're talking about with this CHUCK thing, but I'll take a look." Together, she and Zeke crawl out of the front cab. I watch the Razor Guards take them off into the night. My heart sinks. What have I done?

Evil Lincoln leans in closer. "There's still time to join our side, you know."

When I answer him, I make sure to have my eyes flare red with demonic rage. "Never."

Ethan knocks on the back metal door of the ambulance, grabbing my attention. "Time to get out." Ethan pulls a gun from the pocket of his gas station attendant uniform and points it right at my stomach. "Now."

Every nerve ending in my body goes on alert. Not only is Ethan pointing a gun at me, but he has dozens of Razor Guards around him as well. Not to mention whatever weaponry Evil Lincoln may be hiding, and that guy is right beside me.

This is it. Game over.

My mind reels as I crawl out of the ambulance and into a living nightmare. My husband's still missing, and now I'm about to turn MIA as well. Plus, since everyone in the after-realms already thinks I'm dead, no one will come searching for me.

Crap on a cracker.

24

I stand on a runway at LaGuardia, surrounded by Ethan, Evil Lincoln, and a bunch of Razor Guards. The air feels like it's pressing in around me, but that could just be the humidity from the nearby Hudson River.

As far as I can see, all the tarmacs are filled with locals. Night is falling, but everyone's still here for Ethan's Touch The Tech Event. Mobile spotlights dot the various runways, so the place is cast in a weird daytime glow even though it's getting darker by the second. I scan the crowd for human police. After all, Evil Lincoln has a gun to my back. Humans have laws about this stuff.

I've barely begun looking around when Ethan leans in closer. "Call for help and you're dead."

I inhale a deep breath. *I am so screaming my lungs out.*

Evil Lincoln jams the gun harder against my spine. "Just give me a reason to shoot you," he snarls.

Ethan lifts his hand. A syringe glimmers in his grasp. "Or I can shoot you another way. Your choice."

That line shuts me up and how. So far, I'm lucky they

haven't gone straight for sedation. There's no point poking the bear on this one.

"I'm taking her back to the lab," announces Evil Lincoln.

"You? Absolutely not." Ethan waves his stubby-fingered hand again. "You're far too emotionally attached. Get the H-E Launch ready."

"But—"

"I said, the H-E Launch."

Evil Lincoln lets out an angry huff, and it's just so satisfying that he's ticked off. Angling my head, I give him a snarky grin. Sure, it hurts my neck to crane it this way, but you really have to appreciate the little joys in life. Like pissing off your fake husband.

"Run along now, Clone Boy," I say with a wink.

Evil Lincoln lowers his voice to growl in my ear. "I could shoot you now."

"So do it."

Evil Lincoln talks a good game, but he fools no one. Ethan calls the shots here. Literally.

I hear the click of the gun getting cocked, and that's when Ethan loses his freaking mind. "Lincoln Unit 47-J! I said to move out!"

Evil Lincoln steps aside so another Razor Guard can keep a gun pressed firmly against my back. He's hiding the weapon in the pocket of his Nazi coat. It should be obvious to anyone looking for a gun.

Trouble is, all the humans adore Ethan. He's their savior. No one's expecting him to have a guard threaten random women at LaGuardia. Again, humans excel at avoiding realities, even when those facts are right before their eyes.

I'd be bummed about this, but I'm still stuck on what Ethan said.

Lincoln Unit 47-J? Excuse me?

I'm so stunned I don't even notice when Evil Lincoln slips off into the crowd. I focus on Ethan instead. "How many clones of my husband have you made, exactly?"

Ethan rolls his eyes. "Hundreds. That's the only one that's still breathing, though. Your husband is rather challenging to duplicate."

I narrow my eyes. Makes sense. Ethan wanted to duplicate Lincoln so he could have an ongoing source of angelic soul power. Failing that, he went to the next best sources: my baby and me.

And I'm at this freak's mercy.

Still, I'll figure out something. My father always says: *"Opportunity is eighty percent awareness."* And considering how he's the general of all the archangels, my dad knows his stuff. In other words, I need to stay alert and ready, that's all. My chance will come.

Behind me, the Razor Guard jams the barrel of the gun harder into my back, so I take the cue and start marching across the tarmac. I don't think we'll have to go far. Based on the direction we're taking, I'm guessing there's another portal hidden somewhere in the minivan aisle. Sure enough, Ethan pauses by one of the black minivans with tinted windows. Before, Iggy and I had hidden behind one of the pastel-colored vans. I didn't even know they had black ones on display.

For the record: if I were making a movie about creepy serial killers and someone asked me to find a minivan for the scene where the serial killer in question abducts someone from an alley? This is exactly the model that I'd pick. *Nasty.*

Ethan holds up a key fob, presses a button, and the

minivan door slides open with a *boop-boop*. He climbs inside and disappears. That settles it.

This is definitely another portal back to the laboratory.

With a little urging from my friend Mister Gun, I crawl inside the minivan as well. At first, I find myself a typical back seat complete with one of those fake leather bench thingies.

Suddenly, black smoke swirls through the air in shapes that are definitely not Earthly. The mist forms shapes that are a cross between a pinwheel and a massive snowflake.

That's black magic.

Seconds later, the smoke disappears, and I'm back inside another clone room. This one resembled what I'd I visited before: a massive pod-like space made of smooth black plastic. The huge floor is covered in hundreds of glass pillars. Inside each case, there waits a different clone. But instead of naked Ethan clones, all of these columns hold demons.

My thoughts spin through comments I'd heard before. Felton had said something about it being easy to clone demons. Now, it's one thing to hear that you're cloning the residents of Hell, but it's another to see them in row after row of tanks.

How did Ethan manage this?

The answer appears to me in a flash. Armageddon. Ethan always got so twitchy when I mentioned the King of Hell. Is this why? Did Armageddon help Ethan clone demons? Could Ethan really be that stupid?

I glance over at the guy in question. Ethan stands behind me with a dozen Razor Guards. He's grinning widely and scanning the tanks. Dude thinks what he's done here is the bomb.

Yes, Ethan could really be that stupid.

Another memory appears. Back during his tour, Ethan

said that the Razor Guard clones were almost ready for birth. My mind whirs. These demonic clones are in the exact same kind of tanks as the Razor Guard ones. They must be ready for birth as well.

Ready for birth? That little fact may be just the opportunity I need.

My tail flicks behind me in its predatory shimmy. Most of the time, my backside sways in long arcs like a cat's tail. But every once in a while, it goes all snake-like and rears up behind me, cobra style, as if it's scoping out something to strike.

Mostly because it *is* scoping out something to strike.

And in this case, I agree with the plan wholeheartedly.

I mean, they're walking me through a line of glass cases stuffed with demons and they expect me *not* to start trouble? Sheesh. I quickly scan the exits. There's one with a bright red door. Last time, that led toward the labs.

Bingo.

My pulse speeds up as the plan comes into focus. Now, all I need are some especially nasty demons to release, and after that, the fun can start. Because once I set the demons loose, it will be time to hustle to the back exit that leads toward the labs. After that, I can rescue my real husband and move on with my life. Hope sparks in my chest.

This is a solid plan. It's going to work.

Ethan and his guards march me down another aisle. As I mope-walk along, I subtly scan the nearby pillars. Unfortunately, these are all filled with some pretty lame demons. I mean, Limus demons. Really? They're just goo monsters and not too aggressive. If I release them from their glass cages, they'll be happy to take a nap. Nope, the Limus demons aren't what I'm looking for. My palms become slick with sweat.

We turn down another aisle.

This time, I spy case after case of Reperio demons. *PUH-lease.* These are badass if you want to turn garbage into little elf-like creatures with bad language, but they aren't good for much else. My insides twist with worry. This clone room is huge, but it's not that big. I'm running out of glass pillars, along with decent chances to free something that's really terrible.

That's when I see it up ahead: an entire row of Manus demons.

SUH-weet.

Manus demons are gorilla-like creatures with lots of brawn and even more bad attitude. All Manus have huge tusks and an even larger appetite for death. As I walk along, I swing my hips with a little more shimmy. My tail knows what that means.

Once I give the signal, it's go time.

Finally, our small group passes a line of glass pillars stuffed with particularly grouchy-looking Manus demons. Their eyes even flutter open as we walk by. Perfect.

Here's the deal. Back in Purgatory, we store souls in what are called Ghost Towers. It takes a heavy dose of enchanted mist to keep them knocked out. If the spirits perk up at all when mortals are nearby, that means the mist levels are too low. The ghosts could easily wake up, and when they do? They're always cranky.

Let's hope things with these glass tubes work the same way.

We march close to an especially nasty-looking Manus clone, and I snap my fingers twice. That's the signal.

My tail goes to work skewering the glass. Jagged panes break free from their columns and tumble downward. A great crash fills the air, accompanied by the high-pitched jingle of tiny particles cascading across the floor. A plume of black smoke rises to the ceiling.

The Manus bursts from its clear cage.

The demon lands right atop two Razor Guards, flattening them. It takes the other two in its fists and bashes their heads together. There's a nasty crunching sound as their skulls collide.

Serves them right, holding a gun on a pregnant lady.

That leaves two more Razor Guards and one Ethan to deal with. The pair of warriors unholsters their guns and starts shooting at the Manus, rapid fire.

Clearly, these fighters have never been trained on how to confront Manus demons. Something like a gunshot only pisses them off.

I'm liking these odds. In all the confusion, someone forgot to keep the gun at my back, and that's a mistake I'm capitalizing on, big-time. So while the remaining guards shoot at the Manus, I rush over to another pillar-o'-demons.

As I race along, I hear Ethan's voice. "Stop, Myla. I will shoot you."

Brave words, considering he's two aisles over and can't possibly have a decent shot. Just to make things more complex, I spear the glass in my current aisle as well.

More shattering sounds.

New plumes of smoke.

Fresh Manus demons leap into the battle, and boy, are they ticked off.

Meanwhile, the first pair of guards is still shooting at the original Manus demon. That won't end well.

With the demons keeping Ethan and his forces busy, I race

down a third aisle of Manus, smashing the cases and releasing all the badassness.

"I can see you, Myla." That's Ethan's voice, and it's way too close. A gunshot sounds. The bullet whizzes past my shoulder, actually grazing the fabric of my Scala robes. Yes, I've changed the garment into battle armor for the occasion, but even so, the bullet signed the fabric.

Not a good sign for the effectiveness of supernatural armor on the Earthly plane. I'm at risk, and so is the baby.

I have to get out of here.

My gaze lands on the round exit at the far end of the clone room. Last time I came to this lab, Iggy and I used that passageway to find the labs and Evil Lincoln. I'm guessing we probably passed my real husband somewhere along the way.

I hightail it in that direction. More gunshots whiz by me, and a few more singe my skin. That can only mean one thing.

Ethan is in pursuit.

More Manus demons stomp around. Fresh Razor Guards pour into the massive room. Soon, the place is one huge demonic zoo, crammed with all manner of evil rushing around in a frenzy.

I haul ass toward the exit door. Every muscle in my body strains with the effort. Ethan's footsteps sound louder as he closes the distance between us. More gunshots sound. A bullet grazes my left ear and right thigh.

Damn.

I whip open the door, rush through, and spot the knob to close the access door, which I then twist with my tail. Like the eye of a camera, multiple concentric discs roll into place, sealing off the main clone room.

The circular door closes right in Ethan's face. Yes.

Leaning my forehead against the closed door, I try to catch

my breath. The panel before me shakes with the fury of Ethan's screams. My tail and I bump fists. On reflex, I reach for Iggy's hand. He isn't there, of course. A pang of regret tightens my chest.

How I wish I didn't have to send him away.

Still, I did escape Ethan, and that has to count for something. All I need to do now is find the lab where they are keeping the real Lincoln. I'm feeling pretty good about my chances for success when it happens.

I hear the sound of a gun cocking behind me. There's no mistaking that particular noise. Pausing, I raise my arms. Little by little, I turn around.

The hallway's crammed with a whole legion of Razor Guards.

Oh damn.

"Our glorious leader would like a word with you," says one of the Razor Guards.

"Sure thing." The thud of my heartbeat grows so loud, I'm certain every guard can hear it.

Soon Ethan breaks through the group of guards. He stands before all his troops, his round face pink with rage. The sleeve's been torn off his gas-station attendant uniform. He bares his Chiclet teeth at me. "I lost three dozen Razor Guards in that clone chamber."

"Hey, it's your own fault. Who clones demons?" I bob my brows. Sure, this situation has turned from delicious escape into one massive shit burger, but maybe I can still get something from this disaster.

Like, you know, information.

"Come on," I plead. "Give me something here. What's up with the demonic duplication farm?"

Ethan narrows his piggish eyes. "I'll tell you nothing."

Great. How did I end up with the only bad guy in the history of ever who won't blab his master plan? A girl needs info if she's going to escape.

I hold my thumb and pointer finger an inch apart. "Can't you tell me one ittle wittle thing? I'm just wondering how you got so good at cloning demons when you clearly suck at duplicating anything angelic, other than the one clone of my husband." I lower my voice. "He's got a droopy eye, by the way. You might want to look into that."

"You." Ethan's mismatched eyes gleam with malice. "Ruin everything."

"What can I say?" I shrug. "It's a gift."

"Right." Ethan's so pissed off right now I swear that his entire body is vibrating with rage. It's a good look on him, really. "Let me show you something."

"Show away."

Ethan and his three-dozen Razor Guards then march me through more artery-style hallways. All the while, a Razor Guard keeps a gun to my spine. At the same time, another four guards keep semiautomatic machine guns trained in my direction. I guess after the clone room incident, Ethan isn't taking any chances on my making sudden movements again.

This just keeps getting better and better.

I'm force-marched into a snug black room that's pod shaped and made of plastic, just like other chambers. One wall is a tinted window that overlooks the clone room below. Again, this spot reminds me of the Ghost Towers back home.

Probably a control room of some kind.

I go on tiptoe to peep through the main viewing window to the clone floor. Below us, the place is a total madhouse. All sorts of demons are clawing and crawling in a great pile.

About a hundred Razor Guards are racing about, trying to subdue them.

It isn't going well for the guards.

Ethan's guys are still trying to shoot the Manus demons, which is a dumb move to start with, but infinitely worse to keep doing over and over, despite the fact that it only makes things worse.

I gesture to the floor below. "Let me guess. You brought me here so I could share some battle advice." I give Ethan a mock-curtsey. "Happy to oblige. You need to train your Razor Guards better on how to fight demons. Or at all, really."

Ethan's face has turned a lovely shade that I like to think of as "rage-red." "It's a limitation of cloning, not training, you brainless little lust demon. And it's a roadblock that I will soon eliminate."

My eyes narrow. Human cloning only duplicates the body. Based on what Ethan said, magical cloning must involve trying to replicate memories as well. *Interesting.*

Ethan goes over to the wall to the right of the viewing window, holds up his binoculars, and twists a few dials on the viewing device. Instantly, a console appears on the wall.

I nod once to myself. *Definitely a control room.*

Ethan starts fiddling with the dials at the top of the wall. "Regular DNA doesn't capture the memories and skills of the original."

"You're looking to copy memories and skills too."

There's a long pause before Ethan finally answers. "Yes."

For the record, I'm really happy that Ethan is finally sharing a little information, but I'm not too pleased about the content here. Because if he wants to record and duplicate someone's battle skills, then Lincoln is the best thrax around to clone. I rest my hand against my belly.

Except for maybe our child. With my battle skills and Lincoln's strategic mind, Maxon might be an even finer warrior one day. Is that Ethan's endgame? He said he wants to raise our Maxon. No doubt, he wants to brainwash my child to be the number one player on Team Ethan. It makes sense for him to want an army of super-powerful warriors as followers. Still, that doesn't explain what Ethan wants with demons. That part of the plan still doesn't make any sense.

There isn't time to ponder this mystery because Ethan is pounding on more buttons on the new wall console. "Damned system is still locked down," grumbles Ethan.

I can't help but grin. The system is still locked down? That means Cissy and Zeke didn't fix CHUCK yet. They must be stalling. Go, Cissy and Zeke.

"Ah, here we go." Ethan presses more buttons. "Functional again."

Or not. I sure hope my friends are okay.

Ethan points to the glass wall. "Have a look."

I follow his gesture, scanning past the glass and into the space beyond. Directly below our viewing area, I notice a spotlight illuminate two large tanks that rest against the far wall. One is red while the other's black. They remind me of the two canisters I first saw in the lab with Williamson, only much larger.

As Ethan keeps pushing buttons, a safety light starts revolving above the red tank.

Ethan grumbles as he keeps pushing buttons. Is it wishful thinking, or does it seem like the system isn't working for him the way that it should? Could Cissy and Zeke still be fine and hacking?

"Let the show begin," announces Ethan. "And please know that this is all your doing."

I narrow my eyes. "What is, exactly?"

"This." Ethan pounds a final code into the wall. Across the clone room floor, the top of the red tank disappears, releasing a cloud of crimson haze. The smoke takes on the pattern of howling faces as it races around the room. I set my hand on my throat. Smoke taking the form of a face? That's definitely magic.

I step closer, trying for a better look at the features of the misty face. My body freezes with shock.

It's Armageddon, the King of Hell. There's no mistaking that long face and blade-like nose.

All of a sudden, it makes perfect sense how Ethan could duplicate demons so easily but not anyone angelic. The king of all demons was helping him. And Armageddon is forever making side deals and laying secret plans. Somehow, the King of Hell has gotten himself embedded into Ethan's operation. I wonder what pack of lies Armageddon told Ethan to convince the thrax leader to clone demons. Like there aren't enough of those already.

Screams reverberate from the room below. I step closer to the viewing wall; the guards follow. I pause, pressing my palm against the panel of glass. The mist turns so thick, all I can see is a red haze.

The high-pitched drone of an alarm sounds from the room below. Again, the system reminds me of the Ghost Towers back home. Once the mist reaches a certain saturation level, the auto processes kick in and literally clear the air.

The hum of fans sounds as the room below begins to clear. Little by little, a terrible view comes into focus. Smashed glass pillars. Immobile demon bodies. Faces contorted in pain.

Dead. They're all dead.

And they're not the only ones, either. "You killed your own guards."

"Why shouldn't I?"

I round on him. "You're a thrax. There's no honor in killing the defenseless." Another piece of my Queenly role falls into place. "It's even more awful when you're murdering your own people. They rely on you, and—" I'm not sure what that reliance means yet, though. Well, beyond the obvious. I wag my finger at them. "And you can't just go around killing them!"

"Those Razor Guards just died for a good cause."

I can't believe what I'm hearing. "And what's that?"

"Making a point to you, Myla Lewis." He steps closer and grins his Chiclet smile. "Do not fuck with me again. If I do this to my own loyal people, what will I do to you?"

A chill crawls over my skin. "You really believe that killing is worth it, just to impress me?"

"Of course." He nods to one of the guards behind me, and I feel not one but two guns against my spine. Ethan gestures toward the door. "Your husband awaits."

My stomach flip-flops. Part of me is thrilled by the idea of seeing Lincoln again. More of me feels terrified by what I'll find. Once again, I reach out for Iggy's hand without thinking. He's been calming me for so long, and I've never missed our connection more than now.

A soothing warmth spreads over my palm. Maybe it's my imagination, but I swear, I can sense Iggy with me. The feeling is gone too quickly to be certain, though.

Within seconds, the whole episode with Iggy vanishes from my mind as our little group makes its way down the labyrinth of passages to wherever-the-Hell they're keeping my Lincoln. With every step, I try to soak in my surroundings, just as my father taught me. Releasing the demons in the clone room didn't work, but something else will come up. It simply has to.

I won't accept anything less, not for Lincoln...

And definitely not for our baby.

25

*E*than and his guards force-march me through more artery-style hallways. As we walk along, I take care to look slump-shouldered and pathetic. Ethan is done blabbing plans—at least for now—so it gives me a chance to take stock of my situation.

On the negative side, my Scala robes are useless against human guns, Iggy is gone, and Ethan's a dick.

On the positive side, at least my tail is still free. Plus, it's hanging at an odd angle to look broken. It's one of our best battle ruses.

Long story short, I still have a shot here.

Our small group pauses by a nondescript stretch of passageway. Once again, Ethan lifts his binoculars and points them toward a particular stretch of wall. Within seconds, a round portal opens. My heart leaps into my throat.

This is it.

I'm finally about to find out what's happened to Lincoln.

The world takes on a dreamlike quality as I step through the round portal and into another lab room. Like the ones back at Times Square, the space is medium-sized, pod-like, and made of white plastic. Again, I have that creepy sensation that I'm stepping inside an egg. Two lab tables sit in the middle of the room. Behind them, there stands another pair of tall metal pillar-style structures, one black and one red. Tubing snakes out from each and locks into the base of both tables. This is just like the lab I saw with Felton Weiner. Black puts the subject to sleep. Red kills them.

My gaze locks onto the left-hand table? Every nerve in my body goes on alert.

That's Lincoln.

I move close with halting steps. After the last catastrophe with Evil Lincoln, can this really be my guy?

"Don't move any closer," warns Ethan.

But this is my Lincoln! I step closer anyway.

A chorus of clicks sound behind me as more guns cock and the guards prepare to shoot. Some small part of my mind knows I should worry, but I can't focus on anything but the immobile form lying before me.

My love.

The other half of my heart.

The father of our child.

I stop by the lab table. One of those curved glass coffin-tops covers the surface. Under it, there's Lincoln. His eyes are closed. The lines of his ribs and collarbones jut out from his body. Deep cuts and bruises cover his arms and chest. He still wears only the low-hanging jeans that he slipped on before reading the letter from Ethan.

That was a few days and a million years ago.

It takes everything in me not to step closer. Just a few more feet and I'd be able to touch the glass. "Lincoln? Is it you?"

His eyes open a crack. "Myla." His voice sounds hoarse and dry. "I knew you'd come."

"I'm here." I clench and unclench my hands. My fingers itch to stroke his cheek.

"Family reunion is over. Turn around." That's Ethan speaking behind me, which is both bad and good news.

The bad news is that Ethan's breath is fanning out across my neck.

The good news is that I don't feel a gun at my ribs anymore. I slowly shift to face Ethan, taking care to scan the room as I go. There are seven Razor Guards here along with their Supreme Leader. I'm sure Ethan would have liked more guards in tow, but this isn't that big of a space. All of them have reholstered their guns.

They aren't expecting a fight. That's the best news of all.

Ethan hitches his thumb. "Get on your table."

I shoot a quick glance at Lincoln. My guy gives me the barest shake of his head. I know what that means. *Don't get on the table.* I totally agree.

I fold my arms over my chest. "No."

Ethan chuckles. "I'm going to explain things to you once, nicely. After that, it will get very uncomfortable in here. Do you understand me?"

"English is my first language, Ethan."

"You have one chance." Ethan gestures toward Lincoln. "Your husband hasn't been willing in giving up his soul. I don't like that. I've tested hundreds of thrax; none have his unique angelic qualities. I even tried to clone him so I could drain those units, but cloning angelic material has proven trickier than demonic."

"Especially considering how your trick with demonic cloning is to ask the King of Hell for help."

"As I said before, I only rely on the best." A smug grin winds across Ethan's round face. "Now, if Lincoln willingly gives me his soul, then you can enjoy a comfortable life until the baby is born."

"And after the child is here?"

"I have a rigorous training program in mind for him. He'll be my heir and strongest supporter. And yes, I may need to drain your son at age eighteen—that's when our systems work best—but I plan to have my angelic cloning program perfected by then. Rest assured, some version of your offspring will always be alive and well on Earth."

I can't believe this guy. "And what about me?"

"Once you've given birth, you'll be drained as well. Willingly."

"And that's your super-awesome offer? Lincoln dies now, and I live comfortably until you can take your baby away from me? Oh yeah, and then you'll raise our kid to be a brain-washed nutjob, but hey, he'll probably get cloned, so bonus! Am I missing anything?"

Ethan's mouth thins with determination. "Your family is the key to my plans. I need angelic soul power. Between the three of you, I'll have enough to drive my realm forever."

My eyes widen. The words *"realm forever"* echo through my consciousness. Fresh connections form between the bits of information I've been able to gather. The clone room… Armageddon… How Evil Lincoln said that Ethan will perfect humanity and the thrax… And now Ethan's hopes for an eternal Earthly realm. "You're trying to create your own puppet demons to cause trouble. That's what all the news reports were about. But you're also cloning Razor Guards to fight them. Why?"

"Get on the table." Those are the words that Ethan says, but I know what he really means.

I'm getting closer to his real plans.

I glance over to Lincoln. He gives me the barest of nods. That means he's thinking the same thing I am. *Keep pushing.*

"You need angelic power to do more than drive your machines," I continue. "This is about mind control."

"I don't know what you're talking about." But Ethan says it so quickly, it's clear that I'm on the right track.

"You already have plenty of power for your tech toys. You need something extra."

"Don't be ridiculous."

"You forget I'm demonic and angelic. I've seen this at work. My friend Zeke can easily control human minds, and he's not all that strong. Angels can do something similar as well." I point at my poor husband. "No one is a better leader than my Lincoln. He doesn't consciously use his angelic nature to manipulate people, but everyone senses his inner nobility just the same. You want to control both the evil and the good in mortals. Right now, you have some fine demons, but your Ethan clones? They're the same as humans."

Ethan narrows his eyes. "Not for long."

"That's what you really want our angelic souls for, isn't it? You want to place that angel power inside one of your own clones. With that, your Razor Guards can become more than human."

Ethan mock-bows. "My, my. You're slightly less brainless than I thought. You've hit on the one mistake most leaders make through history: controlling only their own side. You see, I failed out of thrax warrior training, but the entire concept of the thrax is outdated. It's time to bring forth a new kind of demon and thrax, both controlled by a single ruler. I must manipulate the so-called good leaders as well as the evil. I already have the greatest power of evil."

"Meaning Armageddon helped you with your demonic cloning program."

Ethan's eyes narrow. "Why would I settle for less than the best? Now, I need a thrax's power to offset Armageddon's on Earth. Trust me, I've tried tons of souls. The angelic energy from each one was minimal at best. All this time, and I've only gotten enough power to create one thrax clone."

A sick feeling crawls up my throat. "How many thrax did you have to kill to create the single clone of Lincoln? Hundreds?"

"They were all sacrificed for a good cause. And now, I need more power if I'm to move forward."

"With whatever happens tonight at Touch The Tech. You mentioned this to the Earls before... This will be your first demon patrol with them."

"Precisely."

My thoughts start to churn over what that demon patrol really is, but I can only think about the trouble we're in right now.

Ethan stares longingly at my stomach. "Our futures all rely on the baby you carry. I'll craft him into my ultimate source of angelic power." He snaps to his guards. "Strap her in."

The guards pounce on me so fast, I don't even notice it coming. And for me, that's saying something. Seven of them hold me down, and even I have issues with those numbers.

The guards start to haul me to the table. I struggle against their hold, but it's no use. I howl with rage. After everything we tried, I'm still here, in Ethan's damned lab. He's going to get exactly what he wants.

Bastard.

My screams rouse Lincoln. He pounds on the glass. "I'll do it! I'll give you my soul."

Ethan rolls his eyes. "Finally." He turns to me. "And what do you have to say to that?"

My thoughts speed through more options. We're out of time. According to Ethan, my only future is where I get strapped down to watch my husband die.

I can't allow that to happen. There must be something else.

Focus, Myla. Think!

A plan materializes in my mind. It's crazy and will involve physical battle, which I've been carefully avoiding up until now. But desperate times and all that. We need to get out of here.

My gaze locks with Lincoln's. For the barest second, I make a face to him like I'm holding my breath. He gives me another slight nod in return. A sense of joy bubbles up through my rib cage. One puffy-cheeked look, and my guy totally guesses what I've got planned.

Damn, but I've missed him.

"Myla." Ethan taps his foot. "I asked you a question. Do you agree with your husband giving up his soul?" Ethan stares straight at me, his mismatched eyes shining with glee. The creep is enjoying this way too much for his own good.

"Here's what I think," I say slowly. "You should have taken away my Scala robes and put at least two guards on my tail." As it stands, there's only one warrior holding down my backside. And that guy has a really weak grip.

I scan the bandaged faces of the guards around me. "Sorry to have to kill you and all, but you really shouldn't mess with a pregnant lady."

Within my soul, I release my powers of demonic wrath. Every movement becomes so fast, it's a blur. My tail skewers the guard holding it, then arcs forward to take out two more guards by spearing their chests. Meanwhile, I leap up and kick another guard in the throat, snapping his neck. I pull his own gun from its holster, spin about, and shoot the other three guards in quick succession.

Ethan opens the door, calls for more guards, and hightails it out of the room. It's about the most cowardly retreat I've ever seen.

More guards rush toward me. There isn't much time to stop them. I leap through the air, aiming to land on the black canister. Along the way, I make sure to drag my tail across the top of Lincoln's glass coffin. The top gets smashed to bits. Lincoln jumps down from the table.

At the same time, I land atop the black canister and rake the arrowhead end of my tail down the side. Black smoke billows out of the container while I command my Scala robes to transform into a hazmat suit.

As more of the dark mist fills the room, Lincoln attacks the nearest Razor Guard. My guy's cheeks are slightly puffed, just like I showed him.

Lincoln has been holding his breath.

The other guards didn't, so they quickly turn sluggish and wobbly. There's still a lot of them in here, though. I join the battle beside Lincoln. Everything becomes a blur of fighting. My tail snaps a guard's neck. Another enemy warrior tries to grab me, but Lincoln nails him with a roundhouse kick to the head. A few more shoot off their weapons, but their aim is crap. The black mist grows heavier. One by one, the guards drop to the ground.

Through the darkening smoke, I see Lincoln rush over to the table and fiddles with the outtake valves. An alarm sounds.

Fans whir into action. The black smoke quickly clears from the room.

Thank Heaven for air.

With the breathing situation sorted out, I make a quick inspection of the room. All the guards lie immobile on the floor. Did we kill them all?

Ethan is nowhere in sight. Tricky bastard.

I step over to the nearest Razor Guard and set my fingers on his neck. There's no pulse. A heavy sense of dread weighs into my bones. It's terrible to take any life. I pull down the black bandages covering his face. Yup, more Ethan clones. I scan the room. Where's the real deal anyway?

"Did you see where Ethan went?" I ask.

"After he let the last round of guards, Ethan snuck out." Lincoln's hands ball into fists. "We need to find Ethan and kill him." His body shivers with fury. "The things he's done..."

I pause. This isn't like my Lincoln at all. "What do you mean? You want to just kill him without bringing him to justice?"

Please, please, please, tell me I didn't free another clone.

Lincoln gives me the side eye. "Whatever I do, it will always be with full appreciation for thrax law and custom."

I grin. That's my guy, all right.

I start hauling the boots off the nearest guard. "Now, we need to change into Razor Guard outfits and get out of here."

Lincoln keeps glaring at the bodies. "The things Ethan has done are beyond the pale. All the thrax I sent to Earth? He drained their souls to make a single clone."

"And he will pay." I step up to Lincoln and cup his face in my hands. "But right now? We need to escape. If I know you, you've spent the last few days on nothing but recon, listening to guards or subtly pumping them for information. You know how to get us out of here. So let's do that, go back to Antrum, get a real army, and return to Earth and kick Ethan's ass properly."

A muscle twitches along Lincoln's jaw. "It's too dangerous to wait. Who knows if we'll get another chance at Ethan?" He scans the downed bodies. "Some of these guards have binoculars. I know how to use them in order to open a secret passage out of this room. We can follow Ethan easily. I'm sure he's gone into the lower levels of the lab."

Oh, no. It takes a lot for my guy to turn into a mindless rage machine, but when it happens? Watch out. And unfortunately, I think that "rage machine" thing may be happening right now.

So, I do the only thing I can do. I call in the big guns.

Taking Lincoln's palm, I set it onto my stomach. "Get us out of here, Lincoln. Please."

Lincoln's gaze finally locks with mine. Bit by bit, the fury drains from his eyes. "Myla."

"That's right." I rest my hand against his cheek. "Me and the baby. We're here."

"So you are." He leans into my touch. "I know another clone room we can use to access the surface. It will take us back to LaGuardia."

"Fine. More Manus demons. I can handle that."

"It might be Manus or anything, really. Ethan's been cloning every demonic type there is, looking for the perfect puppets." Lincoln starts stripping a uniform off one of the Razor Guards.

"Demon, shmeemon. I know every bad guy in the book." I command my Scala robes into thin underarmor and starting pulling the clothes off a Razor Guard. Turns out, stripping a melty-faced Ethan lookalike is about as disgusting as it sounds. It's over soon enough, though. Within minutes, Lincoln and I are both disguised as Razor Guard disguises.

Lincoln approaches nearby wall and lifts a pair of binoculars to his face.

"Tell me you know how to use those," I say.

"I know how to use them." After that, Lincoln twists some dials. Black sparks fly out from the device. Part of it melts in his hand.

I frown. "Is that supposed to happen?" I'd seen other folks use the binoculars, like Albinia. Iggy made the things melt, but I'd never seen sparks fly before.

Lincoln runs his fingers over the device. "No, this must be some side effect of the draining process. My angelic energy got linked somehow to these metal.."

I snap my fingers. "Williamson said something like that before. He was placed into one of these draining coffins." Reaching under my Scala robes, I pull out the arrowhead that I had stashed by my collarbone. It's a little mushed, but still in pretty good shape. "I found him before he died and he'd almost crushed one of Ethan's arrowheads."

Lincoln arches his brows. "You found Williamson?"

"Long story." I reset the arrowhead under my robes while nervous energy zings through me. How often do those patrols check this area anyway? It feels like we've been hanging out here for too long. I bounce a little on the balls of my feet. "We should get going."

"Agreed. I'll use a gentler touch this time." Lincoln scoops up a fresh pair of binoculars from one of the downed guards. This time, when he fiddles with the dials, the portal door swirls open, revealing another all-white corridor. "This is the fastest path. Least trafficked as well."

It's a somewhat inappropriate thought to have at this

moment, but I think the fact that Lincoln did all this recon while trapped in a glass coffin is kinda hot. What can I say? I'm part lust demon.

I nod toward the hallway. "Any guards in there?"

"No," replies Lincoln. "They don't patrol these areas, but they do have cameras everywhere. So we need to go through this hallway and the adjoining clone room quickly. Otherwise, it will look suspicious."

"Got it."

For the record, it's hard to talk with these face bandages on. Even worse, the Ethan clone that I lifted them from had some nasty bad breath. Yet another reason to put this whole experience behind me.

Together, Lincoln and I step into hallway and jog until the passageway appears to hit a dead end. Lincoln lifts his binoculars again, and a door appears. We cross the threshold; the portal door closes behind us with another *swoosh*.

We step into another clone room. This is a huge space but without any cloning tanks. Odd, but what do I care? Maybe they haven't built the tanks yet or something. My heart beats double-time in my chest.

We're so close now.

All we have to do is cross this chamber, and freedom is ours. As we step forward, I can really focus on the details of the room. What I see makes every nerve in my body go on alert.

This chamber is another black pod-like room like the last one. Only here, the walls are lined with the cloning tanks, not the floor. Unfortunately, each glass pillar holds the same kind of demon, over and over.

Armageddon.

Hells bells.

This is the classic-looking King of Hell: tall and long-limbed with a short torso and long limbs. The elongated face holds a blade-like nose and pointed chin. The only difference I see between these clone Armageddons and the real deal? Their skin is a dull and pasty gray instead of shiny and black as polished stone.

Not much of a comfort.

Ugh. Just when I thought things were looking up, I now have to walk through a room of Armageddon clones. If I thought escape was tricky before, that was nothing compared to this. No doubt, Armageddon had no qualms giving some of his life force to these duplicates. And even if they only hold a smidgeon of the King of Hell's power, these lookalikes could do a lot of damage. On such occasions, there's only one thing a girl can say.

Fuck-fuck-fuckity-FUCK-fuck.

26

*L*incoln gently touches my upper arm. I know he wants to hold me, but I also get that we're dressed up as Razor Guards and about to walk across a clone room floor with about a million hidden cameras watching us.

Since all the Razor Guards are Ethan clones, they probably aren't too touchy-feely as a rule. Best to play it cool here.

"What's the plan?" he asks.

"Where's the exit to LaGuardia?"

"Far wall, third portal from the left."

"In that case," I whisper, "we walk slowly across the floor, looking like we're picking up an extra patrol."

"Long walk."

I carefully scan the room. The Armageddon clones are stacked up on the walls eight stories high. The storage room floor looks about five hundred yards long. Lincoln has a point. I don't even want to think about how many Armageddons we have to pass here.

Besides, I've never been good at thinking. I'm more of an "act now" kind of girl. "Let's get started then."

Stepping in unison, Lincoln and I start across the clone room floor. Our shiny thigh-high boots make snapping noises on the metal floor. I scan the space carefully. The room itself appears to be made from one continuous sheet of Ethan's special metal—all of it must be infused with black magic. It makes sense, though. Ethan must have needed a lot of black magic to make so many Armageddons. The thought of so many close by makes my skin crawl.

Don't think about the demons, Myla. You have to escape.

We pass the first one hundred yards with no problem. I exhale.

This might actually be easier than I thought. Only four hundred yards to go.

As we head toward the center of the room, a sense of unease crawls up my spine. Standing near the real Armageddon is no picnic. Unfortunately, these clones seem to have picked up some of his greater demon aura. Without meaning to, I speed my pace.

Is it my imagination, or are these clones staring at me?

I shiver. It must be my imagination.

Lincoln brushes my wrist. "Steady now."

I nod and slow down again. We can't do anything strange, or the security cameras might pick it up. I focus on the opposite side of the room. The door we want is getting closer by the second. To the right of it, there stand the same two massive pillars that the last clone room had: one red and one black. When Ethan killed all his own guards and demons, he released gas from the red canister.

Good to know that even Ethan has a backup plan here.

It's when we reach the halfway mark that the small hairs on the back of my neck stand on end.

Someone's watching.

On reflex, I scan the Armageddon clones. Moving as one unit, they all open their eyes and stare right at me. Man, do those things ever look like the real deal: short torso wrapped in a tux...gangly arms with three-knuckled fingers...and most of all, a long face with a blade-like nose. Except for the gray skin, these are all perfect replicas of Armageddon.

This time I'm certain. No way I'm imagining things. All the eyes flare red as they follow the two of us across the floor.

My pulse skyrockets. If these clones have some of Armageddon's power, do they have some of his memories as well? In other words, do they know how much they freaking hate me?

My money is on *Hell yes*.

We reach two hundred yards, and I'm sweating up a storm inside this Razor Guard uniform. Those thousand sets of Armageddon eyes aren't helping any, either. With every step, I suppress the urge to run.

That's when it happens.

All the Armageddons tilt their heads as a thousand of them speak at once: "Hello, Myla Lewis."

Crash! The clones leap through their glass cases and race for Lincoln and me at full tilt.

Fuuuuuuuuuuuuuuck!

Lincoln and I run full out for the far wall. I keep my gaze locked on the red canister. "That's not too far from the exit. I can spear it with my tail." And by spearing it, I'll release a deadly gas, but I'm figuring I don't need to add that part.

A pair of Armageddon clones leaps for us. My tail bats the

first away; Lincoln dodges the second, so it lands on the floor nearby. Taken together, those two attacks mean one thing.

At this rate, there's no way we'll reach the red canister, let alone the exit door. We need another plan. My thoughts speed through everything I know about Ethan and his schemes.

For some reason, Williamson's final words echo through my mind.

"This may help our king."

When Williamson spoke those words, he was holding a crushed-up arrowhead. I'd only thought about it as a keepsake, but now? This projectile could open a portal to who-cares-where, assuming Lincoln can activate one again. And if it *is* functioning, the arrowhead could take the Armageddons away, not my Lincoln.

Thankfully, I still have that crushed-up arrowhead. I pull it out from its resting place under my Scala robes. "I have one of these."

Lincoln's eyes glint with recognition. He opens his mouth to speak, but before a word leaves his lips, another pair of Armageddons lunges for us. My tail skewers one through the chest. Lincoln punches the other in the throat.

This isn't going well.

"We can use that to create another transport portal," says Lincoln. "All the arrowheads send captives to the same holding pen. They can be transferred back, but at least it will give us some time to escape."

"Assuming we can keep it from dragging us in, too."

At these words, more memories flicker through my mind. Williamson had smashed the arrowhead in his hand. A few minutes ago, Lincoln almost squashed one of the binoculars by mistake. Both of those things were made from Ethan's black magic metal. Lincoln had said that being in the glass coffins may have changed the way he interacts with the stuff.

"Lincoln, this floor is made from that black metal stuff."

A small smile rounds Lincoln's mouth. "Right. Toss the arrowhead as far away as you can."

"Will it work if I do it?" I'd been thinking Lincoln was the easy bet.

"Anyone with angelic power can activate it. Ethan does that for his guards." Just focus on it opening the portal as you throw it. The magic will do the rest." Lincoln scans the floor. "While you do that, I'll make sure we don't get sucked in."

"Got it."

For the record, a major benefit of having done so many demon patrols with Lincoln is we rarely give super-long speeches on battle plans. Just a few sentences, and Lincoln and I know exactly what to do. In this case, I know exactly how to chuck this arrowhead. I grip the item more tightly in my palm.

One portal to who-cares-where, coming right up.

I toss the arrowhead over my shoulder. My tail catches it and then flings the projectile toward the south wall, snapping like a whip. The arrowhead sails over the demons' heads. A moment later, it lodges in one of the empty cloning pods. For a moment, nothing happens.

Crud.

Suddenly, a wall of black flame erupts from the other side of the chamber. I let out a whoop of joy. The dark fire rolls across the room, heating everything but burning nothing.

The black magic of the arrowhead is working.

Only this time, it's to our benefit.

The Armageddons stop their pursuit to screech and howl. The flames aren't burning them, so I guess the yelling is just on principle. Once the fire dies down, I can see that one of the oval cloning pods is now nothing but an empty hole in the far wall. Just like last time, the world seems to tilt. The far wall becomes the floor. Everything begins to tumbles into the new vortex on the center of that "floor."

And by everything, I mean a lot of broken glass and Armageddons.

My tail spikes through the floor, holding me in place. Meanwhile, Lincoln rams his fists through the floor. Like the binoculars, the metal crumbles for him easily. A second later, Lincoln has a firm set of handholds. Gravity and wind start pulling us toward the hole in the opposite wall. We've only a few hundred yards to go before we reach the exit door.

The howl of wind quickly turns deafening. I can barely hear Lincoln over the din. "Grab on to me!"

I must admit, I like this plan.

My tail acts like a hinge, arcing me over so I can latch onto Lincoln's back. I loop my arms around his shoulders and my legs about his hips. My tail snakes around his waist as well. Lincoln's back quivers under my torso. My guy has been locked up and tortured for days. Is he really strong enough to drag us out of here?

The wind whips faster around us. My long Razor Guard coat snaps in the quickening gale. With a mighty cry, Lincoln lifts his right arm and jams it into the floor, only this time, the hole is a little closer to the door. Lincoln is dragging us across the floor. Love it.

"Keep going," I cry. "You're doing great."

Crunch…Lincoln tears another hole in the floor and pulls us nearer to the door. After that, his rhythm grows quicker. The cries of the Armageddons sound below us as more tumble into the new vortex on the far wall. Lights begin flashing in all corners of the room. A woman's voice sounds over hidden loudspeakers.

"CHUCK master system alert. CHUCK master system alert."

I frown. That voice sounded like... But it couldn't be...

Was that Cissy?

The last time I saw my bestie and Zeke, they were being dragged off to undo whatever Cissy did to CHUCK, Ethan's master computer system. Later on, Ethan complained that he still couldn't get access. Heck, Ethan even acted like the interface had changed. But now Cissy could be doing announcements for CHUCK?

What the WHAT?

Lincoln keeps pounding his hands into the metal flooring. Turns out, the metal floor is way heavier and thicker than the binoculars. It's positively shredding Lincoln's skin. My guy's knuckles turn raw as red meat. Blood trickles down his arms.

But we're almost at the exit.

At last, Lincoln grips the metal beside the round door. Raising his fist, he punches the button to open the exit. Concentric circles swipe over each other as the door opens, reminding me of the shutter on an old-fashioned camera. Lincoln heaves us inside. I regain my footing and stand up straight again. The effect of the vortex is muted here. It feels good to have gravity back where it belongs. I'm about to breath a sigh of relief when one of the Armageddons leaps toward us through the opened doorway. Damned thing was using Lincoln's old handholds to trail us.

My tail does the honors, smacking the button and closing the portal. Based on what Lincoln heard from the guards, this door and passageway definitely lead to LaGuardia. The Armageddon who was leaping toward us gets trapped as the concentric circles closed up again. The demon gets sliced in two. Ick.

I make my tail tear out the big red button and a ton of wires along with it. No one else is getting through that door.

"This way," says Lincoln. He gestures toward another artery-style hallway. Unlike the main cloning room, this thing is made from black plastic.

"You sure?"

"This is the path. A few guards and then we're clear."

Ignoring the half-of-an-Armageddon, we run into the new passage. For the record, there are a ton of Razor Guards here. At least ten block our escape.

Damn.

I've gotten this far without breaking my "no fighting because of the baby" rule. Do I really have to do this now?

As it turns out, I don't.

Lincoln has kept two slabs of the black metal from the floor of the cloning room. He's turned them into makeshift boxing gloves, which he now uses to beat the pulp out of all ten guards in less than two minutes.

You have to appreciate the beautiful things in life. Watching Lincoln in a long black jacket pulverize bad guys is definitely one of those beautiful things. All too soon, the battle is over. I almost wish there were more Razor Guards to fight.

"This way," calls Lincoln.

We race down another artery-style hallway. Then another. Oh, and about sixteen more after that. Each time, I rip out the mechanism so no one can follow us. We're at about the twentieth hallway when Lincoln stops. "Let's take a breather. Are you all right?"

"You're here. I'm perfect."

Lincoln pulls me into his arms. "This feels so good." He nuzzles into my neck. "The whole time they were trying to pull out my soul, all I could think about was you and the baby. I knew you'd find me." He leans back and rests his forehead against mine. "And you did. Both of you."

"I had some help." My voice cracks as I think of Iggy again. More warmth spreads across my palm, right where we used to hold hands. I close my eyes and send out a message with my mind.

"Are you trying to contact me, Iggy?"

A thudding sounds on the other side of the door. I'm pretty sure I hear the rumble of Razor Guard voices accented by Armageddon's high-pitched laugher. Lincoln said the Armageddons could get transported back here from the holding pen. Looks like they didn't waste any time returning.

Uh-oh.

Lincoln and I share a knowing glance.

"Break time is over," I say.

"Agreed."

Hand in hand, we race down the corridor before us. I can only hope that at the end of this tunnel, I'll find LaGuardia and freedom.

Somehow, I doubt it's going to be as easy as that, though.

27

*W*e follow the passageways for what seems like hours, although I'm sure it's only a few minutes. At last, we reach a dead-end wall with a round door set into the middle. It's not a huge thing as doors go, and something about it reminds me of the Touch The Tech event. I run my fingertips over the arched metal surface. That's when it hits me.

"A tank." I grip the round handle. "This must lead to a tank."

Lincoln tilts his head. "What makes you say that? Aren't tank doors generally on the top of the vehicle?"

"You saw how Ethan's magic changed gravity before. Plus, the last portal I used was a port-a-potty at LaGuardia. The door always looked like a port-a-potty, even from this side." I pat the round handle. "This door looks like it leads to a tank."

"Touch The Tech." Lincoln nods slowly. "My guards were talking about it."

"For the record, you have really blabby guards."

Lincoln gives me a sly smile. "Every last one is a clone of Ethan, and that man was always a motor mouth."

"Truth."

Lincoln rubs his chin. "Do you remember where the tanks were?"

"Sure. The far right runway." While we'd been running along, Lincoln had quizzed me on everything I could remember about the layout of LaGuardia.

The intercom system buzzes to life again. Cissy's voice sounds once more. *"All personnel, prepare for attack. All personnel, prepare for attack."*

"There." I point to the nearest speaker. "Does that sound like Cissy or what?" Lincoln had been a little distracted last time, so he didn't really notice the voice in the Armageddon clone room.

"It does sound like her." Lincoln rubs his chin. "You said they took her and Zeke to the main computer system?"

"Yes, there was an access point to the master system set up at one of the tents at LaGuardia."

The voice sounds again. *"Leave me alone. No!"*

My skin freezes over with shock. "Okay, that was definitely Cissy and it sounds like she's in trouble."

"We need to get out of here," says Lincoln.

"Right." At this point, I'm wearing a green high-collared shirt, jodhpurs, and tall black boots. I have bandages jammed in my pocket, just in case I need to hide my face again. It feels creepy to walk around with my face bandaged up, even if it is a better disguise. Lincoln's in full Razor Guard gear. He'd lost his hat in the vortex, but found a replacement along the journey here.

Lincoln grips the round handle and starts turning it clockwise. "I'll go in first. Ethan could have one of his Razor Guards in the tank."

"Agreed." Before, I noticed a lot of guards outside the tanks and such, but no one was in there, waiting to start things up. That said, it's better to be cautious.

Lincoln finishes spinning the handle and pulls up on the small round door. It opens a crack. A stream of stale air whooshes into the hallway. Lincoln pauses, listening. I've no doubt that if anyone is in there, he can hear their breathing or whatever.

"It's clear," says Lincoln.

Stepping up, I peer into the opened portal and frown. Sure enough, the portal is in the wall, but it looks like we're looking down into the tank.

We climb inside. Lincoln takes the driver's seat. A series of clicks sound. I almost jump out of my skin.

"What was that?" I ask.

"I engaged the locking mechanism on the portal. This way, we won't have any unwanted visitors."

"Got it."

I decide to slip into the gunner's station. It's comfy as chairs go and has a large console with tons of buttons and a monitor. Not that I know how to use any of them. Lincoln peers through this periscope thing. The one place thrax go high-tech is one demon patrol. I know for a fact that Lincoln and his warriors use a similar periscope thingy to scope out the enemy while staying under cover. It's not usually attached to a tank, though. Still, I'll take whatever intel Lincoln can get. "Our path is clear. There are no guards around."

"That's odd." I frown. "All the vehicles had guards around them before." I keep hearing Cissy's "no" echoing through my mind. What is happening?

A small speaker inside the tank comes to life with a mechanical hiss. This time, a man's voice sounds inside the tank. *"All units with maintenance issues, report to runway five. All units with maintenance issues, report to runway five. H-E Launch starts in two minutes. Repeat, H-E Launch starts in two minutes."*

Lincoln's gaze stays locked on the periscope. "Some of the other tanks are driving away." He angles his head from side to side. "A few of the Humvees and vans are as well. This is our chance, Myla. We can escape. There's a Pulpitum in one of the closed-up hangars."

I hug my elbows. Isn't this what I wanted? Lincoln and I were going to escape LaGuardia, get back to Antrum, regroup, and return in force. At that point, we'd take down Ethan and his goons, easy-peasy. We could also be far more help to Cissy and Zeke if we had backup.

So why does escaping feel like the wrong move here?

The answer appears to me in a flash: the H-E Launch. It's what all of this has been about. It's why Lincoln was captured in the first place. This is the crux of Ethan's plans to take over both good and evil on Earth.

And it's starting in two minutes.

I stiffen my spine. "I don't want to leave, Lincoln."

He cranes his head to look at me. "What?"

"I want to stay for this H-E Launch."

"Myla. The baby."

I rub my hand over my stomach. "I've been thinking a lot lately. About what it means to be a wife and mother. I haven't really realized what it meant to be a Queen though. At first, I thought it was all about doing different projects."

"Such as improving our oxygen systems. That's important work."

"I know, but it's not leading. What Ethan's doing? It's

about the very definition of what it means to be thrax. He doesn't have all this tech out here for show. These are weapons of death and war. That's what he wants to bring to the human world. I can't leave the mortal world to that."

Lincoln stares at my belly as well. "This is a big decision, Myla."

I absently trace the image of an arrowhead on my stomach. The first time I saw one of Ethan's arrowheads, it was in the library of our honeymoon palace. The thing looked completely foreign then. Who sends arrowheads to their King? It was an odd symbol from one of our subjects. I felt completely separated from my role as Queen of the thrax.

Then Williamson handed me the crumpled-up arrowhead that he'd stolen while helping me escape from Antrum. At that point, the arrowhead came to mean something else entirely. Williamson had offered me that arrowhead because he wanted to help Lincoln and me. And he did help us. Lincoln and I would never have gotten past all those Armageddons without the knowledge that Williamson brought us. Watching Williamson die on that laboratory table, I felt a deep sense of responsibility settle into my bones. I had to save Williamson and others from a similar fate at the hands of Ethan.

"This is about more than stopping Ethan," I say slowly.

Lincoln's gaze turns intense. "How so?"

"This baby is my child. But he's also my subject. I want to bring him into a world where being thrax is something to be proud of. Ethan is going to bring death and destruction to the human world, I know it. And it will forever stain what it means to be a thrax. That kind of dark future is something I'm willing to fight against. I believe our son would want that too."

There's something even bigger at stake. I open my mouth,

trying to find the right words. None appear. I huff out a frustrated breath.

"Give yourself time, Myla. I'm listening."

I give Lincoln a shaky smile. "Thank you."

For a moment, my finger keeps retracing the image of the arrowhead on my belly. *That's where the future lies, and in more ways than one.* My tail slips over my stomach, placing my real arrowhead end onto the outline that I'd drawn. With that, I know exactly what I have to do.

"Here's the thing, Lincoln. I see a thrax future where we adhere to traditions, but we also open ourselves up to being more understanding of other peoples and cultures. Our baby will be more than thrax. Our people need to open their eyes to other cultures as well." I roll my eyes. "I know it sounds naive and simplistic."

Lincoln's attention is riveted to my every word. "Not to me, it doesn't."

"I know it will take time, too. Many lifetimes, maybe."

"Some fights are worth it."

I grip the gunner controls before me. "In that case, I think we should stay, Lincoln. The first step to a joint understanding of our peoples is for you and I to fight injustice together, as quasi and thrax."

The voice comes out on the speaker again. *"Units with maintenance issues, this is your last chance to leave. Units with maintenance issues, this is your last chance to leave."*

Lincoln's gaze connects with mine. Invisible arcs of love and fear seem to move between us.

"If you want to leave, I'll respect that." I straighten my shoulders. "But I really want to stay and fight."

"And I want to battle at your side," says Lincoln. "For all thrax, including our Maxon." The igni told me they wanted our son named after the last Great Scala. The guy was old as dirt when I met him, but he'd been with the igni for a thousand years. They loved the man. We were proud to pass on the name.

My eyes well with held-in tears. "Including our Maxon."

Ethan's voice sounds on the loudspeakers outside. *"Thank you all for joining my Touch The Tech Event."*

Something in Ethan's voice sets my nerves on edge. My warrior sense goes berserk. The monitor before me crackles to life. On it, I see a live video of Ethan that's being broadcast from the H-E TV Channel.

The man has his own television channel? Why am I not surprised?

An older white guy in a gray suit acts the announcer. He holds a microphone in his left hand, while his right presses on his ear piece. Beside him, Ethan stands beside him in his gas station onesie. All around, crowds are streaming and cheering.

The old dude announcer stares lovingly at Ethan. "What an amazing event," he says into his mic. "I didn't think people could learn to love Hunter Enterprises any more than they already did, but boy oh boy! You can sure feel the excitement here."

Ethan grins his gap-toothed Chiclet smile. "It's certainly been another triumph for H-E." His beady eyes widen. "But wait! What can this be? Are those actual demons at my event?" He points across the tarmac, and sure enough, some of the gray-skinned Armageddons are strolling about. These must be some of the ones that transported back after we hovered them away. Argh. Even worse, the humans can see them.

And they're freaking the fuck out.

Screams resound from the monitor. People rush about in

every direction. Their terrified voices reverberate through the tank as well.

Lincoln and I share a shocked glance. "He didn't..." I can't even finish the sentence. It's one of the basic rules of the after-realms that humans do not see angels and demons. That would take away their free will.

"He did," says Lincoln. "Ethan combined humans and Armageddon clones in order to make something that would be visible to the mortal world. I should have suspected something when we saw the gray Armageddons. An accurate clone would have had stone-smooth skin that was much darker. These had flesh that was almost human."

"So Ethan wants humans to see demons. The bigger question is...why?"

On the monitor, I see Ethan grab the microphone from the announcer. "There's no need for panic. As you know, Hunter Enterprises has suspected demonic activity for some time. We have imbued a protective substance into all the black metal products we create. They'll soon flare up with a bit of dark fire. Don't worry—it won't burn you. But it will make you ready to accept what happens next."

My stomach sinks to my toes. I have a yucky suspicion what happens next. It's got to involve all the high-tech weaponry on this tarmac.

Sure enough, small plumes of black flame erupt throughout the crowd behind Ethan. I remember seeing all the black magic hardware on the vid screens from Times Square, including the runway models' jewelry and the swimmer's breathing apparatus. Hell, even my doc's stethoscope in the hospital was made of the stuff.

Now, it's all flaring with dark fire. A moment later, everyone turns eerily calm. The crowds stop screaming. On my monitor, all the faces turn toward Ethan. Pure adoration gleams out from their eyes.

Lincoln shakes his head. "Even the announcer's microphone flared up for a moment."

I rub my neck as I think. "But none of the equipment lit up."

"He's casting a spell on every human who's got H-E tech."

"In other words, he's casting spell on everyone." I grip my neck so hard, I wonder if I'll bruise. "What is his plan here?"

On the small screen, Ethan opens his arms wide. "Behold, my Razor Guard! Now, not all of you have been exposed to the glory of H-E. But those of you who know me, realize that when I speak, I am infallible. My Razor Guards can protect you from the upcoming demonic invasion…and yes, millions of demons will be upon us soon!"

At these words, most of the crowd stands dumbfounded. I watch onscreen as a few dozen humans start to race for the exits. They are quickly apprehended by the Razor Guards.

I tap the screen with my fingernail. "His spell doesn't affect everyone."

"Maybe some humans don't have tech from H-E in their lives. That's how he spread the magic."

I nod, remembering the images I saw at Times Square. "Humans use jewelry from H-E, ventilators, you name it. But no system is perfect. Most people will believe anything Ethan has to say, though."

Once again, the Ethan on my monitor opens his big yap. "My Razor Guards will now restore order and protect you from this terrible demonic threat. Prepare for them to temporarily take over all governments until we have the situation well in hand."

I smack my lips. Temporarily? He's so full of it.

"Now some of you may not be as familiar with Hunter Enterprises. That's understandable. In fact, to you my Razor Guards may seem a bit daunting. But never fear. Our troops are undergoing training. Soon, every last one of you will be compelled to love them as much as you would, say, an angel."

My mouth falls open. That's his plan to catch the extra humans who weren't affected by his spell. *"Love them as much as an angel?"* I repeat. "Ethan is saying that because he plans to remove our angelic power and place it into the Razor Guards." I let out a low groan. "He hasn't given up on draining us, you know."

Lincoln rubs his neck slowly. That's one of his moves that means he's thinking something over. "Still, the fact that Ethan doesn't have our angelic influence isn't stopping H-E from trying to take over the human world." Lincoln looks at me over his shoulder and grins. "That's why you're going to come up with a plan."

"Me?"

"You always do." He winks. "Dazzle me, Myla."

His confidence makes my smile broaden. Closing my eyes, I spin my thoughts through every angle and approach. Finally, one option does appear in my mind. It's been an idea that's been rattling around in the back of my head ever since I felt that ethereal warmth on my palm. It happened back in the laboratory when I thought about Iggy. It was almost as if I could feel his hand in mine.

What if he was trying to reach out to me?

If so, we could certainly use Iggy in this fight.

It's a long shot, but when do I ever have anything else? Keeping my eyes closed, I call out to Iggy with my soul.

"I need your help. You must find my father. Tell him you need more time to mourn me. Get the gates of Heaven and Hell closed

again. Come back to me on Earth. I need you, Iggy. Only you and I can fight this together."

My palm warms with the sensation of Iggy's touch. I open my eyes, ready to see him standing before me.

Nothing.

"About that plan?" I ask.

"Yup."

"I may need another minute."

Lincoln looks at me over his shoulder. "You can do this, Myla."

An idea occurs. It's simple, beautiful, deadly. I raise my pointer finger. "We could drive the tank over to Ethan and blow him up." I make a *psssh* noise to dramatize this option.

"That's a last resort. If we blow up Ethan, escape is next to impossible."

"That's never stopped us before."

"We've never faced a challenge like this before. The problem here is bigger than getting rid of Ethan. Hunter Enterprises has now cast a spell on a global basis. Humans everywhere want his Razor Guards to rule them. Do you have any idea how long it would take for the thrax to clean it up with good magic?"

I wince. "A long time?"

"Weeks. And who knows what will happen in the meantime? The ones under his spell could turn on the humans who aren't affected. This could cause a world war."

The words hang in the air. *World war.* I hug my elbows. "Okay, no shooting Ethan with a tank."

Think Myla, think.

"Maybe it will help to list our assets," offers Lincoln.

"Good idea." I count off our inventory on my fingers. "First, we've got a tank, which we can't use to blast Ethan.

We've already discounted that plan. Second, we could go back to the laboratory, but I don't know what that would do there. Third, we could go outside. There's a tarmac filled with machinery and— Oh crap!" My monitor becomes filled with bodies of Razor Guards, and they march across the tarmac and start boarding every piece of equipment. A knocking sounds on the top of our tank.

"Ethan 1073-J reporting for duty with my team!" The knocking continues. "Who locked down this tank? That wasn't authorized."

Crap. My pulse speeds more quickly. "Moving on."

Lincoln starts rewrapping the black bandages over his face. "I like the tarmac direction. What else did you see there when you first arrived? Do you remember anything we can use?"

My eyes widen. "Cissy."

Lincoln pauses. "I don't follow you."

"There's a tent on the tarmac. It holds the access monitor for CHUCK, the master computer that runs everything for Hunter Enterprises."

Lincoln nods slowly. "That could be good. Go on."

"When we first got here, I was looking for you. Cissy and Zeke explored the rest of the event. Cissy got into CHUCK and did something with the computer to lock it up or whatever. Later on, Ethan captured Cissy, Zeke, and me."

"That was right before Ethan brought you to the lab where they were holding me."

"Right. Cissy had put some kind of block on the computer system. While I went to the lab, Ethan sent both and Zeke off to fix whatever she did to CHUCK. Maybe we can do something to the system, too?" I don't add the obvious point that beyond turning it off, I have no idea how to use a computer.

Above our heads, the pounding on the tank's entrance portal grows louder. I shudder. We don't have a lot of time here.

"Wait a moment." Lincoln taps his chin. "We might not need to do anything to CHUCK. Knowing Ethan, he's probably keeping Cissy and Zeke close by, in case she did something else to the computer and he needs her to fix it again."

"And we did hear Cissy's voice on the intercom a few times." Hope sparks in my chest. "I bet she's still in the computer tent."

The knocking sounds again at the top of the tank. "Open up!"

"There's a lot of chaos with the Razor Guards on the move —" starts Lincoln.

"If we can get Cissy back on CHUCK, maybe she can do something to stop all this," I finish.

A series of clicks sound as the portal atop the tank starts to unlock. Lincoln turns to me. "They overrode the locking mechanism. You better get your bandages in place."

Above our heads, the portal swings open with a long creak. I've just finished setting my last bandage in place when a Razor Guard sticks his head in. "What's going on down here?"

I shrug. Now that I know all the Razor Guards are Ethan clones, I'm not going to risk talking.

Lincoln clears his throat. "Thank you, Ethan 1073-J. The portal was indeed malfunctioning but has since been repaired. My colleague and I ran a diagnostics test, and this unit is ready for service."

My brows lift. Diagnostics test? That's a nice touch.

Lincoln starts to rise from his chair. "We'll get out of your way now." The Razor Guard still has his head stuck down the portal hole. Lincoln lowers his voice. "If you would step back, I could leave."

There's a long moment where the two stare at each other. Even with bandages over his face, it's a really bad idea to get into a staring contest with my Lincoln. Ethan 1073-J backs off. Lincoln and I crawl our way out of the tank.

Outside, the tarmac at LaGuardia looks just like it did on the small tank monitor inside. A dark sky stretches overhead. Tall spotlights cast a daylight glow onto the ground. Razor Guards march in neat rows over to different pieces of war equipment. Mortals stand immobile, staring at a point across the tarmac.

Ethan.

They stare so lovingly at the guy, I'm not sure they're even breathing. Somewhere a baby cries its head off. Must be one of the few beings left at LaGuardia who weren't affected by Ethan's black metal. Huh. Maybe the guy hasn't gotten around to making enchanted binkies yet.

Lincoln and I climb off the tank. I quickly scan the grounds and find the place where the CHUCK tent is located. I gesture in the direction, not trusting anyone to hear a woman's voice from a Razor Guard.

Lincoln nods, and we head off in the direction of the tent. Beyond finding Cissy and hoping we can somehow stop this fiasco with a computer, I really don't have much of a plan B, especially since there's been no response from Iggy.

Maybe something will occur to me along the way.

I ignore the little voice inside the back of my head that says two words: *fat chance.*

28

*L*incoln and I speed-walk across the LaGuardia tarmac. The place is like something out of a nightmare. There are people everywhere, but it's super quiet, except for the stomping of boots and the growing chorus of screaming babies. The air smells of airplane fuel and dead fish, probably a combination of all the H-E tech getting ready to take off...along with the nearby Hudson River.

"All guards report for duty. All guards report for duty." All around us, Razor Guards pour out of the different exhibit tents and race toward the tech lining the runways. My heart lightens. Hopefully, the tent holding CHUCK will get emptied out, too.

Hey, a girl can hope.

We quickly locate the tent in question—it's is a long and low structure made of black fabric. Beside it there stands a platform overflowing with satellite dishes and mini-towers made of mesh-like metal. I'm guessing they're for communications, but what do I know? All that really matters is what's inside the tent anyway.

Please be there, Cissy.

There's a sign on the entrance flap: *"Razor Guards Only."*

Perfect, that means we won't have to deal with the possibility of human collateral damage. This plan is looking better by the second. Lincoln and I step inside the tent. It takes a moment for my eyes to adjust to the low levels of light. These bandages are a bitch to see through, even in the best of conditions.

What I see makes me smile.

The huge tent is all but deserted. There are rows of tables, all of them covered with Ethan's stupid toys. The far wall of the rectangular tent is one massive monitor. A small table sits before a monitor that holds a keyboard and what looks like a black ball. Whatever. That's not what's important.

Nope, the big news is that Cissy's sitting before the small table, typing away at the keyboard. A pair of guards stands behind her. Sweet. Zeke sits off to the left-hand side of the massive monitor. Another set of guards flank him as well. My bestie's boyfriend looks pretty beat up, but still conscious. Considering how things could have gone, I consider Zeke being awake and alive a mark in the "good for us" column.

Lincoln and I pause just inside the tent's entrance. When Lincoln speaks, his voice is so low, only I can hear him. "I'll take the guards on Zeke."

I take care to whisper as well. "I've got the ones with Cissy."

Walking in sync, we march across the tent floor. Considering how we both look like good little Razor Guards, no one says boo as we approach. A few of the guards look over their shoulders at us, shrug, and go back to staring at the far wall monitor. For this first time in hours, I feel the thrill of a good fight coming on. My mind slows down and goes into battle mode. There is nothing but these two guards and the attack vectors to take them down. I'm vaguely aware of Lincoln tightening his gloves.

Wait a second, gloves?

It takes me a moment to remember that Lincoln can mush Ethan's magic metal like it's putty. He's been working on the "Hulk smash" style boxing gloves that he formed while we were back fighting Armageddons in the laboratory. Since then, he's been smooshing them down into what look like sleek black leather gloves.

I'm sure they still pack a wallop, though. Just because the black metal is mushy to Lincoln, that doesn't mean it isn't deadly to everyone else.

It's enough to make me almost feel sorry for the Razor Guards behind Zeke.

Almost.

Lincoln and I march over until we stand just behind the four guards. Zeke's guards turn around.

"Shouldn't you be assigned to a vehicle?" asks the far left guard.

Lincoln shakes his head while my tail taps the shoulders of the two standing behind Cissy. They can't see my tail, being that they're human and all, but they will feel the tap on their shoulders. Sure enough, the pair slowly turn around to face me.

I pull off my Nazi hat and loosen the bandages on my face. "You have a choice between getting quietly tied up or killed." I cup my hand by my mouth. "By the way, that's my best friend and her boyfriend you're holding, so I'm really pulling for death in your case."

Cissy swivels around in her chair. Her lip is bleeding, and she has a bruised cheek. For the record, now I'm really itching to kill.

"Myla, you're here!" Her golden retriever tail wags behind her. I love Cissy.

Lincoln removes his hat and bandages as well. He gestures between the two guards behind Zeke. "Same goes for you two."

There's a long moment that lasts forever where all the guards stare between one another. For a second, I think they might actually not be dumbasses here. After all, I never kill without giving the bad guys an out.

In this case, the bad guys in question are Ethan clones, so I'm not holding out of hope for a logical response here.

Sure enough, they don't disappoint. All four Razor Guards reach into their jackets and pull out their guns.

I leap toward the far right Razor Guard, leap up until my boots hand on his shoulders with enough force to send the guy onto the floor. While the Razor Guard tumbles to the floor, my tail spears the Guard beside him through the chest. Once the Guard beneath my boots hits the floor, I grab his head, twist it to one side and snap his neck.

I look over to Lincoln. He's also gone for a torso attack. Using the extra power of his new gloves, my guy has punched both of his Razor Guards right in the larynx. A pair of round-house kicks later, and the last two Razor Guards are laying dead on the floor. I scan all four of them. I should feel bad about this—after all, all life is precious, even if it is an Ethan clone. But then Cissy rises, and I see more bruises along her cheek and neck.

Nope, not feeling too guilty. They had an out and didn't take it.

Cissy wraps her arms around my neck. "Myla, you're here!"

I lean back and cup her face in my hands. "Are you all right?"

"I'm hanging in there." Cissy rushes over to Zeke. "Are you okay, baby?"

Zeke straightens himself in his chair. "I'm great." It's like he's talking through a mouthful of cotton, though.

The zoom of jets sounds through the fabric walls of the tent, reminding me that Ethan is basically trying to start another world war. "We have to stop Ethan, Cis. We need you to work your magic on the computer."

Cissy leans in and kisses Zeke's head. "Ugh. That Ethan guy is such an asshole. After I unlocked his stupid systems, he made me stay and monitor his plans to rule all the humans." She looks over her shoulder and focuses on Lincoln. "Are you the real guy? Did Myla finally rescue you?"

"We don't have time for chatter," says Lincoln. "Myla and I came here for a reason."

Cissy shakes her head. "You rescued the right one this time. The real Lincoln is always focused on his duty."

I move my grip to her shoulders. "Lincoln's right. We need your help with the computer systems." I gently guide her away from Zeke and back into her chair before the computer console.

Okay, that's a total lie.

I maybe push Cissy back into her chair, but this is a serious situation here. "Look, Cis. You have to stop this. There must be a way to shut the computer down and erase whatever Ethan did to the humans with his black magic." I twiddle my fingers at the console. "Do the thing with the thing. Make the jet planes stop and everything."

Cissy winces. "I don't know how to do that." Another jet roars overhead. "I just got lucky when I locked up the computers last time."

Zeke clears his throat. "Cissy used her envy powers to challenge one of the researchers that he couldn't open up the password systems as quickly as she could. He took her up on the challenge, and she told him to go first." Zeke's beat-up face melts into a loving grin. "My girl totally mind controlled him."

"That's all really special," I say quickly. Now, a bunch of choppers take to the air. The whirring rotors make the walls of the tent ripple in the night. "But there are Razor Guards flying out from freaking LaGuardia to take over the human world."

Cissy slumps in her chair. "I'm sorry, Myla. I don't know how to hack into these systems."

I stifle a groan. This plan is a total bust. The ground shakes as the tanks start rolling out over the tarmac. There has to be something I can do. I close my eyes and call out to Iggy one last time.

"Iggy, are you there? Did you get my father to close the gates of Heaven and Hell again? Can you please come here and help us?"

My hand warms once more. A sense of peace and joy moves through me. *Yes. Iggy is coming.* I call out with my soul once more.

"I need you, Iggy. Please. Hurry."

My palm turns hotter than ever before and then cools to nothing. I rub my fingers over my palm. Lincoln steals up beside me.

"What's wrong?" he asks.

"I tried to call Iggy again. It didn't work."

Lincoln wraps me in a hug. "We'll figure out something."

"Hey." Zeke leans forward. "That one researcher was talking about the failsafe." He turns to Cissy. "What was it, baby? Do you remember?"

Cissy's eyes widen. "He did say something."

I kneel before Cissy. "What did he say?"

A new voice sounds from the entrance flap. "A failsafe. Let me enlighten you."

I turn around and gasp. Ethan is here. He raises his arms, and all the jet models on the tables burst into small columns of black flame. A second later, they all rise and turn toward Lincoln, Cissy, Zeke, and me.

Lincoln doesn't so much as flinch. "Go on."

"Kill me and it all ends. The brainwashing. The Razor Guards. The gray Armageddon clones. The black magic. We're all linked. Take me down and they all disappear. It will be completely over."

Wow. Once you get Ethan going, the guy is a major blabbermouth. Where was all this sharing back when I needed information?

I turn to Lincoln. Our gazes lock. The question is unasked but in my eyes. *Is this true?* After all, Lincoln knows Ethan better than anyone.

Lincoln gives me the barest of nods. Yes.

I round on Cissy and Zeke. "Get the hell out of here." I don't need to tell Cissy how to get back to Purgatory. As the Senator of Diplomacy, she has plenty of contacts that can transport her around.

Cissy puffs out her lower lip. "I won't leave you."

I shift my pleading gaze to Zeke. "Get her to safety. This is for Lincoln and me to end."

Across the long tent, Ethan folds his arms across his chest. "Go get them, my sweet little models. Take down the King and

Queen just like your larger versions will take down the world."

The mini jets stop their hovering and start zooming toward us. I shove Zeke in the shoulder. "Go!"

Cissy protests, but she allows Zeke to guide her into crawling out under the bottom edge of the tent. Lincoln and I could do the same thing, but if taking down Ethan will end this whole nightmare? Then here is where we're staying.

This ends right now, one way or another.

29

The air outside the tent fills with the rhythmic thud of helicopter rotors. The ground rumbles as more tanks roll out. Ethan laughs as his mini jets speed across the tent. The noses of each plane turn deadly sharp. Ethan's plan becomes clear.

He's going to try to stab us with his stupid flying toys.

Bring it on.

I command my Scala robes to expand out. For a second, the threads jut forward like a thousand tiny needles. Within the span of a heartbeat, they've torn off all my Razor Guard gear. After that, I make the threads to reform into the shape of battle gear. The process takes less than a few seconds, and then, I'm back in my chosen battle gear. What can I say? I want to go into this final fight as the Great Scala.

Once my gear is set, I shift my weight onto the balls of my feet. My tail arches behind me, ready to fight. Lincoln races forward, jumps into the air, and grabs two jets. He crushes them in his fists and drags them down. It reminds me of how King Kong takes down planes that go after him. Only replace

King Kong with a really hot guy in a long black coat, and that's pretty much the scene here.

And of course, the hotness factor isn't missed by me. My lust demon side never sleepeth.

The planes stop attacking. All the tiny vehicles hover in place. Lincoln and Ethan lock gazes. I maneuver to stand before my guy. "Wondering what happened? It seems like your attempts to drain Lincoln's angelic nature changed how he interacts with your magic metal. We'll give you one chance to surrender without dying." I gesture to the screen and computer console behind me. "There must be some way for you to shut this whole mess down. Do it and you can live."

Ethan ignores me, the creep. Instead he focuses on Lincoln. "Do you know what really happened to my parents?"

Lincoln narrows his eyes. "What are you talking about?"

"You've felt guilty your whole life for the demons that possessed my parents and killed my sister."

A muscle tics along Lincoln's jawline, but he doesn't reply.

"Of course, he felt responsible," I say. "You've been manipulating him about that for years."

"Well, it wasn't your fault." The way Ethan keeps grinning, I have a feeling we won't like what's coming after this. "Years ago, I met an agent of Armageddon's on demon patrol, and we made a little deal."

Lincoln's face pales. "You let your parents become possessed?"

"Quite right. And I booby-trapped the transfer station so they could get into Antrum while you thought it was your mistake. You all dismissed me as a warrior, but Armageddon thought I had potential. We had a deal to try to take over Earth and remake the thrax. It was almost ruined when Adair made her own deal with Armageddon, but fortunately, she failed. Once I discovered you were pregnant, I knew my time had come. Between the three of you, I would have enough angelic power to make my dream a reality. And I will still drain you, mark my words. One day, my Razor Guards will have so much angelic energy, they'll be able to render humans quiet and easily controlled."

When Lincoln speaks, his voice is deadly low. "So, that's a 'no' on surrendering?"

Ethan rolls his eyes. "Correct. I will never give in to you. The only reason I've paused your demise is to ensure you realize how complete your failure has been all these years. You blamed yourself so deeply for my family's death." He sets his hand over his heart. "I hope the truth doesn't upset you."

Lincoln's eyes gleam with rage. "That's a 'no' on surrendering. Got it." My guy holds a jet in each hand. He curls his fists more tightly. The metal crinkles as Lincoln crumples it into a short baton. Smashing his fists together, Lincoln meshes the two planes into a longer structure.

My brows lift. Lincoln is making a sword, maybe. Or a bat. I wish he could just make a baculum, but those can only be crafted by pure-blooded angels over a period of many years. Long story.

But whatever Lincoln is making, I'm down with this plan.

Ethan roars with rage. The miniature planes zoom toward us once again. I bat them away with my tail, but there are hundreds of these things, and only two of us. A knife-like jet slams into my thigh. The threads of my Scala robes strain, but don't break. Not yet.

More jets come at me, each one focusing on the same spots over and over. One comes at my stomach in slow motion. I fall down into a fetal position. I can't risk a body blow with pregnancy.

"Stay down, Myla," calls Lincoln. "The metal doesn't hurt me."

I peek through my fingers. Sure enough, the black metal planes slam into his body, Kong style. Lincoln keeps a steady path toward Ethan. He plucks more jets from the air, crashing them together into a makeshift spear. Ethan shifts his focus entirely to Lincoln, assuming I'm going to cower in a corner of the rest of the battle.

Bad assumption.

I start crawling under the long tables, making my way toward Ethan. Meanwhile, Lincoln launches his makeshift spear. The weapon strikes Ethan straight through his shoulder. Ethan roars again, but this time in pain.

I'm tempted to yell out, *Nice toss, honey*, but I'm making good progress sneaking under the tables. In a few seconds, I'll be within striking distance. There's no way that I want Ethan catching on to what I'm up to.

Ethan pulls out the spear from his shoulder. Lincoln's grabbed a few more planes and is starting to form a new weapon.

What happens next seems to take place in slow-motion. While I rush at Ethan, our enemy takes out a gun, points the muzzle at Lincoln, and fires. The boom of the weapon cracks through the air like thunder. The bullet strikes my guy in the gut. Lincoln curls forward. It seems to take forever for him to fall onto the ground.

Pure, white-hot rage tears through me. I leap out from under the table and tackle Ethan. Now, I know I've been trying to act more and more Queenly. But seeing someone shoot my Lincoln? It sends my demonic self into overdrive. And in retrospect, being Queenly doesn't mean acting like a priss twenty-four seven. It means leading your people with a vision. And I can certainly lead while flattening someone who shot at my husband.

Straddling Ethan's chest, I wrap my hands around his throat and pound his skull against the ground. "You shot my Lincoln! You shot my Lincoln!"

Ethan writhes beneath me, gasping for breath.

A hand rests on my shoulder. I look up. It's Lincoln and he's grinning. "The gun had black metal bullets." He raises a fresh spear over his shoulder. "May I?"

I release Ethan's throat and stand. As he gasps for breath on the ground, Lincoln stands over him. "I am Lincoln Vidar Osric Aquilus, King of the Thrax, and Consort to the Great Scala. In executing the law of the Arbiter, I hereby sentence you for the murder of your family. I also release all the humans of Earth from your lies and black magic. The sentence for all these crimes is death." Lincoln stabs the spear through Ethan's heart.

Ethan's face contorts in one last look of rage. After that, his features turn slack. His body stops moving.

He's dead.

With Ethan's death, the computer monitor behind us comes to life. A dozen warnings flash across the screen. Outside, a prerecorded voice sounds from all the loudspeakers. "*System malfunction. All Razor Guards no longer operational. System malfunction. All Razor Guards no longer operational. Autopilot commencing. Autopilot commencing.*"

The whir of tanks falls silent. The thud of helicopter rotors takes a steady rhythm, like they are hovering place. The same goes for the roar of jet engines. All the humans, who had been quietly standing about the tarmac, now start screaming their heads off. Whatever spell Ethan cast must have died with him. Everyone is freaking the hell out.

"There's a dead demon on the runway."

"Who's flying those planes?"

"The helicopters! The planes! They're about to crash!"

Lincoln and I share a look.

"Ethan told us about this," I say. "He said his death would get rid of the Razor Guards. It also took his black magic off the metal—"

Lincoln finishes my thought. "But although Ethan's magic has vanished, the machines are still here." Lincoln tilts his head, listening. "They're all in hover mode.

"How long can those things go on autopilot?" My hand pops over my mouth. "And how much stuff did he have in the air over New York?"

"Too much," says Lincoln.

I stare at Ethan's body. That bastard. He planned this out so if he died, he'd take half of New York with him.

I press my fists against my temples. *Think, Myla. Think, think.*

There must be something we can do.

This time, there's just too much at stake. Not the least of which is the fact that if the planes and choppers come down, Lincoln and I will be the first targets.

Damn.

I'm out of things to try. This is really it. I lock gazes with Lincoln. At least, we'll die together. I only wish I had a chance to be a better ruler to my people. Another thought appears.

And a better friend to Iggy. I never gave him a proper goodbye.

Suddenly, the warmth on my hand returns. Looking down, I see that it isn't a mirage this time.

Iggy is here. *Yes.*

30

I can't believe my eyes. Iggy is here. He looks just like he did when I first saw him: a pot-bellied alien with glowing skin and long limbs.

"Great Scala needs Iggy. Iggy came as fast as Iggy could."

Suddenly, the regular thud of helicopter rotors and jet engines falls silent. The computerized voice on the loud-speaker sounds once more. *"Imminent autopilot failure. Imminent autopilot failure."* The humans freak out even harder than before.

I kneel down beside Iggy. "Listen to me carefully. We need to send out little lightning bolts into all those machines in the sky. We have to stop the planes and copters but without hurting any humans."

"That hard for Iggy."

"I'll hold your hand and help you focus. It'll be just like when we knocked out those Razor Guards. Will you help me?"

"Iggy will help."

Closing my eyes, I call out to the igni with all my focus.

"Come to our aid, little ones. Rid us of this threat."

I open my eyes again and scan Iggy. The little guy is scrunching up his face. Suddenly, thousands of lightning bolts go flying off his free hand. Like fireflies, they whip through the night. I can't see this with my eyes, but I can sense them flying off into the night sky, finding all the different machines.

The computerized voice sounds again. *"Autopilot failure. Autopilot failure."*

The human screaming becomes deafening. On reflex, I gasp and let go of Iggy's hand. Lincoln kneels beside us both, quickly resetting our palms together. "You can do this, Myla."

I mouth three words to Lincoln: *I love you.*

He winks.

Now that Iggy and I are reconnected, I can sense the igni once more. A thin tendril of consciousness connects me to each tiny lightning bolt. All the igni on their way, but they aren't yet close enough to any of the planes or choppers.

Iggy fidgets beside me. "Bigga boom."

"Careful, Iggy," I warn. "Not yet. The igni aren't in place."

If Lincoln is worried about the *"bigga boom"* comment, he doesn't show it. He keeps our hands firmly clasped together. "You're doing so well. Both of you. Finish it off."

In my mind, I can sense as my igni enter every engine. I redouble my focus, making the power do something I've never seen happen before. In the past, the igni have made things melt or explode. Now, I need them to make them fly. Energy seeps from my soul as I command the planes and copters to hover in space. A thousand circuits and dials flash through my consciousness. Fuel pipes and cloudscapes. It's too much and not enough.

I have to get these planes away from the humans.

"Iggy bigga boom?"

"Not yet. We need to take the planes and copters far away from the humans, Iggy. We're going to take all Ethan's flying machines high into the sky, Iggy. Can you help me do that?"

"Yes, Great Scala."

Sweat drips down my cheeks as I double-down my focus once more. Iggy's hand shakes in mine. Together, Iggy and I share our consciousness; we direct the small bits of supernatural power. One by one, all the pieces of Hunter technology rise up into the sky, higher and higher. Soon, they are nothing but distant specks in the night sky. In my deepest soul, I know they are far enough away not to cause any more danger.

"Now, Iggy." I say in a low voice. "Bigga boom."

"Yes!" Iggy laughs as the great explosion lights up the night sky. Distant rumbles shake the very air. The humans start to scream again. They don't know that the threat was erased. I exhale and let go of Iggy's hand.

Lincoln kisses my forehead. "Great work."

"All three of us did it." My limbs feel like Jell-O. "Although now that it's over, I could use a nap." I blink hard. "Oh wait. I know the Razor Guards died when Ethan died, but what do we do about the bodies? Especially, you know, the four we just killed."

"They're gone," says Lincoln.

I rise on shaky legs and scan the other side of the tent. There are no more bodies, only empty Nazi uniforms. I glance over to Ethan. He's gone, too. I slump into Lincoln. "What happened?" My guy knows a lot more about black magic than I do.

"It's part of the magic. The price that must be paid." Lincoln's mouth thins. "I'm sure his soul should go to Armageddon, but with this much black magic, I think it will be as if he never existed at all."

"That's fine." As much as I hate Ethan, I'd never wish anyone to be kept under Armageddon's tender mercies. In fact, it's a huge part of my job as the Great Scala to keep every soul I can away from the King of Hell.

Iggy yanks on my robes. "Great Scala see that? Bigga boom! Bigga boom! Scala and Iggy control it all together."

My knees turn watery beneath me. Before I know it, Lincoln has scooped me into his arms. "We need to get you home." He strides out of the tent and onto the tarmac. The place is almost deserted. Say what you want about humans, but they do know how to run.

I try to keep my eyes open. It isn't easy. "How far away did you say that Pulpitum was?"

"Not far. I've got you."

I try my best to stay awake, but my eyes drift shut on their own. Within seconds, everything fades into darkness.

31

I don't know how long I'm in the darkness, but the next thing I know, I hear Lincoln's voice through my mental haze.

"Myla, wake up."

My eyes flutter open. "Yes?"

"We've reached the Pulpitum that will take us to Antrum. It's safer if you're awake for the transfer process."

I blink hard, trying to force my brain to focus. A jumble of images flashes through my mind. "There was a battle…"

"Yes," Lincoln says in a soothing voice. "You and Iggy teamed up to defeat Ethan's army. I'm so proud. But now you need to be awake for the transfer back to Antrum. These platforms can be very unstable. It's better if you're alert, all right?"

I widen my eyes and look around. I know we're in a Pulpitum. This one looks like an empty airplane hangar. A few broken light fixtures shine far overhead. Most of the space is cast in shadows, but I can see a small round disc sits on the floor. Lincoln stands on the center of this circle. I'm still in his arms.

Iggy just outside the metal disc. His overly large eyes are lined with tears. "Great Scala has to go. Iggy goes too."

"Right. We'll be together soon."

"Iggy won't be like this again." The little guy gestures across his humanoid form. "Hard for Iggy to talk with so many voices. Was very hard to tell father of Great Scala to close down gates."

"Did you use double-screech?" I ask.

"More like triple."

"Ouch." Note to self: get Dad a nice thank-you gift.

"Iggy likes talking to Great Scala this way."

"I like chatting with you too, Iggy."

I know what my mini supernatural dude means. When he's in his igni form, Iggy is a million little voices all trying to talk at once. Normally, I have a hard time understanding him.

"Great Scala no more understand Iggy."

"Hey, I always get what you mean in the end." I kiss Lincoln's cheek. "Set me down, please."

"Of course."

Lincoln gingerly places me on my feet, and I quickly crumple onto my knees. It's more because my legs are still watery than anything else, but it's also easier to look at Iggy this way. I open my arms to him. "Come here."

Iggy rushes into my embrace. Lincoln wraps his arm around Iggy as well. When I speak again, my voice cracks with emotion. "You'll always be my little one, too. You know that, right?"

"Iggy knows." He sniffles into my shoulder.

"And one day, you'll be important to Maxon as well. You're a part of our lives, whatever form you take. Do you believe me?"

Iggy nods and steps back. "Iggy sees Great Scala again

soon."

"That's right." I force a smile. "Until then, Iggy."

His little body flares more brightly for a moment. After that, Iggy disappears entirely. I feel the emptiness down to my soul.

Lincoln kisses my forehead. "Are you ready now?"

"As I'll ever be."

Lincoln scoops me into his arms again. I wiggle a little bit. "You don't need to carry me."

He leans in to whisper in my ear. "But I like it."

I grin. "Who am I to refuse you?"

Lincoln nuzzles my neck. For a moment, we're all things snuggly and safe. After that, he scans the darkness and raises his voice. "I am King Lincoln Vidar Osric Aquilus, activating Pulpitum transfer station XXV."

A laser beam brightens from the ceiling, creating a grid of light across both Lincoln and me. A woman's voice echoes through the small closet. "How can this be King Lincoln? You're here in Antrum. I can't—"

"Imperio parendum regis atque."

"That's a mouthful," I mumble. It's also one of those thrax pass phrases. Once uttered, the chick in the transfer station has to do whatever the speaker says.

"Pass phrase acknowledged," says the woman. "Where should I transfer you?"

"Take us to the Arx Hall Pulpitum on my mark," says Lincoln. "Three…two…one…mark."

The Pulpitum lurches into the earth. Lincoln still cradles me in his arms; I lean into his embrace. My heart soars with the triumph of the moment. A single realization moves through my soul.

I have my husband once again, and now, we're going home.

32

*L*incoln and I hold on to each other as the Pulpitum platform hurtles through the ground. Veins of magma, glittering minerals, layers of stone... All these images of Earth fly past us as we're magically transported deeper to Antrum.

With a lurch, the round metal platform comes to a halt. The visions of the inside of the Earth are replaced by the sight of Arx Hall, our underground castle in the thrax homeland. The Arx Hall Pulpitum is basically a round metal platform that sits at the back of a dead-end hallway. Like most things in Arx Hall, this corridor is filled with silver tapestries that hang on matching walls. Even the floors are metallic white tile. Everything looks as it should, except for one thing.

There's no one here.

Normally, at least Lincoln's parents show up to greet us. His mother Octavia probably knew we were en route the moment we set foot into the LaGuardia Pulpitum.

With hesitant steps, I walk off the platform and into the hallway. Still, no one shows up. "So, this is weird."

Lincoln's eyes narrow. "Quite."

"I mean, not that I think I'm so awesome or anything, but come on. I can move everyone's souls to Heaven and Hell. Most importantly?" I point to my stomach. "How about a little love for Mommy?"

Lincoln shoots me a wry look. "They're coming. Give it five, four, three…two…one…"

The door on the opposite end of the hallway whips open. Through it steps Octavia, Connor, and a ton of Rixa guards.

I shake my head. "How do you do that?"

"Do what?" asks Lincoln. But based on the gleam in his eyes, the guy knows exactly what I'm talking about.

"Know when people are about to show up in Arx Hall?"

He shrugs. "Years of practice."

I point at his nose. "You're teaching me that trick. Octavia sneaks up on me way too often."

Lincoln chuckles. "She does do that, doesn't she?"

It's such a normal moment, I could cry. Octavia is descending on us the moment we enter Arx Hall, just like she always does. Connor is begrudgingly coming along for the ride, same as usual. They have a few more warriors along than usual, but these folks are wearing the insignia of Lincoln's personal guard. No doubt, everyone is here to exclaim how glad they are that we've returned safely. And if I'm being honest with myself, I want a little love for Myla, too. I mean, everyone said that I was crazy to go after my Lincoln. And here I am. Totally right.

Not that I'm gloating or anything. I'm becoming way too mature for that.

Lincoln pulls me against his side and whispers in my ear, "Never get too mature, Myla."

My brows lift. "What? How did you know what I was thinking?"

"Your face squishes up when you're telling yourself to act too grown up. I like the life inside you." He places his hand gently on my stomach. "All of it."

I lean up on my tiptoes and kiss his nose. "For you, I'll always stay a semi-impetuous kook."

He gives me one of those smiles that melts my kneecaps. "Perfect."

It takes some effort, but I force myself to turn away from Lincoln and focus on the group marching toward us. *Huh.* They don't look happy. Lincoln must be sensing the same thing, because his body tenses beside mine. After that, he does something I've never seen him do before.

Lincoln steps forward and positions me behind him.

It's a protective move, and normally, I'm not one who needs protecting. But in this case? I trust his judgment. If Lincoln thinks there is danger to me and the baby, then I'll hang back.

I won't promise to stay back forever, though. After all, I just vowed to remain a semi-impetuous kook.

Connor and Octavia pause about ten yards before us. Connor looks red-faced and flustered in his medieval outfit of velvet tunic and leather pants. Octavia appears spotless in her long black gown. She eyes us carefully from head to toe.

Oops.

All of a sudden, I become very conscious of the fact that both Lincoln and I are still wearing Razor Guard uniforms. Not good.

Lincoln scans his parents just as carefully. There's no question where my guy got his strategic sense. "Mother," he says slowly. "Father. I take it you're not pleased to see us."

Octavia opens her mouth to speak, but someone else butts into the conversation first.

Evil Lincoln.

Man, do I ever hate that guy.

The creep busts through the group of Rixa guards and positions himself right in front of Octavia. My brows lift. No one upstages the Queen Emeritus.

This ought to be good.

Evil Lincoln certainly looks the part of King. He's got on the Rixa tunic, silver crown, and leather pants thing going on. It's just…the guy screams conman to me. Sure, Connor is an easy mark. Still, how can Octavia not see that?

Evil Lincoln points right at the real deal. "There they are, just as I said. Clones. You've all heard what happened on the Earth's surface. Ethan and his Hunter Enterprises were cloning demons. Imagine that! Demons! And now, it seems they have cloned thrax as well." Evil Lincoln sighs dramatically. "Thank Heavens that I got here first to explain everything to you. They both must be executed immediately."

My guy raises his hand. "Sermo mihi est lex."

I've heard Lincoln say this before. It's one of the many codes Lincoln has with his Rixa guards. One of the warriors tosses a pair of baculum rods at my Lincoln, who in turn catches one in each hand. These look like two small metal sticks, and sure, that's what they appear to be. However, once baculum rods are in the hands of my guy? They become totally lethal.

This is getting good.

Lincoln moves both rods into his right hand and ignites them as a sword made of white angelfire. When he speaks, my husband's voice is low and growly. "You are the impostor."

Evil Lincoln pales. "How can you say this?" he rounds on Connor. "Dad, you must protect me from this liar."

Connor runs his hand through his shoulder-length white hair. I have to hand it to Lincoln's father, the guy knows who really runs the show. Connor turns to Octavia. "What do you say, my love?"

Octavia purses her lips. "My son *never* asks his father to fight his battles."

I raise my fist. "True that." If anything, my husband is forever covering Connor's ass.

A small smile crosses Octavia's mouth. "It's good to have you back, son. I was starting to worry that you'd somehow had a breakdown and turned into a nincompoop." She shoots an angry glare at Evil Lincoln. "Offense intended."

Evil Lincoln throws up his hands. "How can this be happening? They are dressed as Ethan's personal guard. Why isn't anyone killing them?"

Lincoln turns to me. "I know I promised you the next kill, but..."

I wave him off. "You can have this one. I totally get it." If there were an Evil Myla running around, I'd want dibs on offing her. Fair is fair, after all.

My Lincoln rounds on his evil clone. "I am King Lincoln Vidar Osric Aquilus. You participated in my kidnapping. You threatened my family. I hereby sentence you to death."

Evil Lincoln cowers on the ground, curling his arms over his head. "I'm sorry. I'm just a stupid clone. Ethan made me do it."

Lincoln raises his sword over his head, ready to strike. But I know my guy. My husband would never kill someone who wasn't attacking.

A long pause follows while Evil Lincoln whimpers. At

length, my guy turns to me. "Looks like this one is your call after all. What do you say we do with him? He's not attacking."

"I'll never attack. I don't even know how to fight."

I nod. "We got that, EL."

"EL?" asks my guy.

"Evil Lincoln. It's what I've been calling him for ages. I just decided to shorten it since it looks like he's hanging around for a while.

"EL." My guy nods slowly. "It works."

EL keeps cowering in a ball on the floor. In fact, he shakes so much that he topples over onto his side, still in a fetal position. I stare at him for a moment, wondering what we should do with the guy.

That's when the perfect solution presents itself.

I snap my fingers. "I have it."

"Don't hurt me," says EL.

"We heard you the first two times," I say. "Here's what I'm thinking. It's going to be a real pain, cleaning up the mess that Ethan left on the Earth's surface. We'll have a main team that erases memories and all that good stuff. But someone needs to find every last person who saw what happened at LaGuardia and make sure the memory charms stick. It's boring, time-consuming, and—"

EL looks up through his fingers. "I'll do it."

"No, you won't," I say. "You'll give us lip service and then run off and hide. That's why I say his punishment is a compulsion charm to get the job done."

EL sits up straight. "You'll give me a compulsion charm to do... *work?*"

My Lincoln lowers his sword. "I like it. He should help clean up his own messes."

I raise my hand. "And the Earls should help him. No sending flunkies to do the dirty work, either. They need to realize what it's like doing the heavy lifting." Then, they may not be so jazzed to send other warriors into harm's way.

"But checking millions of New Yorkers," whines EL. "That could take years."

"Good point," I say. "For the *Earls*. After all, those guys do have houses to run. A few months of dirty work ought to be enough to teach them all a good lesson. But in your case? Not so much. Years sounds about right."

"So be it." My guy looms over the cowering EL. "You are hereby sentenced to clean up you own messes for the next hundred years or so, assuming you should live that long." I rub my palms together. "And I know just the guy to cast the compulsion as well. Your old friend Lucas, the Earl of Striga."

EL pales. "He wouldn't."

Lincoln grins. "Want to bet?"

I motion to the guards. "Take the impostor here to the Earl of Striga. Tell him to cast a truth and consequences spell. He'll know what to do from there."

Two guards step forward and frog-march EL away. Lincoln's clone whines the whole time, which is pretty satisfying. Once EL is gone, I turn to my guy. "Wow. One didn't go on the attack. I feel like I should buy a lottery ticket or something."

Before my Lincoln can reply, Octavia rushes forward and loops Lincoln into a huge hug. "My boy, I was so worried. It was obvious that character was a clone, but what if there were more clones of you? The moment you said my name, I knew. You're back."

One of the guards steps forward. "We knew the second

you said the passcode phrase. It's good to have you back, Your Majesty."

Octavia turns to me. "And Myla! I never thought I'd see you again. You can't imagine the grief that's been going through the after-realms. I didn't want to tell anyone when you showed up in the Pulpitum... It would be cruel to get their hopes up only to find out you weren't you." She rushes over and gives me a full hug as well. "I can't tell you how happy I am to have you both back." Her voice actually breaks, which is a big display of emotion for Octavia.

I hug her back, and with that, I decide that I should definitely buy a lottery ticket. The only thing that's more rare than an enemy not attacking is an emotional outburst from Octavia.

"I missed you, my dear." Octavia rocks from foot to foot. "It's nothing but mindless ninnies around here without you. And your parents have been frantic. Well," she taps her chin. "They were frantic until recently. Did you father by any chance get information about your healthy status before we discovered the truth?"

I shake my head. Octavia is smart as a whip. "They did." Octavia opens her mouth to ask a million questions, but I raise my palm to silence her. "It's a story for another day, though."

"You know you won't avoid telling me the entire tale," says Octavia. "I can be very persuasive."

Lincoln's face turns total deadpan. "You don't say."

I start to laugh, but my chortle gets cut off by the biggest pain ever. Agony radiates across my stomach. "Hey..."

"I know," she coos. "Most thrax aren't used to us yet, are they? But we'll change them eventually. You've already made great strides."

My belly expands along with the pain. The waistline of my Razor Guard pants actually pop. One thought appears in my mind, the words written in neon letters.

The baby is coming quickly, just like the igni warned.

It takes a force of will to speak again. "Baby…"

Octavia actually sniffles. I'd be amazed if I weren't in such bone-crushing agony. Too bad I'm leaning over at the waist. No one can actually see how my belly is expanding at terrifying rate.

Octavia pats my shoulder. "I know, we can't wait for the little one to arrive."

Lincoln gently pushes his mother aside. "Myla, what's wrong?" he kneels beside me and gets a good view of my now very pregnant belly. Panic streams through my veins. Didn't I have months before this was going to happen?

Lincoln goes right into action. In a matter of seconds, he has the hall cleared out, my Razor Guard disguise off, and me curled up in his arms. "I'm taking you to the infirmary."

The mother of all contractions rips through my torso. "That's good. Because I'm pretty sure the baby is coming right now."

Lincoln holds me more tightly and then takes off at a run. The good news is, we're both smiling every step of the way.

Our baby is almost here.

*T*hree months ago, I gave birth to the cutest baby ever. Now, I stand at the back archway of the Chapel, the same place I exchanged marriage vows with Lincoln. Like that day, the place is crammed with thrax, quasis, and angels.

No demons this time. Whew.

The three of us are alone in the tunnel, which serves as the access way to the Chapel proper. At some point, I'm going to stop being amazed at the size of this so-called Chapel. The thing is way larger than Purgatory's Arena back home. And today, I don't think there's an empty seat in the place.

Lincoln stands at my side. We're both dressed in our medieval best as King and Queen of the Thrax. Just like with our wedding, my mother agreed that Antrum would be the best place to hold the main event for today, which is Maxon's naming ceremony. That said, our little family is going on a full tour of Purgatory after this ceremony is over. The angelic choir that got together for my wedding is now doing gigs across the after-realms. They even have a badass name: Wrath of Xavier, or Wrath-X. Personally, I think it's kind of an angelic idea of a badass name, but who am I to rain on their parade?

Here's how it will work. Wrath-X will do a quick intro song. Then Lincoln, Maxon, and I will celebrate the naming ceremony. Once the naming part is done, our little family can hightail it out of the auditorium while the band keeps playing. Mom will get her photo opp. The quasi people will get to see the baby. It's a win all the way around.

Little Maxon squirms in my arms. Did I mention he's cute? He's got that awesome baby smell, pudgy limbs with fat rings on his wrists and ankles, and big mismatched eyes. I love him to pieces.

Lincoln leans over, placing his pointer finger into the grip of Maxon's baby hand. "How's my little man today?"

Maxon is already a total operator, by the way. My baby perks right up, blinks in Lincoln's direction, and coos. Adorable, and yes, working the charming factor at a young age.

Footsteps sound behind us. Turning around, I see my father and Cissy tooling up the stone corridor. I have a flashback of them both here once before, as I was getting ready to head down the aisle and marry Lincoln. As it turned out, I was also getting ready to go into a major battle. This time, I hope things will go much more smoothly.

Dad approaches me slowly, like I'm a strange creature he's never seen before. My father's been acting strangely ever since the igni talked to him at triple screech level. "Are you... okay, Myla?

"I'm fine, Dad. And you look fabulous." Which he does. My

father is decked out in his golden armor with his matching wings on display. He looks everything angelic and kick-butt.

"If you're sure." Dad tilts his head.

"They aren't screeching at me. No worries."

My father exhales. "Glad to hear it. You know I went through a lot in Hell and, wow. That's all I have to say. Wow."

My father spent seventeen or so years getting tortured by Armageddon in Hell, and Armageddon is a guy who really, really, really likes to torture. This may sound strange, but it makes me feel good to have my father acknowledge how tough igni are to interact with sometimes. Makes me feel semi-heroic for just interpreting them.

"Thanks, Dad. I mean it."

Cissy steps up; she's in her Senatorial robes today. "I had to see you before you started." She steps around me in a slow circle. Cis helped me pick out my gown for this event. We had the royal clothier work with a quasi designer this time. I'm wearing a pale pink over-dress with my white Scala robes underneath. The lines are a little more modern and fitted. I like it.

"You did a great job, Cis." It was a diplomatic achievement to get Antrum and Purgatory working together on anything, let alone a gown.

Cissy bobs a little on the balls of her feet. It makes her golden curls bounce by her shoulders. "It's all worth it to see you look this awesome."

Outside, Wrath-X starts into the opening riff of "Somebody to Love" by Queen. Lincoln sets his hand at the small of my back. "That's our cue."

Dad and Cissy make their quick good-byes and rush off down the opposite side of the corridor. Before us, the packed stadium rises to its feet. Little Maxon squirms and gurgles. My tail arches over my shoulder to wave at the crowd. We start the slow stroll down the aisle. I pass so many friendly faces, my face starts to hurt from smiling.

Walker looks handsome in his ghoul robes. He shakes his head as we step by. Walker is basically my honorary brother, so I know what that that headshake means. Walker knew both Lincoln and me since we were kids. No one thought Lincoln and I would ever meet, let alone have a family. Now, Walker can't believe we're stepping by him with little Maxon in my arms.

Zeke and Cissy stand by the aisle. She's crying all over her Senatorial robes. For his part, Zeke is almost completely recovered from having taken down three Razor Guards singlehandedly. The guy spent a week in the hospital after coming back from Earth. When I learned that, I decided to take back another chunk of mean things I said about him.

Next, we step by Octavia and Connor. Lincoln's mother looks like the definition of "blissed out." She's spent the last three months recounting how Maxon's every little motion means that he's brilliant and/or a master warrior. *See how Maxon's gnawing on his toe? Genius baby.* It's sweet.

Meanwhile, Connor is keeping his blustering to a minimum. Of all the parents, Connor took it the hardest when we announced we were splitting our time between Antrum and Purgatory. For someone who seems really conflicted about my having a baby, he certainly has a lot of ideas on where the kid should be raised. Whatever. I'm not allowing him to ruin the day for me.

At the end of the aisle, there stand my mother and father. Mom looks Presidential in her purple skirt-suit. Dad positively gleams in his angelic armor, wings on display. Once I started into labor, Mom took a rush Pulpitum to Antrum. She recovered rather quickly from the "my daughter isn't dead" thing and went right into supportive Mom mode. It was awesome.

Lincoln and I finish our walk down the aisle. Before us stands Verus, the Queen of the Angels, who will be officiating the ceremony. She hovers above us in her white gown with matching sandals; her wings beat a steady rhythm. We share a smile.

For the record, I'm glad Verus came today. It was her oracle powers that brought Lincoln and I together in the first place. I'm glad she'll be officiating the ceremony. As we stand before her, the music goes silent for a moment, then the chorus launches into its big finale.

Find me somebody to love...
Find me somebody to love...
Find me somebody to love...
Somebody, somebody, somebody to love...
Anybody find me somebody to love!

As the crescendo hits, Lincoln and I lock gazes. All the love in world shines out in his mismatched eyes.

The song finishes, and the Chapel falls silent. Verus's voice carries across the massive space. "Who brings forth this child to be named?"

Lincoln's gaze stays locked with mine as he speaks. "The luckiest man in the after-realms."

A blush crawls up my cheeks. Maxon gurgles happily in

my arms. And in this moment, everything imperfect and glorious is mine, both in this world and the next.

—The End—

∾

The adventure continues with THE DARK LANDS,
Book 5 in the Angelbound Origins Series

Read on for a sample from THE DARK LANDS…

SHARKIE AND SNICKERDOODLES

AN ANNIVERSARY BONUS STORY

Introduction From the Author, Christina Bauer

Angelbound is celebrating its ten-year anniversary! As a practical girl, I'm using this opportunity to align the print and audio versions of this book (because unmatched content makes retailers grumpy.)

In this bonus story, Myla seeks out frosted snickerdoodles from a bakery that's also 'home sweet home' for Sharkie, Myla's old nemesis from Purgatory's Arena.

I hope you enjoy *Sharkie and Snickerdoodles*!

BONUS STORY:
Sharkie and
Snickerdoodles

oo ne noo. Noo ne noo. Nothing to see here.

I sashay along a cracked sidewalk. The sky threatens rain, which is typical for Purgatory. All around me, empty storefronts look out over the deserted street. My destination for today is a little place around the corner. My mouth waters as I consider the yum that awaits me.

La Ghoule Bakery, aka the only spot in Purgatory that sells freshly-made frosted snickerdoodles.

And today, I shall get those snickerdoodles in my tummy.

I'm not supposed to be anywhere near this bakery—long story--so I'm wearing a disguise. Pausing before one of the many darkened windows, I check out my reflection. My red hair is hidden under a long blonde wig and floppy hat. My brown eyes are concealed by massive sunglasses. Even my tail is in costume. Namely, I've attached a pair of googly eyes to my tail's arrowhead-shaped end.

The rest of my outfit is gray sweats with a matching T-shirt and raggedy sneakers, which is the standard outfit required for all quasi demons. All in all, I look great.

My tail shivers, a movement that makes its googly eyes roll around. My tail happens to have a mind of its own. Shivering is a dead giveaway.

"You're worried."

My tail bobs up and down. *Yes.*

"Hey, I get why you're riding the anxious train to worry town. The chick who runs La Ghoule Bakery happens to have a live-in boyfriend that isn't totally cool." I make my eek face as I say the words, *totally cool.*

In reply, my tail tilts its arrowhead-shaped end up ninety degrees and slides back and forth in a pretty good imitation of a certain aquatic predator.

"Yes, the baker's boyfriend is Sharkie."

I fight evil souls in Purgatory's arena. Sharkie is both a ghoul and the emcee for these death matches. We have a healthy hate-hate relationship.

"But as you can see, we're both disguised."

My tail loops the arrowhead end around my ear. *You're nuts.*

"It's not the greatest disguise, but it's good enough for Sharkie. Probably." My stomach growls. "Hey, a growing girl has needs."

My tail flops down to hide behind my ankle. Clearly, it still isn't convinced we're safe. But me being me, there's a particular piece of info that I've been saving up just in case my tail got cold feet. Not that it has legs, but you get the idea.

"Hey, there's another reason not to worry. We're here at the ass-crack of dawn for a reason. The bakery opens up early today so they can be inspected by a ghoul delegation. No one knows about this. There won't be any lines. We'll be in and out so fast, Sharkie won't have time to react."

My tail slinks out from behind my ankle to point at my nose. *How do you know this?*

"Walker told me." I make little quotation marks with my fingers when I say the words *told me*. "Rather, Walker didn't tell me anything. It's more that I snuck a look at some papers in his satchel." My tail tilts its arrowhead end, which means I'm making progress. "So, you're okay with visiting La Ghoule Bakery, right?"

The arrowhead end bobs up and down. *Yes*.

"Perfect."

I resume my march around the corner and make a beeline for the only nice-looking building in the neighborhood. The La Ghoule Bakery has two bay windows which flank a thin wooden door. I pause outside.

Dark-cloaked figures lurk inside the shop. It's the visiting delegation of ghouls, just as Walker predicted. The only other person inside is the renowned Madame La Ghoule herself. My heart pitter-pats at double speed as I realize the truth.

There's no sign of Sharkie.

My stomach growls again. I rub my tummy. *Soon, my friend.*

2

*A*fter years of imagining, I'm about to realize my dream: *frosted snickerdoodles from none other than Madame La Ghoule.*

I stride inside the bakery. Along the left wall, there stands a shoulder-high glass case of baked yumminess. This display ends in a waist-high combination of counter and register. Tinny speakers play French accordion music. The scent of freshly-baked cookies fills the air.

Grrr. My stomach growls yet again.

I inch closer to the display cases. Sadly, the ghoul delegation blocks my view into the snickerdoodle section. Even worse, these undeadlies are taking for-bleeding-ever to finish their inspection.

A ghoul I've decided to call Tall Guy reads from a sheet of paper in his undead hands. "Let's continue. Again, I read form A-972-B, the weekly update report from ghoul manufacturing in Purgatory. Next question, 162-J." Tall Guy clears his throat. "Are éclair sold at this store?"

Madame La Ghoule is a round she-ghoul who wears a

white apron over her black robes. She straightens her white chef hat before replying. "Oui."

"Why is there an accent mark on the word éclair?"

"Zat eez how zee word is spelled."

"Are you sure éclair needs an accent mark?"

"Oui."

I want tell Tall Guy to move on already, but I'm trying to be in disguise here. So, I bite my lips shut instead.

Tall Guy sighs and turns to the other ghouls. "I can't decide. Do you think we should we list it with and without an accent, so no one is confused?"

This conversation sucks up ten minutes, minimum. It's taking everything in me not to scream.

After they decide to spell éclair two ways on the form, the group finally moves on to other, equally useless, questions. Madame La Ghoule patiently answers each one.

At last, someone in the delegation declares, "We'll talk about this and come back later."

Classic move of ghoul bureaucracy.

The group slowly trudges out the door. Finally, it's just me, Madame La Ghoule, and the snickerdoodles. As I move closer to the display case, I know that an angelic choir doesn't really break into a version of Handel's Messiah, but it sure sounds like it in my head.

Treat of treats!

And snack of snacks!

For I shall eat this snickerdoodle

Snickerrrrrrr-dooooooo-dollllllllllle!

I blink a few times and look around. Madame La Ghoule stares at me with an unreadable look.

Oops. I may have gotten out of myself a little there.

I shift my weight from foot to foot. "Uh, I was just..." *And that's all I got.*

"Allow me to guess," says Madame La Ghoule in her cute French accent. "You were hearing a version of Handel's Messiah in your head, only the lyrics were about snicker-doodles?"

"Yes, how did you know?"

She shrugs. "For some reason, that happens to all my snickerdoodle customers."

At this point, it's important to note that ghouls who spent their human existence in France are a little different from other undeadlies. Namely, they won't eat worm soufflé or any of the other standard ghoul meals. Yes, that makes them way cooler than the average ghoul.

Madame La Ghoule steps closer to the display case. "My customers are the ghouloisie. I only let certain quasis buy from me... as in, ones I know are not scum." She narrows her eyes at me. Obviously, I'm not on the pre-approved guest list.

Now, there's a lot to dislike about what Madame La Ghoule just said. Being called scum may sound nicer in a French accent, but it's still mean. As a rule, I sass off in situations like this one. But for snickerdoodles? I'll make an exception.

"What do you want to know about me?" I ask. "I'm an open book." Even if I am wearing a wig, floppy hat and sunglasses.

"What kind of tail is that? Tell me the truth."

"It's a googly snake."

"I did not know such a beast existed."

"Well, it absolutely does. Duh." And a little bite comes through my tone. I can't make that much of an exception.

Madame La Ghoule nods. At last, she asks the question of my dreams. "What would you like to order?"

"A dozen frosted snickerdoodles."

"What flavor?"

This is a shock of the very best kind. "What do you have?"

"Ah, I make zee Amaretto, Apple, Anise, Apricot…"

Clunk.

For the first time, I notice a door set in the left-hand wall. Someone beyond that threshold is making a ton of noise.

Madame La Ghoule calls out toward the door. "Silence, mon cher!"

My stomach sinks. I'm pretty sure who the *mon cher* is in this situation. *Sharkie.* Time to move things along.

Madame La Ghoule focuses on me again. "Avocado, Acai…"

I hold up my hand. "How many more flavors are there?"

"I'm just on the a's."

"You know what? If you've got chocolate, then that's my order."

"Twelve snickerdoodles with frosting *du chocolat*, good choice. Now, what kind of casing do you want?"

Here's the issue. I've never actually gotten into this bakery before, let alone placed an order. Normally, Sharkie's around, so I couldn't risk it. All of which means the casing situation is a new one.

"Casing? What's that?"

Madame La Ghoule takes out a sheet of golden tissue paper. "I make zee little origami shapes around each treat. It only takes a few minutes for each one. You can have swan, unicorn, parrot, owl, shark…"

"You know what? You can skip the casing."

"But I make zee little origami shapes."

"Buuuuuuuut all I want is a dozen snickerdoodles."

When Madame La Ghoule next speaks, her irises light up

with demon power. "For quasis, I always make zee little origami shapes. You appreciate the effort and pay more, oui?"

"You price gouge quasis for origami?"

"I. Make. Zee. Little. Origami. Shapes."

In other words, there's no way I'm getting out of here without an origami casing on every freaking snickerdoodle.

Clunk, clunk! More noises sound from behind the door.

"Mon cher! Are you all right?"

A familiar gritty voice echoes in from behind the door. "Yes."

If I'd jammed my tail into an electrical socket, I could not feel more of a charge. *That speaker is Sharkie, all right.*

"I'll be out in one minute," growls Sharkie.

Madame La Ghoule turns to me. "Zee poor man." She gives me a look that invites me to commiserate.

"You don't say." *As in, don't say this. Please.*

"He works in zee arena. You wouldn't believe zee trouble a nasty girl fighter gives him. She is foul. Evil. Zee worst quasi scum."

I should ignore all that and get my cookies. However, life's not all about baked goods. Only *mostly*. Plus, this is an unprecedented opportunity for Sharkie-related gossip. "Really? How much does she bug him?"

Madame La Ghoule sighs. "Oh la la. He comes home so upset."

"Huh. How much?"

"He goes into zee bathroom for hours."

"Does he cry in there? Tell me he balls so hard, there are snot strings involved."

"Non, in zee bathroom, he files his teeth to razor-sharp points, all the better to tear out Myla's throat the moment he ever gets the chance!"

More clunking sounds echo in from beyond the door. A weight of worry settles on my shoulders. *I'm really pushing things here.*

"You know what? I'll take one chocolate snickerdoodle in a swan casing, please." I accent this order with a big smile. *One snickerdoodle is better than none.*

"Ah, that will only take me a few minutes." Madame La Ghoule pulls out a sheet of golden paper with an exaggerated flourish. Crinkles sound as she futzes around with the casing. No further noises come from the Sharkie part of the building.

At this point, I'm feeling good about bad self. First, I get into the bakery, no problem. Second, I order a frosted snickerdoodle. Third, I avoid Sharkie. And fourth, I'm now about to escape without incident.

I can't really see what Madame La Ghoule is up to behind the display case. Still, it seems to take for-bleeding-ever for her to finish. At last, she throws up her hands and smiles. Madame La Ghoule sets the wrapped snickerdoodle into another bag and holds it high.

I rush over to the cash register part of the store. "Ready to pay!"

Madame La Ghoule calls toward the door again. "Mon Cher! I need your help with zee register!"

"You know, there's no point bothering *mon cher*." Reaching into my pocket, I pull out a handful of bills and dump them on the counter. It's a ridiculous amount for one snickerdoodle. "Keep the change."

Madame La Ghoule spies the cash. She steps closer. My mouth waters. One more step and Madame La Ghoule will be close enough that I can take the bag and run.

Suddenly, the back door slams open. None other than Sharkie marches into the space behind the counter. He's a lanky ghoul in his tattered black robes. His skin is gray and leathery.

Madame La Ghoule sighs. "Mon cher, it's you at last."

Sharkie winks. "I'll take care of the cash register."

Madame La Ghoule still holds my bag. Only now, she's taken a decided step closer to Sharkie. In other words, my snickerdoodle remains well out of reach.

My tail shimmies beside me, which is its way of laughing. It gestures toward the exit. The meaning is clear. *Want to go?*

I shake my head. *No way am I giving up now.*

*W*hat happens next moves so slowly, it's like we're all underwater. Little by little, Sharkie reaches his bony arm forward until he snatches the snicker-doodle bag from Madame La Ghoule. His head slowly swivels to face me. He grins, showing off his mouth of pointy teeth.

A pang of rage zings inside me. This is the ghoul who's sent me into countless battles, trying to kill me. Sure, I always win, but still, there's a point here. Sharkie's goal was to destroy yours truly. And now, this ghoul is all that stands between me and my freaking cookie.

Sharkie holds the bag high. "What did you order?"

I speak in a high voice, just to throw him off. "One snick-erdoodle."

What happens next is a nightmare. Sharkie opens the bag and basically shoves his undead face in there. He snorts while inhaling deeply. "Is this chocolate?"

"Correctimundo." That's really old shtick, so I hope it acts as verbal camouflage.

Sharkie looks between me and the register a few times.

Since this is Purgatory, the register is one of those old iron numbers that I could use as a projectile if necessary.

Hey, when you're me, you have to plan for all contingencies.

"You remind me of someone," says Sharkie, still in his underwater-slow mode.

I try to keep my voice high and perky. "Did you see all the money I piled up by the register? Hand me the bag and you can keep the change."

"If I cared about money, why would I volunteer here?" asks Sharkie.

I do a double take. "You volunteer?"

"Yes. I'm paid in... *special snickerdoodles.*" Sharkie looks over at Madame La Ghoule as he says the words, *special snickerdoodles.* A sick taste seeps into my mouth.

Oh, Hells. Now I have to wonder what that weirdness means.

"Thanks for sharing," I say brightly.

"You're not... afraid of me?" asks Sharkie.

Madame La Ghoule raises her hand. "I'm sooooo scared of you, mon cher, in case you're wondering."

Eew. Just eew.

Instead of responding to Madame La Ghoule, Sharkie lumbers closer. "I meant you, quasi. You should be frightened. You're about to beg me to spare you, isn't that right? Admit it, and I will give you the cookie."

That crap crosses a line. Something snaps inside me. Even a snickerdoodle isn't worth this.

"Nooooooo," I say slowly. "I want you to hand over my freaking snickerdoodle. Now."

Sharkie leaps over the countertop to land before me. Let the record show that this move exposes his skinny chicken legs. This whole trip is turning out into way more than I ever bargained for.

Sharkie yanks off my wig and hat combo. The sunglasses fall off on their own, the traitors.

"Ha!" A manic gleam shines in Sharkie's black marble eyes. "It is you, Myla Lewis! "

"False! Look at my tail." I gesture toward the appendage in question, which still sports its disguise. "That's a googly snake!"

Fortunately for me, Sharkie can be sharp as a box of rocks sometimes. *Like now.*

"Oh." Sharkie scans my tail. "My bad."

All this time, Madame La Ghoule has been hanging in the background. Now, she rushes toward the register and fishes through the pile of cash. "I'll finish the transaction. Apologies for any confusion."

My tail arcs up to point at my nose. I know what it's thinking. *We shouldn't degrade ourselves any further for a snickerdoodle.*

How wrong my tail is.

I smile sweetly at Madame La Ghoule. "Thank you so much."

And here's where my tail becomes a pain in my ass. It slams against the floor with such force, the googly eyes fall right off.

I groan. *So close.*

Sharkie points at the now-exposed arrowhead end. "Ah, ha! I knew it!"

I hold up my hands, palms forward. "That's my snickerdoodle. Hand it over and there won't be any trouble."

Sharkie clacks his pointy teeth together. "Run away or I'll bite out your throat."

I smack my lips. "Sure, you will."

Sharkie jumps at me, the dumbass. Leaping up into the air,

I curl my legs by my chest and then pump my sneakers right into Sharkie's face. A satisfying crunch sounds.

Sharkie falls backward, unconscious. His ghoul robes fall in disarray. Turns out, he wears boxer underwear with little red hearts on it. *More stuff that I didn't need to know.*

Madame La Ghoule wags her finger at me. "You're the one. The girl from the arena who taunts him. You call him Sammy."

"It's Sharkie."

"I'll call the ghoul correction squad after you!"

I gesture toward the still-unconscious Sharkie. "How about you skip the ghoul correction squad but take the extra cash?"

Madame La Ghoule narrows her eyes. "I accept zees offer."

I've been in enough fights to know one thing. Madame La Ghoule is totally lying.

"If you keep your promise, I'll never tell anyone about the Valentine's Day themed boxers."

Madame La Ghoule purses her lips. "Deal."

One thing about being a fighter: You learn when to retreat. And the joy of having kicked Sharkie in the face is so intense, I really can't imagine how this particular moment could get any better. With my chin held high, I march out the door and into my station wagon. I'm two blocks away when I realize the sad truth.

I pound the steering wheel. "Damn! I didn't get the snickerdoodle!"

My tail arcs up to show me something beautiful: It speared the snickerdoodle bag onto its arrowhead end. I yip with joy and pull over to the nearest curb. Tearing the bag open, I peel off the little swan origami thing.

At last, it goes into my mouth where it belongs.

And it really is the best. Melty chocolate. Sweet cookie base with a hint of ginger and cinnamon. Madame La Ghoule is a nut job to date Sharkie, but she bakes a fine snack.

It's all over in a matter of seconds. My tail moves to point right at my nose while shivering ever so slightly. It's ticked off.

"I get it," I state. "I should have listened to you at the end there. No snickerdoodle is worth groveling to Sharkie."

My tail bobs up and down. *Yes.*

"Although, honestly? Maybe that snickerdoodle was a *little* worth it." My tail freezes. "I'm not serious. And should I mention again that you were right? Well, you were totally right."

In reply, my tail bobs happily with the arrowhead end angled in a way that begs for a certain response. So, I give it a high five before driving away. Three more blocks pass before I realize something important.

I just downed my first frosted snickerdoodle and kicked Sharkie's ass, all within an hour of each other.

That's what you call a good day.

~

—The End—

This is a bonus story for the book, **THRAX** *Book 4 of the Angelbound Origins series.*

ALSO BY CHRISTINA BAUER

THE DARK LANDS

After THRAX, the adventure continues with THE DARK LANDS!

LINCOLN

Enjoy Lincoln's perspective with the Angelbound LINCOLN series!

OFFSPRING

The next generation takes on Heaven, Hell, and everything in MAXON, Book 1 of Angelbound Offspring!

FAIRY TALES OF THE MAGICORUM

A modern fairy tale that *USA Today* calls a 'must-read!' Check out WOLVES AND ROSES!

DIMENSION DRIFT

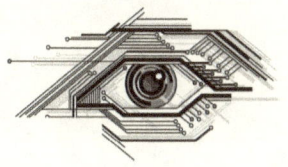

A kick-ass heroine + a swoon-worthy prince + an all-girl heist
= the DIMENSION DRIFT series!

BEHOLDER

Medieval mages ... Slow-burn love ... And heart-pounding action! Check out the BEHOLDER series!

PIXIELAND DIARIES

PIXIELAND DIARIES tells the story of sassy pixie Calla and 'her' elf prince, Dare.

SAMPLE CHAPTER - THE DARK LANDS

BOOK 5 OF THE ANGELBOUND ORIGINS

A perky female voice sounds in my ear. "Great Scala, you're on in thirty seconds."

Blinking sleep out of my eyes, I snap up my head and look around. "What? Who? How?"

After a few seconds, I realize where I am. My husband Lincoln and I sit on the sidelines of the set for *Good Morning Purgatory*, the number one television show in my homeland. Our baby Maxon was up all night—and he's now with my parents—so I've had zero rest. I must've fallen asleep on Lincoln's shoulder. There's even a drool spot to prove it.

The perky girl in question looks in her early twenties. She's average height with olive skin, brown eyes, and long black hair. "I said, Great Scala, you're on in thirty seconds." Her gaze flicks to Lincoln. "And you too, Consort to the Great Scala."

Lincoln nods regally. My guy is also King of the Thrax and an expert demon killer, but my people only think of him as

Consort to the Great Scala. He digs it, actually. Says it's better than getting fawned over as king.

"You know the drill?" asks the girl I've decided to name Perky.

I yawn. "A refresher would be great."

"You'll be interviewed by our new host. She'll ask you fun questions about your baby and that's it. There's no way she'll ambush you with some surprise just so she can get an exclusive."

"What a very specific thing for her *not* to do," says Lincoln dryly.

Perky keeps right on grinning. "Great, then you're all set. After your segment, we have on Cissy Frederickson, Purgatory's Senator for Diplomacy." Perky bobs on the balls of her feet. "I can't wait to meet her. What a natural for television! Have you ever seen her face to face?"

"Yes," I reply. "She's my best friend."

Perky laughs. "That's so funny."

I'd say, *no she's really my best friend*, but I've found it's not worth my breath. My people see Cissy as Mom's ally in the Senate. Guess that's the side effect of having your mother be Purgatory's President.

"Well, I'll leave you to it," says Perky. "Miss Frederickson is in make-up. Can't wait to introduce myself to the Senator. Wish me luck!" Perky steps away and as she leaves, I make note of her cat's tail. She's a quasi demon (part human and part demon) like me. All of us have tails and a power across one of the seven deadly sins. I'm guessing this girl's power is pride. She really seems pumped about her job. *Good for her.*

A voice sounds from the set. "And now, please welcome the Great Scala and her Consort." That would be Becky Tizzle and yes, that is her real name.

Lincoln stands and offers me his palm. "We're on."

I lace my fingers with his and together we enter the set. Immediately, I squint under the heavy lights. Massive cameras the size of water buffalo slowly roll across the floor, taking in me and Lincoln. For a moment, I picture how we must look to all the viewers out there in quasi land. Lincoln is tall and broad shouldered with sharp cheekbones, brown hair, and the mismatched eyes that mark him as a demon-fighting thrax. He's wearing a black suit today, which is his Consort look. *So handsome.* I'm in my form-fitting Scala robes, which are white and fall to my ankles. Other key points are my long red hair, big blue eyes, and curvy body. The viewers probably see exactly what they expect. It's not like Lincoln and I vary our Purgatory style much.

My tail pops up over my shoulder to wave at the camera because *of course it does. What a ham.* I'm part Furor demon, so I have demonic powers over both lust and wrath. My tail is long, black, covered in dragonscales, and all around badass.

Lincoln and I sit in the loveseat across from Becky's chair. For her part, Becky has short blonde hair, thick-rimmed glasses, and a peacock tail, which tells me her demonic power is pride; it's a popular sin with people who work in television. Today Becky wears a tweed suit and a predatory smile.

I recall Perky's not-a-warning.

Uh oh.

"Welcome, Great Scala and Consort," says Becky.

"Glad to be here," I offer.

Lincoln shoots a thumbs-up to the camera. Polls show quasis like it best when he sits there, looks handsome, and doesn't say much. I thought Lincoln might be offended, but he's turned it into a game. How long can he go without saying a word? Last interview, he got away with only saying *'hey nonny nonny'* and that's it. In case you're wondering, he was answering a question about the middle ages (his people are stuck in them) and I guess *'hey nonny nonny'* was a catchphrase back then.

"Let's start with a few questions about your baby," says Becky.

At the mention of the word *baby*, the studio audience lets out a long *ooh*. Everybody loves babies. I glance down at the television monitors by my feet. These things are out of camera range, but they've been placed so that Lincoln, Becky, and I can see the same things as the viewers at home. The picture of a cherub-like Maxon comes on the screen. My boy is all big eyes, chubby belly, and toothless smile.

"Isn't he adorable?" asks Becky to the audience.

More *oohs* follow, this time with a few *ahhs* thrown in. More photos go streaming by. In all of them, Lincoln and Maxon look adorable. I always have something stuck in my teeth or one eye closed. Whatever magic I have, it's not with the camera.

Even so, I settle into my loveseat and enjoy the picture show. Maybe this won't be an ambush interview. After all, how can things go downhill after Becky leads off with baby Maxon?

The camera cuts back to the studio. Becky starts in again. "We heard your parents, the President and First Man, have set up a baby room for little Maxon."

"That they have," I wave at the camera. "Hi, Mom and Dad! Thanks for watching Maxon today!"

"How old is he now?"

"Six months. But he's as large and smart as a toddler."

"You're the Great Scala, so Maxon's the Scala Heir, isn't that right?"

You think?

"Yes, I'm the Great Scala, the only being with the blood of an angel, demon, and human, in case any of your viewers missed it." *Not sure how that would happen, but this is Becky's show. I just answer questions.* "I'm also the only one who can move souls to Heaven or Hell. Maxon also has the blood of an angel, demon, and human, which makes him next in line. As the Scala Heir, my boy develops a little differently from other children."

"That is so precious," coos Becky. She adjusts her glasses and pulls up a clipboard from beside her chair. I've seen that *clipboard raising routine* before.

Danger sign. Ambush ahead.

"This just in," announces Becky. "We interviewed a new victim of the vicious criminal who's been terrorizing the after-realms. This fiend is as mean, slippery, and vicious as a snake, which is why he's called the Viper. Roll the tape, Fred."

On the screen by my feet, a video of an older gentleman appears. He wears a too-large suit coat with thick glasses and a fedora. "Someone snuck up on me from behind," says the older guy slowly. "Knocked me right out. My demonic power used to be gluttony. Now, I don't want to eat anything. Doc says I'm traumatized."

The video of the older man vanishes. The cameras focus back on Becky.

"For months," says Becky. "The Viper has been stealing valuables and attacking the innocent. Victims are knocked out from behind and left weakened. I'm here to ask what every quasi in Purgatory wants to know." Becky focuses on me. "How will *you* stop the Viper?"

I tap my chest. "Me?"

"You're the Scala Mother to our people. The logic here is obvious."

Two things about Becky's last statement. One, the logic here is *not* obvious and two, I hate being called Scala Mother. *So creepy.*

"Not following you, Becky," I say.

"Let me try this another way," says Becky. "You *are* a supernatural being, right?"

"Sure."

"Roll the tape, Fred."

Another video appears on screen. It's the streets of downtown Purgatory City after I went into labor with Maxon. People are camped out on the asphalt with sleeping bags, candles, and signs. For days, my people blocked traffic while partaking of questionable substances. I quickly spot some of my least favorite placards.

Heal Yourself Great Scala

Bring Forth The Baby

Don't Die On Us

Becky raps on her clipboard with her knuckles. "Your followers held a vigil, asking you to have a healthy baby and not die. And that's exactly what you did, isn't it? That was a supernatural response to a quasi request. How is that different from what I just asked regarding the Viper?"

I shrug. "Having a baby is more of a natural woman thing, rather than any special powers related to magical crime solving."

"Oh, I'd say having a baby is magical." Becky raps on her clipboard again.

Crud. She's on a roll.

Lincoln leans forward, resting his elbows on his knees. I know that pose. *My guy is getting in the game. Yes.*

"You're leading up to something." As he speaks, Lincoln's voice turns low and packed with menace. "What have you found?"

True fact: when Lincoln asks a question this particular way, people always answer. It's the *king thing* he's got going.

"New information has come to my attention." Becky holds up her clipboard. "The Viper has somehow broken into the supernatural prison of none other than Lucifer." The studio audience gasps. "Once there, the Viper poisoned one of the guards. It won't be long before Lucifer escapes. Isn't that right?"

Lincoln and I share a confused look. "The Great Scala and I have received no such information. Are you certain it's valid?"

"We received this data from a ghoul named WKR-7," explains Becky. "He's supposed to be very reliable."

"Walker?" It's an effort not to screech the name. "You got this intel from Walker?"

"Why yes," answers Becky. "Have you heard of him?"

"He's my honorary older brother and Lincoln's best friend."

"Then you know this information is valid and the threat is real. Need I remind you why Lucifer was jailed? Roll it, Fred."

Again, fresh video shows on the screen. This time, angels in silver armor fly across a gray sky, their swords held high. These warriors swoop and dive over a retreating crowd of ghouls, quasis, and humans. Angels ruthlessly cut down the innocents. Blood is everywhere. Text at the bottom of the screen says *'re-enacted history'* but that won't matter to most. The facts are true, even if the footage is faked up. Lucifer was a bloodthirsty maniac.

The video switches to show one angel close up. He has

golden everything: hair, armor, and wings. *Lucifer*. He paces before a line of fresh angelic troops.

"My Brimstone Legion," declares Lucifer. "All was peaceful in the universe until the Almighty created ghouls, quasis, and humans. Then we were asked to help these lesser beings. I won't have it! Non-angelic life is worthless. Now take to the skies and destroy what should never have been created." The angels unfold their wings and rise up into the air. The video ends; the feed returns to the studio.

Becky rounds on me. "Now, what do you say? How will you save us when the Viper releases Lucifer?"

I have no idea what to say, but I do know what to think.

Fuuuuuuuuuuuuuuuuck.

—*End Of Sample*—

~

Order THE DARK LANDS today!

APPENDIX

IF YOU ENJOYED THIS BOOK...

...Please consider leaving a review, even if it's just a line or two. Every bit truly helps, especially for those of us who don't *write by the numbers,* if you know what I mean.

Plus I have it on good authority that every time you review an indie author, somewhere an angel gets a mocha latte. For reals.

And angels need their caffeine, too.

ACKNOWLEDGMENTS

If you're reading my freaking acknowledgements, chances are, I should thank you for something. So, for the record: you are awesome, dear reader.

That said, huge and heartfelt thanks must go out to my husband and son for their rock-solid support. Being an author means a lot of early mornings, late nights, long weekends, and never-ending patience. You two are the best guys in the universe, period.

After that, I must thank the extensive network of reviewers, friends and colleagues who helped me build my writing chops in general. Gracias.

Finally, deep affection goes out to my late, much loved, and dearly missed Aunt Sandy and Uncle Henry. You saw the writer in me, always. Thank you, first and last.

ABOUT CHRISTINA BAUER

Christina Bauer thinks that fantasy books are like bacon: they just make life better. All of which is why she writes romance novels that feature demons, dragons, wizards, witches, elves, elementals, and a bunch of random stuff that she brainstorms while riding the Boston T. Oh, and she includes lots of humor and kick-ass chicks, too. Christina lives in Newton, MA with her husband, son, and semi-insane golden retriever, Ruby.

Stalk Christina on Social Media

Blog:
http://monsterhousebooks.com/blog/category/christina

Facebook:
https://www.facebook.com/authorBauer/

Instagram:
https://www.instagram.com/christina_cb_bauer/

Twitter:
@CB_Bauer

VLOG:
https://tinyurl.com/Vlogbauer

Web site:
www.bauersbooks.com

COMPLIMENTARY BOOK

Get a FREE novella when you sign up for Christina's newsletter: https://tinyurl.com/bauersbooks

www.ingramcontent.com/pod-product-compliance
Lightning Source LLC
Chambersburg PA
CBHW051941240626
47153CB00005B/1575